Relaxing after the successful removal of a bullet from his abdomen, Trevor Maxon finds his post-mission tranquillity shattered when the television programme he is watching is interrupted by a Nuclear Alert warning.

Although the alert is rescinded almost immediately, Maxon, whose duty is to safeguard the Global Early Warning System, wants to know what went wrong — and why.

The enormity of what he discovers, and how he and the woman he loves deals with this knowledge is told in THE PRICE OF SILENCE, an exciting and fast-moving story of espionage and deceit on a massive scale.

# The Price of Silence

Stephen Barlay

**CORGI BOOKS**

# THE PRICE OF SILENCE

## A CORGI BOOK 0 552 12260 2

Originally published in Great Britain by Hamish Hamilton Ltd.

PRINTING HISTORY

Hamish Hamilton edition published 1983
Corgi edition published 1983

Corgi Books are published by Transworld Publishers Ltd., Century House, 61–63 Uxbridge Road, Ealing, London W5 5SA

Printed and bound in Great Britain by Cox & Wyman Ltd., Reading, Berks.

*For Trish and Richard*

# The Price of
# Silence

# I

Fog blackened the night and sheltered the shadows that roamed along the border.

'If you survive and I don't ...'

'You must.'

'Nobody will blame you, Maxon. Too many imponderables have gone wrong.' Anxiety thickened the General's precise Muscovite English.

'That's why something must go right. Soon.'

'I can't stomach optimists.'

'It's time to become one when all reasonable hope's gone.' Maxon's view of their predicament was underlined by the asthmatic effort of an automatic. A streak of bullets whizzed past them. It sounded like a whiplash. Another burst followed. Nearer, this time. In the darkness, only the rapping above betrayed which way it had gone. Chipped stucco hailed on the two crouching figures – but they were still alive. 'You see?' Maxon grinned.

'You are crazy. I'll tell London you are.'

So who's the optimist now? Maxon meant to ask but never did. Out of uniform, shivering in cold sweat, General Sarian looked pink, puffy and naked, much too easy to hurt.

A clarinet cried out – and the night scene froze as if the HOLD button of a video machine had been hit.

The wind, the shots, the bated breath of fear – all sounds grew muted except the band's. Glenn Miller's. That's how Maxon knew he was in the ante-room of sleep where memories and nightmares mingle freely. And he could not have been in there for long if the saxophone section was still making 'The Angels Sing'. He tried to will himself to wake up and retreat into the present where he could throttle the verbose DJ who just wouldn't shut up and leave the music alone. Open your eyes, breathe normally, he urged himself, that scene with the General must be three weeks old. A lifetime. But Sarian's voice refused to fade away: *If you*

1

*survive, live fast, Maxon. Moscow will never forgive you for this. And they'll get you. Somehow, some day.* Kill the voice, Maxon told himself. It's over. You got him out. He is safe. Open your eyes, breathe in, breathe out. His lungs and eyelids defied him: what if he would find himself in the past, after all. So he chose to lie still, let his nose bob with the rhythm of the music, and wait for nurse.

*'If you survive and I don't . . .'*

The door opened. Maxon felt the air shift gently all around as Nurse Keenan swept in. You do take up a lot of airspace, he thought.

'Wakey, wakey!' she boomed. 'Time to bare your body and soul.' He refused to open his eyes. Her ding-dong was strangely Irish for a cocksure Washingtonian. Perhaps some padre from Limerick was her confessor who had cornered a chunk of the trade in the capital's black ghetto. She must have had plenty to confess before she came so clearly under the influence.

She soothed away the pricks of pain she had caused by peeling off the surgical tape. Maxon's temptation to submit to her touch blindly equalled the desire to stare at her hands manipulating fresh bandage round his thigh, up his hip, through his legs again. He looked up. Then down. Breasts, jaw, lips, eyes, lips, jaw, breasts, fingers – everything about her was big and joyfully sensuous.

She read his eyes instinctively (her confessions must have been sheer delight for naughty insight and shameless clarity), and nodded: 'Oh, yeah, you are on the mend.' Her teeth smiled, her voice did not. Caught *in flagrante* of intent, he tried to smile back at her, but no, sir, she would play no games. Her staccato 'ah-ah!' would have restrained even a ferocious toddler about to gobble up that irresistible tray of ash and fag-ends. Sheepishly, he sucked his lips in, and she rewarded him with a laugh: 'Remember me when we let you go, sir.'

She turned to dispose of the old bandage. As her hips swung round, something gave a metallic clink. 'Oh, yeah. I almost forgot.' From some invisible fold of her laundry-advert uniform, she produced a small brown vial. 'Here . . . I've managed to get you one of the bullets. You wanna keep it?'

'I collect scrap metal. Preferably with bits of flesh attached.'

'Sorry, no flesh. They dug it out of your bone.' She touched the bandage. 'But now the wound looks real good,' she enthused. She liked patients who responded well to treatment.

'I heal fast.'

'You sound experienced.'

'I was in the war.'

'Which one?'

'Good question.' He hoped he did not sound resentful: her query had not referred to his age in any way. To him, despite his numerous wars, war still meant World War II alone. So what could he say? Arnhem would be as unreal to Nurse Keenan as Mafeking was to him. And it was no less his fault that he was still collecting 'scrap metal' when most of his contemporaries had hung up their boots or rested them on the status-shiny mahogany of a desk in Whitehall.

Nurse Keenan did not press for an answer: she was well enough paid and trained to cope with tongue-tied patients in this place. 'It's stopped raining. You could go for a walk if you like. It's real nice around here.'

Under the window, somewhere among the maze of hedges and trees, the guard dogs stirred. They would soon erupt in throaty furore towards the rustle of leaves and passing shadows – a world they had been taught to see full of enemies.

A breathless disc jockey introduced 'In The Mood', but a few seconds later the hospital radio went dead. Another burst of music followed, only to be killed yet again. Before Maxon could have a chance to curse the whole package, a few bars of some shrill, pulsating tune flooded the room. Then silence. Nurse Keenan's hands seemed to freeze in mid-air. Like the general's mouth. *If I survive and you don't . . . if none of us survives . . .* Without blinking, Maxon stared at the radio, willing it to shut up, never to repeat that sound again. For he knew what the signal meant. And the nurse knew it, too. And neither of them had ever believed they would live to hear the nuclear war alert in earnest.

'Attention, attention.' The voice was dark and mechanical like the captain's on an old submarine, *now hear this, now hear this*. 'Stand by for emergency announcement of national importance. Please en . . .'

The voice was momentarily obliterated by a gush of 'In

The Mood' and an incredulous DJ mumbling, 'What do you mean, for real?'

The electronic signal fought back and screamed to re-occupy the airwaves. 'Stay tuned. Await full emergency announcement of national importance.' The silence that followed was the worst. More frightening than any man-made sound.

Maxon knew it was one of those moments, like President Kennedy's death, that would be recorded indelibly in everybody's mind. The question was, who would live to recall where they were, what they said, what they thought, what they wore, what they did just then, precisely?

Nurse Keenan would remember that her patient had gone barmy: he was grinning.

Maxon would remember that the nurse's black face had grown several shades paler. He felt an excruciating urge to do something. Kick the radio. Bombard the clouds with cushions. Drag Keenan into the bed and screw her for dear life. Write a poem. Put on shoes; strong walking shoes. Have a drink. Tell a joke. Check the time. Phone the office. Yes, phone the office and find out what's going on. He steeled himself not to phone: the lines would be jam-packed with calls to people who were operational, who could *do* something and therefore mattered. He closed his eyes. '*If you survive and I don't ...*' No, general, the chances were infinitely worse than fifty-fifty. With no time to become an optimist. Or listen to Glenn Miller without interruption. A vision of global wasteland filled his mind. A nuclear wasteland with wrecked radios belting out Big Band music, and not a soul, not even a DJ, around to stop or change the endless loops of tape. And it made him grin inanely.

The silence was broken by the nasal sound of the hospital tannoy. 'Er, attention, please ...' Maxon recognised the Admin. Director's voice. Papers rustled through the speakers. 'Er ... turn on your TV or Radio ... and, er ...' She was fumbling for words. A frightful stickler for paperwork who saw unconscious accident victims as the curse of the filing system, she had probably mislaid her emergency drill sheet. She fought hard to find and actually *read out* long-standing instructions rather than recall them, let alone improvise. 'There'll be a government announcement. Wait for it. Do not, and I repeat, do not leave your ward until directed by the medical staff.' She paused, and then blurted out: 'Your evacuation to shelters is in hand.'

Maxon glanced at his watch. They were only thirty seconds into apocalypse. Incoming missiles must be approaching Washington. Closing in on London. Hitting scores of towns in Europe. Through that fearsome window of aggressive opportunity. He knew the scenario. He knew the likely targets. He knew the missiles which had probably been spotted by GLEW, the new Global Early Warning System. He was a cog in the GLEW machine, and he knew he ought to be proud of its success. But he felt no pride. He hoped the counter-punch, too, would soon be on its way. But it gave him no sense of satisfaction. He could not work up a thirst for blood and an appetite for war. Nor a sense of fury, militancy or vengeance. It's just that the books had to be balanced by those who were fit and operational while he could only sing something. A nursery rhyme, perhaps. Or 'Chattanooga Choo Choo'.

The inclination to sing did not amuse him. He calmly noted that, at thirty-two seconds into apocalypse, one would begin to show symptoms of premature dementia.


The road weaved, and weaved gently enough to make the drive seem to dance among the trees. The sun battled to elbow through the clouds, and a warm breeze raced the only car on the road. The tall woman at the wheel slowed down. She did not want to miss an unmarked turning that would appear to lead nowhere. She was sure she had taken the right road out of Washington, she had passed Langley with its sprawling CIA compound, she could not be far now. She wondered what sort of place it could be. Would it be masquerading in the guise of a factory? A warehouse? A cluster of bungalows? With guards? And dogs?

She reached towards the radio, but a strong gust caught her hair and changed her mind. She pulled up over the edge of the road, and craned her neck to inspect her hair in the mirror. She would soon see Maxon. He would help her, she was sure. No, she was not. It had been a long time. She would not tell him how good it was to see him. Would he guess? Would he care?

Thirty-three seconds into apocalypse – countdown proceeding smoothly. Maxon was watching himself from somewhere above, through a telescope. The thoughts that occurred to him were not part of a sequence spaced out in time: they just existed, all at once, out of control.

Stand by. Check the time. Sing something. A calypso, perhaps? Apocalypso? Pardon me, boy, is that the turning to Armageddon?

The signal was played again. The signal, designed to make your stomach turn, did nothing for him. His back was itching. Was it worth the effort to scratch it minutes before the likely end? A hedonist to the last, he could ask Nurse Keenan to do it for him.

She was still standing near the window. She had not moved since the first tune of doom. Leaning slightly forward, as if about to take a step, she looked petrified, lifelike yet lifeless, a relic of Pompei, in total submission to fate. Submissive and alluringly vulnerable – like that Balinese girl in Huddersfield of all places, who had once teased and tempted Maxon in the security of knowing that he would not sleep with a friend's wife.

Maxon rose from the bed and walked towards the nurse. She did not move. He put his arm around her. She let him guide her to the bed. They sat down, and he held her hand to share her fear.

'Attention, attention. The President will soon speak to the nation. Early warning satellites report the approach of missile or missiles, presumed to be hostile. Damage limitation measures are being applied, but meanwhile, you can do much for your own safety. Please follow the . . .'

The voice was cut off. Silence followed. Just what Bert, an American colleague, used to call 'audio vacuum', Maxon remembered, and looked at his watch: fifty-two seconds into apocalypse. Maxon used to call Bert a 'keen listener'. He buried him with all his bloodsoaked electronic gear on the upper slopes of Mount Ararat from where he could listen into Soviet Armenian communications to his dead heart's delight.

Silence yielded to a rhubarb of noises presided over by ringing telephones. And then the voice of that cursed disc jockey: 'What? . . . Can't hear you . . . Oh! . . . Quiet everybody! He tried to laugh. 'Sorry folks.' He managed to squeeze out a guffaw, thick and phoney, that cost him the last vestige of his composure. 'It's ... er ... it seems we've got a real nasty one here ... I mean something got into the system, some gremlin, oh dear, did I say Kremlin? It left me trem'lin', and certainly not in the mood – sorry, Glenn, over to you, Glenn, I mean put us in the mood with "In The Mood" ...' He laughed as the music began to swell under his voice. 'I mean it beats this,' he hummed the nuclear alert signal, 'any time.'

Drained and stunned, patient and nurse were still sitting on the bed. It took time to disentangle their fingers. Then a sudden urge forced them to do something. Anything. She breathed a kiss on his cheek. He turned off the radio with such ferocity that the tuner came off its shaft, then yelled into the telephone, 'Give me GLEW security! Now!'

Seconds later Captain Beck was on the line. 'Early Warning Security.'

'Maxon here. Give me Locke.'

'Your ident code, sir.'

'Don't play games, Captain, not now.'

'I must insist, sir, especially now.'

Maxon swallowed a lump of fury. 'Skylark in Red Square, okay?'

'Sorry, sir, regulations. General Locke insists ...'

'Okay, okay, I want to talk to him.'

'He's on his way to the White House. You wanna know about the alert, I guess.'

'Stop guessing. Is this a safe line?'

'The hospital is Company property. All lines go through the scramblers.'

'So what was it? False alert?'

'No, sir, the real McCoy. Regular last warning with all the extra time GLEW has bought us.'

'Then how come it was called off?'

'We don't quite know what happened. I mean not yet. But it was real scary because we know for sure, I mean the General himself has told me, that GLEW-7 spotted and signalled at least one incoming, unidentified missile.'

'Where was it launched from?'

'Outer space.'

'Then it had to be Russian.'

'But of course.'

Captain Beck's tone irritated Maxon. He had disliked the young American since first sight and never discovered anything about him to soothe his antagonism. Beck was much too handsome and inexperienced to work for General Larry Locke, Junior, a first aide to the President's security adviser. He beamed readily, managed to combine servility with the school-masterly style of a born know-all, and seemed to regard it a compliment that people openly nicknamed him Locke's Beck-and-call. An eternal, keen college kid, he had never lost the puppy-fat, prominently displayed round his chin, and his blue eyes under curling lashes retained the romantic gleam of would-be heroes. He was obviously familiar with Maxon's work record, and tended to treat him as his demigod. So now that he had a chance to inform and lecture Maxon, he was keen to improve his status. My fault, thought Maxon, I gave him the opportunity to say 'but of course' when I had thought aloud and said that 'it had to be Russian' because no other nation had yet the capability to launch a missile from a satellite in space.

'The General himself talked to Omaha Center, sir, and they confirmed it just before we had the second signal.'

'What second signal? Try to be a bit more coherent, Captain.'

'Sorry, sir. The second signal was also from GLEW-7 and it reported the disappearance of the missile. We think it might have blown up.'

'Or else GLEW-7 made a mistake. What if only the first signal was correct and the missile is still on course?'

'Doesn't look like it. Not at all.'

'Then how the hell did the public alert slip through? Retaliation must have been seconds away. People must have been scared to death.'

'That's just it, sir. The General says it must have been one hell of a foozle somewhere down the first green. We must get to the bottom of this. Just the job for you, sir, once you're back on your feet. I guess I can just foresee what your next assignment is going to be.'

'Have you considered taking up clairvoyance?'

'Clairvoyance? . . . Ah,' his voice transmitted the beam, 'I appreciate the joke, sir.'

'Let me know if you have any further news.'

'Right away, sir.'

'And Beck . . .' Maxon could not bring himself to calling him Alvin. But then, admittedly, hardly anybody had ever called Maxon by his first name. Some people suspected that he himself hated it. Others reasoned that he was much too intimidating to be called anything but Maxon.

'Yes, sir?'

'Tell Locke that I'm available. I'm well enough to be discharged. Or I could discharge myself if necessary.'

In fact, there was nothing Maxon wanted more than to leave the hospital. He knew he ought to be but was not flattered by the privilege of being treated in this exclusive CIA establishment. Yet he had no choice. His life's labours had not exactly endeared him to the KGB, and running the defection of the Armenian general marked him as a likely target for revenge.

He caught a glimpse of himself in the small mirror above the hand-basin. He thought he looked like he felt: worn. Tension as a way of life had kept his cheek muscles tight, but even the round-the-year tan could not hide the deep-furrowed pattern of a lived-in face any more. Age had, in fact, done much for his looks. He used to be a skinny lad. Now he was just slim enough to look taller than his five foot eleven. His alcohol intake battled valiantly to deposit a surfeit of fat on him, but a combination of nervous energy and *langlauf* skiing burnt most of it up. He used to be a hairy youngster. Now his thinning and receding hair threatened to make him look distinguished. He definitely saw it as a threat. His face remained chin-heavy, his drooping eyelids lent him a sleepy appearance – a misleading effect he liked to exploit – and there was still no bitterness in his eyes to betray his fifty-six years on the go. Except that he felt spent. And fed up with it all. Liar, he warned himself. After a long and varied career, he still loved the work. Well, most of it. The last year of the War; the Nuremberg inquiries; a stretch with worldwide radio monitoring and intelligence gathering for the code-breakers; missions under diplomatic cover; 'life on the brink' as he called the period he spent on Section K7, the antipenetration unit of MI5; the year he was loaned to the CIA; the counter-intelligence job he was sent to do with 'Phoenix' in Vietnam; and the endless variety of special assignments that would, eventually, earn him the accolade of being invited to join *special projects*, a group of unheard-of independence within British intelligence.

When Global Early Warning satellites became operational, there was a great deal of in-fighting and position jockeying for the new prestige jobs. Everybody knew that GLEW would shut the menacing window of vulnerability in the Russians' face; that GLEW would work for USACAN, a US-Anglo-Canadian outfit authorised to supply early warnings to NATO and other countries at its own discretion; and that the automated system would be operated by robots and a mere skeleton staff. It seemed that all spooks and counterspooks were angling for a chance to work for General Locke's elite security outfit. Maxon never applied – he was asked to join. His boss, Sandy, was not pleased. 'Special projects' was his own pet. He fought against the transfer until Sir Gerald himself, the Prime Minister's security adviser and intelligence overlord, intervened on Locke's behalf. Grudgingly, Sandy gave in. 'It's a golden distinction they're offering you,' he told Maxon in his usual pompous voice. 'Locke is very close to the President, will run the leanest of security networks, and he insists on having you on a long lease as a troubleshooter. I've told him that you're a field-man to the core, and that you'll be most disinclined to mind the shop for security, but he didn't care. A golden distinction, indeed.'

The golden distinction soon turned into leaden disappointment for Maxon. He called GLEW security 'a bloody holiday camp with nothing to do apart from wasting time and exchanging idiotic code routines with people like Captain Beck-and-call, whose appointment as Locke's personal aide was a devastating comment on the whole outfit'. In the first year, Maxon made two written requests for a transfer back to Sandy's 'special projects'. Each time, the request was denied. Locke's argument was that 'if we have nothing to do here, it shows we're doing a grand job. And your presence here will warn all our enemies that at GLEW security we don't just look mean – we mean business.'

Then out of the blue, he was loaned back to London to do 'a one-off job' for Sandy. 'Maxon, it's a platinum-plated compliment to you,' said Sandy, 'that we've asked for you specifically, and that Locke has agreed!' A week later, only six weeks ago, he was briefed about the Sarian assignment. Sandy said he had been chosen because he was known to be an escape and rescue specialist, a distinction Maxon had never wanted or laid claim to, but a reputation he could not deny.

The first experience came at the height of the cold war, in his early twenties, when he was sent into Russia to assist a scientist's defection. The plan was made by others, he was to be just the guide and nursemaid. A submarine dropped him off, and he was to paddle to the shore in a rubber dinghy. It was a filthy night. The freak waves were too much for the small craft that disgorged him as it overturned. He had to swim, playing lifeguard to his boat which he needed for the return journey and to the plastic bag that contained his shoes and set of identity documents.

He managed to hide the dinghy, and walked towards his target village when a police round-up netted him. They were looking not for spies but fishermen who had thieved from their own catch, the property of their kolkhoz. With a dozen others, Maxon was marched to the local police station that seemed to have been built around a red-hot metal stove. It soon transpired he had nothing to fear: rain accounted for his wet clothes, his crumpled papers oozed innocence (Sandy and his craftsmen would have to be praised for them lavishly), and his Russian was impeccable (he made a mental note to thank the cunning elocutionist who had superimposed a Baltic accent for added credibility). After a few anxious minutes, he was free to go – except that order would have to prevail, cleared suspects would have to leave as a group.

The room was small, constant jostling was inevitable, and Maxon ended up near the stove. A chance to dry himself turned into a chance to die. He noticed it in the sergeant's eyes gazing at his clothes. Maxon looked down. On his well-worn quilted jacket and tatty trousers, white rings and patches had appeared: it was a death sentence, written in salt, left behind by the evaporating sea-water. Maxon saw the sergeant's hand reaching hesitantly for the holster. It was a moment he would remember in every detail. He was consciously amazed that his life failed to flash by. And he had an urge to sing. His voice had always been atrociously out of tune, not to be heard even in the privacy of his bathroom, why would he want to sing just then? And why did he remember only the women who got away from him unloved, those who said 'no,' and those who would never get a chance to say 'yes' or 'no'? Maxon was ready to die, but not like that, not without a fight. He wrapped his arms round his head, dived through a window, and ran.

That time he was lucky. He even got his defector. And he earned himself the reputation that would be rewarded by similarly dangerous assignments and chances to risk his life for others over the years. By the time Sandy wanted him to lift Aram Sarian, the Armenian general, Maxon would be trusted to do all his own planning and preparations. At least he would have no-one else to blame if something went wrong. All he knew about Sarian was that he had been a defector *in situ* for several years, and that his escape was worth more than Maxon's life. A rendezvous was arranged in Hungary. Maxon guided and protected him despite the bullet he bumped into during that long, foggy night on the border. It was certainly not the most elegant escape he had ever arranged, but he succeeded in smuggling Sarian into Yugoslavia. The original 'platinum-plated compliment' was re-emphasised by the red carpet treatment they received in Belgrade. The CIA station chief laid on medical attention, cover, clearance, new identities, and a special flight just for two, to jet them straight to Washington. From the airport, a helicopter took them into the security of the CIA hospital, where no assassin from the KGB 'wet affairs' bureau could reach them. A few days later, Sarian was taken away for lengthy debriefing by London and Washington specialists, while Maxon stayed on for treatment and a chance to collect his 'scrap metal'.

The tension of the nuclear alert had left Maxon drained. Lack of action made him feel frustrated. Somewhere, something had gone wrong. War had been seconds away. This was the moment he could really do something important for GLEW. Yet he might have to leave the investigation to others.

The sun was winning. The breeze carried some bitter-sweet wood-smoke. The scenery along the narrow lane was still wild, but the keen observer would detect that yard after yard, nature appeared to be more and more manicured. A dog began to bark, but stopped just as suddenly. It must have been his handler's doing, the woman at the wheel deduced. She drove on slowly, at an even speed. The path surface turned into well-kept gravel. The tyres gnawed at it noisily. The gravel was doing its duty to warn someone. The woman smiled. Something among the treetops glittered. The lens of a closed-circuit TV camera, she guessed.

Beyond a sharp bend, she had to brake hard. The path was blocked by an unmarked van. Two armed guards in the uniform of some obscure private security firm sandwiched the car. They had dogs with them. They looked as friendly as marines making an opposed landing.

'Seems you've lost your way, miss.'

'Don't think so.'

'There's nothing here – and it's not designated as a picnic area.' The man's partner laughed.

'I'm looking for a hospital.'

'Hospital?' He made it sound like some Latin word from an algebra textbook. 'What hospital? This is a dude ranch for geriatrics.'

'Really? With all these dogs, TV cameras, a road-block, and armed heavies playing receptionists you could have fooled me. Now try to play an angel and find me Mr Maxon fast because I have a plane to catch back to Toronto.' she spoke quietly, but something in her voice stopped them slouching. They began to look like marines on parade.

'Er . . . have you got clearance, ma'am?'

'Ask Maxon.'

'I don't know anyone of that name, ma'am.'

'That's why you'll have to find out, won't you?'

The men exchanged glances. 'Come with me, please. You'll have to leave your car here.'

One man marched her to a clearing. He kept half a step behind her because her gait matched her voice of authority – and it also gave him a chance to ogle the tight fit of her skirt. She pushed out long thighs as if walking into headwind. Her dark locks marked the direction of the breeze. The guard took her driving licence, left her in the charge of another two armed men, and went into a small lonely hut to telephone.

'Her name's Jacqueline Kowalski, sir.'

Maxon stayed silent. The name had uncorked a geyser of memories.

'Sir . . . are you there, sir?'

'Yeah. Any means of identification?'

'Driving licence. Canadian.'

'Describe her.'

'Er, very attractive,' he paused with embarrassment. 'I

13

mean Caucasian; about five-nine, maybe five-eight; about a
... hundred and thirty pounds ...' he said the weight
slowly, relishing the sight of every one of those pounds,
probably through a two-way mirror. 'Dark hair ...'

Used to be auburn, thought Maxon. He wondered if the
tint was covering a sprinkle of white hairs.

'... greenish eyes, even teeth, no visible marks of
distinction.'

'Age?'

'The licence says forty-two, but looks younger. Will you
see her, sir?'

'Yes, if she checks out all right. There should be an old,
one-inch bayonet scar on her lower abdomen ... Er ... on
the right hand side ... yes, facing her ...' For a second he
visualised the flaring gleam in the guard's eyes, and added
hastily: 'Get a nurse to check it.'

As he rang off, there was a knock at the door. Nurse
Keenan returned. She hunched her back and looked
sheepishly at the floor. 'I ... just wanted to tell you I
couldn't get the second bullet for you.'

'Pity.'

'And ... er ... sorry I was a bit ... rattled?'

It really worried her that she had been weak when she
had needed to be strong to support her patient during the
alert. It made him smile. 'Don't worry.'

'That's what I say. If we're going to die, what's the point
of being alert and worrying? It's a joke.'

'But that's the point. Your country gave the world the
idea of service with a smile. So now we get death with a
laugh.'

'I'm not laughing,' she said and left to let him answer the
phone that had begun ringing.

Captain Beck was on the line. He reported the confirmation that the alert had been set off by a hostile launch from
an unidentified space vehicle in Moon Sector Seven. In
other words, a Russian missile. The launch had apparently
coincided with dummy satellite manoeuvres and short,
random firing of rocket engines, designed to blind the older
types of warning satellites that could detect only heat
sources. 'But GLEW caught them red-handed, didn't it,
sir? That should spoil their May Day fun!'

'Anything else?'

'Yes sir. The General asked me to let you know that he'll

be interviewed in a special news bulletin for the entire network ... just about forty minutes from now.'

'Thanks.'

'It'll go by satellite to every corner of the globe.'

In a vacant examination cubicle on the ground floor, Jacqueline Kowalski tried to humour the young, apologetic nurse who had checked her out bodily. The girl reported to the guards, and now she was told to show the visitor to Mr Maxon's room. A porter overheard the patient's name and volunteered to do the job: 'I'm passing his door anyway. Lemme save you the long walk, honey.' On the way he proved himself a chatter-box. He mixed a disarming, avuncular smile with a child's shameless curiosity, and asked endless questions about the visitor's accent, life in Toronto, the weather over there and the strength of the Canadian stock market.

The new, low-profile tanks rumbled past Lenin's tomb and made their clumsy exit behind the freshly gilded onion domes of St Basil's Cathedral. A screaming fighter squadron swooped down and by, evoking a faint, obligatory applause, but all eyes in the crowd were on the history museum end of Red Square, waiting for the hard-heralded public debut of the FOB machines. Which was why those eyes missed the belated appearance of Marshal Beryov, Commander of the Soviet missile forces, the man who had taken most of the credit for the development and launching of the FOB network.

One by one, Beryov squeezed past bulky generals and the household names of the Politburo, and nodded gravely towards the Soviet leader even before he could reach the centre of the parapet atop the mausoleum. The leader, known as the *Nachalnik* to friend and foe alike, frowned: he understood Beryov's nod, he was a technocrat, the first man at the very top with real managerial background – and proud of it. It was his wish to be known and addressed (jocularly, of course) as the Manager, and to be recognised as the man who needed few words to understand what his colleagues meant. This time he knew that Beryov was the bearer of bad news.

The *Nachalnik* took a deep breath to control his palpitation. He was in a bad shape and had to fight to remain upright. His fingers closed tight on the railing in front of him: only his hands and wrists remained as strong as they used to be in his legendary arm-wrestling days, still capable of humiliating many a younger colleague and keeping an iron grip on the reins of power.

Beryov stopped next to him and was about to report, but the *Nachalnik* already knew that the launch must have been detected by the Americans, that GLEW must have lived up to its reputation, that the FOBs were losing their domination of surprise attacks from outer space.

'They issued a public alert even before we could announce a "launcher malfunction" as planned,' Beryov whispered.

'A public alert?'

'Yes. It implies they must have been close to full-scale retaliation.'

'They haven't even tried to call me! The hot line has been cold throughout.'

'That's typical of the President's recklessness.'

At the corner of the old Mint, the first huge platform-vehicle appeared, carrying a full-size replica of the satellite that could launch Fractional Orbit Bombardment, the first true weapon of space-wars to come. Cheers rose from all lips of the crowd, and the *Nachalnik* felt disinclined to argue. Not here, not now: Beryov and his cronies had cajoled and pressurised him long enough into authorising that test launch; the KGB had assured him that this new western warning system would not yet be fully operational; the most hawkish of the generals had argued that GLEW might be little more than a scarecrow in the sky, and the test would be essential to discovering its precise capabilities; and they all must have known that the test would be a gamble. What was the hawks' aim? War? Unlikely. Not yet. To boot their leader out? No, comrades, not yet. The *Nachalnik* was not yet ready to go.

He turned away from Beryov and peered at the pale, featureless mask of his most likely successor. He thought of the diminishingly hairy history of communist leadership. The bushy beards of Marx and Engels; Lenin's neat, pointed Vandyke, Stalin's fat moustache; Khrushchev's baldness, perhaps the hallmark of treachery; his predecessor's massive eyebrows; his own full head of hair, so

16

dominant in every picture in the press – and now this Mad Monk of the KGB with a bureaucrat's bare, inscrutable face and gleaming pate that would have to be tanned by paint to show up at all on huge posters one day. No, the *Nachalnik* did not feel like discussing the fiasco here, within earshot of his successors-in-waiting, but Beryov was at it again:

'Of course, they might have been plain lucky. If, for instance, one of their warning satellites in the GLEW network just happened to look in the right direction at the right moment ...'

A flick of the wrist silenced him. 'Issue the usual statement condemning the warmongers' irresponsible reaction to false alarms caused by their own negligence and incompetence, etcetera, etcetera. Then I'll want a full report and explanation right after the parade.'

The crowd roared with delight at the sight of Soviet firepower but, viewed from the top, the mighty FOB looked suddenly as phoney and dead as the effigy with the Vandyke in the belly of the tomb under the *Nachalnik's* feet.


I've never known how hard it could be to chat up an old love, thought Maxon, refusing to admit that the length of separation was a less formidable obstacle than the fact that the affair might be finished but not yet over. He told her that only a few minutes earlier, the world had been on the brink of war, that it was no false alert, that the chances were that neither of them would survive the time it took her to drive the last mile or so to the hospital. Then there was a pause. An embarrassingly long one.

Maxon sought refuge in clichés. 'It's good to see you.' At least it was true.

'Likewise.' She made it sound light. Too light. He could tell.

'You haven't changed at all.'

'May I take that as a compliment?'

'That's what it was meant to be.'

'I would have preferred a kiss, Maxon. Compliments are not your style.'

In the silence that followed, the echo of her words thrashed about desperately until he offered her a drink – the

17

convenient life-belt of any drowning conversation. 'What can I get you?'

'What's this? Washington's most exclusive speak-easy? Complete with bouncers?'

'Hope they weren't too awful to you at the gate.'

'I must disappoint you. I still don't strip readily.'

'I'm sorry. I needed something, but I couldn't think of any other easy means of positive identification.'

'Wasn't it lucky that you knew your visitor so intimately?' Before he could answer, she quickly changed the subject. Maxon wondered whether she was more afraid of a yes or a no. 'Are the heavies here to keep people in or out?'

'Take your pick.' Maxon hesitated. The question was, how had she found him? But since she was here, she might as well know where she was. 'The maniac in charge of security must have decided that if a CIA sanatorium is camouflaged as a CIA sanatorium, nobody will believe that it's either CIA or a sanatorium. Anyway, it helps to keep the oil sheiks out without insulting them.'

'And reserve the beds for really special patients?'

'I'm not that special.' He noticed she was eyeing the brown medicine bottle the nurse had left on his bedside table.

'Modesty won't get you anywhere.' She picked up the vial.

'It got me in here.'

She shook the bottle. The metallic clink confirmed her suspicion. She remembered the 'scrap metal' collection in a shoe-box in his Hampstead cottage. The bullets, the broken tip of a flick-knife some sailor had once left in him, the ugly piece of shrapnel he used as a paper-weight ...

'How did you find me?' he asked casually.

She ignored the question, unscrewed the bottle top, and let the distorted bullet drop on her palm, weighing it. 'Seven-point-one-five Tokarev?'

'A fair guess.'

'Still a KGB favourite? Or was it border guards?'

It was his turn not to hear the question. 'How did you find me?'

'We used to work together – remember? You taught me.'

'What? How not to answer questions?'

'That, too. But does it really matter? Only half an hour ago, the mushroom was about to go up. Mind you at least

18

we'd have died together. That's something, isn't it?' She knew she had failed to turn the prospect of death into a big joke. She looked away. 'You think there'll be war? . . . No, it's a stupid question. If you knew, you wouldn't tell me.'

'Stop it, Jack.'

She looked away. Her voice grew weaker and softer: 'Nobody calls me Jack any more.' He resisted the invitation to play. His eyes remained cold, waiting. She shrugged her shoulders. 'I had to find you. I tried everything but it was no good. So as a last resort, I phoned Edie.' She spotted the first flicker of anger and tried to excuse his old Cerberus of a housekeeper hurriedly. 'She didn't know where you were. She only gave me a box number.'

'She shouldn't have.'

'Blame me. She wouldn't have known that I could trace you from that.'

'That's not the point.'

She knew it was not. She shared Maxon's view that Edie had been born withered, grumpy and ancient, just about bearable at the best of times, senile and pathologically possessive of late. Every now and then, Maxon would exclaim that she was quite impossible and she would have to go, but Jack had never believed him. When she had told him she was convinced he would give up his job and all his women before he would do anything drastic about Edie, he had laughed it off: 'Well, every man needs at least one steady relationship.' And their relationship was nothing if not steady. Fate had brought them together in India when Maxon worked there under diplomatic cover.

Driving from Delhi to Agra, he stopped at a ramshackle hut for a Seven-Up that was a little warmer than his own saliva, then walked across to a vast field alive with vultures. He was about to take some photographs when he noticed a frail woman, curled up and dusty at the feet of the flock, dying apparently, almost ready to make the birds a meal. Maxon pulled her away – the mean creatures gave way grudgingly. He fed her with his last sandwich, bought her a drink, and offered to drive her to the nearest village. From that point, there was no turning back. If Maxon had saved her, she claimed, her life belonged to him. And to his young wife and little boy. Someone named her Edie. Probably the child. When the Maxons were transferred, first to Hong Kong, then to London, Edie went with them as part of the household. Their lack of money was no problem: she had to be forced to accept her pay anyway.

At the end of a particularly eventful period, Maxon was thought to be too vulnerable. It was his superiors' indisputable request that his wife and three years old son should live away from him, under an assumed name, for a while. His boss, friend and mentor, Sandy himself arranged temporary accommodation for them in army married quarters, near Aldershot. Edie stayed in Hampstead to look after Maxon who visited the family regularly, using different cars and routes every time. It was Edie who took the early morning phone call to tell Maxon that an explosion had devastated the house and killed his wife and son. A lengthy inquiry came to the conclusion that a gas explosion had been caused by a faulty central heating boiler, but Maxon would never believe it. On the night when it happened, he was supposed to be there. His plans had been changed only an hour before leaving for Aldershot. Nothing would convince him that the accident had not been engineered.

From then on, he saw everybody close to him in mortal danger. Like a battleship preparing for action, he battened down all his emotional hatches every time he felt he might get seriously involved with anyone. And in Edie, he had a perfect, natural ally. Beyond being her master of life and death, he became her son-substitute to be protected, ferociously, from everybody, particularly women. She knew how to make them uncomfortable and unwelcome in his house. Sometimes it suited Maxon, mostly he just let her grumble and sulk – until Jack came along. Then Edie had made her choice, and she made no secret of it. So it was no surprise to Maxon that she had given Jack the box number. And Jack, who liked the old stick dearly, had to be quite desperate to find him before she would take advantage of her.

'She's impossible,' said Maxon.

Jack said nothing.

'And don't you defend her just because she tried to talk us into marriage.'

She clinked the bullet in the bottle to contrast her emphatic silence.

'And she was very cross with me when you left me.'

'When *I* left *you*, Maxon?'

'Well, whichever way you want to put it. I mean it

certainly wasn't me who married somebody else, virtually within minutes, after we'd broken up.'

'It must be useful to have a selective memory.'

'Can't hurt.'

But it did. She turned away from him and walked to the window. She was determined not to cry but did not quite trust herself. She pressed her cheek to the cool of the glass. The grounds below were now floodlit by the sun. The chatty porter who had shown Jack to Maxon's was pushing a gleaming bike along the path. It looked a much too racy contraption for an old man. Jack hoped he knew how to ride it. He would, she thought, if he really rode out on it every lunchtime on medical advice, as he had claimed on their way up.

She spun round. 'Are you still paranoiac about the danger to all who may ever be close to you?'

'Please don't try to see me as an old romantic.'

'Would you prefer to be seen cold and pompous?'

'Am I?' His voice revealed he had been stung.

'No. But you tried to be just once. When you broke it up and told me *no matter how painful it is, lovers in this post-war period* ...'

'Oh yes,' he interrupted her sharply, 'the good old days of the post-war period.'

'You make it sound as if it was ages ago.'

'It was. We're in the pre-war period now.' He looked at his watch. 'Damn, we might have missed Locke.' He switched on the television set and waited impatiently. If Locke had made only a brief announcement ...


Captain Beck was engrossed in Locke's self-assured performance, and swore when Nurse Keenan's call interrupted his pleasure. 'Make it quick, will you?'

'It's just that you wanted me to report every time Mr Maxon had a visitor and as this is the first time ...'

'Who's it?'

'A Mrs Kowalski. Kay-o-double-u ...'

'It's all right. We know her. Thank you. Let me know how long she stays.' He rang off.

Nurse Keenan frowned. She would have preferred an assignment to report on Beck to Maxon.

'. . . Look, the President has asked me specifically to come to your studio and tell your viewers that this was no false alert. We were threatened and we were warned. GLEW did for us what the geese did for Rome. Why the Russians chose to threaten us at this particular moment in time, we can't tell. Not yet. But now we know that the free world is a safer place under the GLEW umbrella.'

'That's not exactly what the Russians say.'

'Of course not. Moscow claims that our new Global Early Warning system is a tool of the warmongers.' General Larry Locke Jr smiled endearingly at such a childishly transparent propaganda statement. His looks, the battle-hardened face with the innocent twinkle in the eyes, were brought into full play. Viewers would surely understand why gossip-writers loved to speculate who would be best suited to bring one day the Locke legend to the screen – Peck or Stewart? 'There's no justification for the Russian stance. We've always played our cards face up. Nothing underhand.'

He sounded so blatantly sincere that it irritated Maxon as much as the interviewer who was trying to rattle him: 'Cards face up, General? You mean we've told them about GLEW in advance?'

'In principle, yes, because, as I've told you . . .'

'But you still haven't told us precisely what happened. Were we or were we not on the brink of war?'

'The President was in full control throughout and . . .'

'Is that why the Russians call our public alert an outright provocation?'

'Look, I was trying to put this all in proper perspective. You must allow me to complete one answer before you put the next question. And believe me, I'm here to answer any question, whatever you care to ask.'

'I take your point. Go ahead, General.'

'Thank you, sir.' Once again, there was the winning smile. Maxon nodded towards the screen: yes, Locke could sell life insurance to immortals. Locke seemed to stare back at him – he was now peering into millions of homes. 'Look, we maintained a nuclear balance for decades. Although sometimes they got ahead with the bomber gap, then the missile gap, we were still strong enough to protect peace. But then they developed their old favourite.'

'You mean FOB?'

'Precisely. Fractional Orbit Bombardment. It's a truly

space-age weapon because they can launch missiles from free-ranging battle stations in space. It rendered our early warning system obsolete, virtually overnight, and it opened a window of opportunity for them to launch a sneak attack.'

'We still had the radars, General.'

'Sure. But if we waited until a missile came up on the horizon for our radars to *see*, we'd be far too late with any retaliation. That's why we needed a new Global Early Warning system which was quite impossible until we'd created a new generation of extra-high-speed computers. Once they'd been installed aboard our satellites, GLEW was in business, and for the Russians, the party was over. They'd have to stop blackmailing us in every theatre of conflict, because GLEW had shut that window. You see, the old infrared warning system could spot only heat when rockets were fired to put something in orbit, launch a missile or correct the course of some space vehicle. But GLEW can track even a hamburger in flight, hot or cold.'

'And the Russians knew that?'

'We told them. So my guess is that they've panicked. Their economy is in a shambles, and they can't hope to match GLEW or even our high-speed computers with anything for years. They knew they couldn't afford it and they'd have to be good boys from now on unless ... unless we were bluffing. So they tried to call that imaginary bluff – and they were caught red-handed.'

'What if that launch was just a routine test?'

'Without due notification? And on course to hit Washington?'

'Is that certain, General?'

'It would have been a birdie, unless their guidance system broke down or something.'

'So you, personally, would have felt justified to wipe out Moscow?'

'A limited surgical response would have been more appropriate.'

'You mean *one* atom bomb or *one* ICBM?' Urged by impatient signals from his director's cage, he sneered.

'I mean a limited surgical response.'

'Is that why they aborted the launch?'

'Did they? We don't know. But maybe they got cold feet and ordered the missile to self-destruct when they monitored the public alert over here.'

'Ah! A blessing in disguise?'

Locke slowly raised and dropped his shoulders.

'Or a mistake on our part?'

'Unlikely.'

'But possible.'

'I said unlikely.'

'Aren't we supposed to be safeguarded by a series of filters and verifications to avoid just such mishaps?'

'We are.' Locke snapped smugly, and drank a few sips of water – probably for effect. 'That's why we can't rule out any explanation – not even sabotage.'

Maxon tried to guess what had happened: had Locke dropped a clanger or had it been an intentional slip of the tongue to frighten some suspects into foolish acts of cover-up?

'Sabotage?' The interviewer chewed on the word with relish. 'Can you elaborate on that?'

'No.'

'But ...'

'No. It's under investigation.'

'But you'll not deny that the incident was extremely dangerous.'

'I'll concur with you on that.'

'And it took us at least one step nearer to war.'

'I'll have to refer you on that to Moscow.'

'What I mean is that with their problems of food and industrial production, and now the nuclear balance tilting in our favour, they must think about war ...'

'Ask them. If you get an honest answer, tell me.' The old charm was rekindled, but Locke watched the man intently. He could sense that a twist was coming. Which way would it go? Would he be questioned on GLEW techniques and finances? He would have to dodge and wriggle, and it would look bad. Or else it could become an attack on USACAN. Why was only the US-Anglo-Canadian outfit privy to the secrets of GLEW? Didn't the government trust the European and other allies? Locke felt like going into battle the first time. The urge to vomit and relieve himself simultaneously. The fear and joy of life at its simplest. Go on, hit me, hit me hard and see what.

The interviewer tried to read his thoughts during the pause: you're a great supporter of the President – what's your fee, General? What office are you after? But that he would not ask. He followed on with the problems of the Soviet economy. 'Yet they have no choice, they must pursue the arms race, while GLEW will allow us to relax *and* divert funds to shoring up the dollar and fight unemployment.'

'Possibly.' Locke knew he was off the hook.

'Which makes the appearance of GLEW a lucky coincidence, doesn't it? I mean if, and I admit it's a big if, our warning system was ready earlier, ready to be pulled out of the hat, one might be driven to suspect that it was being used as a booster to the start of the President's re-election campaign.'

Locke tried to look suitably grave, as if he cared. 'I think I see what you mean, and I don't wish to seem elusive, but if this was a question, you'll have to put it to the President himself. All I can say is that today, the infant GLEW has scored a great victory for peace and . . .'

Maxon switched him off. He disliked working for GLEW, and hated serving under Locke who played all his cards so close to his chest that Maxon never quite knew what his actual job in GLEW security was.

'Come on, Jack, let's go for a walk.'

She was running out of time, but she did not want to argue.

She took out a cigarette. He gave her a light and made her smile: he was still carrying the battered old lighter – the courtesy of a life-long nonsmoker. It was like 'welcome home'.

On medical advice, the porter cycled vigorously. He turned off the road and carried on along the path through the sparse forest until he came upon a clearing bisected by a brook. He let the bike lean against a tree, and climbed the hump of a pretty wooden bridge that was more in keeping with a miniature Japanese rock garden than the Washington countryside. He unpacked his sandwich, taking care not to grease the outer wrapper bearing a note in handwritten capitals:

J KOWALSKI, PROBABLY MRS, FROM TORONTO: DARK HAIR, 35–40, SHORT VISIT – M. MAY LEAVE SOON, SAID TO BE FIT.

The porter sat down on the bridge, feet dangling perilously close to the water. He munched away and, over his sandwich, systematically reviewed his horizon of trees, bushes, clearing. Nothing moved, no sign of anyone. He carried on with his lazy meal while his right hand, clutching a drawing pin and the note, explored the underside of the plank on which he sat. His jaw stopped involuntarily in the middle of a bite as he concentrated on the minute effort that drove the pin into the wood. His fingers checked that the folded wrapper was securely held in its hiding place.

He finished his lunch unhurriedly, listened to the birds for a few seconds, then got on to his bike and set out towards the hospital, feeling good. The day's drop had been done, he had given them something which was a change after weeks of nothing, and if it was not enough for them, they knew what they could do with it, see if he cared.

'You didn't really want to walk, did you?'

'No.' Maxon stopped to admire the expanse of a vast flower-bed – and ascertain that there was nobody within earshot. 'You wanted to tell me why you needed me so urgently. It sounded confidential.'

'And you think your room is bugged?'

'Not necessarily. But why take chances?'

Yes, it all came back to her. The caution, suspicions, his almost paranoiac fear that his loved ones might get hurt by Them, the Opposition, whoever they might be at any given moment. But then, losing his wife and son must be enough of an experience for a lifetime. 'My husband needs help.' She hoped it did not sound too dramatic.

'My husband and I . . .' he began in a mocking tone, but stopped and changed tack. 'Why are you so formal?'

'Marriage is a formal affair.'

'You mean some marriages are.'

'Perhaps.'

'And what's the correct form when you send your wife to get help from an ex-lover?'

She decided he did not mean to hurt her, so she chose to ignore the cutting edge of the sentence. 'He didn't send me. He must never know that I've turned to you.'

'Is that fair? I mean to share secrets with me about him?'

'I don't know – you tell me.'

'Do you love him?'

'You know, you both know the answer.'

'Poor old Kowalski.' Maxon was angry with himself. He kept saying things unintentionally. He was bitching. He was jealous, even envious. And it irritated him because he thought he had cured himself of both.

Occasionally, Jack also thought about her husband as 'poor old Kowalski'. But a private thought was very different from an actual remark behind his back. Her loyalty drove her to say something defensive about the man she did love in a way. 'We have a warm relationship.'

'Developed along CIA guidelines?' something snapped in him and he longed to retract it but did not quite know how. Yes, Jack had looked after the old scientist's security, and yes, she had married him on the rebound, but her marriage was not an assignment and Maxon knew she was genuinely fond of the man.

Jack came to his help. She meant to say *Maxon, you fool, you still love me, only that can make you so nasty – so why aren't we together, why don't we raise children or funds for a home for stray, old scientists, and why don't I tell you everything you ought to know?* But she only mumbled, 'I'll pretend you haven't said that.'

'And I'll apologise for what I haven't said.' He was grateful. And ashamed of himself. 'Let's stick to the business in hand, shall we? What help does he need?'

'Tell me something first. And please be honest. Are you a party to his destruction?'

'Not as far as I know. Who's destroying him?'

'I don't know. But it's got to be connected with GLEW, and as you're GLEW security . . .'

'How do you know?'

'I was trained by you, in the post-war era, remember?'

'Touché.'

She looked away and listened to the dogs barking among the trees. 'They're throwing him to the dogs,' she said absent-mindedly, then shook her head and made an effort to sound objective and strictly unemotional. 'It began a few months ago. They stopped his research grants one after another. He told me about mounting difficulties in his access to vital sources of information. It began to look as if he had been cut off. But nobody said anything. Then he was thanked for his services as a consultant or adviser to various organisations, and his appointments were "terminated regretfully". After that, it came as no surprise to us that he was suddenly transferred to a quite poor and insignificant research outfit in Toronto. Secretly, I concluded that he was getting too old and useless, that they had put him on ice with a sinecure in recognition of services rendered. But no, the whispers continued.'

'What whispers?'

'All sorts. About him. His work.'

'His integrity?'

'Yes ... in a way ...'

'Has he been accused of anything?'

'Nothing. Not a word. That's why he can't defend himself. How do you argue with whispers you can hardly hear, let alone attribute to anyone? How do you fight the silence? That killing silence that's all around us? It's grossly unfair.'

'Fair, unfair? What a charming relic of the post-war era.'

'Don't play the cynic, Maxon, you're not as rotten as you like to look.'

'Then be more objective and stop playing the naive little helpless housewife I invented for you as cover. You must have some idea what's going on.'

'I can think of only one thing. He must be suspected as a serious risk or an actual traitor.'

'By whom?'

'Your people? You know that his research had something to do with GLEW.'

No, Maxon did not know what Kowalski's job was. He knew far too little about GLEW itself, and it was no secret that he resented that. He objected to Locke's *modus operandi*, his insistence on code-names and boy-scoutish security procedures, and he protested vociferously against excessive 'need to know' restrictions which shackled if not paralysed him. About Kowalski himself he knew that some people saw him as a grand old man, gentle and honest, hateful of politics and politicians which should be no surprise considering that he had been persecuted by every major dictator of the century. But Jack did not need to discover how ill-informed Maxon was, and it would have embarrassed him if she had. 'Oh, I know he's the father of the faster computer or something,' he said airily.

'Godfather. If that.' Jack corrected him. 'His work has always been purely theoretical.'

'It's no good telling me. I'm a technological illiterate.'

'But so is he! He doesn't understand how GLEW works. So how could he give away something he doesn't know?'

The question was begging for a counter-question, but Maxon was reluctant to ask. She was holding back. At least not volunteering essential information. If that was the way she wanted it, that was how it would have to be. He did not ask her to come here. He did not feel like cross-examining her.

She sensed the mood of his silence. Reluctantly, she nodded: 'You're right. I'm sorry. I've done some thinking and I've developed a hypothesis, but it's no more than that. And I thought we could discuss it better in Toronto – I mean all three of us . . . I mean I wanted to ask you to come to Toronto. Just for a day or two.'

'Why?'

'To talk to Joseph. And if you believe him, to help clear his name. I'm sure you can imagine how desperate I must be if I've come to you.'

She seemed humiliated and it gave him no pleasure. 'What's the hypothesis?' In his experience, nothing could restore shattered people's self-confidence more readily than a simple question of fact they could answer with certainty.

'As there had never been any direct accusation, I tried to date the beginning of Joseph's misfortunes. And it seemed to work. Everything pointed to the weeks after an incident in East Germany.'

'Oh?'

'Please don't jump to conclusions. It was all above board. As you know, no, perhaps you don't, he was an accredited expert at the Vienna disarmament conference. But you know how he hates flying . . . no? Well, he does. So once when he had to go first to Hamburg, he took the train from there through East Germany.'

'Without clearance?'

'Oh no! GLEW security okayed it.'

'So he was still in GLEW-related research at the time.'

'Yes, but he didn't tell them anything.'

'Them?'

'East German police. They took him off the train at Dresden.'

'How long did they keep him?'

'Two days. But they didn't even question him.'

'Is that what he says?'

'Don't you believe him?'

'I don't know. I'm not his wife.'

She blushed. 'He's no liar.'

'Perhaps not. Perhaps they didn't *need* to question him. Perhaps they'd already found what they wanted. Has he got a list of papers he was carrying?'

'Yes. There were some research notes, but nothing secret.'

'Anything relevant to GLEW?'

'Theoretically, yes, but nothing that wasn't translated even into Russian a long time ago. It's in every library.'

'Well, I don't want to be unhelpful, but if it's anything to do with GLEW, you must first talk to that old fool Locke. Not that he'll lift a finger without authorisation in triplicate.'

'I've tried and you're right: he stalled and stalled and stalled. but he's no fool. He asks a million questions, radiates sympathy and goodwill – then doesn't do a thing. And I can't understand why. He must know that Joseph is innocent.'

'So what do you expect from me? Miracles?'

'Perhaps.' They stopped at her car.

'You overestimate me. Like you overestimate Locke. Which probably makes you a full-blooded Canadian: you always overvalue the Yanks and the Brits. Sometimes even the French.'

'Not more than all of you tend to underestimate us. We'll talk about it in Toronto.'

'When we're not too busy talking to Kowalski?'

'You need to see him only once or twice. You'd restore his self-respect, I'm sure. You could tell him how to clear his name.'

'I'll think about it.'

'Thanks,' she beamed and suddenly her face was almost touching his.

'Take it easy – I haven't promised anything.'

'I know.' She hesitated. He let her. He let it be her choice. Cheek? Lips? He could feel her breath. She compromised and kissed the corner of his mouth, then withdrew hastily. The porter cycling by nodded towards them with the smile of the man who understood lovers. 'Let me know when you arrive. I'll book you a room. And I'll pick you up at the airport.'

One of perimeter guards came running. 'Call for you, sir. You could take it in the sentry box over there.'

Maxon turned to Jack: 'It shouldn't take long – will you wait?'

'No. I'll miss the plane. and I'd better go before I start feeling soppy, and sorry for myself.'

It was Locke on the line. No, it was not urgent at all, he hoped he had not disturbed Maxon. He was pleased that Maxon had seen him on television, and he was sorry that he had no further information to add. 'I'll keep you posted, don't you worry.'

Maxon volunteered to start the potential sabotage investigation right away.

'No dice, dammit,' Locke bellowed down the line, 'not even if I got to handle it myself.'

'I could . . .'

'No, you couldn't. I'm under orders to make sure that you're safe from the Russkies until they cool down. They must know that it's you who got General Sarian across the border, and they must be hopping mad. In fact, we're all amazed that you're still alive. Usually they're much quicker and more efficient when it comes to taking revenge. Are you in their pay or something?' He laughed with gusto. 'Or are you living on borrowed time?'

'I'll tell you if I live long enough.'

'I should hope so. Incidentally, Sandy sends his regards. He tells me you're in line for some medal.'

'I'm flattered. To the core.'

'It's good to hear you're back to form, Maxon. You're lucky to have me for a chief. Other people might object to your habit of throwing a little acid in your superior's face, but not me, buddy – I was brought up on napalm.'

'It's very reassuring, sir. That's why it's so nice to work for you. How's the debriefing going?'

'Beautifully. Sarian is singing like some bird, whatever singing bird they have in sunny Armenia, and no mocking. He's a goldmine of information and I'm not surprised that Moscow is fuming. They must want your head on a plate.'

'Before it's delivered, I ought to see Sarian to clear up some details about his defection.'

'Naturally. I'll arrange it as soon as it's feasible. But first get well. And that's an order. The white House itself keeps a tab on you, and we're reporting on your progress daily. Your stock over there is real high right now.'

'Would that entitle me to a few days' leave?'

'A vacation? Sure. Pick a nice spot, take someone vivacious, and take your time – if you're still young enough to call that sort of thing a vacation. Then you'll be ready to clear up this public alert balls up for me.'

'I might go to Toronto, if that's okay with you.'

'Why not? You've got friends there, haven't you?'

'It's no secret.'

'No. But you'd never guess who else is in Toronto these days ...' Locke paused for effect. 'Volodya Ellsberg.' He savoured Maxon's silence.

'What's he up to these days?' Maxon hoped to sound no more than mildly interested.

'Not much. He's too old. They put him out to pasture. Trade delegation or something.'

'That's crazy. He's probably the best man Moscow's ever had.'

'I take your word for it. You've had plenty of experience with him.'


The young Russian keep-fit enthusiast was becoming a well-known feature of the forest. Every afternoon in the past few weeks she had parked her car at quarter past four precisely, and rain or shine, had gone for an energetic cross-country run. Now at the half-way mark she rested for two minutes on a small wooden bridge that spanned a lively brook. She took a few deep breaths while her fingers were drumming impatiently on the underside of the plank. She found the note, removed it, pressed the drawing pin into the wood next to a knot to show that the message had been collected, rose and returned to the car in a furious trot. She was intensely unhappy with the arrange-ment. She regarded her new boss, a second secretary in administrative charge of the Embassy cultural section, as an amateur. The drop, the pick-up and her own cover smacked of unprofessionalism that could turn out to be costly even as a temporary measure. She decided to tell the

Resident himself or send a personal report direct to the Centre.

No matter how much light the oak panelling absorbed, there was plenty left to glitter on the immense sheet of glass atop the heavily carved partners' desk which was big enough to accommodate a not too fertile Moscow family – or so the bitchier of the Kremlin wits estimated, with others retorting that if any family had so much living space to themselves, they would stop being infertile. Members of the Politburo inner circle saw that desk as a symbol of 'collective leadership for one', and laughed dutifully whenever their leader declared that the partner's side was reserved for his inseparable fellow traveller.

But this evening, nobody felt like joking. The hawks had gambled against the scarecrow and lost; the *Nachalnik* had gambled on their gamble and so won; and now the select few present waited silently to see which way the heads would roll. Marshal Beryov, the most likely candidate for the axe droned on and on as if afraid that any closing remark would be his last ever.

The *Nachalnik* seemed to be totally absorbed in scrutinising the glass top which was a monument of his fingerprint-phobia. No papers were ever allowed to lie on it any longer than absolutely necessary. The two identical, embossed leather writing sets that faced each other permitted the 'partners' to swap places at will. Tonight he chose to sit facing the window, which meant that not all his guests, his closest acolytes, would be able to watch and gauge every twitch of his features. He half heard Beryov saying something about apologies. That the Soviet Union would have to apologise, in a way, well, to some extent, a mere formality, more a gesture of goodwill than apology, but then the Americans would also have to make a gesture, apologise, yes, why not? – all very confusing, just the way Beryov, a man of cold logic, would want it this time to talk himself off the hook. Because the *Nachalnik* had always seemed to oppose the plan, and deemed the test as being too provocative. So what could be the next step now, after having been caught out? Further escalation? Escalation at a time when GLEW had nullified the winning chance of a sneak attack?

Over the distant chime of the Kremlin clock, Beryov tentatively suggested he should sum up his report. His voice faltered, he waited for some reaction. 'So to sum it up . . . if I may . . .' and after a long pause, a direct question to the *Nachalnik*, 'I mean . . . may I?'

The answer came with a sustained explosion that threatened to sweep the marshal off his feet. 'Yes, yes, yes! You want it in writing? No? That's a change. I'm told that in the decadent, impotent and doomed so-called democracies of the west, millions of things get done on individual initiative or on the authority of a wink or nod or just sympathetic silence. Could that be the greatest difference between them and us? Could it be that our peasants would soon delay the harvest till January if the weather fails to carry written authorisation and they must wait for ministerial approval in triplicate? What have we done to our people, comrades? What have we done to you, Alexei Ivanovich, treble hero of the Soviet Union? . . . I'm asking you . . . What an eloquent silence . . . All right, carry on, you have mighty witnesses in this office that you've been authorised duly by the head of the USSR to complete your summing up.'

Beryov tried to argue yet again that the test had been a success at least inasmuch as clarifying the power of GLEW. 'What I really mean is . . .'

A single glance silenced him. The *Nachalnik* spoke softly but nobody in the room would mistake that for any mellowing of the will: 'We know what you mean, Alexei Ivanovich. You and the other great military brains have been telling us what you meant for years. But what you really meant was that we must spend, spend, spend, because this time, and every time, you had a real final solution. That's how you talked us into the creation of the costly bomber gap to put us ahead in the fifties. They soon caught up with us, so we had to fork out more to achieve the missile gap of the sixties, then even more on the nuclear recovery gap of the seventies, and then bankrupt ourselves to open this window of opportunity of the eighties which is now shut in our face by this . . . this GLEW that did to us what the U2s did to Nikita Sergeyevich in Cuba – and all because you insisted on running this test.'

'We had no choice. We had to devise a test because the KGB, I'm sorry to say, has been unable to supply any reliable information on GLEW.'

The Mad Monk Director of the KGB was on his feet even before Beryov had finished his accusation. 'I must repudiate this totally unfounded allegation. Within the new budget limitations imposed upon the service . . .'

'Ah! Another of our big spenders!' The *Nachalnik* really began to enjoy himself. 'What would the two of you suggest? Shall we increase the defence budget to twenty per cent of our GNP – and issue a begging bowl to every muzhik in the land?'

'Well,' Beryov tried to cool the situation, 'the missile forces, in agreement with the general staff . . .'

'I'm asking for *your* suggestion, Alexei Ivanovich.'

'We can foresee the need to resort, perhaps, to certain other means to counter GLEW.'

'If you mean an EMP test, the answer is no.' He polished a corner of the plate-glass furiously. 'No.'

'It's the cheapest. And just a test.'

'That test is war. Are you suggesting that war is cheaper than the arms race?'

'It doesn't need to be war, not necessarily.'

'That's your guess. And I don't like guesswork. My artillery didn't guess which the key targets were when we had reached Berlin. Just flattened the lot.' He was greatly amused. 'It left no room for errors. So stop guessing, comrade.'

But Beryov was not yet ready to throw in the towel. 'The whole problem is the western aggressors' responsibility. They alone have changed the nuclear balance with GLEW.'

'Is that so? I thought a warning system was purely defensive.'

'With due respect, nothing is pure or defensive in global strategy. And GLEW is such a major break-through that even our best scientists fail to understand how it works.'

That was a fine opportunity for the *Nachalnik* to change tack. 'How come?' He turned to the ghostly pale Director of the KGB and wondered if the man had any blood in his veins. Or was his ineradicable pallor something he shared with his long-serving prisoners? 'Have your primadonnas failed completely to penetrate the organisation that runs the system?'

'We're actively pursuing the matter.'

'But we still can't copy the system because you've failed to break the code they use – is that correct?'

'They use some extra-high-speed computers. That's the key to the system.'

'That's no answer.'

'And their security is quite exceptionally successful. The operators are handpicked only from three countries, that's why our usual NATO sources are useless. But we've initiated certain steps to eliminate some of their key security personnel.'

'Eliminate?' The *Nachalnik* pressed in the knife and turned it slowly. 'You mean you've failed to buy or blackmail them?'

'Our field units have now been authorised to employ certain extreme measures ...'

'Thank you, comrade director. You'll be authorised to put your failure in writing. In triplicate, please.'

Captain Beck telephoned Nurse Keenan but all she could say was that Maxon's visitor had already left. He reported it to Locke who just nodded and said, 'Yes, she's on her way home. But there's something I want you to do urgently.' He handed him a list of questions, demanding detailed answers to every one of them.

Beck's eyes lit up as he looked at the questions: the assignment implied that Locke had confidence in him. 'I'll do it discreetly,' he said lowering his voice conspiratorially.

'No, Alvin, you won't. Your job is to create a goddam stir in the office and beyond. You telephone the London office and demand their answers. Then you call Omaha. I want everybody, but absolutely everybody, to know that the President himself is determined to find out how the public alert slipped through. And if there're further inquiries from the media, you can leak what sort of questions are on your list. Is that clear?'

'Yes, sir, it's just that I thought that you wanted Mr Maxon ...'

'And you were right, Alvin. Eventually, I'll want Maxon in on this because beyond any doubt, he's the best man for the job. It's no reflection on you. None at all. You haven't got the background, the experience.'

'You like him, don't you, sir?'

'Like him? He's a pain in the ass. But he's good. Goddam good.'

Antonin Kobelyev took pride in his work. He knew that many people in the KGB First Chief Directorate would regard a collator's job as lowly, dull and merely clerical, but he measured it by the fact that he kept tabs on many a glamour-boy in the field. *And* he was authorised to handle Residents' relevant messages from every corner of the globe. *And*, occasionally, like right now, he would be required to report to the colonel himself.

Kobelyev stared at Maxon's photographs. He knew much of the man's life story by heart. Fresh information, coming in daily, contained nothing of obvious value, but that never worried Kobelyev. Slowly, little by little, it was bound to add up to something to satisfy his chief's upsurge of interest in the Englishman.

Now and again, Kobelyev would have liked to get on to some agents and demand answers to questions nobody else seemed to ask. There was, for instance, the enigma of the remarks overheard and recorded at an Istanbul cocktail party in 1962: 'Good chap, Maxon – alas, a redbrick man,' and the British ambassador's answer: 'Pity.' Now what did that mean? Somebody once pencilled a note on the margin of the report: 'Low credit limit?' Kobelyev thought he might like to interrogate somebody one day. But then he dismissed the thought. It was more exciting to remain invisible.

The fresh note from Washington lay next to the photographs. A visitor. Female. Mrs? Kowalski. J. J for what? Jean? Joan? He remembered a girl friend ... On impulse, Kobelyev ran a computer check. After all, it was his understanding of the newly installed computer that had secured him his job. He wished they would give him his own terminal. But that was perhaps too much to ask when it took only twenty minutes to get answers. And there it was: J for Jacqueline. He asked for a cross-checking: could it be the same woman? Was there any record of a Kowalski?

Instead of the answer, a colonel from the key disinformation department came personally to him and demanded an explanation: 'Who authorised you to ask for the Kowalski file? And why? In what context?' Kobelyev made a full statement. The colonel took all his notes and warned him not to ask for anything about Kowalski ever again. Which was rather pointless to say, Kobelyev thought, because obviously, there must be some restriction imposed on the computer: that was how the colonel had so promptly been told about his inquiry.

It would have pleased the collator immensely to hear his colonel telephone the Director's office a few minutes later. The colonel explained how he alone had thought about 'putting two and two together' concerning Maxon and Kowalski, listened to the answer on the line, and permitted himself the modest smile of the man who is about to be beatified in his lifetime.

Air Canada had just announced the departure of flight 212 to Toronto. Passengers were requested to proceed to gate number 6. The airport was as busy as if the whole of Washington was trying to flee from some disaster threatening the capital. Even in the telephone bubble the noise was such that the ringing tone on the line could hardly be heard. Luckily, the call was answered right away.

'Sovetskoye torgovoye predstavitelstvo.' In Toronto, the Soviet trade delegation had a good name for friendly efficiency.

'I'd like to talk to Mr Ellsberg.'

'Who's calling?'

'Jack.'

'Hold on, please.'

After a click, a short pause, and another click, Ellsberg was on the line: 'Success?'

Jack felt like crying. 'Yes. He'll go.'

'Thank you. You're a clever woman. I hope he appreciates you.'

'And I hope they'll find something special for you in hell,' she said as she slammed the phone down. She was not sure if he had heard it. And she did not care.

# II

Nothing seemed to be going right for Jacqueline Kowalski.
Following her Washington visit, she had spent three days
trying to contact Maxon, but all she discovered was that he
had left the hospital. Locke's office would say no more than
that he was on vacation, and Edie did not know – or was not
permitted to say – even that. Then came the telegram from
Maxon with the barest details of time and date of his arrival.
The time revealed that it was a flight from London. So
she called Edie once more – in vain, yet again. And
now, it appeared, she had picked the worst cab driver in
Toronto.

Judging from his opinionated insolence and touch of
Newyorkese, not to mention his driving style, it must have
been the Bronx that groomed him as a wheel-whirling
political know-all. His eyes were firmly on the radio –
not the most reassuring sight for a passenger – and in
contrast to his slow driving, he was quick to comment on
the transmission with a mixture of *pah*-s, *so-there* and
*rubbish*.

'Could you step on it, please?'

'You wanna get us killed? Can't you wait for the
holocaust?'

The radio reporter stopped talking. The ominous silence
was punctuated by a few mystifying noises. In the editorial
office of the Atomic Sciences Bulletin, a select group of
experts were about to advance the dreaded Doomsday
Clock towards the projected point of nuclear war.

'I've got to meet an incoming flight.'

'Lady, you'll meet your maker first if that clock hits
midnight.'

The reporter's husky whisper aimed to put the fear of God
into all his listeners: 'Two minutes to midnight. That's what
the clock on the cover of the Bulletin will show from now
on. And the next issue comes out tomorrow. In its thirty-
five years, the Doomsday Clock stood only once that close

to disaster. That was in 1953, when both sides were developing the first hydrogen bomb. So the experts have not taken lightly last week's nuclear alert in the west, the alert that slipped through and became public, causing panic and hysteria, in Washington. It is a fact that the Kremlin was caught red-handed. The question is: what will it do next? And the risk all round is graver than ever not only because of the introduction of the first bits of hardware for a true space war, but also because of the current new thinking. For the first time, to both sides, a nuclear war appears to be thinkable – and actually winnable ...'

That was too much solemnity for the cabby: 'Winnable, shwinnable, who cares if we're dead?'

Jack offered him ten dollars for every additional five miles on the speedometer. She was not going to explain to him that she could not prevent a more personalised disaster if she was late.

Passengers from the London flight had come through but there was still no sign of Maxon. At Jack's instigation, a ground hostess repeated a call for him to contact the airport information desk. There was no response. But the phone rang. The girl picked it up. 'Information ... yes ... hold on ...' She turned to Jack: 'Are you Mrs Kowalski?'

'Yes ...'

'A call for you. Could you please take it in the booth over there?'

Jack ran, squeezed through a bunch of Florida-bound octogenarians, and picked up the receiver, breathlessly shouting 'Where the hell are you?'.

'It's not him. Sorry to disappoint you.' The heavy Russian accent needed no introduction. 'You must be expecting young Maxon.'

'What if I am?'

'I thought we had a deal.'

'Spying on me wasn't part of it.'

'I could have warned you. Young Maxon is no fool. If he said he'd arrive today, he must have slipped into Toronto yesterday ... or the day before ... Does he suspect you?'

'No. Why should he?'

'Oh, I don't know, but I'm sure he's here ... somewhere ... watching you.'

Jack felt more and more uncomfortable. With two

invisible pairs of eyes on her, she just wanted to shout 'go home, Maxon, or join the merry widows on the next flight to Sarasota.'

Safeblower Gerry 'The Bang' Houlihan would not often abase himself to the level of sneak-in burglary. But then his mate Foxy was not all that often skint just on the day of his wedding anniversary. Houlihan had no cash to lend him, and the banks were already closed even to this pair of big-bang-men because they would never try to crack a safe on the spur of the moment without preparations. So they really had no choice.

They drove up to Highgate village, stopped the car in a street of largish, Tudorish semi-detached houses, and waited for the first hall-light to come on in full daylight: although the days were getting longer, many security-conscious owners would fail to adjust the time of their supposed deterrent to burglars. They watched the house with the light on for a few minutes. If anybody was at home, the light would soon be switched off. It was not. A visual double-check confirmed that the house must be empty. Houlihan drove the car to the house, and so covered Foxy who opened the tradesmen's door on the side by the sophisticated means of a single kick. Houlihan drove away, parked the car in the next street, returned and walked through the open door, carrying a parcel of books – a conscientious delivery man who would not want to leave goods in the open.

They helped themselves to a few trinkets to make a decent anniversary present, a 'little something' in the shape of a plated silver ashtray for Houlihan's missus (she would know it was nicked if it was sterling stuff), and a fine pen-knife with mother of pearl handle for the landlord of the Hound and Hare who was a collector of things like that. The landlord was, in fact, so pleased with it that he gave Foxy a bottle of cheap bubbly for the anniversary and a free meal to Houlihan. But Houlihan would never finish that meal. The law came in, went straight for the old safecracker (a most unusual indignity) and focused on the ashtray like a heat-seeking missile on a jet.

Houlihan just knew, and would never believe it otherwise, that he had been fingered. But by whom? That was the big q. The only person who might have overheard their discussion about Foxy's predicament was the geezer who had approached Houlihan a few minutes earlier. He seemed to know who The Bang was and offered to be helpful to him as well as a friend: 'Giv'im a shout on the blower. You never know, you and my pal, Maxon, might do some business together.'

Down at the station when they had turned his pockets inside out, a keen young detective constable spotted the telephone number on the inside of his fancy matches from the Hilton. 'And what would that be?'

'I dunno.'

'It's your matches.'

'No, they ain't. I found 'em. No law against it, is there? The Hilton ain't me local.'

The sergeant laughed as he should, but the young cop got mad. 'It's a Hampstead number. Is it a house you've done or is it something for a rainy day?' He left to find out whose number it was and eventually, returned with the news that the number was ex-directory. Now the sergeant became interested, but he, too, drew a blank: even he would not be told whose number it was.

Houlihan stuck to his story about the matches (he knew they could do nothing to him on acocunt of the ashtray or the matches) until there was a phone call which changed the sergeant's manner completely. 'You're in trouble, old son. A Mr Big Shot from Special Branch is coming over and you'd better call him guv or he'll chew your balls off.'

'Special Branch?'

'That's what I said, didn't I? You're in the shit, old son, so do yourself a favour, tell me the truth, and then maybe, maybe I'll tell them that you're no spy, just a stupid old safecracker who should know better than mixing it with security.'

So Houlihan saw no more reason to protect the geezer who had approached him in the Hare and Hound: 'He knew who I was and what I could do, I mean if I was criminally minded, and he says his mate, some Saxon or Maxon, some funny name, would like to meet me, and it could really be worth something to me, so I says why not, it's not criminal to meet, so he gives me the number and that's that, see?'

Maxon watched Jack leaving the airport. He felt reasonably certain that she was not being followed. He wished he could say the same with the same degree of certainty about himself. Although he had a busy schedule for the afternoon, he was delayed repeatedly by timewasting anti-surveillance routine. No, he had no obvious tail, but professionals with sufficient manpower, a pool of vehicles and some information about him would hardly attract any attention. Stop being so jittery, he scolded himself, what you feel in your bones isn't necessarily superior to cold logic.

He was a little late but managed to keep his 'meet' with a recently retired agent of Mounted Police intelligence. He joined the man in a conveniently 'out of order' service lift at the Chelsea Inn, and together they rode up and up for three minutes. 'No, nothing definite on K., but there's something wrong, and that's for sure,' the man sporting a greasy overall said. 'Fraud? Treason? Nobody says. Not to me. But it stinks. Wouldn't touch the old Pole with a barge.'

A French friend of a friend of a friend had done some checking on Jack for Maxon, but came up with nothing: 'She's clean – politically, *n'est-ce pas*? Morally? Who can tell? If yes, all men in Ontario must be blind.'

Papa Mike of the CIA, who did some photographic moonlighting for Maxon, had assembled a one-man-show, starring Kowalski, in the past few days: Kowalski at home, near the window, Kowalski driving, Kowalski with wife, with colleagues, with and without a hat, Kowalski arriving for work, Kowalski entering and leaving Friends' House. 'You know he's a dedicated Quaker, don't you? He's lecturing, too. You want him taped at the meeting tonight?'

No, Maxon did not want him taped. But he watched Kowalski's arrival, and he knew the meeting would last at least a couple of hours. So he drove round, spotted no tail behind or up front, and chose to pull up near Amesbury Park, some half a mile away from Kowalski's home. As he switched off the engine of the signal-red Chevrolet, a policeman approached him.

'Do you realise what noise you're making, sir?'

'Yes, it's a bloody nuisance, isn't it? I've just hired it for a week but it's going back to them tonight, I can assure you.'

The policeman shook his head in sympathetic despair: 'How can you trust them with the brakes if they don't do anything about the muffler being shot?'

Maxon walked round the block and, following Papa Mike's directions, found the service entrance out of the front porter's sight.

Jack paled as she answered the door. 'You . . . you weren't at the airport.' In the background, a kettle began to whistle.

'I was. Perhaps we missed each other. Aren't you going to ask me in?'

'No. I'll meet you somewhere. You mustn't be seen here.'

'Then you shouldn't let the kettle call the neighbours' attention.'

She ran to turn it off and Maxon followed her in. As the whistling died away, Stravinsky's Fire Bird could be heard through the open door of the living room. Jack's old favourite, Maxon thought. Jack turned to face him: 'You must leave.'

'What did you say?' He tried to act out the conversation of a friendlier moment: 'Did I hear "Hello, Maxon, it's good to see you?" And you, Jack. "Are you well?" Much better, thanks, now that I'm here. "Won't you have some coffee, darling?" Coffee?'

'Please go.'

'No, I'd prefer something stronger.'

'I'll explain everything.'

'Yes, something stronger. "You mean alcohol, my love?" Now that you mention it, yes. "Isn't it too early, darling?" Doesn't matter, I'm a late developer but an early starter.'

'Stop it. My husband . . .'

'No, don't worry, he won't be here any moment now. You know he's giving some lecture tonight. I've just left him at Friends' House.'

'You were with Joseph?'

'Not exactly with him . . .' He started towards the living room. 'Is he still a devoted Quaker?'

The room radiated warmth and friendliness. It was full of flowery prints, crazy antique lamps and eye-catching knick-knacks, with Jack, Jack, Jack written all over it.

'He must never find out that you came here.'

'Why? Would he divorce you?'

'Probably not. But he'd be hurt. Age might have deprived him of everything – except his pride.'

'And I thought there was such a lot to be said for impotence,' Maxon sighed. 'I'd have expected it to make life so much simpler.'

'Flippancy doesn't suit you.'

'But a Scotch would.'

'Okay. We'll have one, and then you go. Okay?'

'Having been dragged all the way to Toronto, I'd have expected a little friendlier reception.'

'I'm sorry, but in fact, I was trying desperately to prevent you from coming here.'

'Why?' He poured two fingers of bourbon into tumblers.

'I . . . I've changed my mind.'

He lifted his glass. 'Cheers. It's good to see you.'

'You weren't on the flight you'd given me.'

'True.'

'What made you so devious?'

'I'm not sure. Perhaps it's an old habit. Perhaps you acted a little unnaturally when you came to the hospital.'

'It was lovely to see you. Was that unnatural?'

'Perhaps not. But there was something you were holding back. You wouldn't have asked me to help Kowalski, not in a million years, without some very special, pressing reason.'

'He's innocent. Isn't that a pressing reason?'

Maxon slowly raised and dropped his shoulders. 'Maybe. And it may be a reason for fighting innuendos or whatever. But it doesn't explain why you came to *me*.'

She drank up, stared hard at the Persian rug until the pattern began to blur, then held out her glass without looking at him: 'Make it a small treble, will you?' Not that she expected their old private joke to win a smile this time. Pity. It would have been nicer if he smiled when she was seeing him probably for the last time. 'All right,' she said as he poured. 'I'll tell you why it had to be you, if you promise me something.'

'No promises. We could have bargained in the hospital. Now it's too late.'

'I know. I'm sorry.'

'Well?'

She took a deep breath. 'Like a fool,' she downed a big gulp, 'I made a deal.'

'With whom?'

'Volodya Ellsberg.'

'What fun.' His voice was flat.

'You don't seem very surprised.'

'I am, I'm not – does it make any difference?'

'Look, I made a mistake,' she swallowed hard. 'I'll understand if you never talk to me again. I don't mind.' She

45

did. She was almost in tears – not her style at all. 'But at the time I felt I had no choice. He held all the cards.'

'Where did you meet?'

'At a cocktail party.'

'Are you sure it was him?'

'He knew a lot about you. About us. He called me Jack, like you, perhaps to prove, that he knew even that.'

'Describe him.'

'Small, plump, in his sixties ... bright eyes ... pudgy fingers, yes, they went quite white as he pressed them together – hard, as if he was praying – when he said, "Please don't worry about young Maxon, he has nothing to fear, we're as close as that ..."'

'Okay, that's him.'

Ellsberg had never stopped calling him 'young Maxon' since the war. In fact, more often than not, 'young green Maxon' was the expression he used – and not without good reason. Maxon was only seventeen when they had their first clandestine meeting in Spain.

Maxon's parents had separated soon after his birth. During the war, he was at school in Switzerland, where his mother lived for a few years. His father was a driver attached to the British embassy in Madrid. In the summer of 1943, at the time when Italian generals approached Sir Samuel Hoare, the Ambassador, seeking a separate armistice behind the back of their German allies, and the Madrid-Lisbon-Tangier triangle was the intrigue-capital of the world, young Maxon had a rare chance to visit his father. On the third day of his visit, a tall and exceptionaly well-groomed diplomat (later to make headlines in a spectacularly scandalous way) approached the boy: 'I hear languages are your great hobby. Splendid, my boy, that's the spirit. Spanish and Russian, eh? Splendid. How about making those languages pay? A few pesetas? What? Or would roubles be more preferable?'

Maxon did not seem too keen: he thought he was being propositioned. But the diplomat quickly changed tack. Instead of financial incentives, he began to play on the boy's patriotism and saw at once that there he had a winning line. He was not asking for much. Maxon would only have to translate a seemingly quite innocuous message into Russian, memorise it, and deliver it verbally, to a man called Ellsberg. Above all, secrecy would be essential, not even his father must be told. Maxon would discover only years later that the diplomat needed him because his regular liaison, his only Russian-speaking agent, had gone missing (presumed drunk) on the most crucial day and, at that time, Ellsberg was so secretive that even his superiors did not know about his fast-improving English.

That one-off mission led to several others, and soon the boy proved himself so reliable that special favours were granted to him. That was how to his father's utter surprise, his mother was permitted to visit them in Madrid. Then father and son were transferred to Tangier (in the wake of Ellsberg), and by the end of the war, young green Maxon was an experienced, agent apprentice, paid quite handsomely from the Ambassador's sizeable fund under the key heading 'miscellaneous'. The plan was to let him go to university, but that had to wait when he was induced to join his friend, Ellsberg, in Germany, until the conclusion of the Nuremberg trials.

'What makes you so sure that it's him?' Jack asked, but Maxon pretended not to hear it.

'He offered you a deal?'

'Yes, he offered me evidence to clear my husband's name in return for a chance to meet you. But he'd give the evidence only to you.'

'Then why didn't he approach me?'

'He said he couldn't track you down. He lacked the resources, he said, he was too far from the centre of things these days.'

'You mean too far from the Moscow Centre?'

'Maybe.'

Yes, it was possible. Locke said he had been put out to pasture. 'And he made his offer at the cocktail party.'

'Yes, he approached me, and when he introduced himself I was intrigued. I remember how highly you had thought of him. But there was no time for getting acquainted through small-talk. He was quite blunt. He knew that Joseph was suicidal because of the mute accusations. And he played up my responsibility for this grand old man who had suffered more than his fair share.' She tried to imitate Ellsberg's accent. '*If he takes his own life, Mrs Kowalski . . .* He let it hang in the air, then switched to another line of blackmail. He said he wanted me to do you a favour.'

'Me? How come?'

'He said I mustn't tell you. It must be a surprise. I said "no dice". He argued I owed it to you to trust your friend.'

Maxon laughed. Yes, the twisted logic was pure Ellsberg.

'And then he produced yet another trump card. *I know I can really trust you, Jack, so I'll be frank* . . . He said it would be vital to meet you. Because the two of you could do something important.'

'What?'

'He mumbled sort of half-sentences. Something about the two of you preventing nuclear war. A pack of lies, obviously, to impress me. And that wasn't all. For he then tried to exploit my divided loyalties.' Her voice had begun to falter and she held out her glass.

Facing Friends' House, leaning against a tree, totally preoccupied with the lighting of his pipe, the man never had a chance. Even the woman who saw the car mounting the pavement had only half a chance to scream before the man in the ancient Burberry was squashed against the tree trunk.

The car reversed, jumped forward again, its bumper hitting the heap that used to be a human figure, reversed for the second time, and sped away.

Cries of anger and horror rose all round. An old man looked sick, closed his eyes and lost the battle to keep the vomit down. A punk-pink teenager ran to find a phone. A young woman fought to get near the tree in the tightening circle of stunned onlookers. 'Let me through . . . I'm a medic . . .'

A man looked around officiously. 'Has anybody got the registration number?' He was positively disappointed with the crowd when no definite answer was forthcoming.

'Sounded like a tank,' a bearded army-type volunteered. 'Brummm-brummm . . . like a tank.'

'What divided loyalities?' Maxon asked, prodding Jack gently to forget the drink and the pattern of the rug she seemed to be concentrating on.

'My loyalties to all of you. To an old man, an old love, an old notion of serving peace. He tormented me. He played out one loyalty against another – damaging them all in the process. I knew what he was doing and yet I couldn't stop listening. Waiters came, drinks were offered, people gossiped and laughed, and I fought not to let him see me waver.'

'I understand.'

'Do you? Do you, really?' Her voice was sharp with the sudden recognition of an old love's new face. 'Yes, perhaps you do. Perhaps that's just how you'd work if *you* had to pressurise someone.'

'He offered you a choice, didn't he? The final decision had to be yours.'

'Oh yes, that was the trick. But the odds were stacked against me, and he knew it – just as you know it. My first duty was to save Joseph. Or so it seemed at the time. And deep down I knew right away what a lovely excuse it would be to see you. So I said yes to Ellsberg, and from then on, it was just a blind rush to find you, go to you, talk to you, make you promise that you'd come and see me ... It was only then, back home, that I had my first chance to stop and think. I began to see the risk I might expose you to. And suddenly, even Joseph ceased to matter. All that mattered was that I should reach you and stop you. But I failed. So please go away. Now.'

'Without seeing Volodya?'

'Please.'

'Does he know I'm here?'

'I didn't tell him.'

'Then do. What exactly did he want to know?'

'Date of your arrival and the hotel where you'd be staying.'

Maxon burst out laughing.

'What's so funny?'

He began to whistle the 'March of the Toreadors'. 'He's incorrigible.' It was in Madrid that Ellsberg and young green Maxon invented a simple code and middleman system for arranging unforeseeable meetings. They knew they were watched by snoopers of all nationalities working for the Germans, and they managed to keep meeting, right under their noses, without a hitch. 'Okay, tell him I'm staying at the Seaway.'

'On Lakeshore Boulevard?'

'Yes, feel free to visit me.'

'I won't.'

'I know. And I didn't really want you to. But you will invite me to dinner, won't you?'

'No.'

'Why? I must meet your hubby, darling. Cosy dinner for three. Long time no see – you know what I mean.'

'Stop it.'

'Tomorrow?' His face told her this was no question.

'Yes, yes, okay.'

'Good. Don't forget to wash and put away my glass. Some men get suspicious when the old lady uses two tumblers in their absence.'

He stepped a little closer, but she backed away fast. 'No, please don't kiss me goodbye.'

'Did I intend to?'

For the first time she relaxed and smiled. 'Shame on you if you didn't.'


The woman who 'had seen it all' became quite hysterical whenever the policeman asked anybody else about the car and the sequence of events. It was her accident, she had to be the chief witness.

'Can you describe the driver, ma'm?'

'I told you. I saw it all. He was a young man. I mean middle-aged. You know what I mean?'

'And the colour of the car?'

'Well, you know, darkish. Yes, nigger-brown.'

'You mean chocolate.'

'I mean nigger-brown. Can't I say nigger-brown? Does it count as race discrimination?' She looked around for support from the crowd, but hostile glances were all she received. Some people claimed the car was yellow, others opted for red, a child insisted it was signal-red. The crowd developed a very poor view of the policeman who seemed to pay more attention to a twelve-year-old than anybody else.

'And you say it was a noisy car.'

'Like a tank,' the child said.

'Didn't I tell you?' The woman asked and earned at last some onlookers' sympathy.

'Yeah,' the bearded army-type nodded knowingly. 'Like a tank. You can tell Seapick it has a faulty muffler.'

50

The policeman took his word for it and radioed HQ C-PIC: the Canadian Police Information Computer would make the clue available to every patrol on the streets.

The red light flashed on Locke's private line. The general answered it at once: the caller might be *anyone from the President upwards*, which was Locke's private joke to say what he meant most seriously, that the few in the know within the international intelligence community were the ones who really mattered.

'San-dy.' Nobody could quite copy the way he said it. The elongated *san* was followed by a comma-long break and short sharp *dy*. Some people said he was born to be non-existent. Few people had ever met him, even fewer could guess what he did for a living if anything, hardly anybody knew that he had a hereditary title, nobody would believe that he was six-foot-four when he was not stooping (which never happened), and although it was generally agreed that he must have some other name or names, nobody would ever call him anything but San-dy – and even that only on account of the sparse growth at the tip of his Gothic cranium.

'Good to hear you. How are you?' Locke prepared for a lengthy conversation because he knew that Sandy equated small-talk with civilised behaviour. But this time, he was wrong.

'Listen, Scotland Yard picked up a safecracker with Maxon's telephone number on him. Any guess what the connection may be?'

'Perhaps both are short of cash.'

'Funny. But Maxon can crack safes. Or he can call on any number of our people. Unless it's, er ... private ...'

'I'm sorry. I don't know the answer. Maxon is on vacation.'

'Busman's holiday?'

'Meaning?'

'He was in London, buzzing around like a blue-arsed fly for two days. He kept bumping into a lot of people "accidentally". Including those at GLEW HQ, over here. And then this burglar connection.'

'What are you suggesting?'

'Nothing. I thought you ought to know.'

'Thanks, Sandy.'

'I mean he might be up to something. Or somebody might be trying to implicate him in something.'

'I'll look into it. Let me know if you have any new theories. But nothing on paper okay?'

'Righto.'


Maxon returned to Amesbury Park, approached his car from behind, swore all the way to the hotel because of the noise the exhaust made – if anything, it had become worse since he had parked the car – and resigned himself to a long, lonely vigil in his room, waiting for a phone call. He had breakfast in bed, upset himself listening to the news which was still full of theorising about the public alert and the proximity of an all-out nuclear confrontation, and it gave him no pleasure to think about Jack. He knew he had been a fool to send her away and ever let her go.

The phone rang at half past ten. 'Maxon . . .' he answered eagerly. After a few seconds' silence, he heard the first dozen bars of the 'March of the Toreadors', a click marking disconnection, and then the return of the open line sound. Maxon showered, dressed and left in a hurry. A few touristy inquiries at Reception revealed that as it was a Wednesday, the main sporting event in Toronto must be ice hockey, particularly now that the Swedish national team was in town. In the absence of bullfights, Ellsberg would expect him to be at the Maple Leaf Gardens, and make himself available to contact.

Maxon decided to leave his troublesome car in the hotel parking lot and use taxis until he exchanged it on Thursday. In the evening he arrived at the stadium a few minutes early, relaxed and tried to enjoy the game. It was no good guessing how contact would be made, but he could not help being more interested in the fans' antics than the players' crippling efforts.

Halfway through the game, he went for a drink. In the tumult around the bar, he found himself crushed against an appealingly fragile woman. She seemed in no hurry to back away, and he was not going to be the first to break contact. Her dress was as tight a fit as a complete skin graft. Her large, sadly empty eyes flitted about nervously to avoid entrapment into any exchange of glances; her sensuous lips seemed to contradict the primness of her expression. She reminded Maxon of the demure and impersonal Chinese housewives who walked the pavements outside Singapore's Change Alley and Raffles Hotel in the balmy hours after lunch to earn a little pin-money and delicacies for the family table. You'd better go, he warned himself sternly, and leaned hard against the crowd making room to turn and leave, when she asked him in an earnest whisper: 'Will you please tell me who's winning?'

'The bull.'

'That's funny. That's what a new friend of mine says.'

'He must be a witty man. I'd like to meet him over a glass of Sangria,' said Maxon absentmindedly. His eyes scanned the crowd: was Ellsberg among them?

'Sangria?' Her forehead aged with puzzled wrinkles. 'Shouldn't you ask my name?'

'I guessed it. Paloma – right?'

'Yeah.' She seemed lost. Definitely a one-off messenger, never again to be used or contacted. Expendable, too. Maxon wondered what sort of cock-and-bull story Ellsberg had dished out to her. 'Will you buy me a drink?' she asked because that came naturally to her.

'Aren't we supposed to go for a drive?'

'Sure. We'll use my car.'

On the way Maxon could not ask her to make inexplicable detours, and he saw no obvious sign of a tail, but he could not dispel the nagging sensation of being watched by shadows as they drove along Lake Ontario. 'We're almost home,' she said pointing towards some ramshackle houseboats beyond the floating palaces in the Yacht Club marina.

'Will my friend be there?'

'No, you'll have to spend a little time with me.'

Not an unattractive proposition, thought Maxon.

'Your friend said you must stay until ten thirty. Then you'll have to row very quietly to that ship . . . over there . . .'

It was a rather large white ship, anchored a little outside the main harbour towards the Toronto Island Airport. Strong beams of light lit up the sheet of water between the ship and the shore, leaving a mass of darkness beyond quite impenetrable to the naked eye.

'Your friend said you must row to the far side of the ship.'

'Yes, he thinks of everything. He's clever.'

'And funny,' she giggled. 'But he's not so clever as he thinks. He say's you're spies. But I'm not stupid. I think you're lovers. I can tell these things. And I don't mind. A little of what you fancy does you good, doesn't it?'

'Paloma's' boat was moored at the very end of a jetty which swayed with the wind and groaned in protest against being trampled on. Maxon stumbled deliberately because he wanted her to take his hand but was unsure how far a homosexual, not yet out of the closet, would go with keeping up pretences on a secret date.

'Give me your hand,' she said, 'I know every loose plank . . . And you may kiss me if you like . . .'

'Perhaps when I'm less in a rush.'

'I understand . . . it's just that people usually kiss me when we get here.'

'Oh. Then we'd better stick to the routine.'

In her cabin, it took him only a glance all round to satisfy his precautionary compulsion and familiarise himself with the scene. The single bed-sit was furnished mostly by a low platform which was packed high with large, soft cushions. There were two more cushions on the floor, a rocking chair, a sideboard with drinks, a few fishing nets and floats hanging from the ceiling to lend a maritime flavour. Two knotted string-curtains led to a shower cubicle and a galley for a most Spartan bachelor. There were three portholes. An enlarged window faced the lake.

'Paloma' put on all the lights, lowered a Venetian blind to cover the window but did not bother to curtain off the portholes. 'Your friend said you must kiss me, then pretend to undress, and then we must switch off the lights.'

So Ellsberg thought that somebody might be watching. It must be unlikely, because otherwise he would not risk the meet, but it was typical of him to think of it.

The girl made similar deductions, though for different reasons: 'Who'd be watching you? A friend? Another boy friend who doesn't mind if you go with a girl but would knife you if it was another man?'

'How on earth did you guess?' Maxon asked in astonished disbelief.

'I told you, I have an eye for these things.'

They embraced near the porthole, separated, began to

undress, then stopped to switch off the lights. Maxon sat in the rocking chair.

'Make yourself comfortable,' she said, 'you have an hour to kill.' She was moving about. Maxon heard the soft drop of clothes. 'You're nice. You may come to the bed if that's what you like.'

'It's all right. Thanks.' He kicked off his shoes.

Maxon was dozing when his ever-suspicious senses signalled that something was wrong. A second later he recognised footsteps outside, along the gangway, passing the window, rounding the bow, approaching the door and the jetty. ... He leapt from the chair and bounded through the door before 'Paloma' could tell him that there was nothing to worry about, there would always be a few harmless Peeping Toms around the place.

Maxon's swinging fist caught a man's cheek with an ugly thud. The man fell. Maxon, driven by his own impetus, toppled over him, and by the time he regained his feet, the Peeping Tom was running down the jetty. Maxon gave chase but a long splinter penetrated his sole, scraping his heel bone. By the time he overcame the pain, the man had disappeared.

'Paloma' demonstrated yet another of her skills: she had gained plenty of experience with the needle and the splinters before she learned to love footwear on the boat.

'If you get a lot of these bastards here, you ought to have an alarm system,' Maxon suggested. 'A few tins on a string if nothing else.'

She laughed at the idea but there was no time to argue: it was ten thirty. She made him promise to visit her again, and assured him that he would not have to pay, but did not watch him row away. Her last job for Ellsberg was to put the lights on and move about a lot, gesticulating and talking to herself as if she still had company.

There were now even more blinding lights on between the ships and the shore. In the darkness behind, Maxon reached the white ship. 'Come on board, young Maxon.' Ellsberg sounded pleased and excited even in that half-whisper.

'Wouldn't you prefer to join me for a midnight frolic in the moonlight?'

'Imprecise as ever,' the old Russian mocked him. 'You ought to know I'd never arrange such a meeting on a moonlit night – and it's only ten-thirty-three, not midnight.'

'And you're a pedestrian at heart, Volodya. No feel for ambience or for words. Frolic goes with dawn or midnight – not ten-thirty-three p.m.'

The ship seemed deserted, with only a few lights burning. Ellsberg led the way, and Maxon tried to memorise the numerous turns they took in the maze of narrow corridors to reach Ellsberg's unpretentious office (desk, two chairs, metal filing cabinet, half a dozen photographs) in one of the smaller cabins – No. 5, starboard, lower deck.

Ellsberg had sent the guard ashore to get some beer, and now he had to go and meet the man on deck to collect it. 'Wait for me, and stay quiet, please.'

Left alone, Maxon tried to look bored. To avoid showing any great interest in the cabin (he noted there was no porthole), he concentrated on the photograph of Ellsberg receiving his second Hero of the Soviet Union medal. Maxon took a closer look. Yes, in the background, the *Nachalnik* himself, not yet boss-man at the time, could be seen. Over the edge of the photograph, Maxon studied the locks on the cabin door and on the strong metal cabinet. The floor began to sway. Through the walls, Maxon heard the hammering of heavy rain.

Ellsberg returned with some beer and vodka. 'We've picked quite a night,' he said.

'Not worse than our last day together, remember?' They laughed. How could they forget it? They had worked together through the Nuremberg trials, rounding up fugitives, winkling out war criminals, investigating details for the court, the military and all the intelligence outfits, and then drunk together throughout that glorious final day when people from all sides danced in a four-hour downpour, got soaked and thoroughly sloshed, swore to remain friends and never to fight another war.

'I'm surprised that you remember,' Ellsberg boomed and produced two mugs: had he still not learned to be stingy with his vodka or were large measures a part of his mission scenario? 'You were so drunk, young Maxon, that you lay flat on your back howling like a jackal in labour.'

'Is that how jackals do it in your socialist paradise?'

'Only if they're members of the Politburo.'

'Okay, comrade Ellsberg, that'll cost you five hundred years in the salt mines, and then we'll see. *Nazdarovye.*'

'Down the hatchet . . . or is it hatch?'

'That's not your little joke.'

'I know.' Ellsberg knocked back his vodka and chased it with the beer. 'I remember pushy Glawchester's little jokes. How is he these days?'

'Flourishing. But his name is still Gloucester.'

'Glowchester is more logical, but I've long abandoned my search for logic in the English language.'

'Then call him Glossie or Glustersky if you prefer to make your own rules.'

'Is he still pushy?'

'He retired from being a pushy Australian and became a pushy reporter.'

'With a foot in the door?'

'No, he's so grand these days that he's said to be working with a footman not a foot in the door.'

Reminiscing, fencing, sparring continued over generous measures of vodka. Maxon did not want anything from Ellsberg, so he had the advantage that he could afford to chat and wait. But what was Ellsberg waiting for? It was the Russian who had initiated contact. Why? It had to be important if he had bothered to use Jack and track him down through private channels. Would that imply that this was not a job for the KGB? The Centre would surely be able to locate Maxon more directly? Or could it be that the assignment had come from the Mad Monk himself, after all, and Ellsberg was now trying to marshal enough of his discipline and determination to do the dirty on a friend?

Maxon decided to help him. 'I thought we were here to save the world or something.'

'You make it sound funny.'

'Then tell me what it should sound like.'

'You underestimate what a couple of good men can do.'

'For the world – or for Kowalski?'

'Both.'

'I hear you want to tell me something about him.'

'Correct.'

'That's a relief,' Maxon sighed.

'Why?'

'I was afraid that Kowalski might be just an excuse and in fact you'd caught old spies' jaw.'

'What's that?'

'Some muscle disease that makes the jaw keep popping

57

open. And the older they get, the less they can keep their traps shut.'

'These days, that's only a western disease.' Ellsberg smiled but his baggy eyes were not smiling with him.

'Why? You've found a cure?'

'We believe in preventive medicine.'

'That's good, Volodya, because if I can't ever be certain about my friends and allies, at least I like to know who my enemies are.'

Ellsberg let it pass and focused on the vodka. Was he trying to avoid eye-contact? Maxon hated the thought that it might be a sign of weakness. He used to idolise the man, and he never quite cleansed his system from a grudging admiration for him. It hurt him badly when the cold war had landed them on opposite sides, and whenever he heard about Ellsberg's exploits, he felt like broadcasting three cheers for him through some ESP channels of the old-spy network. He dreaded the thought that one day some operation might bring him into direct confrontation with him – and yet he longed to see that day like a child hoping to beat daddy in arm-wrestling, like a student craving to be asked to mark his tutor's work and write 'encouraging, more effort needed' at the end. Was this the day?

Maxon stretched lazily to reveal no more than passing interest when he switched the subject. 'So what about Kowalski?'

'I want to help him.' Ellsberg glanced towards the filing cabinet. Or did he? It might have been the muffled sound of distant thunder that had attracted him momentarily.

'Why? Are you feeling charitable?'

'Perhaps. Perhaps it's just that I can't help pitying him.'

'That's nice. A newly developed pity for the weak?'

'He's a silly old man, but an honest one. A typical victim of our times. And he must be completely innocent.'

'Of what?' Maxon shounded sharper than he meant to.

Ellsberg shrugged his shoulders.

'What makes you think that he might be suspected of anything?'

'One hears about these things.' Ellsberg's eyes scanned the cabin and paused on the filing cabinet. Except that this time, there was no thunder to draw his attention that way.

'What else does one hear about?'

'I know for sure that he travelled through Dresden only

to deliver some funds and religious literature for the Quaker underground in East Germany.'

That was news to Maxon. He hoped he had not made it obvious to the Russian. 'Then how come that your people virtually advertised his arrest, praised his friendly attitude and openness, and claimed that all his papers had been returned to him unopened – or was untouched the word?'

'So you know about that.'

'Yes, one hears about these things.' Behind a big wide smile he tried to think hard, pick holes in Ellsberg's revelation, and see if he could find out more. 'What one doesn't hear about is why the Germans let him go so quickly, what happened to the funds and the bibles, why there were no arrests among the German Quakers afterwards, and why Moscow is so keen to show him innocent that it almost proves him guilty.'

'Think, young Maxon, think.'

'I prefer to sit back and just listen when a double-hero of the Soviet Union may be trying to hoodwink me.' He had slipped in the reference to Ellsberg's medals – and it worked: involuntarily, the Russian glanced towards the photograph. 'It was Maxon's experience that people would often look at things, quite unnecessarily, when talking about them.

The moment's pause began to expand into a balloon of silence that threatened to burst the cabin. Both had spoken too many half-truths not to feel a little embarrassed. But once again, Maxon had more time to play the waiting game, and it was left to Ellsberg to open up: 'Try to think. Why would the Germans go through the whole circus act of arresting Kowalski if they didn't want to hold him, if they didn't want to arrest scores of Quakers? Can't you think of any explanations?'

'I think you're dying to offer me one.'

'All right, how about this one?' He paused and his face darkened: he obviously hated saying what he was about to say. Was he reluctant because it was the truth or because it was a monumental lie? 'What if our people want to imply that Kowalski broke under interrogation and gave us information about his research, and about his findings on which your new early warning system is based?'

'Conjectures and more conjectures.'

'But not without logic.'

'Have you come to confuse logic with facts in your old age?' Maxon's deliberately contemptuous tone was not lost on Ellsberg. 'Why would your people go to such lengths to ruin Kowalski? Revenge? No, the KGB never embarrasses old dissidents – you kill them. With cyanide pistols.'

Ellsberg's toes tapped on the floor impatiently. 'What if my elders want to imply that with his help they've broken the secret of GLEW?'

'Haven't they?'

'I can only guess that they haven't. So they're desperate. GLEW is too successful.'

'But you tried to contact me before the successful detection of a missile. Why?'

'Because I foresaw just such a situation. I was afraid of just such a success.'

'What success? The papers still call it our gaffe of the century.'

'Yes, because of that peculiar slip-up with the public alert. But that's theorising. The fact is that GLEW has shut the window of opportunity. And that's a compliment, to you, personally.'

'I didn't invent GLEW.'

'But you might have devised its security. It was ingenious of you to cut NATO out of it, to service them but allow them to play no active part, to entrust the system to only a few Yanks, Brits and Canadians – shall I go on?'

'Do. You're telling me things I've never even heard of.'

'Don't you see how dangerous too much success can be? Our hawks like to believe that they constitute the famous Immovable Object. GLEW has turned you into the Irresistible Force. The question is, what will happen if the two ever meet head on?'

'A mighty big bang, that's for sure.'

'And that's why it must be avoided at all costs,' Ellsberg said earnestly, with slow emphasis on each part of the sentence.

'You mean the status quo ante must be retained.'

'If at all possible.'

'Ah! But if the Immovable Object faces the Irresistible Force and nothing happens, the Object has won!'

'Very clever.' Ellsberg shook his head in despair. 'But you use sophism either to provoke me or to avoid hearing what I really say. I don't know which.'

'All right, spell it out.'

'I'm warning you. The side that finds itself threatened by a sudden, serious disadvantage can be dangerous.'

'GLEW doesn't threaten anyone.'

'But it hurts the pride of the Kremlin hawks! And it makes them unpredictable.'

'So what do you suggest? That we teach them how GLEW works?'

'I only suggest ...' he stopped abruptly, paused, and turned to the bottle and the empty mugs, 'another drink.'

He had gone to brink and pulled back, Maxon thought and decided to change tack. 'Is this your regular office?'

'Only for a few weeks. We've hired the ship for a trade exhibition.'

'What do you exhibit?'

'Mostly our good intentions,' Ellsberg laughed a touch too heartily. 'We want to be friendly traders. That's all we want to be.'

'Except at night.'

'You're too suspicious.'

'You're not thinking about coming over, are you Volodya?'

'At my age? Not even a likely conjecture.'

'Then how about this one: you're trying to tell me something. But you're ashamed for some reason. Or you're afraid of the truth.'

'Truth? What's truth? It's not always comfortable to know the truth.'

'Could be worse to know but not to face it,' Maxon pressed on, knowing full well that Ellsberg was too proud of his pride not to be vulnerable on that level.

'I'll be perfectly honest with you, Maxon.'

'Yes, I did expect you to be devious.'

'That's unkind when I'm about to trust you with my secret thoughts.'

Elusive old bastard, thought Maxon affectionately. He was angry, but powerless: the old man was slipping off the hook. 'In a Moscow court, even a kindly people's judge would give you ten years' strict regime Gulag for that.'

'But would it have exonerated someone at Nuremberg?'

'What? Having secret thoughts?'

'It's a crime in a dictatorship.'

'But not an excuse afterwards, Volodya. I mean we'd

have looked on it favourably if a Nazi volunteered to tell us about his doubts *during* the war.'

'Telling the truth to the enemy is treason, young Maxon,' Ellsberg said, mostly to himself. 'It's against orders.'

'Disobeying unlawful orders is a duty. At Nuremberg we found the accused guilty of failing to disobey criminal superiors beyond a certain point.'

Ellsberg permitted himself a victorious little smile: 'Then why isn't such a let-out clause in your military oath of allegiance? Why do the British have to swear to observe and obey *all* orders of Her Majesty, Her Heirs and Successors, and of the officers set over them? And why do the Yanks solemnly swear to obey the orders issued by their President and all their officers? Why isn't there a built-in excuse? Why isn't it their duty to disobey unlawful orders? And if it isn't their duty, why should it be mine?'

Maxon knew he had been caught out, but he refused to give in. 'Because you have a strong sense of morality. Because otherwise you would have forced yourself to forget all your dangerous, secret thoughts about your government, and would have never taken the tremendous risks of coming here, talking to me, hinting what a desperate Kremlin might do, taking a chance on Paloma's naivety.'

'I trust you.'

'Yes, perhaps – and the girl is expendable.'

'If necessary. But then, aren't we all?'

He was cut short by a tremendous explosion that shook the ship and set the cabin dancing. Maxon needed all his self-control not to be first through the door. He waited anxiously, with a chair in hand, ready to fight.

'All clear . . .' Ellsberg called from the corridor outside, and Maxon joined him. Through a porthole, they saw a massive bonfire, multiplied by reflection on the waves all around it. A few fragments of an old houseboat were still falling back from above into the flames.

'You . . .' Maxon began with choking fury, but Ellsberg protested that no, it had not been his doing. The horror in the Russian's eyes was more convincing than his sworn innocence. Questions, accusations, belated conclusions flashed through Maxon's mind. The intruder on the boat must have been a bomber not a Peeping Tom. If Paloma was the intended victim, the bomb would have been planted before her return. If it was meant to kill Maxon, somebody must have watched his arrival. Or followed him all the way from the stadium. Or had been warned to expect him at the boat – such inside information could have come only from Ellsberg who, on the other hand, would know precisely how long Maxon would stay on the boat.

For a few seconds they stared at the burning boat and jetty. 'Paloma' must be dead. They could do nothing for her. 'Give me one minute,' Ellsberg said. 'I'll make sure that the guard won't see you leave. Row towards the airport. A motor launch will pick you up.'

'You think of everything – well, almost everything.'

'Don't talk to the boatman. Make sure he doesn't see your face. Turn away from the flames.'

'How about the dinghy?'

'It didn't belong to the houseboat, don't worry. Just memorise this.' Ellsberg held up an address on a card. 'Now go. Hurry.'

'You wanted to tell me something.'

'Yes. And I'll show you the Kowalski papers.' Ellsberg hestitated. 'That's why you must do me a favour: stay alive for a few days.'


'Do we presume him to be dead?'

With his back to the room, the major from the KGB 'wet affairs' bureau nodded: 'That is correct.' He stared out of the window. From up here, the third floor of the grey block, the little grey Skoda in the grey street looked quite pretty. He knew it was pure junk, from cam-shaft to shabby upholstery and rickety doors, but it was his, his very own private property – even if run on an expense account. He was oblivious of the aura of hatred surrounding him.

The colonel from 'disinformation' viewed him with open contempt: the major did not belong to the rest of the gathering, a bunch of select manipulators who read Camus and dealt in stealth; the major was nothing but one of the more experienced butchers of the assassination bureau. The trouble was that the major would have never arranged Maxon's death without written orders in triplicate. Such orders would have come from 'above' and therefore nobody would want to initiate a witch-hunt with weapons that might backfire. 'Pity,' the colonel said at last. 'It was not *our* intention to see him dead.'

The major raised and dropped his shoulders but continued to study the drabness of the grey paintwork. He wondered if he could find some 'operational necessity' of having it re-sprayed red or silver by Autocar Maintenance Depot No. 1 which serviced all vehicles for tailing suspects and had, therefore, access even to metallic paints.

'Still, if he's dead, it can't be helped. We'll have to start all over again with someone else,' the colonel concluded and answered the telephone. He listened – and a juicy smile spread across his face. He rang off and his voice conveyed a subtle change in the balance of power: 'Comrade major . . . I've just heard that Mr Maxon's appetite doesn't seem to have suffered from his death.'

Hamburger joints for clandestine meetings and public telephones for intercontinental calls were not Maxon's idea of bliss, but he had no choice. To top it all, both he and Toronto were thoroughly rinsed by several sudden downpours, and the splinter in his heel still hurt. His frustration grew incessantly all that Thursday as he began to run out of likely sources of confidential information. Both in London and Washington, only a few people knew anything about Ellsberg. All of them confirmed that he was now well away from where it all was happening. With Kowalski, there were special problems. Informers pleaded ignorance or simply clammed up when Maxon asked about him. Only one was willing to go as far as saying 'DNT for do not touch' and so reminding Maxon of his Toronto contact's joke about the Pole and the barge.

From time to time, Maxon called his hotel, but there were no messages for him. Ellsberg would probably be busy trying to find out some details about the boat explosion, and to set up another meet. By early afternoon, Maxon had no inclination left to help Kowalski clear his name. But he had no choice: if Ellsberg needed him, he could not walk away from it; if it was a ploy, he would have to uncover it. Once again he called the hotel to leave Jack's number where he could be contacted.

The tension was inescapable throughout dinner with the

Kowalskis. The crêpe Suzette Jack served reminded Maxon of the burning houseboat and the girl who had never had a chance.

Kowalski was furious partly because Maxon had 'poked his nose' into his affairs, partly because he did not want anybody's help, and partly because he did want help badly.

'How did you find out about my work for the Quaker underground?' The implied admission proved Ellsberg right.

'One hears about these things.' The flames were dead, Maxon seemed to devote himself to the crêpes. 'But knowing *why* you travelled through East Germany doesn't prove to me that you didn't give away any secrets under interrogation.'

'But I knew no secrets! My research has always been purely theoretical. And all my findings were published years ago.'

'Don't excite yourself, Joseph.' Jack put her hand on his arm and glanced towards Maxon pleading for peace. 'Let's have coffee.'

But Maxon transfixed the man with an infuriatingly incredulous half-smile, and set Kowalski seething: 'It's your dear friend who's making me excited. He doesn't want to listen. Are his accusations what he calls help?' He brushed aside her hand and stormed out to make the coffee.

Maxon waited for the door to close behind him before whispering to Jack: 'I thought he was not to know that you'd asked for my help.'

'When I told him that you were in town, I mean not that you came here, only that you phoned, I thought it would be easier and more honest if he knew that you could help. I said I'd told you about his troubles and that you'd make some inquiries.'

'How did he take it?'

'He said thank you. And he said yes, he always thought you were a nice man.'

'Nice?'

Kowalski returned and banged the tray on the table. Cups rattled and some coffee went flying. 'Look – look, listen.' Agitation brought back the full weight of the Polish accent he had long tried to eradicate for his students' sake. 'When the Russians developed the new FOBs to launch missiles from anywhere in space, our old infrared scanners were no good to us any more. They could detect only the intense heat from the rocket burns. So early warning was soon to be finished. Kaput.'

'Really?' Maxon hated his self-assigned duty to prod, needle and antagonise, but if he had done it to his friend, he must not be too squeamish with Kowalski. 'Do give me the credit for knowing that much, please. And let's stick to Dresden.'

'Wait. I want to explain. We had to find a way to watch those satellites and orbiting missiles at all times, even when they were just cruising, cold. But we were asking too much from our observation computers in space. Because even when we'd overcome the sensor limitation problem by introducing long-wave infrared systems that could spot anything that moved, the computers still had to distinguish real objects from what we call 'random noise' by analysing every signal they spotted, check it, double-check it, distinguish objects of interest from all that junk that's left orbiting in space, identify each object by a recognition code, check again, then chart and predict the object's course before signalling to us on the ground: there goes such and such an enemy craft! Now that took ages!'

'And that's where you came in.'

'No, I didn't. All I tried to discover was how a computer could deal with signals at a higher speed. If we could double the speed, we could watch twice as much of space within the same time limit. But if the signals came in too fast, they became a blur for the computers. At our existing maximum speed, we'd have needed hundreds, probably thousands of satellites to watch everything in space. Now all my achievement was no more than a tiny, tiny step towards a new generation of computers that could distinguish electronic signals at pico-second intervals. That's a million-millionth of a second.'

'Sounds impressive.' Maxon looked thoroughly unimpressed.

'Are you trying to be flippant?'

'No. Your wife tells me it doesn't suit me.'

'She's right. You only want to reduce science to the level where even you could understand it.' His hands and arms began to shake, and his eyes bulged in an effort of self-control.

Jack tried to rescue him. 'No, Joseph, he only wants to rattle you.'

'It doesn't matter. Not at all.' Kowalski's voice grew coarser. 'He must understand that I had no secret to give away.'

'Then you must be dying to discover how GLEW works,' Maxon sneered.

'It's a miracle to me.'

'Miracle? To you? All right, perhaps you did not actually discover the technique. But are you telling me that you've never even wondered how the big break-through was achieved?'

'I never said that.'

'So you speculated.'

'Who wouldn't?'

'Have you made tests?'

'Just the odd experiment or two.'

'You see?'

'No, I don't! I don't, I don't, I don't! Because all I discovered was that my laboratory measurements could not be translated into industrial applications.'

'That's what you say.'

Kowalski went very pale. Sweat began to glisten on his eyebrows. Jack poured coffee. She knew what Maxon was doing, but she had to stop him: 'You're going too far.'

'Am I?' Maxon retorted. He would not let the scientist off the hook now. 'Am I really? He's beaten the Russians at this game in theory at least. They must be desperate to get all sorts of things from him.'

'He'd never tell them anything. He hates them.'

'Well,' Maxon lowered his voice, 'he's been known as a bit of a pacifist, right? I mean the sort who might like to balance the books. . . . He wouldn't be the first, you know. . . .' Watching the slowly contorting face, the tautly sucked-in lips and quivering eye-lashes, Maxon dreaded the thought that Kowalski might soon begin to cry. No, he did not want to embarrass him, not in front of his wife. But what was the alternative? He could not turn back, not now. And no, he could not afford to be a 'nice man'. So he let the scientist sweat silently.

'Yes, I've spoken about the risk, and I've criticised the arms race,' Kowalski breathed. 'And I know that some-times, preachers of risk may sound like mad prophets of doom because the dividing line is very, very fine, but that shouldn't make me a suspect.'

'Well,' Maxon's voice was mercilessly soft, 'you *have* changed loyalties once ...'

'I've changed *sides*, yes!' All Kowalski's blood seemed to rush into his head. 'But loyalties, no! I've always remained loyal to the human race!'

'And yet you've contributed to the arms race? How do you explain that?'

'Stop it, Maxon.' Jack came between them. 'He doesn't need to explain anything. He's an honest man and innocent until proven guilty. So stop it.'

Maxon could not help feeling angry with her. And with himself because he knew he envied Kowalski for having any of her. He swore to himself to force her to make a choice and lose the comfort of her divided loyalties before the night was out. He knew that loyalty to people was an obsession with her. She spoke about it sometimes, without ever telling him why and how it had come about. But just now, he did not care.

Kowalski put his arm round his wife's shoulder and steered her out of the way so that he could face his inquisitor. 'You're right, my dear, I don't have to explain anything. But I want him to know that I've done nothing for the arms race. *If*, you understand? *if* I contributed to anything, it's GLEW.'

'And that's an anti-war device,' Jack added in support.

Maxon pouted contemptuously. 'Nothing is purely anti-war any more. Not even an ante-natal clinic because it helps to ensure the uninterrupted reproduction of cannon-fodder.'

'GLEW is the exception,' Kowalski insisted with childish stubbornness. 'It minimises the Soviet threat and allows you to turn war-budgets into funds for a war on poverty.'

'Which makes it the hottest military property.'

'Yes, because governments know only one thing: how to turn anything into weapons.'

Maxon shook his head with apparent despair: 'Now why does every tinpot scientist see himself as a Messiah?'

'Stop it, please ...' Jack pleaded, but Maxon was unstoppable:

'Because they can make something, they think they know best how to use it.'

'That's right,' Kowalski nodded repeatedly.

'Are you suggesting that Stradivari was the greatest violin player?'

'Certainly not. But he could have warned against the misuse of his masterpieces.'

'Oh yes, the human race is a pack of imbeciles whose erring ways must be corrected by great men like you. That's the line Klaus Fuchs used in his defence.'

'Don't you dare compare me to that traitor!'

Maxon viewed him with the hard eyes of his trade. The man was close to a stroke or breaking point. Whichever would come first, the end of the road must be reached. 'Then why did you travel via Dresden without telling anyone?'

'I didn't.'

'I know you did. And I've had enough of your pious lies.'

'I had clearance,' Kowalski volunteered feebly.

'From whom?'

'Your HQ. Research security.'

'Where?'

'In London.'

'Rubbish.'

'I went to see them.'

'That's a dangerous lie, old son.'

'Believe me. . . . It would be stupid. . . . I can look up the date . . .'

'Yes, he went to London just before the trip,' Jack testified.

'May be. But he hasn't been to HQ or security for more than a year.'

'They have a log at the gate . . . I was there. They entered my name . . .'

'Too bad,' Maxon turned to Jack as he twisted the knife. 'Because his name isn't in the log. I checked it on my way here.'

'Oh my God . . .' Jack whispered.

The doorbell rang but nobody seemed to hear it.

'I don't understand,' Kowalski mumbled. There were tears in his eyes. 'There must be some mistake . . .'

'Your mistake, yes. You should have told me the truth in the first place.'

'I don't understand . . .' The bell rang again, and Kowalski started towards the door. He might have wanted to answer the bell or just cry in privacy. Nobody asked or tried to stop him.

Jack looked hurt. She had nothing left, not even anger,

no animosity, just pain: 'You said you'd help us.'

'I'm trying to.'

'What's it like when you're not even trying?'

He shrugged his shoulders. She spoke about 'us' – meaning the Kowalskis. So she must have made her choice. No more divided loyalties. What did you expect, you fool? Maxon taunted himself but refused to answer. He would stick to the task in hand. Not for Ellsberg's sake, not to help Jack, simply because it was something somebody had to do. 'I must find out the truth. His name isn't in that log. That's the only fact to go on.'

The door opened and Kowalski returned. He was speaking, functioning in a daze: 'Some detective wants to see you, Maxon.'

Two men came in. The first flashed a warrant card and introduced himself as Inspector Wells from the Toronto police. He made no effort to explain his presence, but asked Maxon if he knew his uniformed colleague.

'No. Should I?'

'Yesterday, in the early evening, he was on duty near Amesbury Park . . .'

'Oh yes, the silencer. You warned me about the . . . what was it? Faulty muffler? Is that such a serious offence over here that you track me down like a criminal? And if yes, you ought to go after the people who let me hire such a rattling heap of rubbish.'

Kowalski hardly heard what was going on. He had enough problems to be preoccupied with. Jack watched Maxon: she suspected that the appearance of the policemen might be one of his tricks to force Kowalski's hand.

The Inspector asked his man if he remembered the gentleman as the driver of that car. The answer was 'affirmative'. The Inspector consulted his notes and turned back to Maxon: 'Would you mind telling me, sir, where you went after you'd parked the car at the Park?'

'Er . . . yes, I went for a walk.'

'In any particular direction?'

'No. Just sightseeing.'

'Not many sights to see along Lawrence Avenue.'

'That's exactly what I thought.'

The Inspector paused to emphasise that his next question would be of particular importance. 'Did you bump into anyone who'd remember you?'

'No,' Maxon answered without hesitation. He avoided looking at Jack.

'Are you sure, sir?'

'Come on, what's going on? Do I need an alibi or something?'

'Not really, sir, but it would speed up our inquiries.'

'Pity I can't help you. It's most unlikely that I should ever bump into any of my few acquaintances in Toronto.'

'But you . . .' Jack started but Maxon stopped her.

'I said no. I walked for a while, but met no one I knew.'

'Didn't you try to come and see us if you were in the neighbourhood?' Jack persisted.

Kowalski suddenly came to life. 'Did you? And if not, why not? Jack told me you phoned. Why didn't you pop in?'

It occurred to Maxon that someone might have seen him in the building. It would be foolish to deny it. 'Well, as a matter of fact, I did both. I mean I came here, but nobody answered the door, so I walked for a while, then returned to my car, and eventually, I telephoned. It was pointless to mention then that I had been here.' He stepped closer to the two policemen and chose a harsher tone. 'That's my story. Now it's your turn, Inspector. Why are you here, what are we talking about?'

'We'd like to ask you, sir, to come with us and help us with our inquiries.'

'Why?'

'Your car was in a hit-and-run accident.' He ignored Jack's gasp. 'There're dents on the front of the car and there're dark patches that may turn out to be blood. And . . . oh yes, the victim is dead.'

# III

Inspector Wells listened to the rain and wondered how long the window pane would stand up to it. His sergeant put his head round the door to ask if a requisition should be made to replace the *fleet* of cars in the station motor *pool* by more appropriate boats, but Wells dismissed him impatiently: he was in no mood for funnies. He had taken it upon himself to stretch his legal rights a little more and hold Maxon without charging him for another day. He felt sure he had the right man in the 'just visiting' cell below, and it must be merely a matter of proving his guilt. Adulterers, fraudsmen and hit-and-run drivers were the Inspector's pet hatreds. They all regarded themselves such clever Dicks. It was fun to catch them out, rope them in, show them up and send them down for a healthy stretch in the bin.

Here was, for instance, this guy, Maxon. He had a British passport that said he was a manager. He claimed he was an international consultant. Consultant in what? This and that. Business? Sort of. With what sort of clients? The sort who needed consultation. The sort who might fail to pay you? Possibly. The sort you might then hit and run down? I might – except that I didn't. That's what you say. Yes, and that's good enough.

Then there was the company he claimed to work for. It had London and Washington addresses. But in twenty-four hours of incessant calling, there was nobody but a machine to answer the phone. Your call will be returned as soon as possible. It never was.

And then the word 'international'. How come there was not a single visa in his old passport apart from a multiple entry American? Clients came to the London office. To meet the answering machine?

What intrigued Wells most was that the victim had carried no means of identification on him, no papers, letters, family snapshots, not even washing instruction tags in his clothes. Wells checked the 'reported missing' lists in the whole of Canada, but found nobody to match the well-built young Caucasian victim. It was a body nobody seemed to miss or claim. So Wells tried the next logical steps: clothes, teeth, fingerprints and – with the help of a clever mortician – a photograph of the reconstructed face for the press. But before he could obtain any answers or release the picture to the media, he received a phone call from the Chief's office: lay off, Wells, concentrate on the driver, inform Chief personally with any findings before, repeat, before charging anyone. Nobody said even indirectly that the case could be important and that certain minor irregularities might be overlooked for the sake of quick results, but Wells had an ear for the finer variations of hinting tones. So he would hold Maxon for another day.

The door opened. It was the sergeant yet again. More jokes coming, Wells frowned.

'A Mrs Kowalski wanna see you.'

'First good news of the day. Show her in.' The Inspector's vanity inflated itself and filled his shrivelled face with a smile. Yes, he had known it all along: there was something that Kowalski woman knew but would not say for some reason; perhaps she was not ready to say it; or she was afraid of something or somebody; perhaps Maxon would run her down, too. He now looked at her drenched clothes and suggested with a marked lack of interest that she might have phoned instead of coming to the station.

'It's confidential. And I must have your assurance that my visit here and what I say will remain completely confidential.'

'Does it concern Mr Maxon?'

'I haven't had your assurance.'

Wells tried to guess whether she would be for or against Maxon. 'It's your duty to tell me everything you know, Mrs Kowalski. On the other hand, if it is not detrimental to our inquiries or the legal process, I can promise you the protection we extend to all our informers.'

She nodded in acceptance of the terms. 'Good. I take it you're still holding Maxon.'

'That's correct.' He guessed she might lie but would not want to perjure herself if Maxon had already been released. Clever.

'Congratulations.' She smiled.

'We're entitled to hold hit-and-run drivers.'

'It's not so much a question of legality ...'

'But?'

'Let's say ... personality? Mr Maxon is not the easiest man to keep behind bars for long.'

'Thank you, that's useful information. Is that what you wanted to tell me?'

'No. I came to give Maxon an alibi. He was with me at the time of the accident. From long before to long afterwards.'

'Well, I must take your word for it, I suppose,' Wells drawled implying that he was most disinclined to believe her, 'but it's a great pity that you did not tell me right away.'

She shrugged her shoulders. 'I couldn't.'

'I understand.' Poor old Professor Kowalski. Wells hated the idea of being in conspiracy with a whoring wife by guaranteeing her secret. Guarantee? What guarantee? It would apply only if he found no reason why the husband should know about it.

'And please don't mention my visit to Maxon either.'

'Why?'

'He doesn't need to know why he's released, does he?'

Women, he thought. Women. He excused himself and almost said 'women', instead of 'Wells', as he answered the phone. He grew paler and paler as he listened to his sergeant's excited gibberish. It was about Maxon. His visit to the lavatory. His departure through a small window. His approach to the driver waiting for the Chief. His warning about a 'flat one' – at the rear. The driver's angry dash to check the tyre – having left the engine running. And then Maxon's driving away ...

'You mean the Chief's car?'

'You bet.'

'Put out a general alert.'

'Too late, sir. He abandoned the car round the corner. But we'll get him.'

Wells felt trapped. It would be embarrassing to publicise the circumstances of Maxon's departure – or the length of his detention without a charge. 'I don't need you to get Maxon. I know where to get him if I want him.' He rang off.

'Maxon?' Jack found sneering quite irresistible.

'It's not funny, ma'am. I understand we're not holding Mr Maxon any longer. That's all.'

'Does it matter? He's innocent, isn't he?'

74

Papa Mike's apartment reeked of the smell-cocktail of chemicals photographers never seem to notice. Maxon decided to stay there only as long as the man would be away to get some fresh clothes and a new shirt for him. It would also give him time to sort out his own position.

A few phone calls (peppered with threats, promises and a recall of favours he had rendered) established that Locke and his sidekick were in London. Locke's private number over there was engaged. Maxon kept calling it while trying to itemise his problems.

First that car accident. Having a car stolen would be plain bad luck. If the stolen car also figured in a fatal accident, it would be a coincidence. That would be suspicious enough in itself, particularly with Maxon's scepticism about coincidences. But this time, there could be nothing haphazard about the sequence of events. After the accident, a thief would try to get away (like any hit-and-run driver) and abandon the damaged car with blood on the bonnet. The last thing he (she?) would want to do was to retrace his route to the original parking slot – unless the aim was to incriminate Maxon. Who would want to do that and why? Ellsberg? Jack? Kowalski? Any of several organisations that would see him as a potential winner of their unpopularity contest? And wasn't it odd that nothing was known about the victim's identity?

Then there was that trifling matter of Paloma's death. Who would want to kill her and why? Would Ellsberg kill her? Was she such a major threat to him? No, and no again. Which left Maxon convinced that someone else wanted to kill and incriminate *him*.

The more Maxon had thought about it, the more certain he grew about Ellsberg's intention: he had arranged the meet to say something. What? Fact or fiction? For some reason, he was reluctant to say it. Kowalski was probably just an excuse. A side issue at most. If Ellsberg's information about Kowalski was true, it could help to prove his honest intentions. On the other hand, it could be the cheese in the trap. Whichever of these was the case, Ellsberg would not want to kill him. Except that he might try to create suspicions that someone else wanted to kill him.

GLEW was the subject Ellsberg seemed most anxious to discuss. It was not impossible (was it likely?) that the information or disinformation he wanted to give concerned

GLEW. Kowalski's troubles were also connected with early warning. Was that the link?

And then there were some aspects of GLEW itself, not the least significant causes of Maxon's frequent annoyance. The system had changed the international power balance, yes, Ellsberg was right. For more than a year, it had released vast western resources which the politicians used for major, far-reaching research projects as well as for bolstering up the economy and winning votes. GLEW was a winner, no doubt, but Maxon never understood or liked the way its security was run, however successful it might be. The skeleton HQ staff, the secrecy surrounding locations, equipment and operative personnel to the extent that even Maxon could not know or visit them. He was given information only about relatively petty specific tasks, such as positive vetting of an applicant or two. He was forced to use amateurish procedures and codes which he hated. And worst of all, it seemed he had been selected – a great distinction! – to twiddle his thumbs on behalf of GLEW most of the time.

Captain Beck answered the phone at last.

'Skylark in Red Square,' Maxon squeezed the words through his teeth but had no choice: it was an open line, and Locke insisted on using correct identification procedures.

'How did you know we were here, sir?'

'One hears about these things. Give me your boss.'

Locke surprised Maxon with questions about Gerry 'The Bang' Houlihan. 'Do you know him?'

'No. Does he know me?'

'No,' and after momentary hesitation, 'no, probably not.' Locke quickly changed the subject. 'How about the spot of trouble you seem to have over there?'

'How come you heard about it? I didn't refer to you or the office in any way.'

'You didn't need to. It was a friend of a friend who told me about the hit-and-run murder.'

'The word is accident, sir. Nobody mentioned murder over here. Not to me.'

'Then perhaps my information is wrong.'

'Doesn't happen very often, does it?'

Locke ignored the question and changed the subject abruptly yet again. 'How about your inquiries about the husband?'

'So you've heard about that, too.'

'You visited the London office.' Locke's voice betrayed self-satisfaction. 'Don't get involved too closely with the guy, not even if the wife is a close friend.'

'I believe him to be innocent.'

'Despite the fact that there's no trace of his visit in the log?'

Maxon had no answer to that. It seemed hopeless to explain to Locke that Kowalski would be a fool to lie about something so easily checkable and disprovable. So instead of answering, he said he needed more time in Toronto because of Ellsberg whom he described as their 'mutual friend from the other end of the world'.

'Have you met him?'

'Yes.'

'At whose initiative?'

'His. My detailed report will go by hand from the Toronto office if that's okay with you.'

'Sure, take your time,' Locke reassured him.

'It's only that . . .'

'I know what bugs you – that Washington shenanigan, right? Well, don't worry, I'm handling it myself for the time being.' Locke promised to use his influence through some 'top level channels' to get the Toronto police off Maxon's back. 'If you want me, I'll be over here for a few days to give a little backing to your old chief against some Parliamentary snipers.'

Poor Sandy, thought Maxon, the government would want some answers from him about GLEW and the Washington alert, civil servants and politicians would want his blood, and one day he would pay heavily for that 'little backing'. If debts were incurred, Locke would never forget to collect in due course. In fact, as Maxon rang off, Locke looked up to face Sandy. Between them on the desk, a greasy notepad was opened on a page where a very heavy hand had scribbled a London telephone number.

'So what do you make of it?' Locke asked.

'I don't know what to make of it. I'm just giving you the facts. Maxon's on your payroll. Do you want a full police report?'

'No, only what's relevant to the number.'

'That I can give you right away. When the police went to search Houlihan's council flat, I arranged that a plain-clothes observer from Special Branch should go with them. That was the man who spotted the notepad with the number which he happened to recognise. It's a direct line to the Russian Embassy, one of the few which are not routed through their switchboard, so it must be used by someone high up, possibly for KGB contacts.'

'What does Houlihan say about it?'

'He claims to know nothing. It's true that the note is in his wife's writing. She's virtually illiterate, but make no mistake about it, she runs his life. She says the caller only left the number, no name, nothing, She didn't like that, so she never gave it to her husband. True or false? Over to you.'

'What do you think?'

'Oh, I've long given up thinking about these things,' Sandy said airily. 'I try to stick to facts. Yes, it is possible that Maxon has something to do with a safecracker. And yes, it is possible that the thief has some clandestine contact with the Russkies. And yes, it is possible that Maxon uses Gerry-boy for a go-between to the KGB. But it is also possible that someone's trying to set him up for some reason. Personally, all I can add is that if you don't trust him as much as I do, I'll be glad to have him back in London – and then it'll be my problem to choose which possibility I accept.'

By about the time Sandy left Locke's office, Maxon had decided he had no way for the time being to understand Locke's interest in Gerry Houlihan or the significance of The Bang in the name. Was the man an assassin? A bomber, perhaps?

Maxon telephoned his hotel. He dreaded the thought that Ellsberg might have wanted another meet when he would not have been available. The switchboard checked it with Reception, too: no, there had been no calls for him. Maxon decided he would soon have to pay a private and unannounced visit to Ellsberg's office: the Russian's reflex glances at the metal filing cabinet had told him that it might contain something relevant to Kowalski's case, something he ought to see, preferably before the next meet. For that he would need some diving equipment and a set of keys as well as a minder to watch his back. With the hardware Papa Mike could help him he was sure, and it was an acceptable risk that the photographer would probably report it to

Locke through the 'electronic toys agency' that represented GLEW in Toronto.

Still waiting for some fresh clothes, he dialled the police and asked for Inspector Wells. He apologised for his 'sudden departure' from custody and declared himself to be available for further interviews. Wells' response surprised him: 'That's all right, Mr Maxon, no need to apologise, technically you've always been a free man, free to leave the station any time. You were here to help us voluntarily, weren't you?'


The computer room, where Maxon found Kowalski, looked fitter for placid robots than fiercely temperamental Poles. 'I still find it quite incredible what computers can do,' he said, marvelling at the old man's toys.

'Presumably you don't understand them.' The professorial tone of the answer made no effort to disguise the contempt that laics deserved.

'I can't say that I do.'

'Then how do you propose to look after their security?'

'Well, I know a little about gates, perimeters, access control and, particularly, about people who are always the greatest security risk. I mean I've yet to meet a microchip that can be bribed, blackmailed or drunk under the table.'

'Is that your latest accusation against me?'

'I thought it was clear that I felt duty-bound to help you.'

'And I thought it was clear that I don't want charity. Not from you or anyone else. Least of all for my wife's sake.'

'Don't you Quakers believe in moral duties?'

'You're not a Quaker.'

'Is morality the Quakers' monopoly?'

'I'm sorry. I didn't mean it that way.'

Kowalski looked sufficiently perturbed to be squeezed a little harder. Maxon knew he had to be shaken and shocked to give away anything. 'Sorry? You? No, you're just fishing for excuses to avoid understanding my position. That I can't help you unless I'm satisfied that you're innocent despite appearances.'

'What appearances?

'You claim you had clearance to go to Vienna via East

Germany. But there's no trace of your alleged visit at HQ. Your name isn't in the log.'

'It's their word against mine. What can I do?'

'You can tell me what the Russians wanted from you.'

'Nothing. They didn't even ask me about my work or about GLEW.'

'Don't be ridiculous. They wouldn't have done their job properly if they let you got without even questions.'

'You make it sound as if you found their keen or even illegal interest in GLEW quite acceptable.'

'Of course I do. GLEW is as essential to them as it is to our response management.'

'Response management!' Once again, his accent grew stronger, revealing agitation, but he was not yet trembling or showing signs of an imminent stroke. 'You mean the conduct of a nuclear war!'

'If you like.'

'How can you use the word *like* in connection with the proposed mass extinction of life?'

'Okay, you care, no need to make such a fuss or to presume that care is yet another of your monopolies.'

'Then why are you ashamed to call a spade a spade?' His voice cooled, he was obviously on safer ground here. 'You're no better than the Nazis who had actual language rules. Deportations had to be "resettlement", words like murder or extermination were taboo. Only "radical solution" and "final solution" were the correct expressions. Now you talk about "military hardware" when you mean weapons. Pinpoint bombing raids are "surgical take-outs", shelters have become "hardened facilities", and it's more palatable to refer to "payload" than The Bomb.'

'Yes, it's disgusting,' Maxon continued the needling, 'particularly because we only try to copy you, scientists. We all want to sound objective and knowledgeable like you.'

'No, you're trying to turn organised homicide into something that's natural in a day's work.'

'It's you who coined the words for us.'

'But the politicians minted them for general circulation. No scientist has ever described an improved nuclear missile as a "newcomer" to the ever-so-friendly and neighbourly "ICBM family". And then those cosy abbreviations, yes. Jolly Little ERWs are so much more lovable than Enhanced Radiation Warheads.'

It irritated Maxon that the man sounded so convincingly sincere. 'You seem to forget GLEW.'

'Oh yes, darling GLEW. The peaceful invention that helps to make nuclear wars thinkable and even winnable. It helps to create the "limited war" concept that the whole affair could be localised because alternatively, we could kill Them ten times over whereas they could kill Us only nine times over. Yes, yes, yes, it's always the new word that offers you the new licence. It's like talking about a "relationship" rather than a dirty little "affair" seems to be a permit to sleep with another man's wife.' The onrush of blood coloured Kowalski's face dangerously. 'Do you have a relationship with Jacqueline or do you only sleep with her?'

'The answer is no to both. Was it the thought of war that made you ask?'

'I just wanted you to know that I wouldn't stand between you. The old and the dying must give way. That's the most positive thing they can contribute to life.'

'And some answers. Now.'

'Tomorrow. Tonight I'm giving a lecture and I'm late already.'

'Timing doesn't seem to be your forte. A few minutes' delay here, a lost day in Germany . . .'

'I think I deserve an honest question rather than hints.'

'True. On your trip to Vienna, a day of your life is missing.'

'Locke has already been through all this.'

This was news to Maxon. A shock, in fact. Why didn't Locke tell him if Kowalski had already been interrogated to that extent? 'Never mind what you told Locke. Answer me. You claim you left Hamburg on Sunday, were arrested in Dresden on Tuesday, the fourteenth, and released on Thursday, the sixteenth. Correct?'

'You know it is.'

'Then where did you spend Monday?'

'On the train, I suppose.'

'The journey doesn't take forty-eight hours.'

'There must be some mistake.'

'Yes, professor, your mistake. Your dates fail to tally.'

'Okay, we'll check my diary. Come to see me tomorrow.'

Maxon answered only with a mocking, quizzical look tinged with the contempt reserved for childish efforts at pulling the wool over his eyes.

Kowalski understood him. His newly-found arrogance was the proof of that. 'Don't worry, I don't intend to make suitable alterations in the diary. My wife is at home, go and tell her to show you all my papers relevant to the Vienna trip. They're in a green folder in the top left-hand drawer of my desk. And tell her not to wait up for me. I won't be home before midnight.'

They left Kowalski's office together, said good-bye, but Maxon tailed the scientist all the way to the University, and left only when the lecture had already begun: no, Kowalski had made no attempt to telephone and warn Jack, and now he would not have a chance to leave and make a call before Maxon got there.

Jack opened the door and said nothing when she saw Maxon. She was wearing a black full-length dressing gown with a silky shine and a soft cling to her skin. She held it together with both hands. Her bare toes tapped the carpet from time to time. They both wanted to embrace, but they knew they would hate themselves afterwards. Kowalski commanded too much pity if not love. 'I was having a bath,' she said apologetically.

'And I came to read the meter.'

'Which one?' she smiled and stepped a little aside.

'All of them.' He marched past her, keeping his eyes from her. 'I'm told that they are in Kowalski's study.' He stopped at a door. 'Is that it?'

'What do you want, Maxon?'

'He wants you to show me a green folder in the top left-hand drawer.'

'Why didn't he call me?'

'He had no time.'

By now, all the sparks had been discharged and he mourned the waste. They found the folder, and holding it, Jack seemed to be dressed in a suit of armour.

'Just where it was supposed to be,' Maxon said only to break the silence.

'I'm not surprised. Joseph has an orderly mind.'

'Has he?' He sounded doubtful. It was disconcerting both to believe and disbelieve Kowalski. He knew he ought to follow his hunch and accept the man's innocence, because he had to admit that his suspicions fed only on jealousy and professional scepticism. He took the diary out of the folder.

'What are you looking for?'

82

'I'm not sure.' Which was not true. He hoped to find evidence of Kowalski's guilt, some terrible skeleton in his drawer. 'It's just odd that a day should simply disappear from an orderly man's life.' He told her about the missing Monday.

'That's odd. Locke never queried it when he started this witch-hunt.'

'Locke? You've never told me that Locke himself interrogated him.'

'Haven't I?' She quickly abandoned that line. 'I mean I'm sorry. I thought you might not help if you knew.'

Maxon found the relevant pages in the diary. There were no marks or notes on the Sunday when, allegedly, Kowalski had left Hamburg for Dresden to meet some representative of the Quaker underground. On Monday, the page-a-day diary showed only a laconic reminder: 'To D.' Maxon shook his head. 'How stupid . . .'

'What?'

'The day is not missing after all. It was his memory that cheated him. On Sunday he must have stayed in Hamburg. For if he left only on Monday, then it figures that he could be arrested in Dresden on Tuesday as he's claimed all along.' The pages for Wednesday and Thursday were left blank. Maxon held them up to the light. There were no traces of erasure. 'Doesn't he ever make notes at the end of the day to remind himself what he's done?'

'No, he's not a diarist in that sense. He only uses advance reminders.'

It figured. Kowalski would not have noted the time and place of clandestine meetings arranged for Wednesday and Thursday. He had planned to be in Vienna by the following day, and the page for Friday was duly full, with entries showing the time and place of appointments and conferences. 'Did Locke see this?'

'No, Joseph relied on his memory. He never even mentioned the diary.'

'And Locke failed to notice the discrepancy of the missing day.'

'That's right.'

'Good.' Maxon was immodest enough to smile: he liked to be one up on his bosses.

She offered to bring him some coffee. Listening to her feet shuffling along the carpet, he forced himself not to watch her leave. When the door had closed behind her, he turned to the phone and called his hotel. This time the operator had a message for him:

'It was a gentleman who called but he wouldn't leave his name, so I only have an address for you, sir, it's number 63, Sheppard Avenue.'

'With S for sugar?'

'That's right, sir, shall I spell it for you?'

'No, thanks.'

'It's only that it's with double-pee . . .'

It did not matter. Ellsberg was proposing a meeting and it would be in their old code established in Spain. If he wanted to leave an address, the message consisted of a set of figures disguised as prices or telephone numbers. The first digit would denote the relevant page of the local telephone directory, the rest would be a simple grid code to spell out the words – the figure 3 for line six on the page, then 2 to pinpoint the fourth letter in that line. But this time, Maxon already knew the address: Ellsberg had made him memorise it just before they parted on the boat.

To decipher '63, Sheppard Avenue' was even simpler. The number had to be divided by three to give 21 or nine p.m. as the suggested time. The day would be determined by the first letter in 'Sheppard' according to a permanent code word, la ESTOCADA, Spanish for the KILL, chosen because they decided on it while watching a bullfight. A local street name beginning with E would have meant the very day the message was left because E was the first letter of *estocada*. S for Sheppard, the second letter in the code, gave the following day, tomorrow evening at nine, to complete the message. The system still worked and brought back some fond memories, but left him only tonight for a secret visit to the ship before the meet. Maxon had hoped to find out more about the ship, the guards, their weapons, but now he was forced to take risks instead of precautions. At least Papa Mike would already have the requested hardware for him.

Jack returned with the coffee. She had changed into slacks and a jumper – it was not her fault that he found this outfit no less tempting. 'What happened?' she asked spotting right away that he looked more tense and anxious. He could have denied it, but he needed a minder that night, and he did not want to involve anyone connected with

Locke: if the general had kept vital information from him, he was not going to give him anything on a plate before finding out facts for himself first.

'It's Ellsberg,' he said.

She nodded as if she had expected to hear just that. 'I didn't ask, and you don't need to tell me anything now, but did he give you anything definite about Joseph?'

'Not yet.'

'You think it was just a lie to force my hand to get you here?'

'I may find out tonight. But I'll need you.' She was about to protest but he put his hand on her arm to reassure her. 'Kowalski said he wouldn't be home before midnight. You'll be back long before that. You'll only baby-sit for me.'

'Okay,' her voice grew a little fuzzy, 'it's a good way to say thank-you for not using me as your alibi in front of my husband.'

'I didn't need an alibi. I'm innocent. That's why the police let me go right away.'

You inveterate liar, she thought with affection but managed to react only with a cool 'Oh, I see.'


Over the din of MPs bleating, croaking, whining *hear-hear, shame, resign*, the Speaker's distinctively elongated 'oarder! oarder!' rose to the visitors' gallery crying for help. But the vocal drowning continued and order remained far from being restored. General Locke enjoyed every minute of the pandemonium in the House of Commons. Sitting behind him, Sandy resented every minute of his visit. He hated playing aide to an American whose office enjoyed no seniority to his own. Locke was supposed to offer explanations concerning GLEW and the Washington alert via Sandy for the government spokesman currently mauled on the floor. It seemed that there was little Locke could or was inclined to say, yet Sandy knew from various sources that the American had been received at Downing Street several times, and that on each of those occasions, he had had a strictly confidential tête-à-tête with the Prime Minister alone.

'We've been told that GLEW costs us virtually nothing and saves vast funds on both sides of the Atlantic,' the pin-up boy of the House began smoothly, only to lengthen the time of his foil penetrating a jugular vein: 'But we still don't know whether the funds so released are really helping the jobless – or some crazy scheme of mutual assured destruction!'

'Better MAD than dead!' a backbencher yelled.

The spokesman uttered some vague assurances.

A youngish old Member of studied inelegance rose to his feet. 'Will the Right Honourable gentleman allow us a glimpse into the current investigation, and will he assure the House that the risk of war was really as remote as the Americans would have us believe?' His voice quivered with deliberate emotion, and his eyes, shiny with the fervour of the sanctimonious and the mad, turned towards some horrific vision beyond it all.

The cacophony swelled but not enough to subdue a horse-faced woman's neigh: 'They say the alert was a genuine error, but if so, what guarantee do we have that this famous GLEW is not too sticky to handle?' She rode the tsunami of booing and laughter. 'And was the warning itself correct? Wasn't it part of the President's re-election campaign to threaten the Russians with ill-conceived retaliation without informing, let alone consulting Her Majesty's government?'

Resignations were demanded. Accusations of cowardice, jingoism, hypocrisy and dishonesty flowed freely back and forth, a faltering voice of reason screamed 'it was a computer error', and an old woman of a senior statesman demanded assurances that 'the American computers' high-handed attitude will not provoke the Russian computers beyond reasonable limits'.

Sandy looked at Locke who answered with his palms turned outwards in a gesture of what-can-one-say. Sandy's face stiffened: he disliked to play the beggar to a man he considered no richer than himself. 'I find the logomachy somewhat discombobulating,' he said finally, hoping that Locke would have to ask him about the meaning of the word. But the American gave no reaction. His eyes were on the press gallery where a Russian correspondent had just returned from the telephones outside as his colleague was about to leave with fresh details of the debate going direct to Moscow.

In the *Nachalnik*'s dacha outside Moscow, the lights had shone all night, and even now nobody bothered to turn them off. From time to time, an aide brought in the latest news from all over the world, but the sheets of papers accumulated untouched next to a massive, ornamental samovar. Facing the leader, Marshal Beryov was beginning to feel pie-eyed and fragile. Drink for drink he could match any man's vodka intake, but as usual, the *Nachalnik* was cheating. The glasses they used looked identical, but the walls of Beryov's were thinner, doubling the capacity. He dreaded the moment when 'a little arm-wrestling' would be proposed to him. Still, the humiliation was a small price to pay for the privilege of being asked, for the second night running, to sit with his insomniac leader whose perpetual work-play cycles had driven many a thriving functionary to drinking, stimulant-gobbling or the ultimate excuse of a nervous breakdown.

Tonight, Beryov was spared from arm-wrestling. He would soon wish he had not been. His leader flicked through the London reports, dropped them on the floor, and turned to Beryov: 'So how about GLEW, Alexei Ivanovich?'

It sounded just casual conversation like all that had gone before it, so Beryov deemed it a good opportunity to drop a few damaging hints about the efforts of the Mad Monk and the KGB, their prevarication whenever the subject was raised, their alleged scheming against known GLEW personnel, and their heavy-handed approach to such a delicate matter in general.

The *Nachalnik* nodded a few times – it was difficult to tell whether he was in full agreement or about to snooze a little – then asked sleepily: 'And how about your own heavy-handed approach, Alexei Ivanovich?' The voice came perilously close to dying away. 'I mean the other day, you mentioned that the missile forces and the general staff foresaw the need of resorting to certain *other* means to counter GLEW.'

Beryov sat up. He knew that the man was at his most dangerous when seemingly half-asleep, and now he had been quoting his own argument almost verbatim. 'We ... we sort of discarded the idea.'

'Why?'

'You and the Politburo were against it. You thought a test would be war. Guesswork at its best.'

'That's right. But does that mean to you that we must remain unprepared?' The leader asked softly, ready to wait for an answer all day if necessary. Beryov looked away, picked up his glass, and tried to look drunker than he was – he needed breathing space, desperately he needed time to think, for they both knew that he was trapped, and lacked the essential information on which to base his answers to questions of his own. Did the leader know about the feasibility studies he had authorised in great secrecy? Had there been a decision made at the very top to carry out some limited tests whatever the risk or was this merely a scheme to expedite Beryov's premature retirement?

It all revolved around EMP, the potentially disastrous Electro-Magnetic Pulse, that could obviate GLEW – and start The War. In front of the Politburo inner circle, Beryov had been crudely reprimanded for mentioning this great unmentionable, and told not even to think about it; but now, in the strictest privacy of the leader's dacha, he was expected to defend himself against the charge of negligently allowing the Soviet Union to remain unprepared. He could thus be made a scapegoat whichever course he chose.

'How much do we actually know about those *other* means?' The question sounded no more than cordial nudging, with the casualness of asking the time. And it was yet another question Beryov could not answer without being accused of just repeating himself or trying to blind his leader with technical gibberish. For it was all in the working papers, and the *Nachalnik* had surely re-read and memorised his technical briefs. So what could he add? Was he expected to summarise it again in lay terms?

He could say that EMP was simply a radio flash which had been discovered as a by-product of nuclear tests in the atmosphere. In 1962, for instance, the Americans exploded a mere one-megaton bomb some two hundred miles above the Pacific, and the resulting EMP played havoc even in Honolulu, more than a thousand miles away, where all the street lights went off, burglar alarms began to ring, and worst of all, computers were damaged. Since then it had become known that a large enough EMP could black out global radio communications, disrupt a continent's electronic systems, cut power supplies, paralyse telephones, knock out computers temporarily, and blank out computer memories permanently, despite the vast fortunes spent both by America and the Soviet Union on developing EMP-resistant circuitries and thermionic valves. In theory, these counter-measures were supposed to protect the most sensitive and crucial systems. But only in theory. For the atmospheric test ban treaty prevented both sides from producing further huge EMPs without which the level of protection could not be measured beyond laboratory conditions.

'The problem is,' Beryov ventured to say at last, 'that the effect of even a limited EMP test is unpredictable.'

'Unpredictability is a spit in the eye of scientific socialism,' the leader snapped, suddenly all awake.

'I did not mean unpredictability in technical terms. We know perfectly well that an EMP would affect the enemy's early warning system. But we can't be sure how big and how permanent the damage would be. And above all, we can't fully predict the Americans' reaction. The President is not particularly stable. He's facing a difficult re-election campaign. He or the White House hawks might regard any test as an act of war because blinding GLEW would surely be an initial part of any all-out offensive scenario.'

The *Nachalnik* nodded. His hypnotic gaze captured Beryov's fidgety eyes. 'You're right, Alexei Ivanovich. We don't want war by accident, and we can't depend on incalculable American reaction. But we still must know how to eliminate GLEW if and when we may have to resort to that. Couldn't you *think* about some tests? Something not too monstrous in effect ... something accidental ... something one could apologise for almost in advance, as you yourself once suggested?'

Beryov knew that this was an order. Tension tightened his neck muscles. Despite his professionally stoked-up belligerence, he felt frightened of going a clear step closer to nuclear holocaust. He also knew that he had not been let off the hook: for him to *think* about EMP would not be enough, to *do* anything about it, war or no war, could be suicidal.

Maxon was carrying a large and heavy hold-all when Jack picked him up in the underground car park. He was concerned about her and wanted to give her the option to back out: 'I don't want to cause you embarrassment. Kowalski may get home early.'

'If he said midnight, it's midnight.'

'The message might have been a trap.'

'No,' she put a cigarette in her mouth, 'there's nothing underhand about him. If he suspects us, he'll say it.'

Maxon whipped out his decrepit old lighter. He tortured his thumb forcing the wheel to grate away at the flint until a smelly flame was produced. Jack smiled: 'Thanks. Won't you allow me to get you a new one for your birthday?' It was a pointless question. She knew the answer was no. It had always been. Even though he had never smoked. 'You've never told me what sentimental value you attach to that stone-age relic.'

'No sentimental value. It's just that at an impressionable age, somebody once advised me,' he slipped into clipped Mancunian with ease, 'that "Don't smoke, laddie, it makes hair grow in your nose. Just carry a lighter." I took his word for it.' He reverted to his neutral BBC-English tinted by the vaguest hint of an accent that Jack had always mistaken for Scottish.

'But why?' Jack laughed.

His accent grew even stronger this time: 'Plain courtesy, laddie. If it's good for a Rolls-Royce to have one, it's good for you, too. Gives you class. And class is harder to come by than brass.'

'Who was the sage?'

'Uncle Dick. Me mum's lover.'

He had never told her anything about his family, and she had never asked because she did not want to talk much about hers either. That was a tacit agreement concerning conversational no-go areas. She smiled to gloss over the unexpected sentence and the uncharacteristic bitter tone.

'And it's not funny, love.' It was not the Maxon she knew.

'I'm sorry,' she backpedalled. 'It's just your unusual accent . . .'

'That's no accent, love – this is,' he switched back once again. 'If you work with Sandy, you speak like Sandy, you hope to make the grade with Sandy – and feel like a whore.'

It was Jack who broke the silence. 'Would you . . .' she stopped, hesitated, then asked shyly, 'how did you know your mother had a lover?'

'We'd better get going. I don't want you to be late.'

At a dark spot behind Union Station he asked her to stop the car, and emptied his bag on the back seat. Among some diving equipment, there was a sealed green plastic bag which he handled with special care. He picked out and plugged an all-black matchbox into a miniaturised walkie-talkie which he handed to her. 'I'll want you to remain in touch with me throughout, and if anything goes wrong, you report it all to Locke.'

'Will . . .' she started but changed her mind: it was pointless to ask if it was likely that anything should go wrong. He would not tell her. But it worried her. Perhaps because of his unexpected mention of his mother and her lover. Was he worried about something? Was age beginning to puncture some inner layers of his armour-plated defences? Better to concentrate on the radio if she wanted answers tonight: 'What's the attachment?'

'Scrambler.'

'Neat.'

He checked the oxygen bottle – it was small, strictly for emergencies – then they set out towards the harbour-front. At the foot of York Street they turned west, and slipped between deserted wharves and warehouses near the water to avoid the night-lively brighter route. Approaching a building site he asked her to switch off the headlights and edge her way behind a motley of cement-mixers and trailers. He picked up the green bag. 'I'll leave this under your front wheel. If anyone approaches you, if I ask you by radio or if you must leave for any other reason in a hurry, you drive over it and go as fast as you can. The first turning on the right will take you back towards Bathurst Street.'

'What's in the bag?'

'Insurance. To help you get away and to warn me. If I'm in trouble, you do nothing to help me. You can't. Your job is to get the hell out of here and report to Locke.'

'Yes, sir.'

'Don't talk to anyone.'

'No, sir.'

'Don't even open the window to anyone. Just go.'

'Even if it's a nice gentleman who offers me some candy?'

'I'm serious.'

'So you do expect trouble.'

'If I did, we wouldn't be here.'

He collected his diving gear. As he was getting out of the car, she leaned across to pick up something from the floor – and kissed his sleeve, almost accidentally. 'For luck,' she whispered.

His swim was peaceful: he would risk going under water only near the ship. In the distance, he could see some police activity on the jetty and around the wrecked houseboat. The exhibition ship was almost completely dark. Maxon floated motionlessly and watched it for a few minutes. Eventually, he saw a lone figure making his round on deck. The guard was dragging his feet, a heavy holster dangled from his hip.

Maxon dived, reached the ship, and threw a length of rope towards the railing. At the second attempt, the rope caught on something. He tested it, and it held. He climbed aboard. Puffing and blowing hard he had to rest: after his hospitalisation, he would need time to regain his fitness. In the maze of corridors of the lower deck, he found 'starboard five', Ellsberg's office. It was locked. At the edges of the door, no lights came through. From his belt, he detached two short lengths of pipe that formed a crude jemmy, every thief's best friend. He could have used his set of keys from Papa Mike, but he preferred to cause damage. It would not give Ellsberg the impression that the break-in had been the work of some top-notch burglar, the sort intelligence services would employ. To support the same misleading clue, he quickly broke into Ellsberg's desk, scattered some papers which were of no interest to him, pocketed a handful of roubles from a petty-cash box, then returned to the door to listen for any noise of footsteps.

The door itself confronted him with a choice. Closing it would have given him greater privacy – keeping it open offered him more immediately audible warning. He compromised by leaving it slightly ajar, and attached his rope firmly to the brass bolt at the trailing edge of the door. He then called Jack: 'I'm in cabin number 5. Going smoothly. Everything okay?'

'Snap.'

The metal cabinet resisted the jemmy and Maxon did not want to cause excessive noise. The keys weighed a ton but contained every variety, bless your heart, Papa Mike. When the drawers were already open, Maxon quickly damaged the locks to look as if they had been forced. He remembered which drawer had had a magnet for Ellsberg's eyes when talking about Kowalski. He was pleased that he had been right. An old-fashioned, faded blue folder of doubtless Russian origin contained a stack of papers in German and Russian – all about Kowalski. There were photocopies of Kowalski's own notes, lectures and articles. Maxon wanted to look through the rest of the drawers, too, but to photograph the Kowalski documents had top priority.

'One roll completed, second started. Film recovery by standard signal if inevitable.' Locke would have the equipment to locate the watertight container with a radio responder to mark its location.

'A light's come on in an upper deck cabin, port side, midship to aft,' Jack reported.

'Just watch it.'

'And there's some movement beyond the trailers.'

'Go if approached.'

'It's all right.'

Photographing the last few documents, Maxon was half-way through the second roll of film, when he heard some noise. He let go of the camera which had been attached to his belt throughout, and put his radio to his mouth. 'Visitor,' he whispered, 'go at once if you hear me apologise.'

The door swung open. The rope attached snaked with it. The light came on and Maxon faced an elderly guard and his Colt. 'Don't try anything funny, son. I've no compassion for thieves.'

'Isn't it sad?' Maxon moved half a step back to stand on the end of the rope. 'I need a few bucks badly and what do I find? Some wretched roubles.'

'To me you're a thief, just the same.'

'I apologise.'

A few seconds later, an explosion could be heard. The guard stiffened but would not move his eyes from Maxon. But it was only then that all hell let loose on shore. In the wake of Jack's car, fireworks, bangers and smoke cannisters exploded. The flashes lit up the corridor behind the guard and distracted him momentarily. Maxon ducked and pulled hard on the rope. The slamming door smashed into the guard's temple and knocked him down. As the man fell, the gun went off. He was clearly harmless and unconscious, it would have been pointless to make doubly sure. Maxon kicked away his gun. The temptation was great to finish photographing the documents, but he could not tell how much time he had before other guards might appear. He quickly replaced the papers and the folder in the metal drawer, switched off the light, and ran.

He was already swimming away when a gun was fired behind him. He glanced back: resting his shaky hands on the railing on deck, the old guard loosed off another shot. It ricocheted from the oxygen bottle on Maxon's back. He knew he should have killed the man in the cabin. Ellsberg would laugh at his predicament. He dived under water and tried to swim a zig-zag pattern. His first lesson from Ellsberg, a warning, came back to him: have no pity for the weak; they don't deserve it, you can't afford it if you want to do the job *and* survive.

He knew the police at Paloma's wrecked home would be busy investigating the apparent shooting match on shore, but the last thing Maxon wanted was to bump into one of their boats and get himself arrested yet again. So he had to surface. As soon as his head bobbed up, the old guard renewed his target practice. It seemed he needed it too, but Maxon could not take chances. He dived again, but he had difficulty with his air supply. The small bottle might have been running out, or the first shot might have damaged it – or he ought to have left such exertions to younger men.

Jack was in bed, trying to decide whether she should ring Maxon's hotel or not, when Kowalski arrived home. It was three minutes past midnight. She switched on the light and asked how his lecture had gone. But he was more anxious to hear about Maxon's visit: 'What did he want to see?'

'Just your diary.'

'The Monday before my arrest?'

'Yes. But it only said "To D". He was surprised.'

'So am I.' He left and soon returned with the diary. 'How peculiar. I always thought I had left for Dresden on Sunday.'

'You should have looked up the dates before you spoke to Locke.'

'Yes, my memory must be failing. How stupid.' And after a pause: 'Anything else?'

'No. He left soon after that.'

'Did you go out with him?' He began to undress.

'No. Why?'

'As I parked my car next to yours I noticed that the hood was warm.'

'I'd run out of cigarettes and went to get some.' Not his logic, only his attention to practical details surprised her. Was he suspicious?

The cab driver needed a great deal of convincing that the thoroughly wet and apparently drunken man he had picked up at the quayside would be both able and willing to pay the fare. Papa Mike looked no less suspicious or displeased when he opened the door to his late-night visitor, but had the discipline to offer Maxon a bourbon, make some coffee, and ask no questions.

Maxon hoped he would get used to the stink of chemicals, but he found the cramped little darkroom more and more suffocating by the minute. The quality of his photographs were his only consolation. He asked for some enlargements, and sat studying the pictures of the documents till dawn. Everything seemed to bear out Kowalski's story as confirmed by Ellsberg's account. Kowalski's papers, photocopied by the East German police, contained no secrets. The interrogation sheets revealed that only the most basic personal details had been asked, nothing about his work. There was a list of the religious literature that had been confiscated together with the two thousand dollars he had been carrying in cash, presumably for his Quaker contact. His traveller's cheques had been returned to him as acknowledged by his signature. On the edge of one of the interrogation sheets somebody had scribbled in German: 'No further questions; release tomorrow; revalidate his ticket.' That was a slight discrepancy. Maxon remembered clearly that the folder had contained an actual railway ticket, not a photocopy. They must have had some problem with revalidation, so they kept his original ticket and gave him a new one. This was the original. He took a closer look. Even before he had consciously registered it, he had a warning cramp in his stomach. Yes, there was something odd. The seat reservation was attached. It had been issued in Hamburg. For the evening train on the 12th. The 12th was the Sunday. He must have left for D. on that day, not Monday the 13th, after all. He had lied. And not only that. He had falsified the entries in the diary to show 'To D.' on the Monday.

Papa Mike returned with some fresh coffee, and looked at the picture in Maxon's hand: 'Ah, so you've also noticed it.'

'What?'

'The marking on the edge of the ticket. I've tried a big blow-up but it's no good. It's only an indentation. It's handwriting, that's obvious. Somebody must have used the ticket as a pad while writing on some other sheet of paper. Is it important?'

'I don't know. Can you do anything with it?'

'Nope.'

They studied it together but magnification only blurred the indents. They agreed that most of it must be figures in two distinct groups. In the first, they identified three deeper impressions that looked like slanting strokes. Between the first and second obliques, there seemed to be just one figure which was odd: *something, stroke, something* rather than strokes sandwiching a solitary number would look more natural in a reference number, for instance.

'That first figure could be an 8 or a 3,' Papa Mike suggested.

Maxon was still puzzled by that first oblique. What if it was a figure 1 without the little flag in front? It would turn the first number into 18 or 13 and eliminate the oddity of starting with a stroke. Read like that, the first group could be a *date, stroke, month, stroke, year.* 18th or 13th of a month. Kowalski's missing Monday was a 13th. Maxon resisted the lure to jump to conclusions, but the idea was very tempting. If Kowalski needed some reminder for the Monday, a note he did not want to put into his diary, he would use a separate sheet – atop the ticket.

'There's only one way to find out,' the photographer said holding the print between yellowed fingers. 'If you get me the original for a couple of hours, I could work on it with a friend in the police lab. Perhaps ultraviolet will show up more, I don't know, but I could ask someone who deals with forgeries. Can you get it?'

'No.' It was most unlikely that Maxon could steal or

borrow the ticket even if Ellsberg kept his promise and let him see the Kowalski papers. 'But I may have a chance to take a closer look.'

'You could try it with some graphite powder. If you rub it into the indents, it might make them legible.'

Maxon shook his head. 'Doesn't work. But a bloke at Scotland Yard invented some fluorescent powder for the job. Your police friend is bound to have access to the stuff. Get me some. I'll need it tonight. And I'll need a Durex.'

'Why? Is it going to be a fuck-up?' Papa Mike could not stop laughing long after Maxon had left.


KGB collator Kobelyev duly noted with undue pleasure the ever-growing frustration of Moscow's Canadian Maxon-watchers. It seemed they had discovered virtually nothing about the purpose of Maxon's Toronto visit apart from meeting Mrs K. (something Kobelyev was careful to take no notice of because he never needed to be told twice what was and was not his business). He gleefully listed the various occasions when Maxon had given his tails the slip. The English agent's artful disappearing acts were no news to him, in fact, he remembered with pride that it was a Russian – Ertyakin? Ekarin? – who had taught Maxon some of the basic tricks of the trade in Spain. Yes, it must have been during the war. Because Kobelyev delighted in such details, he was upset beyond reason whenever his memory failed him. Who was that Russian agent? Ekman? Eckmann? A German sounding name, he was sure. He asked for a computer check and waited impatiently, hoping that nobody would query why he needed it. Generally, nobody asked him to justify his research, but sometimes, the overworked computer handlers kicked up an embarrassing fuss over the most trivial requests.

A half an hour later, Kobelyev received the answer – and felt like kicking himself. Ellsberg. But of course. How could he forget? He had never met Ellsberg personally, even though the old agent was one of his idols who had worked, he knew, for a few years in Moscow Centre, perhaps a few doors or only a couple of green corridors away.

Ellsberg. Ellsberg. The name needled him for some reason. He tried to put it out of his mind but it would not go away. Angrily, he decided to call it a day. The reports in hand concerning Maxon and some others could wait until the morning. At this late night hour, nobody would read them anyway. He began to lock his papers away. When he shut Maxon's file, his eyes picked out the word 'Toronto'. And it clicked, at last. Now he really felt like kicking himself. I must be getting senile, he thought as the gossip he had overheard in the KGB club came back. A couple of young louts had been talking about Ellsberg's transfer to the Toronto trade mission, and they upset Kobelyev with using adjectives like 'feeble' and 'big-headed' about the man who had more famous exploits to his name than those two together would ever accomplish.

Ellsberg and Maxon in Toronto. A coincidence. And then Kobelyev remembered what he was supposed to forget: Mrs K, (J. for Jacqueline) was also in Toronto. Another coincidence? If he mentioned it all in his analysis, he would be told off for failing to forget about the Kowalski name. But there was a way to handle it. He quickly completed his memo on Maxon without any reference to Ellsberg or Kowalski, made a phone call to discover that the colonel in 'disinformation' to whom he was reporting was still in the building, and chose to deliver his memo by hand. In lieu of thanks the colonel dismissed him with a contemptuous wave of his fingers, but Kobelyev mentioned, just in passing, that the watchers had not reported anything about Maxon meeting Ellsberg of the Soviet trade mission.

'Why should they meet?' The question revealed that the colonel knew nothing about the old friendship between the two. It had all happened before his time. Young blades equally disliked reading dusty old files and endless computer print-outs. Kobelyev answered as casually as he could, and revenge for the earlier majestic dismissal was sweet in the form of a sudden deluge of interest from the colonel.

An hour later, a hastily summoned midnight meeting took place in the colonel's office. The 'wet affairs' major (now the proud owner of a metallic blue Skoda) was also present. The colonel summarised the coincidences he himself claimed to have discovered. The consensus of opinion was that no great significance should be attached to them, but orders must go to Canada that if any contact between Ellsberg and Maxon was noted, 'executive action would have to be taken forthwith against one or both men

. . . the methods to be chosen for greatest expediency in the prevailing circumstances.'

The colonel would make some prudently discreet inquiries to satisfy his own curiosity about Ellsberg's current intelligence role, if any, but unless something startling and crucial emerged, the decision would stand because his own Kowalski operation in progress must retain precedence according to directives from what he liked to call 'the heavens above.'

The KGB Resident at the Soviet embassy in Ottawa received the coded 'personal and urgent' cable at half past seven in the evening, local time. Typical of the Centre, he thought, they would make such tentative decisions at midnight or beyond. They just loved to demand immediate attention at all hours even if the matter had no urgency at all. Only to be on the safe side, he called his best man in Toronto who apologised for losing Xerxes (office code for Maxon) from sight and promised to pick up his trail 'any moment now'. The Resident's new instructions in code would be delivered by hand to Toronto, but it could wait, surely, until morning.

Maxon followed a strict anti-surveillance routine. With the help of Papa Mike and another two local contacts he kept swapping cars, retraced his routes, wasted time in the open only to disappear in buildings with emergency exits. Crouching on the floor of Papa Mike's cruising car, he studied the district chosen by Ellsberg. It was Cabbage Town, a demolishers' paradise under redevelopment, with scores of deserted, tumbledown turn-of-the-century tenements and new chic boutiques. Shortly before eight in the evening, an hour before the appointed time, he was already hiding behind a boarded-up window opposite the house where the *meet* was to take place. He knew he was 'clean' and he was certain that there were no fresh arrivals to watch the street, so he could not be seen crossing the road except by someone who had inside information in advance – and that could have come only from Ellsberg. For his final approach, he was relying on Ellsberg's help anyway, and he was not to be disappointed.

One minute before nine, a bulky truck parked in front of

the house, blocking the narrow road almost completely. Seconds later, a large saloon car raced in from the opposite direction. In the ensuing noise, excitement and vehicle manoeuvering, Maxon slipped into the building where Ellsberg was waiting for him.

The Russian apologised for the derelict meeting place, and offered him his hip-flask. Maxon could tell that he was upset, even angry, perhaps. 'Good to see you,' Ellsberg said.

'We'll drink to that. *Nazdarovye.*' Maxon drank and returned the flask.

'Down the hatchet.'

'It's "hatch", Volodya, don't you ever learn?'

'Perhaps this time I meant hatchet.'

'I didn't realise we were fighting ... Were we? Don't keep it a secret.'

'I have few secrets these days.'

'Poor, poor Volodya.'

'It's not funny. I was hoping to get some documents for you. It was important.'

'What's it about?'

'It's best if we talk when you see them. You don't seem to believe me without evidence. But I've got you this.' Ellsberg pulled the faded blue Kowalski folder out of a plastic shopping bag, and paused, watching Maxon. It was an old trick to get a tell-tale reaction but Maxon would not fall for it: he maintained a strictly faint interest only. 'It's the Kowalski papers, as promised,' Ellsberg said at last. 'Photocopies of everything he had on him when they took him off the train, and the interrogation sheets. Pretty innocuous stuff, as you'll see.'

'May I borrow them for a few hours?'

'Can't risk it. And I'd rather you didn't even photograph them. We're lucky to have them anyway. Some hooligans visited my cabin last night.'

'Anything missing?'

'Nothing of value. But I don't keep valuables in that office. This was there because I wanted to show it to you when the explosion interfered.'

'How come you have it anyway? I mean if you have few secrets these days.'

'I have dealings here with various scientists. Exchange visits and things like that. So I had a pretty good excuse to ask for Kowalski's file ... through a friend.'

'And why show it to me?'

'Can't I do you a good turn?'

'It's not your style, Volodya. You taught me, remember?' He began to look through the papers trying to display due interest. He noticed that each had been numbered since his visit: it would give Ellsberg an easy way to check that nothing was missing after the meet. The rail ticket was numbered 17. The indents were visible but illegible. While Ellsberg watched the street from behind a torn curtain, Maxon slipped the ticket into his pocket.

'Anything?'

'It's all quiet,' the Russian assured him.

'Good. Is there a loo in this place?'

'Upstairs. Not very clean.'

'I'm desperate.' Maxon left the door open behind him to let Ellsberg see that he was going up. If the Russian glanced through the papers in his absence, he would discover that No. 17 was missing. It was a risk Maxon had to accept.

On top of the rickety lavatory seat cover, Maxon dusted the rail ticket with the special powder which, he knew, had the peculiar characteristic of losing its fluorescence when it was rubbed gently. He then half inflated the condom Papa Mike had found such a hilarious idea, and began to roll it lightly, back and forth, over the ticket. The fluorescence faded gradually all over the smooth part of the paper but not where the powder had settled in the fine grooves of the impression because in there, the large, flat surface of the balloon could not reach it.

The first oblique was clearly different from the other two. Yes, it had to be a number 1, turning the first two digits into 13. The date of the missing Monday. The month and year that followed it, separated by obliques, confirmed that the note referred to Kowalski's missing day.

The second group of figures seemed to be a telephone number with a code prefix of 5831. Of the number itself, only the last digit was blurred. The impression might have been too light originally or careless handling and overall pressure might have evened it out. Still, Maxon could consider himself lucky: one missing digit gave him only ten possible numbers to try ranging from a 0 to 9 ending; whereas two missing digits would have offered a hundred variations, and three missing digits would have left him with the near-impossible task of sifting through several thousand combinations to call and test. But whatever the mystery number might turn out to be, the most worrying discovery remained that Kowalski did seem to have a secret after all. And if that was the case, it would reduce, even wipe out Ellsberg's credibility: most probably, his 'doing a good turn' and attempting to buy Maxon's confidence with the Kowalski papers would be just a part of some operation on behalf of the Centre.

Maxon did not forget to pull the chain, and then complain about the filth on his return to the room. Ellsberg showed no sign of having noticed the short absence of the ticket, and Maxon slipped No. 17 back into the folder while reading the rest of the papers. The pretence of interest and a reasonable length of reading time had to be maintained even though he would have liked to run and find out what the telephone number was. It might well be an East German secret police contact. Poor Jack.

Staring out at the dead street, Ellsberg began to talk about Nuremberg, a memory that had been haunting him more and more frequently. Maxon remembered he had also mentioned it during their first meet on the boat.

'You have a saying, young Maxon, my country, right or wrong – correct?'

'Yes. Do you want to apply it to Nuremberg?'

'Why not?'

'I'd prefer to question – how wrong? The Nazi state was much too wrong to deserve blind obedience.'

'It's not that simple. The people we convicted had been brought up not even to question authority.'

What was he getting at? Was he talking about his own problems? Was this a preamble to undermine Maxon's loyalty? There was only one way to find out: Maxon had to play along, whatever the game was, and try to steer the conversation towards the real minefields of basic beliefs. 'Never mind their upbringing, Volodya, we convicted them for being criminals. For failing to disobey unlawful orders issued by other criminals. So never mind the wording of our oath of loyalty, if you obeyed the Eichmanns of this world, you'd be a murderer and you'd know it.'

'Strong words, young Maxon.'

'But true. The sentences we passed at Nuremberg would be plain murders if we now recognised one law for the losers and a different one for the victors.'

'So how would you compare my position with theirs?' Ellsberg's voice softened. He might have been talking to himself. 'Their leaders were patently malicious and dishonest even to their own people. Mine aren't. Despite their numerous failings.'

'Including their imperialistic dreams and paranoiac suspicions towards the outside world?'

'Yes, perhaps, but these are inherited diseases. And not completely without real historical causes, you must admit.'

'Okay, I buy that. What else are you selling?' Maxon closed in on him.

This time Ellsberg accepted the challenge of making eye contact. 'Selling? No, it's free to you that some of our madmen are dangerously agressive in order to defend.'

'But if that was your defence at some future Nuremberg where you were the accused, I'd remind you of a big difference.'

'What?'

'That this time we're not talking about petty, mischievous misdemeanours like genocide and mass-extermination – this time round it's the real McCoy. There's no excuse for not stopping your madmen.'

'Why do you want *me* to judge everybody and everything? Who am I to know what's right and wrong?' Ellsberg turned away.

Maxon rounded and cornered him. Provoke, provoke, provoke, he urged himself. 'That was Eichmann's defence in Jerusalem,' he raised his voice, 'and that's what showed him up as an animal. Humans can tell right from wrong, honour from dishonour.'

'And how do you want me to measure my honour against my loyalties – the loyalties I owe to myself, my nation, my kind? Mankind.'

Maxon felt like embracing his friend to share his agony of facing the truth and trying to make the most painful decision a man could ever be asked to reach. But he could not afford to let him off the hook. 'Yes, you got the ascending order right,' he said acidly. 'You only left out the family, perhaps because neither of us has any. But yes, you owe it to yourself to survive, yet you'd kill yourself for your family and you'd die for your country. With that you recognise that the greater good of the larger group must have priority. And your country is *not* the top on your list.'

Ellsberg shrugged his shoulders.

'Is it or is it not?' Maxon pressed on. 'It's your list.'

'So what the hell do you propose? Treason?'

'It's got to be *your* answer.'

'I know. But it helps talking to you. You're the only friend I've ever made.'

'Then use me. Talk.' Maxon turned his right foot to give the tape recorder in the heel of his shoe the best chance to pick up even whispers. 'Talk, Volodya. Take your time.'

'There may not be enough time.'

'Then tell me now.'

'Would you believe me?'

'I'd try.'

'Thank you for your honesty, young Maxon. You could do no better than to try. You wouldn't be a pro if you believed me without some evidence ... and you couldn't convince your own people ... your leaders.'

'About what?'

'That I was telling you the truth. I was hoping to have some evidence for you tonight. But it hasn't arrived. I need more time anyway.'

'To think?'

'That, too.'

'Then don't delay it, Volodya. Occasionally a man can change the course of history. It takes a great man to recognise his moment of destiny.'

'You're a friend. And a real pro. I mean professional enough to break into my office before our meeting to see for yourself what I might have to offer ...'

They both smiled hesitantly, then began to laugh with growing conviction. They stood close to each other without touching, and the warmth of shared laughter enveloped them. It was good to be friends. And it was tempting for Maxon to tell his friend about those curious indentations on the rail ticket, but he held back: Ellsberg might still be play-acting, laughter and all. 'You once told me that beyond a certain point, you wouldn't trust yourself. Is it still true?'

'Yes.'

'Then how can you trust me?' Maxon probed again.

'I have no choice. I think.'

'That's a good enough reason. So go ahead, give me a hint ... I don't want to push you ... I mean I do ...'

'I know. But it's not easy if you're not accustomed to being a ... how shall I say it? With my poor English I almost said "traitor".'

'Oh yes, the poverty of your English and a whore's virginity.'

'Okay, I purchase that.'

'No, Volodya, you *buy* that, and you know it. So what am *I* supposed to buy? Are you playing for time or just waiting for an outright offer?'

Ellsberg seemed hurt. 'I wish it was that simple.'

It was time for Maxon to prove himself to his tutor by demonstrating that he had learned lesson No. 1 to work and live without pity. 'I understand. You must find it embarrassing to set some KGB trap for me.'

'You really think I'd do it?'

'No, I don't *want* to believe that. But then, I don't know the circumstances. You may have no choice. You haven't unearthed me for nothing, that's obvious. You bore gifts, but you'd taught me to beware of the Greeks bearing gifts and being charitable. And then you hinted that GLEW might endanger peace. How could it?'

'By upsetting the balance. By disarming a threat. It's a weapon some of our generals may find too dangerous to live with.'

'It's as much a weapon as weather forecasting is a cause of rain.'

'What if the gods don't like to have their intentions exposed? They may get mad and choose to send down thunder instead of rain to prove the forecast wrong.' Ellsberg regained his composure and sank the folder into the shopping bag.

Maxon knew him well enough to see that right now, it was no good to press him for more, yet he had to keep trying. 'Their thunder could of course be a bluff,' he said at last, 'and a bluff too many could easily be the end of all bluffing.'

'Yes, it could be that, for instance,' said Ellsberg absentmindedly. 'For instance? I mean for example. I never know which is right. You tell me.'

'If you tell me more about the thunder.'

'Thunder? No. It's a clear night. Just the night to take a long stroll with you. I'd really enjoy that.' His eyes and voice came as close to being emotional as they probably ever could. 'What a crazy world where two friends mustn't be seen walking together ...'

Papa Mike called a friend at the Mounted Police in Ottawa to get a quick check on the possible telephone numbers for Maxon. The contact reported back an hour later that the prefix indicated Wittingen in West Germany. Of the ten possible combinations two were spare reserve lines, five belonged to individual desks through an automated switchboard in the local tax office, one was an exclusive mental home, and two were private subscribers.

Maxon knew that a lengthy security check on each of them might be too slow to help him in any way. So he invented a plausible story and called one of the private numbers. It was engaged constantly. The operator said there might be a fault on the line. The tax office would have to wait until morning. He called the mental home.

'Sanatorium Schulberg,' a male voice crooned down the line.

'Er ... shprecken zee Da-ich?' Maxon struggled, 'I mean English, bitte?'

'Sure thing,' came the answer in caricature American, 'go ahead caller.'

'This is Air Canada from Toronto.'

'Oh yeah.'

'We've got a piece of lost luggage here with no name tag, nothing. But inside, there's a note with your phone number and a name.'

'What's that?'

'Does the name Kowalski mean anything to you?'

'Kowalski? You mean Drusilla?'

'Who?' Maxon swallowed. 'Could you repeat that?'

'Yeah, Drusilla. Mrs Drusilla Kowalski. But she wouldn't travel,' the voice smiled, 'most unlikely sir. She's one of our patients ... Hullo? Are you there, Canada?'

'Yeah. I'm here ... just checking ... the luggage contains only men's clothing ...'

'That's what I thought. It must belong to her husband. He lives in Canada – Toronto, I think. You want me to check? ... Hullo? ... Hullo?'

# IV

Designed to offend no one, the hotel room failed eminently to please anyone. The position of the radio button, the sailboat in the pale frame, and the siting of the dent in the mattress followed the traveller from continent to continent, as if creating a home for the homeless, continuity, dependability, in the distinct style of the nondescript. Maxon always thought that the portrayal of absolute vacuum would have to take the shape of such a hotel room because the mere *nihil* would inevitably be furnished by the onlookers' imagination which, on the other hand, would gladly annihilate the sight of sailing boat & co. After a sleepless night of encoding his long report to Locke, even the dreary prospect of breaking Kowalski seemed preferable to staying in the room for an unnecessary second longer. Maxon was about to leave when the phone rang.

'Hi. Guess who?'

Maxon recognised the voice right away. It belonged to the inimitable Gloucester, the most popular/unpopular 'Glossie Aussie' news hound of Fleet Street (unwanted adjective or the subject himself to be deleted according to editorial taste).

'Glossie! Good to hear you.' Maxon liked him. He could never explain to himself why. Perhaps it was just an intriguing experience to like someone despite everything. Particularly despite his striving to imitate The English Gentleman modelled upon Sandy's mannerisms and sartorial style. 'Are you in Toronto?'

'Alas, no. Still stuck in London 'm'afraid.'

'How did you know where to find me?' Maxon asked more with admiration than suspicion.

'I bumped into your dear old chief the other day.'

Maxon was now on his guard: nobody, not even Gloucester would just accidentally *bump into* Sandy. 'Is that why you've called?'

'Well, you could put it that way, I s'pose. We talked

107

about old times, and you, of course, and then he asked if I could give you a message.'

'Couldn't he call me himself?'

'Ask him, old sport, do. But he said it's off the record.'

It had to be if Sandy used a scribbler as his messenger boy. 'Okay, stand and deliver the message.'

'It's just that he heard that you'd sort of branched out into this and that lately. Know what I mean? I think he mentioned "irregular" or perhaps "off-duty" activities. Do you know what he meant?'

'Did he object to those activities?'

'Didn't say.'

'He never does, does he?' Maxon nodded.

'No, but he thought it might be more *prudent* to stick to your main, regular job.'

'You mean safer?'

'That's something else he didn't say,' Gloucester laughed effortlessly. 'He just stressed that he's sorry, but ... er ...'

'But what?'

'But from now on, you're on your own, old sport.'

Maxon was dumbfounded. If Sandy knew something and wanted to warn him, why didn't he spell it out? And why do it through Glossie? Is it against the rules of the game to help people on your own side? Was somebody stirring the shit? Was somebody knifing him in the back? Maxon saw the room in a new light: he had never checked it for bugs, he had had no reason to. And the phone – was it safe? For a start, he wanted to test Gloucester's reaction. 'I understand, I mean I don't but I do, you understand?' he tried to joke to disguise the onrush of thoughts and doubts the message had triggered off. 'Does it also mean that I can't ask you for a small favour?'

'Don't be daft, man, we're friends whatever your game is. Go ahead, ask.'

'Thanks, I'll come back to you.'

Maxon left the hotel in a hurry. This time he took no precautions to shake off his tail if he had one. After Sandy's warning, it was best not to alert whoever might be watching him. It would make it easier to get away on other occasions when he really needed it. That he was about to pay a visit to Kowalski would not have to be a secret. But the timing mattered: he wanted to see the scientist on his own, and he knew that Jack would be out all morning, showing the sights to her weekend visitor, a childhood friend from her desolate past in the North West Territories. Maxon found it difficult to imagine Jack as a child, and she was never keen to talk about her 'cold years up there'.

Hoovering to Vivaldi could be heard through the door as Maxon rang the bell. The machine stopped, the music did not. Kowalski opened the door and made no attempt at concealing how displeased he was to see Maxon and have the peace of his Sunday morning interrupted.

'Hello,' said Maxon with a false smile. 'We seem to have similar tastes.' He meant Vivaldi.

'I know.' Kowalski sounded bitter: he had mistaken the remark for a crude reference to Jack. 'She's out.'

'Good. I came to see you.' Maxon moved the vacuum cleaner and walked in, noticing that the old man was blushing: he belonged to a generation of mid-Europeans who would admit more readily even to being impotent than to helping with housework.

The shame of appearing to be henpecked fuelled Kowalski's hostility. 'So what do you want?'

'I wanted to give you another chance to help yourself by helping me.'

'Don't be absurd. I've told you everything I could except what I remembered only yesterday. It's just a tiny detail about my London visit to get clearance for that train journey.'

'Are you still claiming you visited the London office?'

'I don't *claim* things! I state facts, no matter what's in the doorman's log.'

'Because you suddenly remember that there was no log. Right? Not that day. It was the log's day off.' The best of the Borgias would have envied the sweetness of Maxon's smile. He knew it would infuriate Kowalski and drive him further and further into irrevocable lies.

'I know nothing about the log. I'm not a concierge. But I know that the day was Friday, and I remember the doorman on duty. And he might remember me. Because he was waiting for news about the birth of his first grandchild. He already knew that it would be by Caesarian section, and he was desperate to get some reassurance.'

'From you?' Maxon's contemptuous tone disguised his surging doubts: Kowalski was no fool – why would he lie so blatantly about something that could be checked?

'Yes, from me. It was quite funny, really, because he must have decided that a scientist is a scientist is a scientist, so I must know all answers to all such things. Well, I did my best to explain that it was a routine operation these days. Nothing to worry about. And I was still there when the good news came through. I was lucky. He might have killed me if he thought I'd misled him. As it turned out, he said we must wet the baby's head.'

'Which pub did you go to?' Maxon knew all the likely places in the area.

'He couldn't leave his post because he was on his own. But he had a fair-size silver hip flask . . .'

'What? On duty?'

'He said he never drank when he was on duty but he was used to carrying one because of his long and often shiverish trips with his racing pigeons. He said he felt sort of naked without the flask.'

So that was it. Kowalski had finally put his head into the noose, quite voluntarily. Would he break down when Maxon used his trump? A condemned man deserved a last chance at least to prove honest intentions: 'Look, I'm serious when I say I'm trying to help you. So if there's any, even the slightest doubt in your mind . . .'

'What doubt?'

'That this tale may not check out . . .'

'He'll remember.'

'I hope so. For your sake. Because it would look really bad, much too bad, if you were caught out yet again.'

'And what is that supposed to mean?' Kowalski's indignation seemed so genuine that Maxon was ready to apologise for any insinuation, admit that he was guilty of jumping to easy conclusions, and confess to allowing himself to be influenced by a sentiment he was in no way entitled to – jealousy. You're a pig, Maxon, he railed against himself, you try to drag an honest, much-suffered man down into the swill in which you wallow. But Kowalski did not stop. He cursed Maxon and his likes, their dirty secrets that allowed them to see everybody else 'only through a filter of shit,' and ordered him to 'get out and don't bring the breath of the gutter into this house ever again'.

Maxon found it upsetting to have it all spelt out for him by somebody else, very different from telling the same to himself, yet at that point, he was still ready to withdraw, continue his investigations, and delay the decision whether a confrontation was really inevitable even if the old scientist might suffer a stroke or a heart attack as a result. But then Kowalski made a mistake. He brought Jacqueline into his rambling outburst: 'How could she remain so clean after having been touched by you?'

Maxon's momentary compassion for him evaporated. His *mea culpa* for his emotional involvement was no match for his lust for revenge: no man was ever to smear the happiness he had destroyed in a mad act of self-sacrifice to protect his love. 'Thanks. You've been a great help,' he said and turned as if to leave. He had no wish to witness Kowalski's potential death throes. 'As for an answer to your last question . . . I suggest you ask Drusilla.' He stopped and listened to the silence behind him. 'Yes, ask Mrs Drusilla Kowalski,' Maxon repeated and started towards the door. Would Kowalski beg him to stay? He did.

'Please . . .'

Maxon led him to a sofa and let him collapse. 'Okay, let's have it straight this time.' Kowalski seemed to have difficulty with speaking, so he poured him a good three fingers of bourbon and impelled him to drink up.

'Jacqueline . . . *Czy ona wie* . . .' In a state of shock, Kowalski began in Polish.

'You may find English a richer language for lying your way out of bigamy.'

'No . . . no bigamy . . .'

'Trigamy? How many have you got? Are you a Muslim?'

'Jacqueline . . . does she know?'

'I haven't told her . . . yet.'

'You mustn't. Please.'

'Well, let's say it's up to you.' Don't you get soft with him, Maxon warned himself. 'What have you got to trade?' He hoped against hope that nothing would come out to prove Ellsberg guilty of betraying their friendship.

'How did you find out?' It was the voice of a broken man.

'None of your bloody business.'

'But Locke promised . . .'

'What?'

'That Drusilla would never appear on my record.'

Locke? Locke knew about Drusilla? It was Maxon's turn to be shocked. But Kowalski was not to know it. 'I hope you're not foolish enough to lie that Locke promised you anything like that.'

'I swear.'

'Not good enough.'

'Look ... look, listen ...'

'Only if you talk about Drusilla.'

'A man is entitled to a scrap of privacy.'

'Yes, until he's found out. And you are. You've fabricated evidence to imply that "To D." meant Dresden not Drusilla. So who is she?'

'She was my wife.'

'Was?'

'Yes. She was tortured by the Nazis. Then by the Bolshies. But she was strong and brave. They never broke her. When we escaped from Poland, she broke down. And now she's mad. Incurably mad.'

'So you divorced her. Hope you're proud of yourself.'

'You wouldn't understand.'

'I don't even want to.'

'I've always looked after her. She's in the best hands. And I visit her whenever I can.'

'She's deeply touched, I'm sure.'

'She doesn't know. Her mind's gone.'

'And what if one day ...'

'No! They told me. Specialist after specialist. And Locke had it double-checked for me. He understood. He knew I'd suffered too much. I was entitled to a little happiness.'

Maxon found he was getting more furious with Locke than Kowalski. The general knew he was interested in the scientist. Why did he withold such crucial information from him? If Locke had known the secret, and if D's existence had not been seen as damning evidence against her ex-husband, why wasn't Kowalski cleared? Just to maintain the pressure, Maxon made a u-turn. 'Why didn't you tell Jacqueline?'

'Locke said it wasn't necessary.'

'I thought it was you who married her.'

'I agreed with Locke. I wanted to. Was I wrong? Don't you understand? I'm old. It was my last chance to be happy. And I love her.'

'But not enough to tell her the truth.'

'I was afraid of losing her.' Tears filled his eyes, and he made no attempt to hide them. 'I thought she might despise

112

me for the divorce as much as I despised myself. That divorce is the only shameful secret of my life.'

'And you'd do anything to protect it, wouldn't you?'

'Okay. You win. How do I buy your silence?'

'Have you ever put this question to anyone else?'

'No. Why?'

'Think, professor, think. Shall I try to help refreshing your memory?'

'My memory?'

'Okay. Let's try. Close your eyes ... I said close your eyes! ... There. ... Let's think about a small room ... a hotel room? Perhaps a cold shed full of police at a railway station ... "Won't be long, sir," they promise, "just a formality. Police formality." ... You're afraid that you'll miss the train ...'

'What train?'

'The train to Vienna.'

'No!'

'They took you off, didn't they?'

Kowalski nodded painfully.

'You see? It all comes back. They make you wait. And wait. Until other men arrive. Faceless men in fur hats. Or Fedora hats. You can hardly see them because there are sharp lights. ... And they make you look at papers, photographs, copies of your marriage certificate, medical certificates ...'

'No! It's not true.'

'Yes, yes, I can see it ... you deny everything, you put up a good front ... "no! It's not true!" But then they change the tune. They trot out with threats. They'll tell Jacqueline about it all. Perhaps they show you a buff envelope, large enough to take all the documents. It's addressed to her. But they drop a little hint. A deal may be possible. You understand. It's the first ray of hope. And then you ask "how do I buy your silence?" Like you asked me ... remember?'

The change was quite sudden: the tears dissolved without being spent, the voice regained the ring of composure, the fingers let go of the glass spilling whisky everywhere. Drained of emotions, Kowalski stated 'not true'.

'But you still want to buy my silence, don't you?'

'Yes.' He was either a great actor or an honest man.

'Then answer me one question: don't you love Jack, I

mean Jacqueline, enough to protect *your* secret from her by giving away just a few lousy, possibly worthless secrets about GLEW?'

'No. Why? Because I hate them. The faceless men in the Fedoras, and the rest of them. And believe me, my sort of hatred of the other side is a greater deterrent to would-be traitors than any woman's love or any oath of loyalty.'

Right now, all Maxon could hate was his own job: it forced him to do things for his side he wouldn't do for himself. On his way out, he flicked the handle of the Hoover towards Kowalski, offering him a chance to finish his chores. He knew it was a petty though irresistible gesture – and he was shamed of it.

Maxon went directly to the Toronto HQ of GLEW. It consisted of two rooms for a grand bored man of the Navy and his secretary. 'As you know, all operations are centralised,' Locke would explain at the slightest provocation, 'and local HQs are only to liaise with governments.' Maxon's arrival caused a welcome stir of expectations only to be followed by the inevitable let-down: nothing disappoints like thwarted goodwill and spurned offers of service. The old sea-dog would have risked his life for GLEW, but all Maxon wanted was the use of his safe line to Washington. He spoke to Locke and asked to have Kowalski under round the clock surveillance.

'What makes you think that we were waiting for your recommendation?' the general retorted sharply.

'I'll tell you tomorrow. I'm taking the early morning flight to Washington. What time can you see me, *sir?*'


An inconsiderate wind got up just when the President of the United States was about to putt on the second green, and earned itself the collective frown of his entourage: was there no respect in this world for moments of presidential concentration? After the brief delay, he was about to apply himself to the task once again when yet another, even less forgivable noise interfered: the bulk of Chuck Parkin approached with a bee-like whizz aboard an electric dune buggy which was reserved for the larger players of lesser mobility. Bodyguards, golf-buddies, hangers-on and other presidential lackeys were uncertain how to react: Chuck

114

was unknown on the course, but he did belong to the White House hierarchy, well, he did in a way, only none of them quite knew how. He had been brought in by the President himself as a coordinator of all intelligence briefings for the Oval Office, but it was rumoured that senior people regarded him as just a nag and a relic from the presidential campaign period. So they waited for a cue, and when it came, 'Hi, Chuck, good to see you,' they all echoed the sentiment.

The President putted, missed, tried again, and won his due reward, though a sharp observer might have found his modicum of success not quite commensurate with the applause.

'Good shot, Mr President,' Chuck mumbled because he felt he had to say something.

The President smiled: 'I was right, wasn't I? Didn't I predict that you'd take up golf one day?'

'You did.'

'So what's your handicap?'

'Only that I still don't play.'

'Then what are you doing here?'

With some effort, Chuck descended from his driving seat and approached the President until he was close enough to answer in a whisper. 'I had to talk to you.'

'Why here?'

'It's not easy to get access to the Oval Office these days.'

'Rubbish.'

'It's a fact, Mr President.'

'Come. Walk with me.' He put his arm round Chuck. 'And at least between you, me and the third green, stop calling me Mr President.'

'Thanks, Bob. You make it easier for me. I miss working with you closely like in the old days.'

'Oh yes, you remember Boston?' the President burst into unstoppable reminiscences. Eventually, he teed off again (a few appreciative mm's greeting the modest drive), then continued his walk down memory lane – and towards the thicket where the ball had landed. Yes, oh yes, those were the days, the wild, early days on the campaign trail, when people like Chuck earned themselves future presidential favours and appointments. Not that Chuck's job was superfluous in any way at the time of its creation, and not that the President failed to glance through his summaries,

115

but these were hard and busy times, no wonder that Chuck had not enjoyed unlimited personal access lately. Chuck understood – at least until lately.

'You're still in the habit of picking on words, Chuck.'

'It's you who made it my job, Bob. But my work is wasted if I can't get any reaction from you even when I mark reports for your *immediate* attention.'

'You mean somebody's stonewalling you? We can't have that. No, sir, not that.'

'Whatever it is, you've never reacted to my most serious concern.'

'About what?'

'GLEW.'

'Oh.' The President's reaction went no further than that. He asked no questions. He had to be 'reminded' of reports he had obviously never read. He noted Chuck's worries about the accidental alert that had stunned the capital, about the apparent lack of serious investigation into the slip-up, and several points Chuck saw as being 'fishy'.

'Well, this isn't really the place, Chuck . . .'

'I know. But we were on the brink of war.'

'I didn't press any buttons, did I?'

'Not this time. But next time it might be very different. Because this couldn't have been just a goof. Not just something technical. And if my reading of various clues is correct, there may never be a next time.'

'What clues are we talking about?'

Chuck knew that the President was growing impatient. Probably on account of the golf ball in sight now. So he had to use his trump: 'It is my strong impression, to say the least, that the security of GLEW has been compromised through blackmail and other means. The Soviets may already possess all the information they need.'

The President's face went blank, the eyes explored the thicket where the ball sat in deep grass. 'That's something you must discuss with Locke.'

'I've tried. He doesn't want to know. He acknowledges my reports, and does nothing else.'

'What are you trying to imply, Chuck?'

'It's just that my analysis and interpretation of combined intelligence sources must be checked and proved or disproved rather than ignored. For if I'm right, and if the secret of our early warning system is broken, the consequences could be disastrous.'

'And I agree, Chuck, I do. But Locke is your man. You must convince him. ... Ah, here we are. ... You really ought to take up golf, you know. Would do you good.' He patted Chuck's mountainous belly with the head of his 7-iron. 'I bet that's what Gwen keeps nagging you with. Am I right or am I right?'

'You're right, of course, her concern about my weight is the only thing that hasn't changed since the Boston days, Mr President.'

'Okay, I'll take the call,' said Locke. 'Ask Maxon to wait ... and Alvin, apologise to him, will you?'

Inspector Wells was on the line. 'Returning your call, General.'

'Oh yes, very good of you, Inspector. Just wanted to thank you for all the details you sent me about that fatal accident. I take it there's no doubt whatsoever in your mind that it was the car Mr Maxon had hired.'

'None whatsoever, sir. But the presence of his fingerprints doesn't prove that he was at the wheel when the *murder* was committed. It's like with that houseboat explosion. The computer recognised his prints on some pieces of wreckage, so we know that at some stage he must have visited that call girl, but it doesn't mean that he killed her.'

'Good reasoning, Inspector. And I'm very grateful for your co-operation.'

'It isn't voluntary, sir, I must confess. If I wasn't *asked* by Mounted Police security to lay off, who knows, I could be ready to bring charges against certain individuals.'

Wells rang off, and Locke looked at his notes: Maxon had never mentioned his visit to the girl's houseboat or the explosion. He locked away Wells' report, and buzzed Captain Beck to show in Maxon, who seemed to be in a filthy mood.

'I'm glad you've come over, Maxon, it's better to discuss these things face to face. So what's your impression about Kowalski? Is he a traitor?'

'I don't know. But it would have helped me a great deal if

you had told me about your earlier investigations, the interviews you had had with him, and above all, about Drusilla.'

'I'm sorry. You didn't need to know.'

'But now I must know if I'm expected to form a useful opinion. So how about his clearance for that train journey? Did he or didn't he get one?'

'The London office has no record of his alleged visit there. That's all I can tell you.'

'Wouldn't any of the doormen remember him?' Maxon found it harder and harder to contain his anger. 'The man on duty was allegedly waiting for news about the birth of a grandchild.'

'Is that Kowalski's new alibi?'

'He says he's just remembered it. Should be easy to check. I'll get on to the London office.'

'Leave it to me, Maxon.'

'I'd like to know.'

'Well, let me put it this way: you're on vacation; you've used your time to engage in some unauthorised investigations . . .' Locke paused, noting Maxon's consternation, 'I mean it was unopposed, but certainly not authorised, was it? It wasn't an assignment. How could it be? You're still recuperating, right? So okay, you've picked up some information, you've duly passed it on to me, now you must leave it to us. There's no specific reason for you to know the answers.'

'It concerns GLEW security, so it concerns me.'

'In a . . . shall we say, personal way?'

Maxon offered his resignation at once.

Locke refused to accept it. He emphasised that he had no *reason* to question Maxon's integrity. But he could not allow anybody's feelings to come into play. 'Not when another, let's say semi-authorised and vastly more important investigation is still in progress. You've got to concentrate on Ellsberg. Squeeze him. Hard as you can.'

'Impossible. I said it in my report. He must be given a lot of rope. Then he may say whatever he's got to say, but only in his own good time.'

'Well, he may have all the time in the world, but we haven't. Some presidential security co-ordinator for instance, thinks that GLEW has been compromised.'

'Ellsberg says they haven't got a clue.'

118

'He may be lying.'

'Not impossible.'

'We must find out. That's why he's got to be squeezed. And if anyone, it's an old friend who can do it. You.'

'I can try, but then he may really start lying.'

'Even that could help us,' Locke insisted, 'if we interpret his lies correctly.'

'Yes, if.'

'What can we lose?'

'His confidence.'

'But you'll be doing him a favour. You think he's trying to tell you something. Something he finds hard to say. And I agree: otherwise he wouldn't have gone to all the trouble to contact you through Mrs Kowalski – and I mean Jacqueline, not Drusilla. So help him. Squeeze him. Set him up if necessary.'

Maxon hunched under the weight of the unpleasant prospect. He knew that Locke was right: if there was urgency, he would have to get the answers – now. But he could not operate a squeeze to full effect, unless he was able to gauge instantly the truth content of anything Ellsberg might say. For that he needed to know the state of the investigation into the nuclear alert in Washington. Locke disagreed. Was that a signpost to lack of trust or to poor thinking, Maxon wondered. He tried to argue. Locke remained adamant: slip-up or sabotage, the alert was quite irrelevant to the Ellsberg operation. How could he be so sure? How could anybody be so sure about anything in this damned business?

Kowalski was late for dinner without any warning. Jack found that in itself most unusual. Yet even more exceptional was his behaviour when he did arrive home at last. He would hardly utter a word and seemed to have lost his usual hearty appetite. She knew it was no good to press him for an answer, and her patience paid off over coffee.

'I've spoken to someone about Maxon,' he looked at her and paused. 'And about the car accident, of course.' When his wife remained silent, anguish flooded his eyes. 'He mentioned that you'd given Maxon an alibi.'

Bastard! He promised not to tell him! So why did he?

Jack could have strangled Inspector Wells. But she looked calm, and only said, 'I see.'

'Did you invent his alibi?'

'No.'

'Why didn't you tell me that he had been here?'

'It was such an innocent visit . . . I didn't want to hurt you.'

'You think I wouldn't have believed you?'

'I don't know. I've never been unfaithful to you.'

'Thank you.' He touched her face lightly. 'It must have been an awful strain . . . I mean to have a secret. It can be quite horrible to live with. Worse than a millstone round your neck when they drop you into the river. It not only pulls you down into the darkness below, it also makes you feel dirty. . . . And in turn you dirty everything you touch.'

The phone rang and she answered it.

'Maxon. Say sorry, wrong number.'

'Pardon? . . . You must have the wrong number.' She tried to look suitably puzzled as she raised and dropped her shoulders for Kowalski's benefit.

'I need you right away. I'm at Eddie's.'

It was the bar round the corner. But how could she get away? 'That's impossible . . . I mean this is a private apartment.'

'As soon as you can, Jack. Please.' And not to give her a chance to protest, he hung up.

'Wrong number?' Kowalski asked.

Jack nodded and began to look for a cigarette. 'I must have run out,' she grumbled.

'It's the second time. . . . It's not like you at all.' He offered to go and get her some but she was already on her way out, promising him not to be too long.

Eddie's was probably the cleanest, homeliest, least crowded, smokefree bar in the neighbourhood – in other words, it was heading for early bankruptcy, and Maxon's glass of Carling was unlikely to keep the creditors from the door. Enjoying Eddie's undivided attention, Maxon knew that the bar had been a bad choice, but it was easy for Jack to reach quickly. He had less than a day to put his scheme into operation and bombard Ellsberg with mysterious little clues which would compel the Russian to find some meaning to the meaningless, add *dva* and *dva* together, obfuscate and interpret the 'danger signs' according to the ways of his own suspicion-ridden mind, and build up some imaginary pressure like a man fattening his own shadow to frighten himself. It was to be a fallacy to think like that, but it was a ploy that had been used on Maxon once or twice, and he hoped that Ellsberg would be no less susceptible to it.

Jack arrived out of breath. 'I thought I'd find you in a pool of blood.'

'Does that make you a pessimist or an optimist?'

'Don't be a fool. What's wrong?'

'I need your help. You'll have to call Ellsberg's home number in great excitement and say you must meet him, but ring off before explaining anything as if you were cut off. That's tonight. Tomorrow, you tell Kowalski that you've just taken a message for him to call a Mr Ellsberg who might help him to clear his name. Say it sounded most urgent, no name was left but the caller spoke with a Polish accent. Tell Kowalski to phone Ellsberg's office number right away.'

As she was disinclined either to refuse or to comply with his request, she sidestepped the answer with a question: 'Why do you keep calling him Kowalski?'

'He and I have always avoided the embarrassing familiarity of first name terms, and I don't like referring to anybody as your husband.'

'I'll remember that. It could cheer me up some day.'

'Wish I could believe that.' Then he added hurriedly to kill the subject: 'And now something to cheer *him* up. Could you persuade him to go to London with you?'

'Not very easily.'

'Try it. You'll have to take a note for pushy Gloucester ...' He stopped because he noted Jack's querulous eyebrows rising and drooping asymmetrically, but he did not want to reveal that since Sandy's message he had seriously begun to feel being on his own, and had grown reluctant to trust the telephone or even the post. Why did Sandy need to spell out the obvious? Why now? 'Glossie will help you,' he said finally.

'How?'

'He'll find the porter I want Kowalski to identify.'

'What porter?'

'The pigeon-racer he's remembered suddenly. ... Expecting the first grandchild. ... You know ...'

'No, I don't.'

'Let's not waste time, he'll tell you. The main thing is that at this stage, I don't want Locke or anyone else to know that we're trying to locate the man who could clear Kowalski. That's why we'll need Gloucester.'

It was obvious she knew nothing about his Sunday visit, but only her expressive, lizard-quick eyebrows questioned him. She looked very beautiful. The temptation to tell her about Drusilla felt as welcome and repressible as vomit. Yet afterwards, he was sorry he had held it down. What the hell did Kowalski do to deserve pity? And why shouldn't Jack know that Drusilla might not be his only secret because otherwise Locke could long ago have cleared the old Pole. At least if he wanted to. But did he want to?

Jack seemed to understand his silence. 'Thanks. For helping him.'

'I'm helping you.'

'I thought you'd never forgive me for luring you to Toronto.' She leaned across the small bar table.

'Don't kiss me,' he whispered, 'not unless you stay with me tonight.'

'I can't. It would be betrayal. And there must be one I don't betray.'

'I don't understand.'

'I'll explain one day.'

'Another Carling?' Eddie crooned and snatched away Maxon's glass to demonstrate his special talent for sensing and propagating *ambiance*.

By lunchtime, Ellsberg had begun to identify the rat he could smell. For some reason, somebody was after him. He was in danger, and in his line of business, danger never came in half measures: it was either mortal or temporarily non-existent. If he was under fire, even innocent by-standers could be hurt from the spray of shrapnel. And Maxon was not even innocent: he had to be warned. But Maxon could not be reached, and Ellsberg could not risk leaving him messages.

The first sign of potentional calamity had come to him the previous night with Jack's unfinished telephone call. It would have been madness to call back. He had to wait.

In the morning, Kowalski rang him in the office asking for his help with reference to some mysterious message he had received. Ellsberg denied, of course, any knowledge of Kowalski and did his best to ridicule this inane 'hoax or provocation by some imperialist hater of peaceful trading,' but he knew then, that the game was up. The first question was, *which* of his numerous games was up. He looked out of the window and saw a small Japanese car. It had followed him to the office and it was still parked a few yards down the road. The driver seemed to have all the time in the world for reading the Toronto Globe. (Ellsberg had never met Papa Mike, the avid reader whose job was to make himself conspicuous.)

Jack might have called him of her own volition. Or she might have tried to make contact on Maxon's behalf. Both versions would be bad news. Kowalski's approach had to be instigated by somebody else. Jack? Maxon? No. Moscow was Ellsberg's prime suspect. But why would the KGB want him? Yes, they would know he had obtained Kowalski's papers, but his excuse for it was convincing and legitimate. The help he received from Colonel Vorodin? Vorodin was still Marshal Beryov's aide, and he would not be if they knew anything about their contacts. How about the unauthorised meetings with Maxon? Yes, that was a crime. But how would they find out? They couldn't, not unless he had been under surveillance. And even if they knew, he had well prepared explanations in hand. His real crime was only a thought as yet. Yes, the KGB knew how to make people reveal their thoughts, but mind reading was not among their weapons. Not yet. Which left Ellsberg with the possibility that there was some vague suspicion against him. Now that could explain everything.

Ellsberg knew he could be convicted without any new evidence. Moscow had plenty of readily available dirt on him to dig up. There was, for instance, his mother's death. She was seriously ill, right after the war, and the doctor, fearful of the young and rising KGB operative, slipped him the information that some new wonder-drug, called penicillin, did exist and could cure her. But it was a western drug. A drug that was available in Moscow to the Kremlin hospital alone. Could Ellsberg get some? He could not. He was just too junior to be entitled to such privileges. And so she died. Ellsberg got drunk and roamed the corridors of the KGB club screaming 'murderers' and explaining to everyone who cared to listen (and to those who pretended not to listen) that he meant the doctors, the KGB, the Politburo and Stalin himself. It was noted and mentioned to him only once, but he was warned that it would never be forgotten.

Or there was the episode soon after the 20th Congress of the Party where Khrushchev had denounced Stalin and his 'cult of personality'. Euphoria spread fast among those least guilty of KGB 'administrative solutions', but intelligence staff at the Centre knew the value of caution. Ellsberg was still half a field man, recently brought home to Moscow, and in his elation he thought he could see the end of a long dark tunnel. In the presence of three colleagues, his best friends in the service, he recalled an evening just before the war, in his last weeks at the Higher Intelligence School 101 on the outskirt of Moscow. The students were dining in the sumptuous hall where they were trained in the art of ordering meals from classy menus in French and selecting wines for each course, when Ellsberg noticed a commotion at the door. 'I couldn't believe my eyes,' he told his friends, 'Stalin was paying the school a surprise visit. We stood to attention, unsure whether we should cheer or salute him. He was passing behind me when he stopped and grabbed my chair. Then he collapsed at my feet. In a panic, I tried to lift him, thinking he was dead. But he wasn't. And I'll never forgive him for that: he robbed me of my rightful place in the history books as the man in whose arms the great man died. Because he was only drunk – and you don't get a mention in a footnote for comforting a dipsomaniac.' The story was received without a smile. One of Ellsberg's friends warned him in private the following day: 'You've been abroad for too long, Volodya.' And he was right. The blasphemous episode had remained on Ellsberg's file ever since – and the friend was now the supervisor of all operations on the North American continent. The same man would now be in charge if the Centre demanded 'something' to discredit the head of the Toronto trade delegation.

Ellsberg looked out of the window. The small Japanese car disappeared. Any of the other parked vehicles might have taken over its job. He rang the hotel once more, and this time, a chatty operator asked him if he was to take care of Mr Maxon's luggage: it emerged that Maxon had checked out of the hotel in such a hurry that he only asked the maid to pack his belongings and hold them until he would send for them.

That seemed to confirm the worst of Ellsberg's fears. Apart from shaking off his tail, he could do little for himself, but somehow he had to warn Maxon.

The phone rang. It was his direct line. He picked up the receiver. 'Ellsberg.' The caller said nothing – but whistled the 'March of the Toreadors'. After a few bars, the whistling stopped and the call was terminated. The sound of open line returned.

Exhibition tennis with a galaxy of stars at York University was the main sporting event of the day, and Ellsberg was lucky to get a ticket at all. He could not blame Maxon for not giving him due notice – it seemed a case of emergency. As if to emphasise the risk of watching eyes and lurking assassins (never too far from Ellsberg's mind) the fans seemed to have stopped breathing to perfect the silence – and hear every syllable of McEnroe's outburst. The player railed and ranted against line judge, umpire, and not least himself, then stopped his own brand of exhibitionism as suddenly as he had started it, resumed playing, and hit a service return to bring forth a whirlwind of oh-s and ah-s.

At the height of the noise with delighted customers jumping up and down, Ellsberg felt a light touch on his shoulder, then heard the familiar whisper: 'Don't turn round, Volodya.'

Maxon, you young, green fool! Ellsberg cried but only inwardly, wasn't it enough that you set up a hasty meet? Why are you here in person?

'I'm sorry. Where can we talk?'

Ellsberg's choice fell on the large underground parking lot at Eglinton and Yonge. 'I'll pick you up at the far end of the second level if all's clear. If not, try again every fifteen minutes.'

The audience roared and Ellsberg was not sure if his last words had been heard because when he looked back over his shoulder, Maxon was not there any more.


If anything might have ever seemed masculine about Jack, it was her driving in town. Like any demented male

125

chauvinist, she could not bear being overtaken by anyone, she swore at them all heartily, gesticulated, showed them fingers and fist in turns, cut in and out of traffic creating havoc at the best of times. Today she was in a hurry, too. Her only saving grace and chance for survival was that she had the reflexes of a Neapolitan bagsnatcher on the run.

Maxon had asked her to come to York University wearing a huge blonde wig to cover her face, and photograph Ellsberg with a flash light ensuring that he knew all about it, but before she would set out, she telephoned her husband at his office only to be told that he had gone home feeling unwell. She then telephoned the apartment, but there was no answer. At the risk of missing Ellsberg, she had to go home first to find out about Joseph.

The door was locked. Kowalski would never lock it from inside. The light was on in the hall and the study. 'Joseph . . .?' There was no answer. She ran from room to room. He was not at home. But he must have been there not all that long ago if he needed the lights. It was unlike him to forget switching them off. She noticed his old briefcase. Its presence was yet another oddity for he would not go even to a wedding reception without it by choice, and she often teased him that it was a virtual extension of his left hand.

She called the garage attendant. No, Kowalski's car was not there, it had been out all day. The hall porter had a vague feeling that he had seen Kowalski coming in early afternoon, but could not remember him leaving at all.

Jack checked the apartment once more. He was definitely not there. As she could do nothing about it for the time being, she ran to her car, and really stepped on it this time to catch Ellsberg. She knew she was late and it would be pointless to wait and wait if he had already left. She thought she would give it an hour and call their family doctor in the meantime. No, Professor Kowalski had not rung or visited the doctor, the nurse was quite positive about that.

In the twilight of the underground parking lot, Ellsberg opened the door of his metallic brown car. 'That was a stupid arrangement, young Maxon.'

'It was an emergency.'

'That much I could guess without you telling me. Get in.'

Sitting side by side, they did not look at each other: their eyes were on the cars entering and leaving. Maxon knew that Papa Mike would soon arrive in a Japanese gadget-collection he called a car, take a long, hard look at Ellsberg, and speed away. That might be the final touch to push Ellsberg over the brink. All Maxon had to do now was to prepare the ground. He hoped to look suitably agitated when he said: 'I may have to leave Toronto. I think I'm in trouble.'

'Is that why it was so urgent to meet me?'

'Partly. I had to warn you.'

'Thanks, but don't worry about me. I'm becoming expendable anyway. It's sad, because one can be abused. But it's good, too, because the less you matter the freer you are to make your own decisions. What's your other reason?'

'I must know whether you lied to me or were just wrong about GLEW. I've discovered that GLEW has been compromised for quite some time.'

'Not by us, it hasn't!' Ellsberg exploded. 'That's why the Centre dreamed up those harebrained schemes.'

'What schemes?'

'First the smear-campaign against Kowalski. They want you to believe that he gave away secrets. Now they're trying to discredit *you*. I'm amazed that you and your people haven't seen through it.'

'All I can see is that you're betraying either our friendship or your country. And you're taking a bloody great risk either way. Why?' His eyes were on the entry ramp: where the hell was Papa Mike?

'A doctor may be sworn to secrecy and loyalty to his patient, but isn't it his duty to warn the airline when their pilot has heart trouble?'

'Except that you're proposing to tell the competitors instead of the airline. And that's a high price to pay for a principle.'

Ellsberg shook his head. 'What choice have you got when your own airline wouldn't listen?' His face seemed to age fast with pain. 'Have you ever tried to put a price on silence? Wouldn't silence be the greatest betrayal in some circumstances?'

An old Buick came down the ramp. The driver reversed into a slot diagonally opposite. In the absence of Papa Mike, Maxon decided to pile on the pressure and use the

Buick as an unwitting ally. 'Forget the circumstances, Volodya. We are both in trouble. You might have been followed.' He glanced repeatedly towards the Buick. 'And you're playing games when it may be your last chance to say what you really wanted to tell me. Something about GLEW if I'm to believe your heavy hints. Something too horrible to remain a secret.'

'But would you believe me before I had the evidence for you?'

'I've told you before: I'd try.' He now stared at the Buick continuously: it's driver had still not emerged from it. Was he asleep? What was he doing in there? Such an obvious and willing ally could be an enemy. Although only some thirty seconds had elapsed since the arrival of that car, Ellsberg, too, was clearly aware of its presence. His eyes narrowed, his face contorted into a wrinkled maze of tension.

'Moscow can't copy GLEW. Perhaps we can't afford it. Perhaps the *Nachalnik* refuses to cripple an already over-stretched economy.' He paused to take a deep breath. 'The hawks press him to cripple your precious GLEW instead. And that comes from a colonel on Beryov's personal staff.'

So that was it. Although Ellsberg had not yet spelt it out, his message was clear – and it *was* treason. He must have come through hell to say that much. And he could do it only because he knew that if Moscow succeeded and did manage to interfere with the early warning system in any way, it would be war. Maxon felt sorry for him. He wanted to embrace and comfort him. But he could not afford the luxury. He could not allow Ellsberg to stop halfway. How would they do it? What did he hope to achieve by coming here? But before Maxon could press him for details, an elongated Mercedes rolled into view. It stopped, clumsily, blocking the ramp. The driver opposite, still at the wheel of the Buick, now attained a truly sinister significance.

Ellsberg looked at Maxon who answered the unasked question with a nod: they would have to find out if only their carefully nurtured suspicions made them see ghosts and menace everywhere. The Russian started the engine, waited for a few seconds to demonstrate how unhurried his departure was to be, then drove slowly, further down into the belly of the car park.

The ramp turned and twisted incessantly and so they could not see if they were followed, but having been warned by the familiar tingle in the spinal marrow, they raced through matters of life and death.

'How would they do it?' Maxon demanded. 'Killer satellites? Sabotage? Electronics?'

Ellsberg turned the wheel. 'EMP.' He was choking on it.

'You're crazy.'

'Not me. The hawks at the top.'

A nuclear explosion in space with EMP to follow meant war. Every modern war scenario began with knocking out the early warning systems. If that happened, all missiles would be fired with no questions asked.

Ellsberg read Maxon's mind. 'It's not *meant* to be an act of war. Just a test to paralyse GLEW temporarily.'

'With a nuclear war to follow *temporarily*.'

'Not if you warn your people not to overreact.'

'Sure. I just tell them: wait! Do nothing.'

'Just warn them. They'll have a few minutes in hand. Give the Kremlin time to grovel and prove it was a mistake.'

'Why don't *you* prevent *your* people from doing it in the first place?'

'You think that greater men than me haven't tried?' They reached the bottom level, a vast expanse built to the glory of The Car, with a nave, a transept, metal columns and structural recesses as if for private worship. Ellsberg stopped behind a massive central pillar where they were half hidden from the entrance and had the freedom to move in any direction. 'You think I would have come to you if I saw any other way?'

The Mercedes nosed into the hall at a cautious, cruising speed. Behind its tinted windows, some passengers could be seen. There were so many free slots for parking that the driver seemed unable to make his choice. He began to reverse into one at last, but stopped – blocking the exit route. Then the Buick appeared on the entrance ramp.

'Run for it,' said Maxon quietly. 'I'll take the wheel and cover you.'

'You're more important now. Convince your people if it's the last thing you ever do.'

The doors of the two cars were flung open. Maxon's eyes were on the men who began to emerge – which was how he missed the shadow of a spanner crashing down on his skull from behind.


The duty officer was full of apologies for calling General Locke's home number at this ungodly hour of dawn. But he began to feel a little better when it was Captain Beck who answered the phone: yes, it had been rumoured that the general's aide was expected to work incredibly long hours. 'A Mrs Kowalski called from Toronto. She said it's an emergency and she must talk to the general right away. Her number is . . .' He began but the captain cut him short.

'I've got it.' Beck hung up without another word. He woke up Locke and made the call for him.

Jack sounded near-hysterical, controlling herself with everything she had left: 'My husband's been missing all night.'

'Contact Maxon right away.'

'But that's just it! He can't be found either!'

# V

The woman on the bridge could hardly talk from constant sobbing. 'It was horrible ... horrible ... horrible,' she kept repeating. The police tried in vain to comfort her, but she could not keep her eyes away from the divers working near the bridge.

'Was it going fast?'

'No. Yes. I don't know. It was still dark ... the lights came ... and wham! I'll never forget that ... that horrible sound ...'

'Where was it coming from?'

The woman gestured vaguely in a half circle.

'Port Perry?'

'Just out of the bend, up the bridge and bang! Right through the railings.'

A diver signalled towards the bridge: they had found the car. The Inspector left the witness in the care of a sergeant, and jumped into the boat waiting for him. The diver met him half way to report that it was an Ontario registration.

'Anybody inside?'

'Male in the driving seat.'

'Dead, I presume.'

'Seems he never had a chance. There's no sign of trying to escape. Perhaps he was knocked unconscious by the fall or even before.'

Or it might have been a heart attack due to the car going out of control or the same sequence the other way round, thought the Inspector, but said nothing. It was no good to speculate. They would know soon enough once the cumbersome job of taking pictures in murky waters was completed. He only hoped it would be a simple, routine case, something like drunken driving, because he had been on duty for almost twenty four hours and he had well and truly had enough of it all.

Two bungled murders in as many weeks was quite unprecedented as far as anybody could remember in the KGB 'wet affairs' bureau. And as if that was not enough to make a full chapter in the never-to-be-written history of the Centre, it was now rumoured that the man responsible for the failures had already been recommended for instant promotion.

Less than twelve hours later, British intelligence heard about the great stir in Moscow. By the end of the thirteenth hour, the information was in Sandy's hands. He deemed it an odd coincidence that Maxon had just survived exactly two 'events' which might have been clumsy attempts on his life. Was he lucky or was he spared? Sandy did not pause to theorise: if Locke was so keen on having Maxon, let him have the headache too.

The report had already been decoded, read and filed by the time Maxon arrived at Washington. Captain Beck picked him up at the airport, congratulated him on his lucky escape, and told him there was still no news about Kowalski. 'Do you think he's defected?' Maxon chose to ignore him and pretended to sleep all the way to the office. Locke welcomed him with a big smile, good coffee and friendly questions about his well-being, but Maxon had no time for civilities: 'So what's the reaction?'

'Well, my first reaction is ...'

'With due respect, sir, I'm more anxious to know what the White House or USACAN or Number Ten thinks about my report.'

'Well, I guess it's a little premature to involve executives at that sort of level.'

Maxon was stunned and stupefied. He was on the verge of accusing Locke of treason, but kept his cool and tried to reason. 'Perhaps you've misunderstood my report, sir. Admittedly, I put it together in a hurry and my head hurt from that blow. But the point is that if Moscow sets off an EMP ...'

'It's war.'

'But only if we over-react, as Ellsberg said.'

'Don't you trust our leaders?'

'It's not a matter of trust. We must give them the maximum available time to prepare our correct response. That's what Ellsberg was trying to give us: extra time through advance warning.'

'He must have had a very poor opinion of our governments.'

'Haven't you, general?'

'That's immaterial.'

'Ellsberg would have agreed with that.'

'Ellsberg, Ellsberg, I've had a bellyful of Ellsberg.'

'You don't trust him, do you?'

'I have doubts, Maxon, haven't you?'

'Not since he risked everything to warn us and not since he died to protect me.'

'For some reason he was also protecting Kowalski. Any idea why?'

'To prove him innocent, to prove that Moscow is desperate and afraid of GLEW. Which means that the system is safe – for the time being.'

'But is it, Maxon, is it?' Locke tapped a green folder which sported the presidential seal and the code that allowed 'sight only' to no one but specifically named personnel. 'Here, for instance, presidential adviser Chuck Parkin argues that GLEW has been compromised. So who do I believe? Friend Parkin or enemy Ellsberg?'

'Parkin did not die for his conviction.'

'No. But what do we know about Ellsberg? Yes, it is a fact that he is dead. And it's another fact that his body has been pumped full of bullets. But why? How? By whom? You only remember the Buick and the Mercedes. About the rest, you know as much as we have in the initial report from the Toronto police. Here, have a look, see if you have anything to add.'

According to the first witness on the scene 'it was like a shooting gallery down there ... It sounded and looked so realistic that I first thought I'd stumbled on to the set of some motion picture ...' He stopped his car on the ramp, unable to reverse because of another incoming car behind him, and 'observed a metallic brown car driving like crazy at men with guns, and crashing into a Mercedes'.

The second witness, behind the first driver, also reported shooting, the 'mangling of a gunman against the wall, sickening like that airplane scene in Catch 22,' and the final crash of Ellsberg's car wrapping itself half round a metal column.

Papa Mike's statement was brief: he had been delayed by traffic; on arrival he heard shooting, guessed what might be going on, and alerted the police without ever entering the bottom level of the parking lot.

The first policemen on the scene were almost knocked down by a Buick racing blindly up the exit ramp, trailing blood from a half-shut door, 'burning tyres as it crashed through the barrier at the pay desk'. The car was found, eventually, in a street nearby; it had been stolen; there were pools of blood inside.

'Downstairs, it was sheer carnage,' the report continued. '... Three men with extensive, gruesome injuries, disembowelled or flattened apparently by brown car (showing potentially corresponding dents, damage and blood stains); ... its driver sustained fifteen (rough count) bullet holes some of which might be exit routes ...'

'Fifteen,' Maxon mumbled, 'doesn't it help to make you believe him, General? Would you have done the same for me? Would you?'

'You're tired.'

'Yes, sir, I am tired. I'm tired of shadow-boxing. Of doing nothing. Wasting time.' Maxon's eyes were darting wildly from file to folder to the general's face. His pupils were closing and opening like motorised camera shutters. He was obviously under tremendous strain. 'I'm tired of the impossible conditions you've imposed. I know virtually nothing about the very system I'm supposed to protect.'

'Which only shows how well this outfit is run,' Locke smiled. 'It's a sad state of affairs when security needs to be active and plug leaks day in day out. I know it's unusual at your level ...'

'Unusual? Unheard of. I've never questioned the need of secrecy or the limits of the "need to know" principle, but now I can't take a single step, let alone run, without bumping into limits.'

Locke reacted only with some avuncular nods of tolerance. Shell-shock, that's what's wrong with you, his eyes seemed to diagnose. 'Was Ellsberg armed?' he asked ignoring Maxon's outburst.

'Don't think so.'

'And you don't know who were in the Buick and the Mercedes.'

'No.'

'Did Ellsberg know?'

'I doubt it.'

134

'So they could have been KGB watching you,' Locke speculated aloud, 'or our people watching him . . . or even Canadian counter-intelligence watching both of you.'

'No. Whoever they were after, him or me, they simply had to be KGB.'

'Why?'

'Because if they were ours, including the Canadians, you'd know about it.'

'Don't overestimate me, Maxon,' his voice sharpened, 'I don't claim to be privy to everything. It's you who suddenly wants to pick up, process and transmit intelligence single-handedly *and* tell everybody at the top how to use it.'

Which was true. It was not Maxon's job to do all that. But could he tell his superior that he just couldn't trust his judgment? 'All I want is that it should be considered at the proper level.'

'Because Ellsberg is dead and your nerves are shot.'

'But did he need to die? Did he need to come and warn us? Did he need to knock me cold and stand and fight to save me instead of running for dear life? Apparently he created such havoc that those gunmen never had a chance to find and kill me in the recess with a fire exit where he'd dropped me.'

'I know how you feel.'

'Do you, General? Do you really?' Suddenly Maxon had enough of it all. Somewhere, something was wrong. Sandy's message: you're on your own. Ellsberg's desperate effort and last stand. The Russian attempt to test the efficiency of GLEW so soon after Sarian's defection. Their vast propaganda campaign. The carbon-copy demos they were organising against GLEW all over the world. They dubbed the warning satellites *panic-mongers*. *Pravda* christened GLEW the *Bomb of the Eighties*. These were signs that they had been injured. That's what made them even more dangerous. That's why they planned to resort to a disastrous blast in space. Ellsberg couldn't have been their instrument. But those who tried to block the information channels could. Locke? The thought both frightened and disgusted Maxon. He had known enough traitors before and after Philby – he did not want to meet another one ever again. Except Sarian who did not count because he was from the other side.

Maxon got up to leave. He knew he was not in a proper

state to play cat-and-mouse with Locke. The time would come, must come, he thought. Gloucester was already making some inquiries for him in London. And General Sarian might be useful. 'When will you need me back from my so-called vacation, sir?' he asked, his voice trying to substantiate the lie that he was ready to apologise for his tirade of disrespect.

'Whenever you're fully fit again,' Locke put his hand on Maxon's fingers as they were clutching the edge of the table. He dropped the avuncular and adopted a fatherly stance. His hands were heavy yet tender and damp – an altogether unpleasant sensation of unwelcome familiarity.

Maxon withdrew his fingers. 'Thank you, sir. Incidentally, I'll probably go to London for a short while. That might be a good opportunity to meet Sarian.'

'Sure. As soon as an opportune moment arises.'

Maxon blew up. 'Here we go again. You know perfectly well that I'm best qualified to question him on several crucial points. We've agreed and everybody agreed with us. But no. No access. Why?'

'Let's not go into that if you don't mind.'

'I'd prefer an answer, sir.'

'Well, okay. Before I let you see him, I must clear up . . . er . . . certain aspects of your recent activities.'

'And what does that mean?'

'You must try to see facts from where I sit. First you indulge in some unofficial investigation into Kowalski's affairs.'

'You knew about it from the start.'

'Almost, yes, let's say almost. Then the car accident, and the boat explosion with your fingerprints on pieces of wreckage, then the meetings with Ellsberg who suddenly dies before he could supply any evidence of his allegations. Yes, it could be read the way you suggest, but nobody witnessed his death, you alone were present, and although you have an ugly bump on the head, it all could add up to something most ambiguous.'

'Ambiguous?' Maxon's coolness returned. He began to feel good. If it was to be a showdown, his hands would be freed at last. 'I agree, sir, most ambiguous. Particularly if you trace it back to my moment of madness when I let Sandy persuade me to come and work for your comedy outfit with its shameful amateurism and childish code-words.'

'Now listen, Maxon . . .'

'Ssh. Call me Skylark in Red Square if you must address me at all.'

'Oh yes, "address" reminds me of yet another peculiarity,' Locke parried the thrust. 'Why would Gerry the Bang have your address and telephone number? I know, I know, you claim you have no idea, but isn't it odd to say the least?'

The buzzer of the intercom interrupted Locke who flicked the switch furiously and vented all his pent-up selfcontrol yelling, 'Haven't I told you, Alvin, no calls, none whatsoever?'

But Beck did not apologise. He knew he had a good enough reason for this minor disobedience. Kowalski had been found dead. Drowned, to be precise. In a borrowed car that had run off a bridge near Port Perry. An accident, apparently.

'Was he . . . alone?' Maxon asked.

For a second, until the answer came, Locke seemed to share his anxiety, but having heard Beck's 'affirmative', he switched off the intercom, and turned to Maxon with a deliberate drawl to make him sound indifferent: 'I guess Mrs Kowalski, I mean Jacqueline, not Drusilla, could do with your moral support for a while. Feel free to stay as long as necessary.'

'Thanks.'

The showdown had been postponed, now they both had extra time to choose the weapons and the occasion. But the delay brought no advantage to Maxon: a truce is a part of war not peace, it never removes the knife poised to plunge, and if Maxon's hands had been tied before, he was now bound by the most debilitating of thongs – a kind of gratitude.


The echo of steps along endless, stone-clad corridors only emphasised the silence of the mortuary. The police Inspector refrained from questioning Jack on their way to the vaults in which many people attain at last the status of valuables, thanks to the doubts surrounding their deaths. The attendant was busy serving another positive identification party, but the Inspector was not proud, he himself yanked the metal container on the left open. A quick flush animated Jack's pale face, but her hope was short-lived: it was the wrong container. The Inspector apologised and tried the next one. This time Jack nodded.

'You're sure.'

'Yes.' She cleared her throat. 'It's my husband.'

'Shall I leave you alone for a moment?'

'No, thanks.'

The container ran back into the wall smoothly and clanked shut. 'I'm sorry. It had to be done.'

Jack understood. And yes, she understood that some papers would have to be signed. But why was she not told about his death any earlier?

Leading the way to a small office, the Inspector explained that it had taken a couple of days to identify Kowalski: 'It was not his own car, and he carried no means of identification.'

'Yes, that's him . . . that was him,' she said with a grimace between a half-smile and a painful twitch. 'He hated all ID papers. To him they were symbols of oppression.'

The Inspector claimed to understand, but that was not true. He saw the information as a cause for caution and suspicion. He had never lived in a country where for decades, an ordinary driving licence could be proof of being an enemy of the working class and so the state itself, and where failure to carry a residence registration document on one's person could provoke a free and instantaneous application of martial law. 'Did he drink a great deal?' he popped the question hoping to catch her off her guard.

'Hardly ever. Why?'

'There was alcohol in his blood. And bottles in the car. Brandy, mostly.' And when Jack said nothing, he demanded to know what sudden inducement Kowalski might have had for getting drunk. She claimed she could not think of any such reason. But she thought she knew the reason: Kowalski disappeared soon after hearing from Inspector Wells that she had given Maxon an alibi.


It rained all day in Moscow. The Soviet leader did not want to see any more of it. He sat with his back to the window, and stared at his own reflection in the spotless glass top of the immense partners' desk. He had finished reading

138

Marshal Beryov's latest report on the progress of preparations for an EMP test. It was full of technicalities, practical details, problems and solutions, racing on and on breathlessly, without ever pausing to think about morality, consequences or justification beyond the narrow needs of the moment. Beryov's heart had been set on an EMP, and the *Nachalnik* knew the difficulty of arguing with him was that only the soldier's blinkered, single-minded determination could win wars and avoid hesitation – the burden of the humanist, the intellectual, and all the other decadents.

He replaced the report in a drawer and took out the KGB Director's weekly summary of international assessments. What interested the *Nachalnik* more than anything was the tone, because the assessments had 'I know better than thou' written in invisible ink all over them. The writer's pale eyes in the hairless face were spying on him through every page: was the chief ready for the push?

The assessments were full of bad news. 'We are under great pressure in the Far East ... The Middle East situation is swinging in favour of the West ... In every theatre of conflict, at every table of international negotiations, we are subjected to the pressure of newly-gained American confidence built on GLEW ... Savings through GLEW finance costly vote-winning measures by the President and truly long-term western research in space ... We're running out of time ...' Implied comment after comment on the impotence of the leadership.

He read the attached note on 'operations in progress'. There was a great deal of emphasis on fighting western reliance on GLEW. If they were led to believe that the warning system had been compromised, an EMP might not be necessary. Ah! The Director was beginning to feel that he might have to play the passenger while Beryov became navigator in the seat next to the driver's. A pleasing thought, but not an easy decision for a leader who, despite all the oft-professed collectivity of leadership, knew only too well the exceptional loneliness exceptional powers impose on the tyrant. And it frightened him more than ever that with old age and infirmity, he had dwindling qualifications for remaining the acrobatic middle-man atop the see-saw on whose single slip the holocaust might depend. His support for one warring faction or the other might cost him his power or even his life; graceful retirement was not one of the perks of life at the top in a dictatorship. His silence might cost him the human race, but not yet, not quite yet. No man should ever be asked to commit suicide for the survival of the species, he thought and decided to initial Beryov's report. The fact that it would be returned to the marshal with no comment on the margin amounted to tacit approval of the continued preparations for an EMP test.

To escape the solitude of the room the *Nachalnik* changed places with himself and sat facing the dripping windows. He wondered if rain would help to cleanse the atmosphere or spread more deaths after a nuclear war.

The aircraft hiccupped as the undercarriage retracted, the starboard wing dropped a little to reveal a vista of the meandering Potomac below, and Maxon wondered what consequences a crash and his untimely death might have. The thought was cold and clinical: like most seasoned air travellers, he was an incurably optimistic fatalist. Ellsberg had thrust upon him a responsibility that he did not want and that no man should be asked to carry, and Locke had refused even to share it with him. Which left him in the position of the Olympic torch bearer who has just been told that it is not a relay after all. And it made him face the old, old question of all his life: whom should he believe and why?

Although he was unable to distil his thoughts clearly at the time, he had been taught early, much too early on, that in order to survive, he would have to understand people's motives, discover their secret plans and embryonic intentions, then learn to gauge and predict their likely reaction even to unlikely events of the future. Unfortunately, if such were the tasks and if the penalty for failure was unacceptably high, he could never afford to shun the inadmissible face of discovery – not when he was a child, not when national interest justified it, not when the good of mankind glorified it. That was why he never needed the usual pompous and pretentious excuses for digging up secrets. Some colleagues had dreams of secret powers to be achieved through prying. Others were gossip-gobblers who got their kicks from knowing. Not Maxon. Like drunks who swallowed prairie-oysters to dispel those morning-after blues, when Maxon suffered the inevitable snoopers' jitters after the intoxication of a mission, all he needed was a dose of childhood memories summed up in one word: mother.

She was a lively soul and a soulful churchgoer who could reconcile merrily her pure biblical admonitions to her only son with her only true love for her gin-and-it. She was no drunkard, she sought solace after her husband had left her. And then there was, of course, Uncle Dick to help her. He was a large, laugh-a-line lover of life, who played a crucial part in Maxon's discovering the importance of whispers.

Maxon was not yet five years old when Uncle Dick, husband of a sickly second cousin on his father's side, began to visit mother more and more frequently. They usually went into a huddle in the living room and sent him to play or sleep or wash, but that was all right, because Uncle Dick's jokes were not funny to him anyway. One nauseously hot summer night, when all the windows were open, the child listened to the inexplicable giggles and unintelligible whispers until dawn. The meaning of it all hit him only when mother and Uncle Dick disappeared in the morning, leaving him with a neighbour, a widow with the pungent air of old age, who used the child as a fetch-carrier, shoe-remover, back-scratcher and lapdog-substitute. And like a dog, unable to distinguish death from temporary departure, the child grew convinced by the end of the first day, that he had been orphaned, mother would never return. When, eventually, she did return a week later, young Maxon had already decided that no whisper must ever remain a secret from him.

The first time mother caught him eavesdropping, she cried, 'What will you be? A snoop? A spy?' and made him kneel in the corner for hours on end. But that did not matter, what alone counted was that she looked shocked and frightened, and that meant that snoopers and spies were creatures to be feared, never to be whispered about, and never to be left in the charge of smelly neighbours.

By the age of six he would never be caught eavesdropping again. He developed the techniques of playing music or running the tap to disguise his movement outside doors and under windows. That was how he once heard mother whispering to Uncle Dick: 'I don't want to be with child'. Maxon withdrew fast in great alarm: there was no other child she could refer to, and the sentence would have to mean either death or adoption for him – adoption by the neighbour, presumably. So he devoted himself to finding out more about their scheming. From an older boy in the street he heard about lip-reading, and spent weeks on trying to master the technique. Meanwhile, he devised a six-foot dental mirror. With some practice he could lower the weird contraption from his room to outside the open window of the back room which mother called the 'front room' on account of the large settee that seemed to fill it. To facilitate lip-reading was beyond the might of the device, and it allowed whispers to remain mysterious, but its peeping potential manifested itself on the very first occasion it was used in earnest.

Lying motionlessly, the child upstairs fought off sleep well into the night (a feat he would often have to perform in his adult life), until he could hear the familiar muttering and giggles. He lowered the mirror, resisted blinking when the reflection of the light in the 'front room' shone into his eyes, and discovered right away that mother and Uncle Dick must be stark, raving bonkers – stark remaining the operative word in his recollection of the night. Straining his eyes he saw that they rubbed and clapped their bodies together like cold hands. The child was baffled: if they were cold despite the heat of July, why would they warm themselves in this peculiar way when they could have kept their clothes on in the first place? No, there was positively no answer to that. The only possible conclusion was that the two downstairs were crazy. And dangerous. Now he knew what sort of people he was dealing with. From then on, he slept with a rusty old bread-knife under his pillow. No, they were not to be trusted. And Locke might be one of the same ilk. Maxon wished he still had the bread-knife.

'And what will your tipple be, sir? . . . Oh, I'm sorry, sir, I hadn't realised that you were asleep,' the stewardess babbled with no trace of resentment because the moment had been designated for drinking – not sleeping or musing or dreaming – by the almighties who ruled the rhythm of life in transit.

Jack met him at the airport. She touched his arm, his lips brushed against her forehead, almost accidentally. They were all too aware of the difference from his previous arrival at Toronto. Now there was no great urgency, no hide-and-seek, no Ellsberg, no Kowalski to reckon with.

This time she drove herself, and did not need the chatty cab driver to remind her how dangerously the Doomsday Clock was poised to strike the midnight hour of eternal darkness. This time he ignored the rousing joy of meeting her, and let his masochism savour a strange embarrassment: it is easier to deceive an old man than a dead one. On their way to town and the cemetery, their exchanges were muted, covering only the barest necessities.

Waiting for the funeral to begin, Maxon called London. It was a bad line, and outside Gloucester's Fleet Street office, a massive flow of demonstrators seemed to be bent on shouting their protests all the way to Canada: Ban the Bomb! Ban GLEW! 'It's a demo!' Gloucester shouted, and had to shut all windows before he could hear Maxon.

'What's it in aid of?'

'War? Peace? I dunno. Something trivial.'

'Ban the Bomb?'

'Ban the Bomb, ban GLEW, Ben Gurion, Ben-ghazi — who cares?'

'You do, Glossie, but we won't go into that.'

'That's a deal old sport. I think I've got what you wanted.' Gloucester's first discovery seemed to destroy Kowalski's alibi, but the rest held out some hope: all the gate staff were new. Apparently, there had been a sudden clean sweep less than a month earlier. Who had initiated the change? Locke? Why would they do it? To destroy Kowalski? To squash Maxon's interest?

Gloucester volunteered to trace the old staff.

'No, thanks. I'll do it.'

'Then I hope to see you, old sport. I'll buy you a beer to cheer you up. You sound half dead.'

A hurried service was followed by a record-breaking cremation. Apart from Jack, only two old Poles had come to pay their respects. The officially assigned delegation of three from Kowalski's lab did not qualify as mourners. They kept their cab waiting, presumably to get away as soon as possible and not to appear to be associated with the man who had lived out his last few months under some unspecified cloud. Even his funeral was overshadowed by the presence of some unattached by-standers who did not seem to belong to any of the other funerals, and could not mingle with Kowalski's sparsely peopled farewell party without calling undue attention to themselves, yet seemed to have

143

plenty of time to kill. Any one of them might have been a participant of the shooting in the underground car park, Maxon thought. It infuriated him that he could not recognise them unless they drew their guns on him. If they shot me, he pondered, at least it would clear me completely in Locke's book. But would it? Did proof of innocence clear Kowalski? Did Locke want to show him innocent?

Once again, Jack drove in silence after the funeral. Only after they had rolled through the gates did she comment that humanist funerals were 'cold, heartless and awful'.

'I don't know . . . Wouldn't mind having one myself.'

'I'll remember it.'

'Thanks.' Maxon watched her knees. He wanted to kiss them. He longed to make love to her. She wanted it, too, he was sure. It would be good. And natural. Excitingly familiar like homecoming after a war. But could they still wake up together? And get up together? Would a gnarled old Pole sit on their bedside, looking away discreetly, with kindly understanding, forever?

'Might have been suicide,' she said.

'No. He'd have used the gun the police found in the glove compartment,' Maxon argued.

Jack shook her head. 'It's fraud. The gun was the red herring. The alcohol level in the blood was not high enough to give an excuse to the insurance company, but enough to convince the cops that it was an accident. So they'll have to pay me.'

'He obviously loved you.'

'Yes. But mostly he wanted to make sure that there would be enough cash to keep mad Drusilla in that sanatorium.'

'How come you know about her?'

'I read the will. Not the nicest way to find out.'

'No.'

'You knew it. Why didn't you tell me?'

'It was his secret not mine.'

'He must have appreciated your discretion.'

'It really shook him that of all people it had to be me who had discovered her existence. I mean apart from Locke.'

'Locke?'

'All along.'

'And he didn't tell you? Isn't that odd?'

'It is.'

144

'At least you tried to help me.'

Maxon answered with a bitter guffaw. 'Sure. I did my best to prove him innocent for your sake. But boy! Didn't I love seeing his long face when I told him? Didn't I wallow in his humiliation because he was ...' he hesitated, then forced himself to say it, 'your husband.'

Jack braked hard. She pulled up but did not bother to park properly. She turned to Maxon and held his face with both hands. 'It's incredible,' she whispered.

'What?'

'That you had it in you to love me, to love anyone that much.'

'You mean enough to kill him?'

'You didn't kill him. I did.'

'Go on, let's have a nice, guilt-sharing party. Anybody may come, dips into the past will be provided for starters, but you must bring your own guilt.' He peeled her hands off.

Yes, this was the Maxon she used to know. Except that now she knew him better. So she waited patiently for him to finish his display of being cold, callous and sceptical. And then she told him of her visit to Inspector Wells, the alibi she had given him, the Inspector breaking his promise not to tell her husband, and Kowalski's shock on being told about it nevertheless. She argued that if anyone, she was the one who had pushed Joseph over the brink. But Maxon could hardly listen. The alibi surprised him, but what shook him even more was the fact that Wells must have revealed his alibi to Locke, too – yet Locke kept up his insinuations of Maxon's guilt in that car accident.

Kowalski's innocence seemed to matter no more. His own career and life, and probably a lot more were at stake. It was imperative to find out if the pigeon-fancier Kowalski had mentioned did exist. Maxon concluded that he would have to go to London right away.

'Okay,' Jack nodded, 'I'll need only half an hour to pack' – which left no room for argument about her staying behind or accompanying him.


London had never been so unkind to Maxon: everything there seemed to be going wrong for him. Rain hit him every time he stepped into the street. Edie was first inconsolable because Jack had arrived with Maxon without warning; then Edie was deeply hurt when Maxon made her leave by presenting her with a surprise holiday package to Düsseldorf where her only known relative lived. The worst was Maxon's steadily growing sensation that he was floating and bouncing about in a vacuum.

Sandy seemed inaccessible. His secretary took messages in an impersonal tone as if she had never cried on Maxon's shoulder, but Sandy did not call him back once in three days. Friends in intelligence circles were obviously stalling him. He had apparently insurmountable difficulties in tracking down the doorman who had been retired or transferred from London HQ so suddenly. The GLEW office itself was most unhelpful or incompetent or both: they had no instructions from Locke to offer special co-operation to Maxon. The general himself distanced himself by using Captain Beck – who was only too pleased to act as a buffer: 'Oh, it's you, Skylark in Red Square. I'm sorry, sir, no direct contact is possible until further notice. Would you like to leave a message for the chief?'

Maxon locked his Ellsberg tapes in a small, red leather case which he deposited with Samantha, an old friend, for safekeeping: he knew that her blue film business needed virtually impenetrable hiding places. Parting with the tapes seemed to be the final severance of the ties that bound him to Ellsberg in friendship, and the act added to the mounting stress though he knew that he was clutching only at imaginary crutches.

The tension poisoned even his relationship with Jack. It was as easy and exciting to spend the nights together as he had expected, but they found it increasingly hard to talk. She was most probably in a state of delayed shock, he was too preoccupied with his problems that reached far beyond his own situation. The main question was how long he could delay passing Ellsberg's secrets to people of the highest authority. If he wanted to do it behind Locke's back, the information would have to go through the right channels to be taken seriously. Channels he could trust. Someone like Sandy. Or Chuck Parkin in the White House. Or perhaps Gloucester.

Maxon arranged to meet the journalist in a Fleet Street pub. On his way there, he spotted a potential tail, a weasel of a man of marked insignificance, the sort Sandy might rope in perhaps from the police to do a specific one-off shadowing job. Alternatively, the man could be working for some foreign service.

Maxon was late. He did not want to miss meeting Gloucester, and to double-check properly that the tail was a tail, indeed, would have taken too long. Maxon turned abruptly into a narrow lane. The man was still behind him. Maxon bent down, pretending to pull up his socks. As the man tried to pass him, he stood up, caught a fragile neck with a vicious squeeze on the throat in the crook of his arm, and whispered urgently: 'One sound out of you and you're dead.' The man believed him, and obeyed readily to the point of being docile, but he did not look frightened. That, and that alone told Maxon that his hunch must have been right: the man was a pro. But then why did he not do a better tailing job on him?

The man's pockets contained nothing that would incriminate him. It would have been pointless to ask questions. He let go of the neck and mumbled something apologetically about some mistaken identity. The man did not seem to be angry. Had he been picked for his very ineptitude? Was he meant to be spotted by Maxon?

'Good to see you, old sport, what will you have?' Gloucester welcomed him boisterously. Maxon asked for a half of best bitter, his mind still on his unjustified assault on a tail who might well have been an innocent passer-by. 'Best bitter? In here?' Gloucester looked truly astounded. 'You stupid Pommy, don't you know that you can get Fosters in here now?'

'Ah. That's really good news,' Maxon said with no real enthusiasm. 'It seems I've been away too long.'

'You can say that again.'

'Meaning?'

Gloucester ordered two Fosters, and Maxon had to press him for an answer. 'Well, I don't know, people who are away for too long, cease to be with it, if you know what I mean.'

'No, I don't. You're not referring to the beer, are you?'

'Well, it's hard to put my finger on it.'

'Try.'

'Okay. If you don't know about the beer, you may not know about the mood of the old town.' He noted Maxon's irritation, and nodded with submission. 'Well, I hoped to put it more gently, but you're bad news in London just now. Or so it seems. I mean your name comes up at a cocktail party at the FO, and people shy away from me. Because they know we're friends? I don't know. But then I try to get the info. you wanted, and within a couple of hours, my editor summons me. He says he's got a call about "some unexpected complications" affecting my clearance for a story I'm working on ...'

'You mean a lay off or else ...'

'Do I need to tell you how *delicately* you security boys tend to play these things?'

'And you blame me.'

'Blame? No. But you stink, sport. Occupational BO, that's what you got. I ought to keep away myself.'

'But you're here. And I appreciate your help.'

'Just don't forget that it's within limits. I can't risk anything beyond that.'

'Okay. Would it be within those limits to by-pass all the Downing Street filters, mandarins and Mamelukes, and slip some information directly to the Prime Minister?'

'Couldn't you?' Gloucester frowned.

'I stink, old sport, remember? Occupational BO makes me feel a bit cut off, right now.'

'Say no more, I know the feeling: I lived in Melbourne for two whole days and an hour. Drink up, our next beer is overdue.'

'Will you do it for me?'

'Well, if there's no other way ...'

'Thanks, pal, I'll ask for it only in final despair. Maybe tomorrow?'

Retired detective sergeant Loveday did not do favours to people outside the force because he saw all such things as corruption. And not without good reason: favours always implied reciprocation before or after the act. He did not like to regard Maxon's requests as exceptions to his lifelong principles. But Maxon himself was an exception. Loveday could not refuse to trace a couple of people for the man who had once risked his own reputation to save him from a security mix-up concerning his appointment as a bodyguard to the Prince of Wales.

One of the two people Loveday had tracked down was Foxy, the burglars' mate, who turned out to be most co-operative when confronted with Maxon's eyes and all fourteen stones of the sergeant. After all, no great treachery was required: the gentlemen visiting Foxy's favourite pub only wanted to know where Gerry 'The Bang' Houlihan lived these days.

Mrs Houlihan was much less co-operative when Maxon turned up on her doorstep: Gerry's associations with better class people always meant larger safes, bigger hauls, and infinitely longer stretches in the can. 'I told you, he's not 'ere.' Maxon shifted her as gently as he could out of the way, and she screamed. If that sound failed to bring Gerry to the door, he was surely out. 'I'll be back,' he said. 'Tomorrow morning, okay?'

'Drop dead.'

'Tell him my name is Maxon. Tell him he has nothing to fear, he should not try to go to ground, I only need to know who gave him my phone number, okay? But I'm going to give you both a lot of bother, and I mean a lot, if he's not here tomorrow morning.'

She believed him. So now she said nothing, just watched him leave, all the way down the road, until he disappeared round the corner. She stayed at the window, hiding behind the curtain, waiting impatiently for her Gerry, her brainbox who was stupid enough to get into more trouble than anyone else. He had promised to be back from the boozer within the hour, and she was anxious to warn him about Maxon whom she classified as too dangerous for Gerry to associate with. She blamed the boozer and the whole wide world where everybody and his neighbour would be after Gerry's brain and delay his return home. At last he appeared from behind the corner: in the dark street only his awkward gait identified him. Prepared to give him a fair chunk of her mind right on the doorstep, she was about to leave the window when she noticed a shadow peel away from the blind stick of a vandalised lamp post. A second later, the shadow hit Gerry on the head and went on hitting him, always on the head, again and again, ignoring the screams from a window.

Mrs Houlihan reached the lamp post too late to see that weasel of a man being picked up by a car. There was a lot of blood, and she just stood and stared. She cursed the stupid head that had always dreamt about a bigger bang, and she was pleased that his thick skull was broken like an egg because at last she and the whole world could see that there was nothing special inside it, nothing anyone should ever care for or respect or love, and then she cried and howled because the pain was too much to bear silently.

Loveday's other find, Fergus McPherson could hardly contain himself when that bitch of a wife burst into his shed yet again. She knew bloody well, and if she didn't, she bloody well ought to know by now, that the pigeons would stir and shit on everything ankle-deep in fright, but she couldn't care less, could she?

'Come out, Fergus, come on out.'

'Oh, you speak to me again! I hoped it would never happen. Is the house on fire then?'

'Some lady with the envelope from the Pigeon Gazette wants you.'

'Me? Why?'

'Don't give me that, Fergus McPherson, not me. I know you too well, remember? You know you'll never keep no secrets from me.'

'What secrets?'

'Aye, what secrets, he asks me. What about the prize money she brought you?'

'Prize money?'

He followed her meekly to the house to meet Jack, posing as the lady with the envelope. She asked him to come outside with her to be photographed in the park nearby. His wife suggested that he ought to change first into something more respectable, but Jack claimed to prefer him as he was, and he was keen to agree with the lady, get outside and pocket at least half the contents of that envelope before the bitch could lay her hands on it.

Maxon was waiting for them in the car a few doors away. McPherson recognised him at once: 'Oh, it's you, Mister Maxon, sir,' his face lengthened, 'no prize money then, I take it.'

'You may keep the envelope. Tell your wife the prize is for the letter you wrote about your birds.'

McPherson thanked him for it and kept fingering the

envelope. What could be inside? A fiver? Tenner? Maybe two? A windfall, certainly, but not big enough for him to be expected to kill for it. So he relaxed, felt reassured as he listened to Maxon's innocuous questions, and never realised what a stirring effect his answers had.

'It was quite a job to find you,' Maxon said.

'Couldn't the office give you my address? I've never moved nowhere since my retirement.'

So he had not been fired – Maxon glanced at Jack urging her to press him gently on this point. She smiled at McPherson: 'Retirement? Aren't you much too young to retire?'

'A wee bit too young, perhaps, but Mr Maxon must know what happened.' When he saw Maxon nod knowingly, he carried on quickly to impress the lady a little more. 'There was this security reshuffle, aye, that's what they called it, a security reshuffle on the gate. Why? Don't ask me. Nobody ever does. They just gave all six of us the choice between a transfer and early retirement.'

Six? That meant the lot of them in the three shifts. 'And you chose retirement,' Maxon confirmed as if he had known it from the start.

'The choice was to go back north, but you know how it is, sir, once you become a real Sassenach, you don't want to leave the big smoke, do you?'

Maxon reached into his inside pocket. He pulled out his handkerchief and *accidentally*, Kowalski's picture dropped out. 'Ah ... You remember him, don't you?'

'Oh, aye, it's a fine photo, and a fine gentleman Professor Kowalski is.'

'He also remembers you,' Maxon said and ignored that his reference to a dead man in the present tense had made Jack wince. 'He has a little story about you ... something about your grandson?'

'Oh that. He'd remember that. He had just come down from the office and I was dead scared about the birth to tell you the honest truth, and he was very kind, and kept me company, half the night, didn't he?'

'So you're sure he was just coming down from the office, right?'

'Yes, sir, sure I'm sure ... why are you looking at me like that, sir? ... I tell no lies ...'

'No, perhaps not ... I just want to be sure that what you

remember didn't only happen inside that hip flask of yours.'

The old Scot blushed. These wily men at the GLEW office were all alike. Hadn't General Locke himself called him in? Hadn't he mentioned that damned whisky flask as if that alone could rid them of him without a pension? Hadn't he asked the same sort of questions about the professor? So what was Maxon after now? Could he stop the pension after all? McPherson complained about it all in one go and, egged on by Maxon, he blurted out that Locke had forbidden him to talk about the office or Kowalski's visit or the night of the grandson's birth to anyone at all. Now it was too late to take it back, but Maxon did not seem angry, one could expect him to know about these things anyway, so it would be best to shut up – and keep the contents of the envelope whatever it had paid for.

Maxon's house in Hampstead was crowded with ghosts. A distant Doomsday Clock threatened to chime midnight at any hour of the day. Maxon played Glenn Miller louder and louder against it.

Ellsberg chose to haunt all things made of glass. He lurked behind windows, stared back from mirrors, tried to speak but emitted only bubbles from the palms of champagne goblets, yet Maxon could hear his urging demands – go and do it, don't wait, don't hesitate, do it.

Kowalski knew best how to make himself visible most unexpectedly. He would take the non-existent third seat at the small Georgian table for two, keep drowning in the bath tub shared by two, or sit on the edge of their bed, protesting his innocence, claiming that he had been framed, and begging to know why Locke would cover up the smear-campaign against him.

Edie, alive and well though absent, could do no better than play poltergeist. She had left little notes tucked away everywhere – perhaps to be helpful, perhaps to make her presence felt. There were notes hidden in the kitchen calendar, in the bread bin and among cutlery, with strict instructions what to eat when from the small freezer, notes for the milkman and the window-cleaner, a reminder of laundry opening hours and lists of items for which the local grocer would tend to overcharge, messages of welcome for

Jack under the pillow and in the bathroom, with innumerable tips for Jack on how best to handle Maxon, what to give him for breakfast, and where to hide the drinks whenever he was about to embark on a binge.

Maxon opened another bottle. Was it the third? Could it be? Judging from the glaze in Jack's eyes, and from her subtle attire of the briefest of briefs with a matching red sandal only on her left foot, yes it could have been the third bottle. Easily.

Maxon marched to the bed and fell on it face down, but the world set out in such a spin that he had to open his eyes and sit up quickly if he did not want the centrifugal force to splash him against the wall. With bottle in hand, Jack limped after him and cursed the shop that had sold her unevenly heeled shoes. 'You think you are a gentleman?' she addressed his penis that sported Maxon's polka-dot tie round its neck. How it had got there was a mystery neither of them cared to puzzle out.

They lay on the bed, side by side, skin stuck to skin by moisture, sleeping a little, drinking a little, aware of each other as well as the ghosts. The band struck up 'In The Mood', and the tune launched them into peculiarly lonesome monologues that ran parallel to each other, without ever becoming unrelated, and even touching here and there, like their bodies.

'You still love Glenn Miller,' she said.

'I still love you.'

'This was the record we played, remember?'

'That moronic disc jockey played it in Washington. I could have killed him.'

'It was the last time we were here, together, before you broke it up.'

'They interrupted the programme. It was the public alert.'

'It was such a serene night.'

'In such a balmy afternoon, the alert was an anachronism.'

153

'I thought it would last forever.'

'I thought it would be war.'

'We made love.'

'Somebody made a big mis-
take.'

'We laughed.'

'I seethed with horror.'

'Then you turned serious.'

'Then you turned up at the
hospital.'

'You said I must go away.'

'It was wonderful to see you.
I thought if war came, we
might die together.'

'I couldn't understand. I
didn't want to.'

'It took time to understand,
and accept, that it was a false
alert.'

They stopped talking at cross purposes. The monologues
fused into a conversation. Gazing at the ceiling, she asked:
'Was it a false alert?' She turned and her nipples skated
across his chest. 'Was it? In both cases?'

'You tell me. You visited me only to help Kowalski. And
Ellsberg. Now they're dead.'

'Can't you forget them?'

'You think you can?'

'Yes.' She kissed him. 'With your help.'

He embraced her and whispered lips to lips: 'I'd forgotten
how good you taste.'

'Shame on you . . .' And when she had another chance:
'I'll have to remind you.'

Kowalski was invisible now, but he was there, somewhere
in the room. Maxon turned to find him. 'I thought you'd
mourn him,' he said.

Jack rose on her elbow and drank from the bottle. 'I do.'
She drank. 'Like I mourned my father.' She kissed Maxon's
chest, spilled champagne on his skin, and her lips followed
the rivulet snaking downhill.

'I like the way you mourn,' he said, but it was not funny,
it was not what he meant to say, and he would have liked to
take it back. Too late.

She sat up and looked now painfully overdressed in her nakedness. Her voice, too, sobered fast. 'Shocks and emotional upheavals are aphrodisiacs to me. Should I be ashamed of it?'

'Why did you marry him?'

'Some people lose their appetite when they're worried – others eat non-stop when something's bothering them.'

'Why did you marry him?' He repeated with quiet persistence.

'You made me. When you went away. On what you called a sticky job.'

'I'd have come back. You knew I would.'

'If you survived, yes. But then there would be just another "sticky job" and another until you failed to return. It was you who was obsessed with the risks my loving you might mean to me. So finally you convinced me. I began to see the light. And what's worse, I knew that if somebody killed you, instead of me, I'd be back to my loneliness in the NorthWest Territories yet again.' She stopped, she always did when it came to her childhood memories, and raised the bottle. It was empty. And the little on Maxon's chest had dried up. She kicked off the solitary sandal and went to fetch the whisky. She could not have looked more fully dressed in a crinoline and velvet robe.

'All right, you had to escape. But why to Kowalski? Why into marriage? If you were looking for a father figure ...'

'No. I was looking for peace. With myself. With the world.'

'In marriage?'

'In that marriage. I'd just shut the door on sex. Once and for all.'

'How? You must tell me about the technique,' he said disbelievingly. 'We'll make it compulsory in the training of agents.'

'You think it's funny?'

'No, definitely not. It would save lives. So tell me the secret.' He noticed the dotty tie and tore it away. It made him wince. She did not see it. She concentrated on the whisky.

'Well, first you make sure your prospective agent starts his-stroke-her sex life at thirteen. Preferably earlier, to be sure.'

'Thirteen? ... you've never told me.'

'I'm not advertising it, no. Perhaps I'm not proud of it.'

'Was it rape?'

'No. He was too big and strong for me.' She laughed freely, but stopped as if her vocal chords had snapped. Then she added in a matter of fact tone: 'So I had to seduce him.'

'At thirteen?'

'Twelve and a half.'

'But . . .'

'You mean *why*? He was my get-away. He was my father's friend, in his mid-thirties or so, and he was big and ugly.'

'What do you mean, ugly? You wouldn't have seduced him if he was that ugly.'

'You're wrong. His ugliness was an essential part of the attraction. He reeked of whisky and foreign tobacco, and had a front tooth missing. The gap was big enough to take my finger. Real horrid if you just looked at it. But he had a tale to go with every feature. The missing tooth was left in a fight in Yokohama – and in my Arctic boredom Yokohama sounded like sunshine and romance and fairyland. He had quite incredible, overdeveloped forearms, disgusting perhaps if I now think about them, but he made me see them in a different light. He'd hold them out straight, nod a sort of can't-be-helped nod, and tell me, "Yeah, that's what you get from pulling too many ropes, thick as your waist". And just to check himself, he'd feel my waist with the span of his hand, and leave me with the images of thick ropes dangling from white pirate boats as they sailed through the mysterious East.'

Suddenly, she seemed shiverish. Maxon found his jacket under the bed – how the hell did it get there? – and wrapped her into it. Somehow it made her look more naked.

'My father told me to call him Uncle Steve, and I never called him anything else. For me the name became synonymous with heat.'

'You mean warmth.'

'No. Heat. If he had any warmth in him, I never saw it. But the heat was there, sometimes stifling and humid, sometimes desiccating, but always overwhelming heat in all his stories. Perhaps in those cold nights he needed to remember the heat when he spoke about his "dancing girls in darkest Africa", his "buddies on the Rio Grande" or his "vicious enemies in Kota Baru". I didn't care if none of this was true. What mattered was that he was on first-name terms with the whole wide world, that he had lost an opium pipe or two in every port, that he had gambled away his girl in Macao but traded his best two goats for a Senegalese beauty in Casablanca. And when I crawled into his bed at the black of the night, I made him talk and talk about his adventures at places I still cannot find on any map.' She lit a cigarette, her umpteenth in the chain, and when it made her voice coarser, she gargled a little with the whisky – an act befitting Uncle Steve, Maxon thought. She gazed at the first light seeping through at the edge of the curtains. 'He taught me more about dreams than sex,' she said without regret, 'and then I betrayed him.'

'You what?'

'Not that I meant to do any such thing to him, but then, how many betrayals are really meant to be that from the outset?'

'What happened?'

'I don't think he had too many scruples about sleeping with me, but he knew it would do him no good if anybody found out. So he warned me to keep my trap shut, and I did, for a while. But then it seemed silly not to talk about the one good thing in my life, and I told my father I was going to marry Uncle Steve.

'The following day there was a frightful row, and then Uncle Steve disappeared. Nobody spoke about him, and I kept telling myself that some "old enemy from the East" must have caught up with him, but I think deep down I knew that my father had killed him. What it left me with was that unspeakable yearning for something, something unknown and mysterious, which I confused with sex, a yearning that remained unquenched wherever I went and whomever I loved – until you came along. By then I thought I was forgetting it all, including sex, but you reeked of mystery, and even a touch of foreign tobacco.'

'I didn't smoke.'

'I know. It was part of my dream.' She pulled up her legs and buried her face in her knees. The jacket slipped off her back. Maxon kissed the skin before covering it once again. 'And you always had that rickety old lighter. I imagined it kept getting lost and found in every corner of every continent, like Uncle Steve's opium pipes. I just wallowed in the mystery around you – and when you made me leave you, it was the NorthWest Territories all over again.' The whisky bottle had run dry. She let it drop. 'The old yearning was back, and I ran from it. The search, the thoughts of suicide, the foul affairs and the one-nighters which were mercifully too short to be fouled up, and finally, the haven of Kowalski's love, purified by his impotence. His dull rationalism made me forget that you'd used up all my dreams and left me with nothing but cold nights, lingering smells, and the frightful shadows of your "old enemies from the East" . . . Now get me a drink, and just let me curl up and sleep.'

While he was rummaging for another bottle in a walk-in cupboard, she took a deep breath of his jacket, then kissed and dropped it on the floor. By the time he returned to the bed, she was between the sheets. His silence apologised for all his questions and probing – hers for not answering one question: why did she marry Kowalski? He asked if she wanted another drink, if she was comfortable and warm enough, but she knew what the real question was. So she blurted out: 'I had no choice. I had to marry him if I wanted to prove to myself that I wasn't a born traitor, that not all my betrayals had been my fault.'

'What betrayals?'

'I betrayed everyone I loved.' She smiled, not because she was amused, but it was easier to say it all that way. 'First Uncle Steve to my father, then my father himself. He had been hurt, and he really cared for me, but I left without ever telling him where I was, dead or alive. Then I betrayed you by looking for substitutes and trying to love others, and betrayed them all by pretending that I had forgotten you. When Joseph asked me to marry him, I couldn't admit that much of what he called "our beautiful nearness" was just one aspect of my security assignment. I couldn't face it that I'd cheat even such pure love. And I married him in good faith. He was my final solution to sex. Or so I thought.' She stretched, making her breasts hill up.

'But fate caught up with you,' he said lightly, only to be struck by her fierce reaction.

She sat up with fear and tear infested eyes, her mouth agape, her voice shattered. 'I know. Not to betray him and to defend him from those groundless accusations, I almost betrayed you. Because I was weak and never up to the task. And it hit back. When I tried to defend you from Ellsberg

158

and the police, I had to betray Joseph. It killed him. And now I have only you to betray. So go away. Run.'

'I think I'll take a chance.' He climbed into bed and switched off the light. They huddled together in a newly-found glow of belonging. He had never pitied her before. Like sometimes he pitied himself. A feeling of weakness and inadequacy was the trigger of many heroic deeds. He knew that from experience.

'You're crazy,' she whispered.

'We both are. Let's try to sleep it off.'

'I'm not sleepy any more.'

'The sun is almost up.' He looked around. The ghosts of the night had gone. The ghosts of the day began to gather. Locke was there, guilty of something. But what? His conduct in the Kowalski case verged on the treacherous. So did his blocking of Ellsberg's revelations. Was he a traitor? Was Chuck Parkin the right man to do something about it? Had Chuck received Maxon's message in Washington? And Sandy . . . why was he such an elusive spirit just now?

'Talk to me,' she pleaded.

'About what?'

'Something about faraway places full of your buddies, enemies, lost lighters and dancing girls.'

'Gloucester sends his love.'

'Which category is he?' The doorbell rang. 'Do you expect visitors?'

He jumped out of bed and, through the gap of the curtains, tried to see who was downstairs. There were two shadowy figures standing too close to the front door to be recognised. He looked for his tattered kimono, once the prize possession of an affectionate Japanese agent's husband, but could not see it. He wrapped himself in a blanket. 'If it's a girl friend,' she whispered, 'tell her I'm here to stay.' She noticed how silently he moved, closing the door behind himself without even a click.

In the hall, he grabbed a snake-wood walking stick with an antler handle, then looked through the spy hole. First he saw a stranger. A car with two men inside was parked opposite. The stranger moved, and his companion came into view. Before they could ring again, Maxon opened the door to an old friend, spy-catcher Major Fred Sleet. 'Fred! What's up?'

'Sorry about the early hour, Mr Maxon. This is Captain Ross. May we come in?'

'Sure. What's the Mr bit?'

'Er . . . it's kind of official business . . .'

Maxon showed them into the living room. Sleet came to the point right away. 'We must take a couple of statements from you, sir.'

'Now?'

'Yes. Before the police get here. Could you tell me when you saw Gerry Houlihan, known as The Bang, the last time?'

'I've never seen him in my life.' Maxon noted that Ross was recording the conversation. 'Never seen him, never talked to him. But just for the record, I was very keen to do both. So I visited his home yesterday, saw his wife, and left him a message that I must see him tomorrow morning.'

'But you didn't return later on.'

'No.'

'You didn't wait for him or . . . bump into him.'

'That's right. Has anybody objected to my visit?'

'No.' Sleet watched him without blinking. 'But he's dead.'

'Oh.'

'His wife saw him battered to death.'

'Is she accusing me?'

Sleet ignored the question, 'We need a full statement from you, sir.'

'Okay. I think I have a good enough alibi if that's what I need. But you mentioned two statements. What's the other?'

'About that fatal . . . er . . . accident in Toronto.'

'Not that again!' Maxon was really annoyed. 'Inspector Wells and Locke himself have more statements from me on that than anybody could ever want.'

'I'm sorry, sir, but they couldn't question you fully because they didn't know or couldn't reveal at the time who the victim was.'

'But you can, is that it?'

'And they couldn't foresee that Mrs Kowalski who provided your alibi would come and spend the night with you.'

'If you were watching me last night, and you had to be to know that, you must have my alibi in the Houlihan murder.

Besides, Mrs Kowalski's presence would be ominous if the victim of that car accident was her husband. But he wasn't.'

'It's worse. He was tailing Kowalski.'

'For the KGB?'

'No. Canadian counter-intelligence. And it was your car that hit him. Did you kill him, sir?'

During the long pause that followed, the two men watched Maxon closely. His first reaction would be noted precisely. But his mind was elsewhere. Locke had to know who the victim was. There could be no doubt about it. So what was his game? Was he trying to eliminate – on trumped up charges if necessary – the one man who might see through his scheming?

'You want to take me in, Fred?' he asked at last a little absentmindedly.

'No, two statements, that's all I need ... for the time being.'

They agreed to let him put on something more becoming than a blanket, but accompanied him right to the bedroom door. And before Maxon went in, Sleet warned him that he had men outside the house.

Jack waited for him with a heavy metal table lamp in hand. Maxon smiled: 'Thanks for the thought.' While he searched for his kimono, he quickly told her in a whisper: 'I may have to go away with these guys. I don't know. You must stay here. If I fail to call you or return within twenty-four hours, talk to Chuck Parkin. He'll be in touch, I hope. If not, you can reach him in the White House. Arrange to meet him, and tell him everything about me, Ellsberg, Kowalski and Locke. Everything.'

He was on his way down the stairs, accompanied by the two men, when he remembered that Jack never knew what Ellsberg's message was. But she knew that he had given his report to Locke, and Parkin could demand to see it if he chose to.

# VI

Major Sleet was down to scraping the barrel for information on Maxon, who had dropped out of sight as if the four men watching the Hampstead house were rank amateurs. According to Sandy, they were real babes in the wood. What infuriated Sleet most was that he could detect a little laugh in the corner of Sandy's eyes: was he rooting for Maxon at his expense?

Had Sleet known how simple the explanation of Maxon's mysterious disappearance was, he might have been tempted to resign. Having taken the two statements at dawn, he had left the house about to position and instruct his watchers, safe in his convinction that Maxon would return to bed or need to get dressed before attempting to slip out. He was wrong. Maxon had grabbed some clothes, stepped through a bedroom window, dropped three feet down on the roof terraces of adjoining buildings, run along, jumped, and made a rather flat-footed landing on the soggy slope of a disused cemetery with an exit two streets away. Mutely he apologised to the old corpse on whose grave he dressed.

In the days that followed, the watchers did a most conscientious job. Their brief was to let anybody from the house go wherever they pleased, but to report every movement to Sleet. In the morning, Jack was tailed as she went shopping, and she was seen making a phone call from a public booth. The men could not have known that she was not making but answering a call from Maxon who gave her some instructions and a daily contact schedule for a week.

In the evening, the listening station reported a phone call to the house from 'an American identifying himself as Chuck. Call was answered by Mrs K who agreed to meet him in Washington.'

The day after that, Jack was tailed all the way to Heathrow, on to TWA flight 701 to New York, and then on to a connecting flight to Washington where she met a man, identified as presidential aide Chuck Parkin. (The report suggested that 'the rendez-vous was probably meant to be surreptitious,' and Sleet made a mental note to clarify, eventually, if this observation was correct or just something to enhance the tail's reputation of efficiency.) The same evening, she made a call to General Locke ('call identified by number obtained from operator – see $50 tip among incidental ex-es').

Meanwhile, the Hampstead house appeared dead. There were no other arrivals or departures, no incoming or outgoing phone calls, no movement behind windows, no lights, no sounds, no opening or drawing of curtains. Three days after his initial visit, Sleet ran out of patience. Maxon would not answer telephone calls or the door bell. Sleet forced his entry without a search warrant – and reported his shame to Sandy by telephone from the house. Now he was down to working through Maxon's 'secondary' contacts, particularly those who would be obliged to give information if they had any about Maxon's whereabouts. He reached the letter G and dialled Gloucester's home number.

'Sorry, I'm unable to help you, Major,' said the journalist, 'but I'll tell Maxon to call you.'

'I'd prefer to know where *we* could call *him*. We wouldn't be ungrateful to you, sir.'

'I know. But as I say, I'm unable to help just now.'

Gloucester rang off and turned to face Maxon: 'So . . . Have you been a bad boy, old sport?'

'Who was that?'

'A Major Sleet. Sandy must be anxious to find you.'

'A few days ago I was anxious to find Sandy. Now I'd prefer to delay a little our finding each other.'

'I see.'

'I appreciate your help and discretion.'

'You didn't give me much of a choice, did you?' Gloucester smiled as he referred to the surprise on his arrival home: Maxon had broken into his flat, helped himself to a clean shirt and underwear, and asked him for some cash just before Sleet had called.

'You deserve an extra dose of thanks.'

'Don't mention it, old sport, I mean don't ever mention it to anyone. Last week you were bad news – now you're front page disaster.'

General Locke's impeccable attentiveness made Jack feel uncomfortable. His exceeding sympathy evoked her worst suspicions. He offered her tea and biscuits, she said she would prefer an explanation. She was just as aggressive as Maxon wanted her to be. 'How come, General, that you knew all the facts that could have cleared my late husband, yet you did nothing for him?'

'All the facts – that's a bit of a sweeping statement, wouldn't you say?'

'You certainly knew that he went to the London office to get clearance for the German trip. You knew about Drusilla. You arranged the transfer of the doormen. You silenced them. Shall I go on?'

'I can assure you that poor Kowalski's name will be cleared in due course.'

'*Due course* would have been while he was still alive.'

'I'm sorry.'

'That won't bring him back. Or reduce your responsibility for his death.'

'I know. And between you and me, I recognise that one day, you may be entitled to apologises and even some compensation.'

'I'll settle for clearing his name *now*.'

'Well, let me put it this way, Jacqueline. It's not in the national interest to follow the course of action you suggest at this point in time.'

'That's criminal.'

'Not if it's born out of true patriotism.'

'I doubt if the court will accept that when you're charged with murder by negligence or design. I'm in the process of taking legal advice but I thought I'd give you a chance first.'

'That's very good of you. And in return I don't mind warning you that if, and I sincerely mean *if* you can prove that our failure to protect his good name drove him to suicide, you'll never be able to cash his life insurance.'

'You think I care?'

'No, I thought you might not. But then you must remember that you're still bound by Company regulations. Because technically speaking, you're still an operative on a job, and technically speaking, your entire marriage was a mission.'

'Don't you ever let go?'

'Of course we do. But right now, I hope most earnestly that you'll resume work for us in a more active fashion.'

'No, thanks.'

'Not even for Maxon's sake?'

'What do you mean?'

'Well, I'll level with you.'

'That's what I was afraid of.'

Locke tried to laugh it off: 'That's good. Very good. You have spirit and integrity. I like that. You have a great future with us. All you need is to recognise where your duties and best interests coincide.'

'And you're offering to help me.'

'And Maxon. Because you are in touch with him, aren't you?'

'No.'

'You don't really want me to believe that, do you?'

'I do. Because it's he who is in touch with me, and that's a big difference.'

'Yes, if you want to avoid telling me where he is. Very clever. But it's no news to me. I know he's gone to ground. The question is why? What is he up to?' He paused, but she looked so blank that for a moment he fell out of his chosen role and whispered in a husky voice: 'You know something? I envy him for you. A partner like you could help a guy go a long way – might even change his ways ...' It appeared he needed another few seconds to pull himself together. 'I just wanted you to know that he might be in trouble. And you could help him through helping me to find him and clear his name.'

'You mean the way you cleared Kowalski?'

He shrugged his shoulders and offered her a drink. She would accept nothing but answers about Maxon's position. In what way was he in trouble? Was there anything specific against him?

'Against him? No, I wouldn't put it as strongly as that. I mean there's nothing he doesn't already know about. Just a few matters to clear up. But technically, he's still on sick leave, and in his absence, while he remains out of touch, it's quite difficult to give him physical protection or even full moral backing in matters that may arise, such as some questions about an irregularity concerning his account with the Schweizerische Bankverein which we've just heard about ...'

Maxon holed up in an offically non-existent boarding house near the Stadium, in Wembley, where the terms were strictly cash in advance (the owner did not believe in paying taxes), but the facilities were excellent, including several entrances and emergency exits, ideal for the select clientele.

Maxon went over and over his memories of the conversations with Ellsberg. He had no doubt that Kowalski's interrogation in East Germany had been a show. So was the smear campaign. Not unlike the campaign against himself. When it came to sowing suspicions, Moscow Centre was the indisputable master of the art. Question: why would they be after him? There were, of course, several feasible explanations. For example, they would never forgive him for spiriting General Sarian out of Hungary. Like British intelligence had never forgiven Ellsberg for masterminding Blake's flight from a top security prison. But there was one major difference: Blake was clearly their man – Sarian might still turn out to be a plant. Except that Sarian would have played a key part in their moves against GLEW if he was assigned to defect. On the other hand, if Sarian carried a genuine warning (like Ellsberg!), why would Washington be panicky enough to let that public alarm slip through? And why were they so reluctant to let Maxon meet Sarian? They? Or was it only Locke? Maxon decided he would have to find Sarian and talk to him, with or without official blessing, whatever the risk.

After twenty four hours in his Wembley haven, Maxon grew restless. He had tried hard not to recognise a wellknown snatcher of armoured cash delivery vehicles who was using the same hideout and seemed to be striking up a friendship with a probable Lybian terrorist who was, Maxon guessed, on the run from his own cronies. The most obnoxious character Maxon encountered was an Indian who was smuggling in scores of compatriots illegally and using them as virtual slaves, employing them without a work permit, paying them a pittance, and deducting extortionate sums for their shared bed in the Wembley 'hotel'.

Maxon decided to expose the smuggler as soon as he himself was in the clear – but that was not yet the case. Far from it. He tailed his own potential tails for hours on end, watched the watchers surrounding his Hampstead home, contacted a few old friends, and came to the conclusion that although Sleet was hunting him, a general alert against him had not yet gone out: that was why he could still approach some colleagues who felt free to gossip with a man of Maxon's seniority about virtually anything, even the location of the Lincolnshire safe house where Sarian was probably kept. By the time Jack was due back in Britain, Maxon had already spent a day on recce.

Meeting Jack had to be an arduous procedure, but he could not take chances because he was sure that apart from Sleet, KGB agents would also be looking for him. He went through strict routines to shed potential tails, changed hired cars at pre-arranged points, drove to Cambridge and along the town's tedious one-way system several times until at a well-chosen intersection he jumped the red lights: nobody could have followed him without revealing himself.

Having swapped cars yet again, he picked up Jack's trail near Burwell on the B1102, ascertained that she was not being followed, and decided that her haystack of a blonde wig was not becoming at all.

The news she had for him was not very reassuring: Chuck Parkin had listened to her attentively but could not or would not promise to do anything about Ellsberg's warning and Locke's delaying tactics; Locke's insinuations had been predictable yet disturbing, and the dirty hint about the Swiss banking irregularity infuriated Maxon. For Locke knew about the numbered account Maxon kept for operational funds. 'If he can't get me on a stupid murder rap,' he fumed, 'he'll dig up two and a half Cambodian piasters I've failed to document in my expense account.'

'Locke mentioned a "sizeable surplus". It sounded serious.'

Sizeable? That was not the usual nit-picking, more like a proper frame-up. But by whom? Even if Locke, the Russians or anybody else discovered the number, the account would remain untouchable – except that anybody could pay money into it without leaving any trace of the source. So if somebody wanted to stir up more suspicions ... Maxon left the thought unfinished. They were approaching Windyridge, and Maxon expected that the entire hillside would be crawling with Sarian's minders – if, indeed, the Russian was kept there. He asked Jack to drive, and he sat on the floor in the back from where he could take a final look, this time in daylight, at the house on the edge of the village.

The road took a lazy turn in deference to a clump of veteran oaks, and emerged in open country. With a decent pair of binoculars, any approaching vehicle could be scrutinised from the Old Factory at the hilltop, and a decent pair of binoculars was one of the few luxuries extended to the minders. Sandy always maintained that in sleepy surroundings like this, birdwatching helped the men to stay awake. Maxon looked up – and yes, there it was, a solitary kestrel, hovering on the horizon, perhaps the same old bird he used to watch as a minder, he had no way to tell, he did not know how long its lifespan would be. It swooped down and disappeared from his field of vision. Damn. In a dead window of the Old Factory something glittered, at least he thought he had seen what might have been a pair of binoculars trying to track the bird's dive. It brought back the long forgotten frustration that he had never managed to catch a glimpse of the prey. He knew how the man in the window must be feeling, he knew his routine, the lay-out of his post, the endless hours of the security rigmarole that dulled his alertness, the incurable hazard Maxon was banking on.

The car began to climb the long, gentle slope. Maxon told Jack to play the carefree tourist, open a window, let the radio blare and the blonde mane flutter.

Nothing seemed to have changed. The village on the ridge was still exposed to the whistle of every wind that roamed the county as if to drive away all but the most tenacious lovers of the view, the isolation snobs, the snooty who would pay any penalty for exclusivity, and the humble who could not afford to go anywhere else. Why the building of romantic neglect was called the Old Factory, nobody knew. Maxon was convinced that nothing but lies, conspiracies and cover stories had ever been manufactured there. The walled, overgrown gardens to be glimpsed at through crumbling V-shapes of stone and mortar, the blinds on all windows, broken or not, the gaping tiles of the roof, and the drunken chimneypots advertised all too loudly a marked lack of life. But Maxon knew that if Sarian was in there, the waist-high nettles would hide audio and body sensors, infrared cameras would scan the grounds day and night, and the gaps in the wall would serve as an easy invitation for intruders who would soon be confronted by the 'eccentric, trigger-happy owner' who was said to prowl about with his friends and double-barrelled shotguns night after night.

Most important of all, the vicar's potting shed adjoining the back of the house was still there. That was one of the escape routes, and Maxon saw no reason why it should not be used as a point of entry.

The car passed the house, the junk shop and the pub at the leisurely speed of the sightseer. Beyond the next village, Jack dropped off Maxon. He had a bicycle hidden in the hedge. 'I want you back here at oh-two-hundred,' his voice sharpened to a military clip. He checked himself, apologised, saying he meant two in the morning, and asked her to bring along a dozen empty tins, a few silver balloons, and a couple of cats. He ignored her quizzical look: 'I don't mind what sort. I'm not fussy. You could buy them in a pet shop in Grantham or pick up a couple of strays in Lincoln. They always congregate behind the cathedral.' Her eyes grew a shade darker. It made him smile: :Don't worry. I won't hurt them ... I hope.'


Yet another round of sabre-rattling swamped the headlines and news time on the air in Washington. The Pentagon declared that under the GLEW umbrella, the west could win a limited nuclear skirmish or even a protracted, full-scale, no-holds-barred war. Moscow answered that 'survivability' and 'speed of recovery over a few decades after a nuclear war' would still favour the east. The Americans proclaimed that the Russians might be on the brink of breaking the test ban treaty in outer space. The Russians 'revealed through reliable sources' that the allegedly reduced American defence budget (the second since GLEW had come into play) only disguised the diversion of funds to new secret weapons research. Caught in the cross-fire of all these claims and accusations, it was not entirely surprising that the rhythmic 'Ban the Bomb! Ban GLEW!' chants of a CND tidal wave, sweeping down Pennsylvania Avenue, confounded some of the onlookers with the equation of the two *menaces*.

None of this printed and televised clamour penetrated the White House, where the President sipped his favourite though unseasonal julep, and found that 'the silence can be quite deafening on a sunny day like this'. He raised his glass with a sad smile towards the man whose bulk posed an endurance test for the dainty armchair on the left of the massive Presidential desk. 'Wish we could throw the windows open and let the birds sing for me, Chuck.'

'Oh, I don't know. ... Bullet-proof glass is a status symbol, Mr President. Just one of the trappings that make the Oval Office awe-inspiring.'

'This is not an office – it's an oval fish tank, and I'll drown in it, I know.'

'Come up for air some time. Have dinner with us, like in the old days ...' He hesitated: it was difficult to call even such an old friend *Bob* when the man was sandwiched between the flags of the highest office in the land. Yes, he did look like a man gasping for oxygen, and Chuck wondered if anyone in a fairly advanced state of hypoxia could be trusted with the fate of the earth. The more warning he had, the better the chance that his finger on the nuclear button would not slip.

'Would be nice, Chuck. Haven't seen Gwen for ages. Yes, we'll have to arrange something.'

'You know, just the four of us, Bob – you, Gwen, me, and a quart of good claret ...'

'We may get a better chance in the next few months when we'll be working much more closely together.'

Just what Chuck Parkin had hoped for, but his delight was not to last. The President wanted him to be more closely involved with his re-election campaign rather than security. Like in the 'old days' and in the 'old style' when Chuck Parkin recognised no frontiers, no limitations to the means that would guarantee success. The President owed him a great deal and was about to increase his debt even more: 'Make it your first job to deal with this goddamn Doomsday Clock. The jokers who operate it choose their own private interpretation of every word I say. When I declare myself yet again on the side of law, order and peace, yes, peace with the greatest possible emphasis, they scream blue holocaust – and push that front page clock yet another twenty seconds towards midnight. Now why? Are they paid by Moscow? If they need funds, I'm sure we could arrange something. But you've got to stop them, Chuck, stop them with a jolt from which they'll never recover.'

'We can't stop them now. The magazine has already hit the streets.'

'Just talk to them. You can speak those jokers' language when you want to. Perhaps they could apologise to me, personally, in the next issue. We could then litter every sidewalk, every shopping mall with the scrapped issue, full of their mistakes, and if it coincided with the launching of the campaign, their endorsement of my platform could do a lot for us.' The President raised his hand to silence Chuck's argument. 'I'm counting on you, Chuck. Like in the old days.'

'You can count on me, Bob, but don't bank on my success in this case. They're a pretty independent and objective bunch.'

'Objective? How can they be objective *and* accuse me of responsibility for the current crisis when all I said was that we continue to stand by the letter of the space treaty? And I spelt it out for them: no nuke tests, no EMP in space; if the reds try something out there, whatever it is, however it comes about, it's war.'

'Unless that tip from Toronto was correct.'

The President turned away from Parkin. 'What tip?' he asked staring at the Old Glory which some hostile cartoonists, who should long have been censored forever, had depicted as a Jolly Roger ever since the beginning of his Presidency. 'What tip from Toronto, Chuck?'

Parkin felt like kicking himself. He had planned to test the water in a more subtle way than just blurting out what he knew. 'The one from that KGB agent . . . Ellsberg.' Now there was no way back. The President pressed him hard to tell what, how and where he had heard about Ellsberg. Parkin would have liked to protect a useful informer, but not at all costs. So he revealed all he knew about the Toronto affair, and that his information came from Maxon.

The President exploded: 'It was none of his goddamn business to tell you or anyone outside his normal reporting channels.'

'All he wanted was to ensure that you'd know about his report. I mean you, personally. I mean to help you decide how strongly to react to a potentially disastrous situation.'

'Great. Thank you. All I needed was yet another big-headed, objective and independent joker flashing cue-cards for me everywhere I turn! All right, he got out that

Armenian general. He did well. Right. But that doesn't entitle him to dictate to me.'

'The way I see it, Bob, the guy is desperate for some reason.'

'Why? Because he thinks that I'm an incapable ninny who needs ages to make the right decision?'

'No, but it helps a lot to be forewarned. That's why he's played his last card.'

'As I see it, he's tried to play a card he's never held. I don't trust people who go behind the back of their bosses. Would *you* trust such a man?'

'The question is: can we rely on his source?'

'Chuck, I'm not going to discuss this.' He spun round and opened a thick blue folder as if to emphasise that the subject was closed. 'If you have any further questions concerning GLEW, Maxon, Ellsberg or Toronto, you must turn to Locke.'

'Then let me rephrase my question, Mr President: do you trust this General Locke?'

The President was so fully absorbed in reading an EYES ONLY/NO COPIES document that he did not even look up. Chuck Parkin left the room quietly, weighing various possibilities: perhaps Locke had never forwarded Maxon's report to the President or any of his top aides; perhaps Locke had mentioned the report to some people but with insufficient emphasis; or he might have claimed credit for the information by leaving Maxon's name out of it. . . . No, in that case, the President would have known about Toronto. But did he? He certainly asked no further questions about Ellsberg's warning. Perhaps he did not take it very seriously. Perhaps he was simply more concerned with Maxon's irregular approach. Yes, that would have been typical of Bob, thought Parkin.

'If you survive and I don't . . .' 'You must, General.' '. . . I can't stomach optimists, Maxon.' 'It's time to become one when all reasonable hope's gone.' Bullets whizzed past his ear, chipped stucco hailed on him.

Maxon willed himself to wake up. It was almost time to meet Jack. He felt shiverish. The Windyridge gravedigger's tool shed did not offer much protection from his own nightmares and the elements of an English early-summer night. He climbed and sat astride the massive cemetery wall. Through light-intensifying binoculars he surveyed once more the Old Factory. Occasionally, a lone figure would stumble over bushes and tall grass, stop, listen, and perhaps pee with abandon in the knowledge that he must be invisible to the naked eye. Then an Alsatian would begin to bark or growl only to be silenced sharpishly by some command Maxon was too far to overhear.

The main building itself was completely dark and seemingly dead. If Sarian was, indeed, kept in there, the central areas of the house would be governed by strict black-out regulations. Deep down Maxon hoped to be wrong. He was under orders not to approach the general, and if Sarian was not in the Old Factory or if Maxon was forced to escape before he could find him, the order would not really be disobeyed.

He thought about Ellsberg whom he had urged so earnestly, with such fervent conviction, to disobey, to break his lifelong loyalties in order to serve some higher loyalty. He never knew if Ellsberg's oath of allegiance contained a let-out clause authorising disobedience towards unlawful and immoral commands. He suspected it did not. He knew his own oath had not provided him with any such comforting sanction. He also knew that subconsciously, he dreaded the meeting with Sarian. A frightened reception would indicate that the man had come over with a mission, as a plant rather than a defector, to mislead, lie, spread disinformation, perhaps against Maxon as well as others. Except that the discovery would come too late for Maxon to use: Sarian would be within his rights to shoot him, in 'self-defence', on sight. And yet he knew he had to go in, face the general, and find out at least some of the truth. There was no other way. Not even if loyalty, reason and caution combined to warn him against it.

Maxon climbed off the wall and walked along the no-man's-land between fields and the village, on the blind side of the houses where drawn bedroom curtains would provide privacy both ways. The rain came down hard as he reached the hedge where he would meet Jack, but he was early, leaving himself with time to shiver and think even longer. And the thoughts were as cold as the wind. Since very soon after his successful mission, so many strong suspicions had accumulated against him, that he himself was sometimes tempted to believe that he might have done something wrong. How could he be certain that he was not a sleepwalker or schizophrenic or someone acting under hypnotic control or a traitor who had developed a comforting refuge of amnesia? What if he did kill that Canadian agent watching Kowalski? What if he did blow up Paloma's boat? What if his mind did help him with the erasure of anything unpleasant to make it easier for him to side with the one real friend he had ever made and win back the woman he loved?

Jack's arrival saved him from courting madness any more. She had the cats, and watched him with repugnance as he tied tins and balloons to the backs and tails of the reluctant strays. 'Promise not to hurt them,' she said at last.

'Don't worry. They can shake everything loose as they run, and run they will, I can promise you that.'

The clouds broke into a southerly race. In ghostly moonlight, the cats caused a mighty pandemonium with the tins on the back seat. The balloons, that would create peculiar bleeps on the guards' monitoring screens, drew menacing shadows and drove the cats to hysterical rolling and jumping. Jack was not happy with the plan, and Maxon could offer her only the hope that the cats' plight would not last long. 'Give me four minutes precisely, then drop them over the wall.'

Before they reached the Old Factory, Maxon got out. 'Four minutes. Then go. Fast. If I fail to contact you in Lincoln before first light, get on to Chuck Parkin and tell him everything.'

He skirted the grounds of the safe-house and waddled across a slippery vegetable patch without incident until the vicar's poodle mounted a ferocious attack on the inside of the kitchen door. Maxon stopped to swear but then realised that the cursed animal was on his side: the barking awakened the Alsatians in the Old Factory and they all joined in heartily. He entered the potting shed, moved a few planks to reach a concealed door that looked like the rest of the old bricks in a mouldy wall (he had often wondered if the vicar was privy to the secret), and waited to hear Jack's approaching car in the distance. The car stopped, cats mewed and cried, tins clattered awakening the dead at the far end of Windyridge, and provoking all dogs within earshot to join in a cacophony of righteous indignation. By that time, the well-oiled emergency exit had opened and closed under the slightest pressure – and tripped the internal alarm. Maxon was racing up the stairs. The bells followed him all the way, but he knew that the peculiar bleeps would puzzle the men on the monitoring sets (if they were not asleep in the first place), and everybody's first concern would be the upheaval in the grounds, a search of the outside for intruders and the point of entry, in the secure knowledge that the alarm had automatically locked all doors – except the emergency exit most guards would not even be aware of. Eventually, the inside of the building would also be scrutinised: he had to find Sarian before that.

Lights came on and went off at random, illuminating every inch of the corridor only to plunge it into darkness yet again. It was part of the security routine to worry the intruder, but it also confirmed Maxon's belief that somebody of importance was being kept in the safe-house. Listening to muted shouts, door-banging and the patter of running bare feet in the distance, he opened door after door, but the fusty smell in room after empty room told him that the first floor was unoccupied.

He was about to climb the stairs when the lights died yet again. Simultaneously, someone came running. A torchlight flickered in the runner's unsteady hand. Maxon knew he had nowhere to hide on the landing. If the lights came on or the beam of the torch caught him, he might be recognised by a guard. He could not risk it. If he attacked the man, he might still be recognised. He would have to fight and perhaps kill a colleague. He felt reluctant to do either. He remembered the fire extinguishers on each landing. Dropping to his knees, he groped along the wall. He touched cold metal. The runner reached the landing. His torch flashed overhead. Maxon pushed the extinguisher – and the red cylinder rolled into the man's path. There was a bone-crushing knock, a cry of pain and anger, a swipe by the light across the ceiling, and then the tumbling of a body down the stairs. Maxon hoped that only the man's pride would be hurt by his supposed clumsiness.

By the time some lights flared up again, Maxon had reached the second floor. If Sarian was there, he would be in the principal bedroom with the barred, bulletproof windows. He tried the door gently. It was not locked. He slipped inside. The room had a lived-in smell. As his eyes adjusted to the faint moon-light, he could make out the shape of the bed. It was empty, but it had been slept in. He moved closer. The linen felt warm. A heavy whisper with a Muscovite accent warned him: 'Don't move. I have a gun.' The disembodied voice came from a dark corner.

'Don't be rash, Aram.' Maxon tried to make it sound light. He knew he must not sound frightened. It would alert Sarian to non-existent dangers. If the man was in any doubt about his visitor, and if he really had a gun, he could afford to switch on a light. If he recognised the voice, and if he was guilty of complicity in some move, perhaps character assassination, he could now shoot without questions. The visibility was good enough for pumping bullets into a target from close quarters, and Maxon would not live to deny the accusations. The worst was that Maxon could do nothing about it. He had to allow Sarian to take his time, wake up fully, recover from the shock of the alarm, and sort out the options for himself. Maxon used the long pause for trying to work out where his host could be. Behind the cupboard? Or the heavy armchair? Maxon decided that if there was any sudden movement or sound, he would dive behind the chair and hope to land on top of Sarian. It was not even a half a chance. But his impotent exposure to a gun had been his own making with nobody else to blame.

'Maxon . . .?'

'Who else?'

'Is this what you call visiting time?'

'I'll explain.' Running steps could be heard approaching down the corridor. 'Just let me hide.'

'Under the bed?' The voice was smiling. The accent puzzled Maxon even at this moment: the wily Armenian must have lived all his life in Moscow – if he really was an Armenian in the first place. What if Sandy had been misled when he accepted Sarian's voluntary services as agent *in situ* all those years ago? And what if the old routine of using no bugs in safe houses had been changed? What if they were monitoring every word? They would be coming for him – about now . . .

There were knocks at the door. Maxon dropped to the floor and slithered under the bed. A few quick puffs of air told him that Sarian was laughing soundlessly. 'It's not funny,' Maxon mumbled angrily. As soon as he was inside, the place darkened: Sarian pulled down the blanket to touch the floor and cover him. A guard asked to be let in. Sarian delayed him by saying that he would have to roll down the black-out blind first. A ratchet began to click. Sarian opened the door and switched on a small reading light. Maxon knew the guard would glance round surreptitiously: the men were trained not to trust even their own charge. The guard explained that probably it had been a false alarm. 'Nothing to worry about, sir. We're still checking. Just keep your door locked.'

Sarian laughed when Maxon crawled out from under the bed. 'You okay?'

'It's been a long time since I had to hide like this.'

'In my country, they'd cut you a little shorter where it hurts most if the husband found you in there.'

'You must tell me all about it.' Maxon noted that Sarian was still toying, as if absentmindedly, with an old service revolver. 'But right now, we haven't got time.'

'That's what I thought. Shoot.'

'First of all, do you trust me?'

'Who should I trust if I don't trust you? You risked your life to save mine. Have your wounds healed?'

'More or less.'

Behind the door, the house went relatively quiet: the dogs were still at it, but the alarm had stopped. 'Did you start all that noise?'

Maxon nodded and gestured towards the corridor: he had heard the approaching steps before Sarian who answered renewed knocking with an irritated 'Yes?!' through the door.

'Just wanted to report that it's okay, sir. A couple of cats dragging tins tripped off the system.'

'Ah! Children. Naughty children are naughty children everywhere.'

'Probably, sir. But we're still checking, so don't open your door, sir.'

'No, I'll just sit here *trembling*. Good night.' They listened to the receding steps outside. 'Now then. What's the excitement and the secrecy? Couldn't you come and see me offically? I've been expecting you for a long time. But they kept saying that you weren't well enough.'

'They were lying. The truth is that you're in trouble.'

'Me? How come? Didn't I do enough for your people?'

'It's not that. You must have said something that makes them suspicious of you.'

'That's crazy.'

'I know. That's why I came unofficially.'

'Thank you.'

'I was afraid you might not be pleased to see me.'

'Why? Are you crazy?'

'What if you were frightened?'

'You *are* crazy! Why would I be frightened of you?'

'No reason. Not unless you said something . . . something damaging about me.'

Sarian scrutinised Maxon's face: he wanted to be sure that it was not his notorious lack of humour that rendered him unable to see some joke. When it sank in that Maxon was serious, his lips and nostrils began to quiver in anger. His voice slipped out of control and though his face might have petrified seasoned troops on the parade ground, his falsetto, a credit to a comic opera singer, would have ruined the desired effect. 'I knew it! I knew it right away. That fucking Locke. I never trusted him. If anyone, it must have been he who twisted something I said.'

'Any idea what it could be?'

'No. I'd never say anything bad or damaging about you.' He turned away. Maxon tried to tell himself that it must have been some mirage conjured up by the reading light, but he could have sworn he saw tears in Sarian's eyes. 'I just wouldn't do any such thing to you.' His voice was so solemn that Maxon feared Sarian might hug and kiss him on the left, the right, and the left again. But the moment of overflowing sentimental comradeship passed, and Sarian realised quite suddenly the risk Maxon had taken: 'You must be desperate, my friend. If I'd played some dirty trick against you, I could have shot you when you turned up, as you said, unofficially.'

'I know. You'd have called it self defence. Not even Locke could have questioned it.'

'Why was he brought into this at all?'

'You tell me.'

'I don't know. At first it was such a friendly debriefing.'

Maxon felt a little sorry for him. Sarian had swallowed every bait Sandy had offered up for him. Special treatment. Elocution lessons to help him fit into the new, high-class

178

identity which was being prepared for him. A generous pension in acknowledgement of his status and services. Personal visits from Sandy and the invitation to Sandy's 'country home' for a long weekend. He had been absolutely overwhelmed by the beauty and homeliness of the place (a government guest house for distinguished visitors to be impressed by their own importance). His only resentment was that 'this man, Locke, had to be brought into the debriefing process'.

'Do you know who he is?' Maxon asked.

'Some big shot in the new early warning set-up, correct?'

'Yes. Perhaps you said something that might be of special interest to him.'

'No . . . don't think so. . . . In fact, I had very little for him apart from the fact that this GLEW frightened the hell out of Moscow.'

'Why?'

'Obviously because they couldn't break the system or even the code it uses. Your new computers and signals are too fast for them. They have nothing to match that speed. That's why Moscow was full of rumours that the *Nachalnik* might try to do something really desperate and dangerous.'

'I'm not interested in gossip.'

'Neither am I, Maxon. And I left with you on this little vacation before anything specific had filtered through. Mind you, some of these rumours must have been correct. Such as about the test . . .'

'Test? You mean . . .'

'Sure. The missile to test the efficiency of GLEW. Didn't they burn their fingers with it?' He gloated over the launch in space that had ended in the spectacular failure by detection and the Washington public alert.

'You knew about that test in advance?' Maxon asked as if only to fill a gap in a casual chat.

'Of course. But it wasn't important to Locke, I knew anyway and he told me himself it wasn't important, because GLEW would pick up the information more precisely than anything I could predict from my limited inside information.'

'How come you knew about the launch in advance?'

'You forget what my position used to be. Besides, I have friends – haven't you?'

'But . . .'

'No. Please don't ask me any more about my friends.'

'Wouldn't dream of it. It's none of my business. But GLEW is. How much did you know about the test?'

'Can't you look up Locke's report?'

'I have read it. But let's pretend that it's all new to me. ... No, I won't play games. You're too sharp. You'd see through the old trick-technique right away, and I don't want to be caught out by you yet again.' He could see that flattery was still his most effective weapon. Sarian's face mellowed: he was anxious to help. 'So I'd better come clean,' said Maxon. 'When I found out that for some reason they'd begun suspecting you, I kicked up a hell of a fuss. I told them I trusted you, and I laid my own reputation on the line. The result was that they tried to cut me off from some sources. Locke's report was one of them. They wouldn't let me re-read it.' Maxon concocted his story as he went along according to Sarian's reactions. Now he was on the right track. The prospect of a hug and kisses loomed large as Sarian's high regard for friendship and his Russian sentimentality about martyrs began to work in his favour. 'So I'm really at your mercy when I'm trying to help you secretly.'

'I appreciate it. And your visit will remain our secret.'

'Good. Then we may find out what's going on. We must consider all possibilities. Even ridiculous ones. Like that you may be a plant and I may be a fool. Or that Locke may be a traitor. Or that I could be the victim of some Machiavellian KGB plot.'

'Sounds fun.'

'Let's go back to your inside information, however trivial it might have been. Would the Kremlin have any way of knowing that you had advance knowledge of the test?'

'You're crazy! If they had the slightest suspicion that I knew something about it, they'd have changed both the time and location of the missile launch as soon as they discovered my defection. Correct?'

'Tell me the location. Where in space did they plan to launch that missile?'

'That's something you must know yourself. It's history by now.'

'But it's never been published. And if you didn't know in advance, you wouldn't know it now.'

'Okay. I'm not telling you anything I haven't told Locke. It's what you call Moon Sector Seven. Correct? ... Answer me. . . . No, your face is the answer. I know it's correct. I'm no liar. Go on. . . . Admit it.'

Sarian was hurt and agitated. Maxon was too benumbed to open his mouth and utter a word. 'I apologise,' he said at last. 'You're no liar.'

'Thank you. I accept your apology.' He watched Maxon and guessed his thoughts. 'Hey. . . . You say they suspect me? Shouldn't it be the other way round?'

'I don't know.' And that was the truth, by now probably obvious to Sarian, too. For if GLEW detected the launch and approach of the missile, the public announcement in Washington could have been a slip-up, a genuine error in the system or even sabotage – unquestionably a case for thorough investigation. But if Locke knew about the launch in advance . . . Maxon did not know what to make of it, but he dreaded the answer whatever it might turn out to be. He felt disgusted with himself, Locke, Sandy, and the whole affair. But disgust would not free him from the tangle that threatened to throttle him. 'What did Sandy say to your advance info?'

'I don't know. Locke told me never to mention it to him. You think that . . .'

Maxon did not want to hear the questions spelt out. He told Sarian it was premature to jump to conclusions. 'We're still investigating every angle.'

'Then learn from *us* to do it faster, my friend. In my country, we'd first arrest you, me, Locke, Sandy, and everybody else even vaguely involved to be sure that the guilty man, if there was a guilty man, was among them. Then we'd have time, plenty of time, to question them all. Or maybe shoot them. One by one. Starting with the B-man who actually pressed the OVERRIDE.'

On his way out, Maxon found the alarm deactivating switch above the emergency exit. He closed the door behind him, and rearranged the planks to cover it in the potting shed. This time, not even the vicar's poodle paid any attention to him.


It had always been an enigma to Maxon how specialists he called the doomsday-men preserved their sanity. In a way, he was, of course, one of them since he had been assigned

181

to Locke's peculiar outfit, but devoting his time to GLEW security differed vastly from the lifestyle of those who circled the earth in shifts seated astride The Bomb, and those who cruised for weeks without daylight in their floating tombs under the polar ice-cap with an eye on the gaps where their missiles could slip through, or even those who had been singled out to be last survivors waiting for an all-out enemy attack in their underground silos with half-keys and quarter keys to the box marked *Ignition*.

Yet to Maxon, the most soul-destroying of it all was the B-man's lot. Day in, day out, night after long night, through the 'happy hour', Yom Kippur and Christmas Day, the B-for-*button*-man's sole concern was a keyboard with a lonely key which was gently hollowed to accommodate a fingertip like a cradle, a key known in the trade as the 'override'. These days, every country had one. To depress the 'override' was a strictly controlled, checked and double-checked ritual which had to be rehearsed daily by real B-men at a mock-up console, with a dummy key and simulated emergencies. Some politicians argued that the act had been over-rehearsed like a grand society wedding without a bride. But those in charge dismissed this as a fatuous argument even if they knew that the 'override' would never be activated more than once, just the first and last time, in the life of any country. They were proved wrong when the impossible happened: the United States survived the day when the B-man actually depressed 'override' to silence Glenn Miller and all other radio and TV programmes, expropriate all the airwaves, and transmit the feverish signal of the nuclear war alert on every wavelength and every channel.

Sarian had been right, Maxon knew he must start with the B-men in search for the truth: was the alert a mistake or sabotage? He knew a few of the B-men personally, but in his current predicament he could not question any of them officially. Not without the authority, nor without calling unwanted attention to himself. He had to find a back door. That was why he contacted Saul Robinson, a Washington G-man, who owed him a favour or two. Maxon gave him a couple of names without telling him that these were B-men. His demand was blunt, and he offered no explanation: dig up some dirt, any dirt, on at least one of them. It was a tall order, he knew, because B-men and their families were security vetted with the most irritating frequency, but to succeed, he needed some sort of leverage.

For his long wait and vigil he holed up once again in the dump in Wembley, and Jack joined him to share his misery. He was grateful but behaved most ungratefully. He vented his pent-up frustration on her, apologised, and could not help doing it again. Maxon was completely preoccupied with the B-men's plight: what do they think, what do they do when they're told to press the 'override', release the signal, and announce the end of this world? Do they cry? Do they contact their families? Do they sit back with a special last bottle of bubbly they hoped they'd never open? Maxon tried to shoo away the thoughts but they kept swarming in. Suddenly he had had enough of the shabby room with the dust-riddled curtain and furniture that housed the largest ever collection of broken springs. He'd had his fill of the hiding, the self-imposed limitation, the urge to behave sensibly. He wanted to walk. Breathe. Do something before it might be too late. And if one side or the other wanted to shoot him, so be it. He knew it was crazy. Jack knew it, too, but she understood. She would not do anything to stop him. Fortunately, the telephone would.

Saul Robinson was on the line. 'Hi, man, can we talk?'

'Within limits, yes.' Maxon blessed the owner of the dump who knew his customers well and provided them with a direct line in each room so that they would not have to worry about some switchboard operator listening in. 'Got something for me?'

'Not really. I mean not unless you call it dirt that the older guy, Henry, visits a cheap callgirl every other Thursday.'

'Mm.' Maxon was disappointed. He was clutching at straws. 'Is he married?'

'Who isn't, man?'

'That's something.'

'Depends what you wanna make of the visits. His old lady may even *know* that it's her fault, after all.'

'How come?'

'She belongs to some dotty sect of religious maniacs who're against sex.'

'Must be tough on poor Henry. Why doesn't he leave her?'

'Loves her ugliness, I guess,' Saul chuckled. 'They have

kids from the days when his darling Evelyn was not too upright to go horizontal occasionally. Yeah, maybe it's because of the kids that he doesn't want to leave her.'

'That's promising.'

'I'd have never guessed, man!'

The longer Maxon thought about it, the more cheerful the prospect looked. All he needed was some gentle lever with which to unhinge the B-man's defences. 'Where does he meet the girl?'

'A small motel out Chevy Chase way.'

'Good. Will you do something for me, Saul?'

'What?'

'I want you to hit the place next Thursday.'

'Well . . .'

'You owe me, Saul, you soulless cop, and don't you forget it.'

'You drive a hard bargain, man.'

'But you love me just the same, right? See you on Thursday. And Saul . . . I'll want a lot of noise to rattle our Henry.'

'You've got it. But then we're quits.'

Maxon rang off and rubbed his hands together: life was beginning to brighten up.

'I sometimes wonder why I love you,' said Jack.

'That makes two of us.'

'Thanks. At least you trust me.'

'I have no choice.' He meant it as a joke. It did not sound like one. Who do I trust if I don't trust Jack? he asked himself, fearful of the rising ghost of paranoia with visions of Jack betraying him to Locke and Sandy or the Russians or all of them in turn. Nevertheless he asked her to contact Gloucester: 'I want him to pick up a plain brown envelope from my safe. I'll authorise them to give it to him.'

'Can't I . . .?'

'No. If my bank is being watched, they'd pick up your trail and you'd lead them to me. Besides, you couldn't deliver the envelope the way I want him to. Tell him to be in the second cubicle in the number two loo in the Oceanic Building at Heathrow at 19.15 tonight.' Neither Jack nor Gloucester had any need to know that the sealed envelope contained a spare passport.

Maxon entered cubicle Number Three at ten past seven, and waited, feeling uneasy, because if Gloucester had been followed by Major Sleet or anyone else, he would miss his flight and the show Saul Robinson was organising for him.

At quarter past seven the door was opened and locked in the adjoining cubicle. Maxon coughed twice, Gloucester answered with an echo. Only a few words were exchanged. Gloucester slipped the envelope under the partition. The seal seemed unbroken. Maxon opened it. The passport, retained for just such emergencies, was inside. He made Gloucester promise to leave the airport right away because it could be a risk to be seen together. He waited a few more minutes before leaving the cubicle. Gloucester was nowhere in sight. But he was still in the terminal building. Twenty minutes after the handover, he put his head inside one of the perspex bubbles and dialled a London number. 'Gloucester here. ... Yes, he's just left for the States, travelling on a London-New York-Washington ticket and a Canadian passport in the name of Cotter. ... That's right, A D Cotter. ... No, he's wearing tinted glasses and a black leather trilby ...'


Henry Claymore considered himself a lucky man. Having avoided the lure of great dreams and expectations, he would never need to learn how to cope with life's great frustrations. He had a secure job for life (there would be no life beyond the expiry of his job), and he was well adjusted to what fate seemed to have in store for him. He knew no vanity, so he would not crave for being called clever or handsome; he found pleasure in repetitions, and enjoyed living without surprises because the thrills were in the anticipation if he knew precisely what to expect. He liked dancing, and the paso doble was his forte (even the imported, professional *cancanières* gave him and Evelyn a big hand when they performed it on their honeymoon in Vegas all those years ago). But this girl, tonight, was no good at it. She had no feel for the rhythm, no eye for real talent. However, she was big, and a man of Henry's modest height found it easy to slip his hand under her short skirt. She wore nothing underneath.

'Don't crease it, lemme take it off,' she whined, to his great disappointment.

'No-no-no-no-no!' He stopped the tape, his own, angrily.

185

'Now what?'

'Evelyn, Evelyn, you don't understand.'

'No, I don't. And I don't even like to be called Evelyn.'

'Tough shit,' Henry said with great authority. 'Didn't they tell you at the agency what the scenario was? They oughta know it by now. We dance, I try it on, you say no, then I get more aggressive, you can't stop me, but you gotta resist me ...'

'You wanna fight? Get Mohamed Ali not me next time.'

'Don't worry. I won't hurt you. I don't wanna hurt you or mess up your fine frock, it's just that you gotta follow the scenario. Everything in life gotta have a scenario. First you find me just a pushy little fella, keen but cute, then I kinda overwhelm you, and then, only then you begin to give in ... co-operate ...'

'Okay,' she sighed and looked at her watch. 'Let's try.'

He shook his head. It was no good. Things ought to work out more naturally. 'Why didn't the other Evelyn come? She knows it's *my* Thursday.'

'She's down with flu.'

'Who's flu?' he quipped only to introduce the missing lighter touch.

'Ha, ha,' she said unimpressed.

'What's eating you Miss Straightface? Is your religion against having a laugh?'

'You wanna get on with it or shall I go? I ain't got all night.'

But it seemed that she had got the message at last, for the second time round, things began to work out better. He overcame her token resistance, removed her clothes (he took special care not to tear or crease anything), and began to enjoy himself especially because he found confirmation of his belief that a well-planned scenario and practice make perfect. And Evelyn had a good body, too, maybe even better than Evelyn's. He undressed, and she was waiting, by now impatiently. He climbed into bed and reached out to restart the tape with the paso doble when the screams of police cars stopped him. They were approaching fast, slashing through the silence of the countryside and the small motel. Then brakes began to screech, and the ugly noise of skidding wheels completed Henry Claymore's fright. 'Oh my god,' he whispered as car doors were opened and slammed shut.

'What's the matter? It's only the fuzz.'

'They mustn't find me.' Footsteps came running. The banging of doors was now only a few rooms away.

'Hey, I thought you were regular ...'

'I'm married.'

'Most tricks are. That's no crime.'

What did she know? He jumped out of bed. 'I'll hide in the closet. Pretend you're alone.' Clumsily, he tried to gather up his clothes.

'Don't worry.' She felt sorry for him. 'If they wanna take anyone, it's gotta be me. Believe me.'

The door was kicked in. 'Police! Freeze!' Saul Robinson looked a big black nightmare even in daylight. His reputation was that he would obtain confessions without flashing a muscle or gun, even before asking the questions. Maxon was among the few who knew that Saul Robinson was liable to faint at the sight or smell of blood. Henry Claymore began to tremble. The girl got up to hold his hand. Robinson bellowed: 'You wanna die? I said freeze!'

'And we will, too, if you won't let us get dressed,' she shouted back.

'You gotta be searched for narcotics first.'

Five massive plain-clothes men and two more in uniform crowded the room. Robinson stepped back into the corridor and whispered to Maxon who was hidden from those inside: 'That's the guy, man. We're quits, right?'

'More or less.'

'He's all yours.' Robinson returned to the room, followed by Maxon who was recognised by Claymore right away. Before anything could be said, Maxon signalled to the naked man to keep his mouth shut, and turned to Robinson with the voice of authority: 'You'll have to let that one go, officer.'

'Is that an order, sir?' Robinson asked respectfully and, on Maxon's nod, shouted at Claymore: 'You! Get dressed and get out.'

'You see?' the girl made a gesture of resignation, 'tricks always get away.' She could not foresee that after a few minutes of free ogling, the whole ferocious bunch would leave quietly and let her go, too.

Henry Claymore finished dressing in Maxon's car. Maxon did not care much for his incessant tirades of gratitude, and even less for his inane excuses mixed with slimy man-to-man intimations. It obliterated any pity Maxon might have felt for the man on whom he had played a dirty trick. 'I mean it's no crime to be found with a girl, is it? You need a work-out now and then – and my way sure beats jogging.' He laughed. 'She doesn't know my real name, and we didn't do anything GLEW security wouldn't approve of, right?'

'You're damned lucky that I was there.'

'Lucky? I thought it was your job to look after people like me.'

That did it. Maxon pulled up braking so hard that Henry Claymore bumped his head against the windscreen. 'I'm not your fucking bodyguard, you know.'

'Now listen . . .'

'No, it's you who's got to listen, old son. You may not realise, but your secret whoring is a security risk.'

'I may have minor failings in my private life, but nobody will question my professional integrity.' He used strong words but they sounded like a cry for help.

'Well, what if the press got onto this little scene in the motel?'

'I won't be blackmailed.'

'Of course not. We'd never do such things. It's in our mutual interest to prevent headlines such as MAN WHO PRESSED NUCLEAR ALERT BUTTON CAUGHT IN VICE RAID. We can't have that, can we?' Maxon started the car again and let him stew. After less than a mile of silence, Henry Claymore grew soft and acquiescent.

'So what do you want from me?' he asked meekly.

'Co-operation.'

'You've got it.'

'Good. And it must remain strictly confidential. One word about our meeting, and you've had it.'

'I understand. Is it in connection with my job?'

'What else? And because I like you, Henry, I hope to God that you have nothing to hide. I mean that public alert might have been due to sabotage and we must be sure that you played your part right.'

'I've already been checked out and they know I did everything according to the book. So you're late.'

'Yes, old son, sometimes we're late, but we tend to catch up. So now you'll be checked out for the second time, and if I feel you're reluctant to co-operate, there'll be a third and a fourth time, and I promise you that you'll beg me to *let* you co-operate. So we'll just talk now for my peace of mind and your peace of home. So tell me, how exactly did it happen?'

'Just like a rehearsal, except that it was for real. You know the routine.'

'I do. But I want to hear it from you.'

'Well, I get the coded alert call from GLEW Center, SAC Omaha on land-line and radio simultaneously, check it back with the White House on a hotline, double-check it with my Number Two who receives the same signals independently, then we hook up the national network – and hey-ho, press override.'

'How long does that take?'

'In all? Ninety to a hundred and twenty seconds. Each move is clocked and logged every time to prove that every stage of the exercise ran smoothly.'

'Except that this was no exercise. So I'll have to see that log.'

'You can't. I ain't got access.'

'Then how will I know that the mistake wasn't yours?'

'What mistake?'

'I'm trying to help you, but I'm not authorised to put you in the picture. I hope you understand. But I must see proof that there hasn't been any slip up in the procedure and your efficiency. Because at some point there was, well, some mix-up.' Maxon was fishing. 'Kind of delay . . .'

'Not at our end. Look, the job is a bit of a bore at the best of times, thank god. We check, re-check and double-check all equipment, and rehearse routines so that we'd do it fast and right even in our sleep. So how can we can go wrong when we have a full hour to do it instead of ninety seconds?'

Maxon stared ahead in a state of shock without seeing the road. Luckily, nothing was coming from the opposite direction. The car began to slow down – he did not even notice that his foot had slipped off the throttle. 'An hour? What do you mean an hour?'

'The advance warning. You know, to make sure that this time the public alert was coordinated perfectly.'

An hour warning meant that the B-men had been alerted long before the missiles were launched and GLEW satellites detected the attack. The information must have come from Sarian – via Locke! But then . . . then how was it possible that the public alert *did* slip through? Was it meant to? The car stopped. Maxon's eyes tailed the windscreen wipers as if expecting to read off the answers from some miraculous head-up display. But only one name kept flashing through his mind: General Larry Locke Junior ... General Larry Locke Junior ... Maxon hardly noticed that he had started thinking aloud: 'And you got the advance warning from the general ...'

'What general?'

'Locke, of course.'

'But I couldn't take orders from him. It's against regulations. You know that.'

'Of course I do. But that must have been the mistake you made. You broke the regulations. You accepted Locke's word and now you must accept responsibility.'

'Listen to me, please. I've never even talked to the general until he came to inspect the log *after* the alert! After! And I can prove it. Because this time, when the advance warning came through, I checked back, well, sort of privately with SAC Omaha, I mean GLEW Center.'

'Who did you talk to?'

'Tucker.'

'Biggles Tucker?'

'Sure thing. He confirmed it. .... Hey! You oughta know all this! You look surprised ... I wanna see your authorisation ...'

Maxon reached across. Claymore backed away as far as he could because he thought he would be punched. But Maxon only opened the door for him: 'Get out.'

'What? Here?'

'Yes. And you mention this conversation to anyone even in your sleep without my permission, and you're dead.'

'I won't. I promise.'

'Good. Now get out.'

Reluctantly, Claymore put one foot through the door. 'It's raining. ... We're miles from anywhere ...'

'Walking does you good. You missed your work-out back at the motel.'

Maxon drove off at high speed. He had already forgotten about Claymore standing helplessly in the rain. His mind was on Locke. It had to be the general who gave Tucker the order. But that was impossible to prove. GLEW Center personnel was far beyond Maxon's reach, even if he knew Tucker, even if it was on his recommendation that Tucker got the job.

# VII

Maxon knew it was crazy to walk into the forest, unarmed, at night, offering an opportunity to anyone who cared to take a pot-shot at him, but he had no choice if he wanted to meet Chuck Parkin without any further delay. And time was what he could least afford when he felt that an EMP, predicted by Ellsberg, and war might be imminent.

It was Saul Robinson who obtained Parkin's unlisted home number for him. The presidential aide began to sound jittery when Maxon identified himself, but to his credit, did not refuse to listen. When he hesitated and tried to stall, if only to make better arrangements for a rendezvous, Maxon trotted out with a wild statement to demolish his reluctance: 'I've got proof of sabotage at high places.' Beyond that, Parkin would be only too anxious to get off the line. His problem was how to get away from his driver/bodyguard. The solution he could think of was not entirely satisfactory, but it had the persuasive merit of being the only one. He was due to play his weekly poker game with friends that night. He would explain, evoking winks of approval, that he had to meet a 'demanding lady' urgently, would slip out of the house with their connivance through the garden, and borrow a car that would be of no interest to his CIA watcher. He would meet Maxon a few miles away, at a spot they both knew because it was close to the road leading to the CIA hospital, near Langley.

Maxon was early. He parked his car in the bushes and walked the last half a mile, hoping that only a professional tracker could stay on his tail. But a meet is only as safe as the precautions taken by the least careful party, in this case, Chuck Parkin, who left the red, borrowed Porsche in full view on the road, and charged through the trees in total oblivion of the patrols in the area. He arrived at the picnic spot puffing heavily from the short run, collapsed on a bench, put his foot on a brick barbecue, and opened with the off-putting remark: 'I've got no time.'

In the distance, the friendly Alsatians ringing the hospital barked in wild bursts, and Maxon needed no other encouragement to be brief. He gave a précis of his conversation with General Sarian. He emphasised the fact that advance information on the missile test had been available from the defector, and he made no attempt to minimise the heavy insinuations against Locke. It was Locke who had received the advance warning, it was Locke who had prevented Maxon from interviewing Sarian.

Chuck Parkin looked as stunned as Maxon had been at Windyridge. And Maxon's report on Henry Claymore and the seemingly deliberate public alert was yet to follow. Parkin stared into the darkness as if forgetting Maxon's presence. But when he spoke, he voice was crisp and his tone had a cutting edge: 'You do realise that what you've just said is bound to ruin either you or General Locke.'

'I know. That's why I must prove or disprove my suspicions. And that's why I need your help.'

'What help?'

'Henry Claymore checked back the advance warning with GLEW Center, SAC Omaha. He spoke to Tucker. Squadron Leader "Biggles" Tucker. The question is, who gave the advance warning to Tucker? My guess is that it came from Locke. Tucker could confirm or deny this. That's why I must talk to him. I know him. I know I can get it out of him. But I need help to get to Omaha.'

'Forget it. That's the one place where even I could go only with a long preparation and full justification. It's not on, Maxon. You'll have to meet Tucker elsewhere. Can't you set up a rendezvous?'

'No. That's an essential part of the job. And I know: I got it for him. He had to agree to a life of almost total segregation for five years. But you may find it easier to get me in there than go yourself. If you used your White House influence and CIA contacts . . .'

'Yes, Maxon, if. But I can't decide this here and now. I must make some inquiries. And you must accept that I may have to hand this over to the relevant authorities.'

'Agreed.'

'Because Locke may have a perfectly legitimate explanation for everything.'

'I know.'

'And in that case, you'll be accused of treason, slander,

subversion, the works, you do understand, don't you?'

'I do.' Maxon smiled: his answers sounded like marriage vows. Although he did not feel like laughing, he was too tired to do anything but smile.

Parkin shifted, preparing to leave, but fired a last salvo of questions at Maxon: 'Why did you come to me?'

'Because I've run out of choices.'

'Because you trust me?'

'Yes, that, too.'

'But why me? Why not someone else?'

'Because I happen to know that you pressed for answers when you believed that GLEW had been compromised. And I know that you weren't afraid to reconsider your interpretation of facts. And I know that you may have access to everyone, including the President. And above all, you're not the only contact in high places I've tried, but you're the only one who's been willing to listen, at least, to my messages. Through Mrs Kowalski, for instance.'

'I'll see what I can do,' said Parkin gravely. They both knew that a patriotic pursuit of this kind was bound to verge on treason. And there was no way to tell how high up in the Administration they would have to reach for evidence. 'You must promise me to do nothing until you hear from me.'

'I can't wait *ad infinitum*.'

'Give me three days.'

Maxon was willing to promise that much. He would not keep his word, but in the circumstances, he was ready to lie, cheat and kill if necessary. He gave Parkin the number of a London telephone answering service that would take messages for a Mrs Welles. 'The message must contain nothing but details for a meet, the place in Britain, America or wherever, and we'll meet five days and three hours *before* the appointed date and time.'

Major Sleet was furious: he was pressed incessantly for reports on Maxon, but every time he managed to pick up the scent he was told to hold back. This time he complained to Sandy himself who turned out to be uncharacteristically discourteous, reminding him in no uncertain terms that he must do as he was told, that was what he was paid for. Sleet could not guess that Sandy himself might live under similar pressures, and feel equally frustrated, being unaccustomed to acting as anybody's messenger boy. Sandy was, in fact, exceptionally rude to his subordinate because life was exceptionally rude to him. 'Mine is not a service department to any security upstart,' his thoughts screamed, 'and I'm no unquestioning executive arm to any foreign con-man who seems to enjoy the blessing of Number Ten itself for whatever reason.' What the hell was Locke's game, anyway? What was his power base? Why couldn't he make up his mind about Maxon? Was there something wrong with Maxon or not? Should he or shouldn't he be pulled in and interrogated?

No, Sandy had no doubt that Locke was the newly-rich in the high society of intelligence circles. And he had less than no doubt that the man would do anything to get ahead. He recalled a conversation with Maxon. Over lunch at the Reform, he had mentioned Lord Acton's famous observation that 'power tends to corrupt, and absolute power corrupts absolutely,' and Maxon had argued that it was 'the *lack* and *desire* of absolute power that corrupt absolutely'. So what power was Locke chasing when he already had or at least seemed to have the President's ear and the full backing of Sir Gerald, intelligence overlord, the PM's security adviser?

It had been an extraordinary week in KGB collator Antonin Kobelyev's life. It had begun with the delivery of a BC202, his own, personal computer terminal – a distinction he regarded as being on par with a Hero of the Soviet Union medal. The terminal was the toy of his dreams, a status symbol, a lover. He spent two days and two nights pressing keys, conjuring up old files, 'dead' items of gossip, data sheets, fact boxes, 'suspicions' proven and unproven.

On the third day of his exuberant affair with the keyboard, he had rechecked the files on Maxon. He had stumbled onto Ellsberg's name again and again. His curiosity drove him to look up Ellsberg's records and learn as much as possible about his now dead idol. Under the heading 'Toronto, Trade mission', Kobelyev found a complete list of Ellsberg's secret communications with the Centre and other Soviet authorities. There was all the agent's 'input', the reports he had submitted, and the 'withdrawals', information Ellsberg had asked for. Tucked away among endless routine traffic and trivia (secret only by habit), Kobelyev found an exciting item: Ellsberg had asked for and received the Kowalski file – and Kobelyev remembered that this was under severe restrictions. He also noted an unexplained upsurge of communications between Ellsberg and Lt Colonel Vorodin who had once been, Kobelyev remembered, an Ellsberg protégé. All the dates but not the contents of these communications were recorded. That in itself was no oddity, and it was mere routine for Kobelyev to run a cross-check, nothing but yet another game with the new toy.

Vorodin's file was not particularly extensive. A bright young man, he had been moved from military to home intelligence, highly praised by Ellsberg, and eventually transferred to work on Marshal Beryov's personal staff. The record did not show if Vorodin continued to have a KGB assignment in his new position, but Kobelyev assumed that inevitably, that would be the case. There was, however, something else the record did not contain: any reference to the communications with Ellsberg. If the exchanges had been deleted as something of no importance, why were they not deleted from Ellsberg's records, too? Kobelyev wrote a brief report about it for no good reason other than providing further proof of the terminal's value to him.

On the sixth day of this week of happiness, the colonel from disinformation told him to stay in his office until further notice. Soon after ten in the evening, the colonel and two guards brought in a virtually unrecognisable prisoner. One of his eyes had completely disappeared under hugely swollen, dark bruises, the other eye was red, watering incessantly. The mouth was lopsided, it kept drivelling through the black hole where teeth should have been. The hands were shaking, the body had to be kept upright by the guards, and there was little to reveal that this was supposed to be a young man. The wreck was addressed as Vorodin. Kobelyev was not a squeamish man, he knew that in this building, enemies of the state would not be treated kindly, but he had never come face to face with any prisoners.

All Kobelyev had to do was to help the colonel checking some dates, references and contacts in Vorodin's confession. The prisoner needed hardly any prodding by now, but in the next fifteen minutes, Kobelyev would learn to hate his new love and curse the day when computers and terminals had been invented. The machine proved Vorodin guilty of lies, omissions and forgetfulness. He apologised. Before leaving, the colonel gave Kobelyev the usual warnings to keep his mouth shut, and praised him lavishly for his good work uncovering the traitor Vorodin. Kobelyev could not afford to show how embarrassing he found it to feel responsible for it all.

Vorodin was then taken back to his cell. He had already confessed that it was one of his duties to brief Beryov on the daily progress of preparations for an EMP test, that he was fully familiar with the plans, that he had told Ellsberg about them, and that he had sought Ellsberg's advice on how one could prevent the test and the likelihood of war. He claimed that Ellsberg had never told him what he would do with the information. But that had still to be confirmed. He also confessed to the colonel that he had promised Ellsberg some sort of proof of the plan, but insisted that the proof had never been obtained or delivered. That, too, had to be checked, and so the colonel knew that there would be many more questions Vorodin must be persuaded to answer.

The colonel had no doubt that Ellsberg must have passed the information to Maxon, but beyond that he could only guess to whom Maxon would have reported it and how seriously it would have been taken without actual proof. And guesswork was not good enough. As far as he knew, the best chance to find out would be through Maxon himself, a man who had already been compromised, rather successfully, according to reports from London and Washington. Question: was this the right time to approach Maxon? If yes, question: who should make the approach? Certainly not that stupid Vanek: he had once been caught by Maxon; he had created the embarrassing legend of a Maxon-Gerry-the-Bang connection but panicked and, fearful of recognition, battered the safe-cracker to death; and he had made a bit of a mess of the killing of Kowalski's Canadian watcher. No, Vanek was out of reckoning for making the crucial contact with Maxon.

Five times a day Maxon left dummy messages with the answering service for Mrs Welles, and five times a day Jack collected them – but there was still nothing from Chuck Parkin. Using public telephones, Maxon also called Edie at least once a day (and rang off every time well before anyone could trace the call), but she had nothing for him either (except complaints about her own health and various ill-mannered visitors who would not leave their names or any messages).

Maxon tried to make some inquiries but found most of his channels blocked: people seemed to dodge him or refused outright any contact with him. His bank account had been blocked by Major Sleet, and although his bank manager, an old friend, sounded apologetic on the phone, his tone indicated that Gloucester had been right saying 'you're bad news, sport'.

Halfway through the third day after the meet with Chuck Parkin, Maxon began to drink heavily and consider the last resorts open to him, including some of the craziest schemes he could think of. Jack tried in vain to slow down his rate of alcohol intake, and as *her* last resort, she drank with him to leave less to him in the bottle: their Wembley hide-out had only limited supplies. She also suggested a final attempt at approaching Sandy, the Prime Minister and the White House.

'Too late. Who'd believe me?' His bitterness frightened her. 'Maxon stinks, you remember? Doesn't everybody seem to know that I'm in trouble? Suppose I broke into Downing Street, what would I tell the PM? That something looks fishy, that I suspect Locke of something which I can't fully define, that there's something wrong with the timing of that public alert – who'd believe me? And why should they? Leaders at the very top are always disinclined to accept and act upon the best intelligence reports because the best is always the most unexpected, and the truth tends to be the least palatable. These things don't fit in. They're a nuisance. Didn't Hitler refuse to believe that D-Day was the real McCoy? Didn't Stalin pooh-pooh reports from Sorge *and* the Red Orchestra that the Nazis were about to attack? The information had come from the best, it was of the highest quality, and it was disregarded again and again, like the warning about Pearl Harbour. No, it's no good to go to anyone without irrefutable evidence.'

Looking for ways to find and contact Tucker, Maxon drew up basic organisation charts of GLEW – only to burn and flush them down before even Jack would catch a glimpse of them. Unfortunately for him as well as, presumably, for the Russians, the very simplicity of the system reduced the number of possible penetration points. Most of the work was automated anyway, computers communicating with computers, checking themselves and their correspondents, cutting out the frail and fallible human element.

Maxon recalled one of his security visits to the GLEW station on Diego Garcia, the minuscule atoll in the Chagos Archipelago. He had had to travel under commercial cover to Port Louis, in Mauritius, from where a local agent, the owner of some dubious flying machine, was to arrange his passage halfway across the Indian Ocean. Maxon had been on time and sat, as arranged, in a cafe opposite Government House, facing a corpulent lady of stone. The inscription at her feet declared proudly that she was Queen Victoria, 'Our beloved and much regretted sovereign,' which was Maxon's only cause for amusement; for he did not find it funny at all that the agent failed to turn up that day, and the next, and the third. Maxon sent a cable to Locke – and it took a full twenty-four hours to get the answer which, on decoding, made his blood pressure surge: 'Skylark in Red Square. Stay put. Your contact usually survives his crashes. Good luck.' So Maxon had to wait, with a flimsy cover story, at a time when Mauritius must have been swarming with Soviet agents anxious to find out more about GLEW.

Eventually the intrepid pilot materialised and arranged a nightmarish journey to Diego Garcia, where another shock awaited Maxon. The entire staff of the key GLEW station consisted of two half-coherent drunks and their garrulous Irish-American technical expert who kindly intimated to Maxon that there was no security risk there, because nobody knew, indeed, needed to know, anything: 'We receive signals from satellites direct, and also from other listening stations in Guam, Fylingdale, Miami, Iceland, the Cape – you name it, sir, we receive from it and also send to it. Yes, sir, we also send direct signals even to Omaha, if you please. We're part of the grand circuit that transmits and exchanges information of the greatest value, just don't ask us what it is, no, sir, because it's not for us mortals to know. Only the computers are privy to it all, and only they, may the Lord bless them, are accountable to holy Strategic Air Command, Omaha.'

That was the first time that Maxon submitted his request for an immediate transfer or, alternatively, offered his resignation. Then, as on several other occasions, Locke, Sandy and once even the Prime Minister's office talked him out of it.

The state of affairs was no better at other GLEW stations Maxon was required to check out but, he had to admit, the system functioned without a hitch. There were no complaints, not a single suspected security leak had ever been reported until the Russians tried to implicate Kowalski, and when Maxon took computer tape samples to the leading specialists outside GLEW, they remained baffled by the transmissions. (The experiment had been unauthorised, and it caused a great deal of embarrassment when the experts he had consulted began to demand access to GLEW technology and, particularly, the magical breakthrough with these high-speed computers.)

So now, facing the problem the Russians must have faced, Maxon was at a loss: the circulating GLEW satellite communications remained nothing but electronic garbage until they were decoded; this was done only at Omaha; while access to SAC Omaha seemed impossible, access to GLEW Centre within that was a non-starter of an idea; yet it was only at Omaha that anybody could confirm or deny that Locke himself had warned them in advance, and that the alert had been a premeditated one by him alone. It was a vicious circle. Maxon decided that it was time, once again, to resort to optimism: that was how bad the situation looked to him. He asked Jack to call the answering service more and more frequently, but there was still no message from Chuck Parkin.

After the departure of the last group of processed tourists, the Kremlin was at its silent best. A paling sun, cooler than a winter moon, lent some glitter to the gilded domes. The sheet of glass atop the *Nachalnik*'s partners' desk reflected a balmy skyscape surrounded by eyes of anxiety that might befit a Goya execution scene. The *Nachalnik* glanced from face to face around the inner circle of his Politburo. 'What would Josip Vissarionovich do with this bunch?' he asked himself. 'Would he eat them alive or make them stars in Comrade Obrazcov's unique puppet theatre?' He found himself thinking more and more about Stalin. It gave him a masochistic pleasure to recognise that he was no Stalin, and to recall the all too obvious moments of his rule whenever he had failed to consolidate his powers through killings. Now it was too late, even though he liked to hold his immediate associates responsible for what was to come.

'We need a Sorge, comrades, a man who's not afraid of telling us the truth, who'd bring us the fresh air of intelligence.' The eyes around the table refused to meet his. 'Yes, we need a new Red Orchestra, but until we find at least a red string quartet, we'll have to rely on your *expert* recommendations.'

It had already been agreed that a minimal EMP explosion remained the only option to retain the momentum of their global peace-time strategy, because an EMP alone could cripple GLEW and regain Soviet space superiority. But EMP needed a test to tell them how small a force could be regarded as minimal to do the job of knocking out GLEW without incapacitating Soviet warning and communications systems, too. The test would be done within seven days, depending on the elimination of last-minute hitches in the programme.

About the potential consequences nobody in the room had any doubts. The missile forces would go on full alert only three hours before the test to avoid detection by spies on the ground or satellites. The rest of the vast war machinery would simply be ignored: if the west reacted in the extreme, there would be no build-up, no threats and mobilisation of conventional forces, it would be an all-out exchange within fifteen minutes after the EMP. The question was: how much room had remained for political manoeuvering?

'Although *technically* we'll be in breach of the space treaty,' the *Nachalnik* appeared to be thinking aloud, 'we certainly don't want war. We don't want to start it, but we do want to minimise the chance for the American warmongers to unleash their nuclear hounds.

'We have two courses proposed to us. Comrade Beryov, the missile forces and some of our best military thinkers would like to see a strictly political move. It is suggested that in the last possible moment, I should call the President on the hot line, beg his forgiveness and assure him that the test about to happen is not really a test but a technical hitch for which heads will roll.

'On the other hand, the security services would prefer a timetable to allow the test to coincide with the Chinese space flights next week. We could then blame Peking for the EMP and support the west wholeheartedly in the condemnation of the Chinese warmongers. In fact, we could warn the President, saying that we have information on Chinese plans for an EMP. An appealing concept – more's the pity that our missile forces object to it on technical grounds . . .'

'No-no, it's not quite technical,' Beryov protested.

'Then is it perhaps on ideological grounds?'

'Certainly not. Most certainly not.' Beryov paled: ideological objections would have meant he was siding with the Chinese, a capital sin. 'Our objections have been due to the . . ,' he paused for a deep breath: taking on the director of the KGB was a risk he did not relish as a prospect, 'to the question about the quality of the intelligence available to us. After all, we've been told that GLEW personnel could be approached and GLEW itself could be compromised. Yet we still know nothing about GLEW, we've not managed to entice a single man in the know, and we're now given to understand that traitors on our side might have warned the Americans that an EMP test was imminent. I'll not go into the question of the traitor Vorodin's KGB credentials, because the main problem is: what is happening on the other side? If they know about the EMP, they must be ready and waiting for us to move. They would have an excuse to hit us with everything.'

'You mean you want us to hold back?' the *Nachalnik* asked with surprise in his voice for the first time. But Beryov was not to disappoint him with unexpected sobriety:

'On the contrary. We must go ahead in that case. We can't afford not to. For they'd see us as cowards, and treat us as such in the future.'

'You're forgetting,' the Director said quietly, 'that our operation concerning GLEW personnel is still in progress. We may, in fact, achieve fruitful contact with a key man in their security network.' He viewed Beryov with open contempt: the man still failed to understand the powers at

201

work or guess that the Mad Monk had enough information on the skeletons in his life to 'tread on him and crush him like grapes in a tub until pips of shit came shooting through his ears.' He now turned to the *Nachalnik*: 'As for comrade Beryov's concern about the secrets which Vorodin, *his* personal aide, gave away, well, it's understandable ... but not quite logical. It fails to take a number of points into consideration. For we've still got serious doubts that *any* information on EMP has ever reached the President. We have some means to interfere, now and then, with their internal transmission and evaluation of intelligence, and we've got our ears to the ground over there. Yet we've heard nothing. Don't you think there would have been urgent security conferences, consultations with their allies, major policy decisions, military preparations and the commencement of an alert count-down, etcetera, etcetera, if they really knew about our plan?'

This was a good opportunity to cut the Director down to size. 'On the other hand,' the *Nachalnik* said in his best headmaster tone, 'they might think that we've merely planted false information through *apparent* traitors, and decided that this time, they'd try to call the bluff.'

Nobody ventured to answer that and break the silence of collective responsibility. Besides, nobody knew if all this essential bluffing was about to go a bluff too far.


Gloucester regarded it as an exceptional favour that Sandy was willing to see him so promptly. When he said as much, Sandy dismissed it with an airy remark that he liked to return favours, but initially refused to give his visitor a chance to talk about anything but the quality of tea he served – Darjeeling, as always.

'Look, I do not wish to interfere with things that are none of my business ...'

'Good,' Sandy interrupted before the sentence could continue with an inevitable 'but'. 'I'm glad. Is that too weak for you? I like weak tea.'

'So do I, Sandy, so do I, indeed, but ... er ...'

'All right,' Sandy sighed, reluctantly, 'say it if you must.'

'Look, you know I help you gladly every time you ask me to, but I don't enjoy doing the dirty on a friend.'

'Nobody does, dear boy, no, but sometimes, we all have to make sacrifices, willingly or unwittingly. And I can't allow exceptions even for Maxon. More tea?'

'But you could . . .'

'Do something? Yes, perhaps I could, but would it be right?' And he resisted mouthing his next question that had long been on his mind: would Sir Gerald and the rest whom Sandy called the headboys and prefects of the service allow him to do something for Maxon? For he knew the answer would be 'no', at least until he could prove to them that Locke was the wrong man to use, treat, maltreat, clear, smear, promote or eliminate Maxon.

A peculiar whizzing sound invaded the room. A small, piercing light began to flash on a red telephone. Gloucester volunteered to leave the room while Sandy took the call.

It was Locke on the line. He wanted to know if there was any news about Maxon.

'He's dropped out of sight yet again, I'm afraid.'

'I'm surprised that you let him, but I'm sure you'd have a perfectly good explanation if your Prime Minister asked you for one. As a matter of interest, have you got one? Or would it be easier to offer some excuses?'

Sandy tried to put his answer as softly as possible, but to his annoyance, this was the second time that his words sounded uncharacteristically sharp: 'I do not think that I'm actually accountable to you, general.'

Locke laughed. 'No-no, no offence, but it can't hurt to be prepared. Mind you, an organisation that managed to produce an "explanation" for Philby and co. would surely find excuses for letting Maxon drop out of sight.'

Sandy was now in full control of himself and refused to engage in any slanging match. When the time came, and it must, he knew, he would make up for lost ground. 'I'm sure we'll pick up his trail when necessary. Would you like me to pull him in?'

'No. But I want to know where he is and what he is up to. I'll contact you when I get to London.'

'I'll leave a message for you, Larry, in the Needle on Sunday morning. You'll have your usual suite, won't you?' Sandy could not resist that: he was pleased that Locke sounded surprised about his advance knowledge of the visit – it helped to even the score.

As soon as Locke was off the line, Sandy decided to take

it upon himself to put a few questions to Maxon. He called Major Sleet: 'I want you to bring in Maxon.'

'But . . .'

'No buts. I know you've lost him. Find him. You said he calls his housekeeper every day. And I know he cares about her. Well, think of something. If, for instance, you arrange for her to go into hospital, he may take the bait . . .'

Chuck Parkin used to do voluntary work in hospitals. He now reaped the benefit of his good deeds: he recognised symptoms and knew he was on the verge of cracking up. Only three days ago, he could not have believed that he would ever stop enjoying food, lose his appetite or need to resort to handfuls of valium. But then, only three days ago, he had been just an ordinary highly-strung administrator, feeling the weight of the world's future on his shoulders, and scared by the threat of war, whereas now he knew that he, perhaps he alone, might get killed. He tried to cheer up by telling himself that a bullet in the back would be quick and painless, and the thrust of a knife might at least loosen up that dreadful cramp in his stomach, but it was no good, he knew he had nothing to joke about. He wished he had never joined the Rotarians through whom he met Bob, the local guy with big ambitions, never organised a presidential compaign, never heard of a man called Ellsberg, and if all this was impossible to undo, at least that he should have never talked to that man Maxon.

After the meet in the forest, Chuck Parkin made some urgent inquiries. The more he discovered the less he liked the news and his own predicament. First he put out feelers to see if he could get Maxon into SAC Omaha, if not GLEW Center itself. The result was a flat 'negative'. He then had dinner with his cousin, his only trusted sterling contact in the CIA. The dinner was excellent – Parkin could not have eaten more if he had known that it would be his last decent, fully appreciated meal for a long time – and the cousin was full of deliciously malicious gossip about the life of the highest echelons in the Company. But when the two men returned to the chic Georgetown apartment which Parkin retained for extramarital engagements, and settled down with a bottle of Remy Martin VSOP, the light mood of the night took a dramatic turn. The cousin first refused to discuss anything connected with General Locke, then took Parkin so excessively in his confidence that the presidential aide wished he had never suggested dinner in the first place. For apparently the cousin had had his own personal clashes with Locke, and there were several other high-ranking spooks who would have liked to peep a little deeper into the general's status and affairs, but the consensus of White House watchers' opinion was that 'any dirt on Locke could easily rub off on the seat of power itself'.

'You're not suggesting . . .'

'I'm not suggesting anything. But once Bob shared a tent with Larry Locke, and they've been like this,' he interlocked his hairy fingers, 'ever since. Now some people would suggest that there might be a mighty lot to be discovered about the ways of the Oval Office, but would *you* like to be the one to try?'

'I don't know anything,' said Parkin, and it was almost true. For he did know that his nervous indigestion suddenly reached up to his throat and he would have to commit the ultimate sacrilege of drinking Alka Seltzer as a chaser to a good cognac.

On the second morning after the meet, Parking worked on his weekly security summary for the President, although he did not believe that Bob would ever bother to read his briefings: it was no secret any more that Parkin's real job was to work on the re-election. In the reports he now summarised, there were two independent references (from usually reliable sources) to Soviet preparations for 'some atmospheric test that, it is rumoured, may turn out to be an EMP'. That would support the information from Ellsberg, and strengthen Maxon's case.

Later that day, Parkin chatted up the most talkative White House aides. With blatant flattery, he asked them about *their* views, as opposed to the President's, on the international scene. He knew full well that either their views prevailed in decision-making or they were merely a presidential echo-chamber, but certainly they would never say anything that would clash with the Oval Office. The answers were yet another devastating blow to Parkin. It became clear that if the Russians did anything 'extraordinary', anything to rock the boat or upset outright the status quo, the President would want to hit them hard. He could not afford not to. He had been elected on a 'stop the Russians, not a step back' programme, and now it was re-election time. Parkin knew that Bob was a born leader, a man to whom leadership meant more than the direction in which he led his flock, he would lead them always straight ahead even if the route was circular, and his motto was that 'if the Red Sea won't part, we'll have to swim across or drink it dry'. Which was good for elections, but would it be good for shaping a response to an EMP? It puzzled Parkin why nobody around Bob seemed to take a view of greater gravity of the EMP rumours.

In the evening, the CIA cousin showed Parkin a confidential file on Locke. There was nothing definite against the general in there, but his Middle East career background could be construed to spell out a potential motive for acting the way he seemed to act.

Parkin was now paralysed with fear and disinclined to help Maxon in any way. But that night he had a totally unexpected and ill-explained telephone call from Locke. No, no special reason, just wanted to check Parkin's views on this and that as a security information co-ordinator. The call was so pointless that it could not fail to be menacing. Did Locke know about his recent inquiries? Or about his access to the file? Was this alertness a proof of Locke's guilt? A guilt of some kind shared with someone at the very, very top? If so, they would have ears everywhere and could get any Nosy Parkin killed before investigations got anywhere. At this point, Parkin got so frightened that he became ashamed of it – and shame was often the decisive factor in his life. No, he could not run away from the challenge and live with the memory.

On the third day after the meet with Maxon, he arranged a London visit as a surprise for his wife 'to celebrate the twenty-second anniversary of their sleeping together for the first time.' (She was delighted and praised him for remembering: there was no point in ruining the trip by telling him that he had got both the date and the year wrong.)

The reason for delaying the call to Maxon's message service was that Parkin had to choose a meeting place. He persuaded his wife to give an embassy friend's son a treat and take him to the Zoo. He then suggested that perhaps the child could be entertained by the monkeys – while he, on his own, could look at some other attractions that might frighten the little boy. It was, of course, a silly excuse, but he knew his wife was too wise to ask questions.

Parkin greeted Maxon with apologies in the green light of the reptile house: 'I hope it's not too inconvenient ... I mean the venue.'

'On the contrary. In my line of business, one gets summoned to venues like the Zoo all too infrequently.'

Parkin hesitated, then allowed himself a smile. 'If I didn't find your remark amusing, I'd think you were impertinent.'

'I'm glad you know I wasn't, sir. Because I take it you're here to help me.'

'It's rather limited what I can do, but I'll do my utmost. I've just seen further reports that Ellsberg might have been right. It seems they're actually preparing an EMP. Wish I knew why.'

'They're trying to restore the balance. GLEW opened a gap which they won't be able to close until they launch their battle stations with laser guns in space. The test is just another lap in this Marathon.'

'Marathon? It's a downhill race which can't be stopped without a terrible jolt. And if we can't stop, we've got a war nobody wanted. Like the First World War. Henry was right.' Parkin disliked Kissinger whom he saw as everything he was not. He was, however, frank enough with himself to admit that he envied the man for some of his thoughts. He now tried to resist getting carried away on one of his favourite hobby horses, but he blurted out some of it. 'Yeah, Henry said the trouble was in 1914 that military planning drove decisions, while bluster and posturing drove diplomacy. Now I'm not keen on political wheeler-dealers who can't leave philosophy to the philosophers – or on philosophers who fancy themselves selling panacea to the natives,' he chuckled, 'but for once, Henry got it right and got me scared.' Behind the glass, a boa constrictor moved, and Parkin backed away.

'Perhaps you scare easy.'

'I guess so. Particularly when the roles are reversed and presidents dabble in military planning while the military start posturing and spooks like Locke play politics.'

'Any reason why?'

'Just a guess. He's been associated closely with key Moslem powers throughout his career. His best friends and contacts are Moslem leaders and oil potentates, I hear.'

Involuntarily, Maxon glanced around. Nobody was standing near them, nobody had been tailing them. The entrance of the reptile house was watched by Jack, and there had been no warning from her. He did not want to stay long with Parkin, but he had to find out more, if possible, about Locke. 'That's a pretty serious accusation, sir, I'm sure you realise.'

'In the America where I hail from, we don't treat accusations lightly. But originally, it was you who tried to hint things about Locke. So now I offer you an explanation. It may help you to keep in mind that all underhand activities must have beneficiaries. So what about the Arabs? Wouldn't it serve the wildest dreams of the oil-powers to be spectators at an east-west confrontation in the extreme?'

'You mean war.'

'If you like.'

Maxon tried to provoke him to say more: 'No, Locke couldn't swing events on such a scale even if he wanted to.'

'He has the President's ear.'

'And you resent that, sir, do you?'

'That's bullshit. And you're wrong if you think that this meeting is some position-jockeying among bickering presidential advisers. I made up my mind to help you. But I can't get you into Omaha. So what can I do?'

'First you must stop doing any investigation on your own account. No, please, don't be offended and don't interrupt me. You're not trained to do the job. You'll only call attention to yourself and then you won't be any good to me.'

'Now listen, Maxon, the fact that I happen to concur with your conclusions . . .'

'*You* concur, sir, but *I* beg to differ. I haven't drawn any conclusions. Not yet. And if we're to work together, it must be on my terms. Because it's me who's already risked everything. It's me who's on the run and has even had his bank account frozen. So it's you who must listen and stay in the clear if you really want to be of any use.'

Parkin began to sweat profusely. He did not even try to blame the heat of the reptile house for it. 'Okay, what do you want from me?'

'First I'll need some money. Say, three thousand will do for starters. No, make it four, I must buy new passports in the open market, and they must be good. Then I'll need some info. on a Squadron Leader J G "Biggles" Tucker. He's a widower, working at GLEW Centre.'

'I don't think I can get access to GLEW personnel files.'

'I know you can't. But if you play your cards right, you may get a chance to see his basic RAF service record. Find some reason for it.'

'I can do it through the air attaché at the embassy. And I don't need to give him excuses. So what do you want from it?'

'His daughter's address. She's at some boarding school.'

'School? How old is she?'

'Eight? Nine? Ten? Does it matter?'

'It does to me if you want to get to Tucker through the child.'

'Don't worry. She wouldn't even know where he is. But she'd have a post box address and a phone number, probably MoD, for emergencies. ... Don't look so disgusted, I won't wring the kid's neck ...'

'It's just that if you can get to key personnel in such ways, what's the guarantee that the Russians couldn't?'

'None whatsoever. They could do exactly the same if they knew as much as I do about the system.'

'Judging from experience, that would leave us with very slender hopes indeed.'

'Judging from experience, their best intelligence would be disregarded.'

The cramp in Parkin's stomach turned into a vice, squeezing his guts towards his throat. The green light did not improve his sickly appearance. If he dies, Maxon thought, his green ghost will haunt me forever. He gave him the number of another answering service to memorise. 'Leave only a date and time – and we meet two days and four hours before. Let's make the venue the aviary this time, okay? It'll be a change, I hope you concur.'

In the first of the past twenty-four hours, the London underworld had stirred like the fauna of dry forests at the initial whiffs of smoke from a distant, invisible bushfire. Ears were pricked up, heads turned nervously, favourite haunts remained deserted as if the beer had run out, old lags lay low forgoing the best chances of rich pickings, petty thieves went hungry, and juvenile delinquents retreated in all directions having no idea from where the threat had come. By nightfall everybody knew the heat was on. Police seemed to swoop on suspects, likely wrongdoers and temporary innocents alike. Nobody had any doubt that the law wanted someone badly, and that there would be no peace until that someone was in the net.

Narks were activated from both ends: police pressed them hard and offered to pay extra for information on a man called Maxon. Hardly anybody had heard of him but moneyed grey eminences urged the informers to give freely anything they could pick up – a harassed, hungry police force was bad for business.

Major Sleet, guest of the Special Branch, sat in a cell-bare room at the Yard and kept gazing at a dusty telephone until his eyes began to water: perhaps if he showed enough resolution, the phone might ring before he had to blink. The ploy with using Edie had failed. Incoming calls had been misrouted from Maxon's home number, and when Maxon's daily call came through to an office at the Hampstead police station, it was answered by a policewoman's death rattle and pleas for urgent help. Maxon took the bait, his immediate despair was obvious, but instead of running to the house, he alerted the police, the ambulance service and, for good measure, the fire brigade with some cock-and-bull story of an old woman being trapped, injured, in a burning room. If Maxon was there to witness the wailing arrival and angry departure of all the services, he would now be warned to be on his guard even more.

Maxon, in fact, had been at the house. The sight of the commotion and the presence of Sleet's men convinced him he must leave the Wembley hide-out as soon as better arrangements could be made. Samantha, that delightfully devious friend offered him her luxury pad inside the marina at the foot of the Tower. Maxon decided to move in there the morning after his meet with Chuck Parkin.

That night, at two in the morning, the Hendon police CID duty sergeant received a courtesy visit from Foxy, the late safecracker Houlihan's mate. He said he might, just might have information on Maxon's whereabouts.

'Let's have it then.'

'People say it could be worth some readies, is that true, sarge?'

'Could be.'

'They say a hundred, maybe . . .'

'Maybe . . .'

Foxy gave him the address: the death of Gerry the Bang would be avenged. The sergeant paid him fifty and made him sign for a hundred pounds. Foxy went through the motions of looking disappointed, but he did not really care for he had already pocketed fifty pounds from the Indian slave-merchant who was keen on restoring peace in Wembley by flushing the intruder out of his lair.

Sleet was alerted. He left the Yard in a hurry to make the arrest. This time he would leave nothing to chance. The 'hotel' was surrounded by police and his own men who were told that only Maxon would be taken. Sleet insisted on this, despite police resentment, because he was afraid that in a more general upheaval his own quarry might slip through the net. The preparations went smoothly: the hotel-keeper was asleep, his minder on the gate never had a chance to warn any of the guests.

Just before dawn, Maxon was awakened by quite polite knocks at the door and subdued calls from outside: 'Open up, Maxon, this is Sleet. Don't give us trouble.'

Maxon jumped out of bed. One look through the window told him all he needed to know about the situation. 'Sure,' he shouted, 'just putting on some clothes.'

'You have thirty seconds,' answered Sleet who had unpleasant memories about Maxon's need to dress. In fact, it would have been wiser for him to kick the door down. For Maxon did not bother to dress. He picked up a large, heavy-duty fire extinguisher from the corner, moved it to face the door, uncapped it and pulled the lever. Thick foam flooded out, engulfing half the room like some monstrous djinn just released from the bottle. Jack took over from him. 'Fifteen seconds!' Sleet shouted through the door.

'We'll meet as arranged,' Maxon whispered grabbing a pair of trousers. 'Stand clear when they break in.' He pushed the huge wardrobe, expecting resistance, but it moved with amazing ease. He squeezed his body inside the dumb waiter, and Jack yanked at the rope that started him on his agonisingly slow downward journey. He heard the shattering of the door, the shouts, the swearing – the foam would prevent them for a while from searching the room, reaching the window and figuring out what happened.

In the cellar, Maxon got out but did not allow himself the luxury of a gesture to modesty: naked as he was, trousers in hand, he ran. He reached the coal bunker under the adjoining old bakery. Above him, he saw the coal feeding window. As expected, there was a ladder right underneath it.

The service road, connecting workshops and derelict buildings, seemed deserted. He ran, stopped to pull on his trousers – and took the wrong turning. Two young policemen spotted him. He did not want to retreat into what might be a cul-de-sac, so he ran against them. With an element of surprise, he managed to knock down one and push away the other, but they soon recovered, gave chase, shouting in their walkie-talkies, and gaining on him with every step. Maxon swore at himself: as he was past the age of enjoying such exertions, he should have taken better precautions. His breathing grew heavy. He heard the men closing the gap behind him. The cracked pavement cut his bare soles. His heart pounded as if trying to break out of his chest. He began to feel dizzy. He knew his chances of winning would be nil if he stopped to fight.

'Hold it.' The frail figure stepping out of the shadows did not appear particularly authoritative or ferocious, but backed up his command by the hissing sound of two shots through the silencer of a large handgun. Maxon halted, so did one policeman. The other, perhaps carried by his own momentum, lunged at Maxon, but another shot stopped him short of his target. 'This way, sir. Move.' The gun motioned Maxon towards a dark doorway. 'Run.'

Maxon did not feel like arguing with the gun. He ran. It was a short passage to the main service road. A bakers' delivery van was waiting for him. The door slid open and the gunman prodded him through the gap. The van took off as if it was ready to fly. A torch lit up Maxon's face. It also revealed that the gun was pointed at him.

'I'll be to the point, Mr Maxon.' It was a husky voice with more than a hint of a Slavonic accent. 'The circumstances don't give us time for courtesies, you understand.'

'Okay, okay, what do you want?'

'I want to help you. We want to help you.'

'Who's *we*?'

'Friends. Your friends.'

'In Moscow?'

212

'Yes, maybe there, too.'

'Where else?'

'I bring you greetings from Stockholm. Nadia Buzinova – remember her?'

'Yes.' Over the high-pitched road surface noise and the labouring engine of the speeding van, Maxon tried to hear if they were being given chase. No, probably not. But he was not sure what he wanted less: a chase and capture by Sleet or the continued ride with the Russian whose face was invisible.

'Oh yes, you must remember comrade Buzinova. She's still as beautiful, perhaps, if possible, even more beautiful than she used to be. And she remembers you very well. She said to me: "Please, give my greetings to Maxon, I have very fond memories of him". If you want to get in touch with her, she's now in charge of our Baltic Fishing Commission delegation in Stockholm. I'm sure she'd receive you with, how shall I say? open arms?'

Maxon knew that Nadia was now in a very senior position in the KGB European network. Why she would sit in Stockholm rather than London or Paris he could not tell, but the message was a clear invitation to defect. Throughout a long winter in Copenhagen – was it '72 or '73? – they tried to pump each other for snippets of intelligence. They both failed. What they gained was plenty of drinking, dining out in style, luxury weekends in Oslo (Sandy insisted on the best hotels to infuriate the Centre's expense accountants), and an insomniac affair with both of them fighting to stay awake in fear of the words they might utter in their well-earned slumber. 'You've gone a long way to deliver her greetings,' Maxon said at last. 'Thank you.'

'All right, Mr Maxon, we know you're a clever man. We respect you more than you think. So I won't insult you with playing games. We know a great deal about what's going on. We know that you're – now I must try to remember the word *our* friend among *your* friends used . . . oh, yes, you're ostracised, and you're hunted by this Major Sleet who's a stupid man. He's never even noticed that he led us to your hiding place. So you see, we know a lot. And we'd like to help you if you want us to. Give it a try, yes? As you say, no commitment on either side. If, after all you've done for your friends, they can play dirty against you, why should you be loyal to them?'

The other man made a backhand smash with the gun against an invisible ping-pong ball and spoke for the first time: 'At least we can protect you, see?'

'Shut up!' the man in charge exploded. He was furious with Vanek on several counts. But Maxon's pick-up had topped them all: despite his strict instructions, Vanek had fired warning shots and, eventually, shot and killed or wounded a policeman. Yes, Vanek had become a liability. 'I think we'd better drop you somewhere here, Mr Maxon.' He tapped on the driver's back. 'Would you like to borrow my friend's jacket and shoes?'

The gunman was obviously appalled by the idea and Maxon would have liked to cause him at least some discomfort, but wearing anything borrowed from them could be interpreted as proof of his treachery if he was caught. So he refused the offer.

The van stopped. 'Once again, Mr Maxon, you'd be most welcome. Please contact Nadia. Or make your own arrangements if you wish. We'd hate to see you end your life in the gutter when you could still do so much for all of us, I mean the whole world.'

'Thanks for the ride,' said Maxon and opened the door. They were in a short, dark street, at the end of which he recognised Camden Lock. An ideal place to shoot a man he thought. His back tried to contract to present the smallest possible target. Perhaps he ought to have held out some hope for the man in the van. Now it was too late. He ran. His bare toes kicked a broken milk bottle.

Inside the van, Vanek was told to hand over his gun. He was then shot twice in the head, the barrel touching his temple. As the stolen van made yet another flying start, Vanek's body rolled through the side door. By that time, Maxon was inside a boarded up house that awaited demolition and served as the last refuge of a bunch of meths drinkers. He stayed with them, waiting patiently for them to awake from their stupor. They would be an ideal decoy for a man in his scanty attire.

When the Saturday market opened, this swarm of sleepy stumblers descended upon the Lock. The drunks reactivated yesterday's methylated spirits in their stomachs by drinking plenty of water, while Maxon took a good look at the second-hand clothes stalls. He decided to use the technique he had learned from the experts, the street urchins of Naples, and promised himself to pay, eventually, his would-be victim for the loss. He began shouting 'thief! thief!', chasing the phantom wrongdoer through the thick of the crowd. People soon joined in the hunt, stall-keepers were up in arms to protect the tribe – where? where? get him! – with all eyes on the milling multitude, suspending standard precautions which was, perhaps, quite logical: statistically it was unlikely that *two* thieves should be operating simultaneously in the vicinity, and one was already chased by everyone. Maxon helped himself to a canvas jacket and a pair of yawning boots, and swore that next time in Naples he would give generously to Father Borelli's charity.

From Sleet's anger and embarrassment when reporting to Sandy on the phone, Jack gathered that Maxon had got away. But it took her most of the day to make sure that she had lost her tail, collect Chuck's message from the answering service, and pick up Maxon in a quiet mews behind the goods entrance of Harrods. By then she was driving a hired Rolls, the car least likely to attract suspicion and roomy enough for Maxon to change into his own clothes. That left them barely half an hour not to miss the rendezvous with Chuck before the closing of the Zoo.

The American looked pale and extremely agitated, unnerved by the incessant twitter of the aviary, ready to take flight if a child, impressed by his bulk, deemed him worth a second look, but he did have the money for Maxon in cash, and the address of the school where Tucker's child was a boarder. No, he did not want to know how Maxon intended to go about his unsavoury business. But something that bothered him a great deal was what he and Maxon could do if Locke turned out to be guilty of some form of treachery. 'I mean if he is, his backing in ... er ... high places,' he forced himself to say, 'could implicate someone like ... I mean anyone ... I mean how would you go about that?'

Maxon had no answer. And it worried him that even if he found an answer, eventually, he might not have time to go all the way with his investigation before at least some of this earth was blown away through bluffing, or the ongoing numbers game with a stockpile of sixty thousand nuclear weapons when two hundred could destroy all the major cities – or the brinkmanship that drove politicians to demand and scientists to provide the means to kill nine instead of merely eight out of every ten people in every country.

Off the B-road out of Windsor, tucked away behind the blanket of beechwoods on gently heaving Berkshire hills, the school stood among meadows and playing fields. Its extensive lawns alone could be responsible for the top fifth of every bill unfortunate parents had to foot for every child fortunate enough to be accepted as a boarder.

The arrival of the maroon Rolls caused no great stir as it rolled to a halt on the finely crunching gravel path, but the calculated combination of Jack's elegance and subtle sex appeal guaranteed the opening of all doors despite the early hour on this Sunday morning. The headmaster, a notorious stickler for regulations, was eager not to appear what he was by nature, and waved away all formalities when Jack apologised for her unannounced arrival. She explained that she had just 'spoken to Biggles, I'm sorry, I mean Squadron Leader Tucker, who's a great friend of mine, and promised him to give his little girl a day's outing – with your kind permission, of course.' The headmaster permitted himself some feeble jocularity over fliers' luck in choosing friends, waived the rule of all rules concerning church attendance, ordered that 'little Kristina form-two Tucker' should be delivered, suitably dressed, to his office henceforth, and issued an exeat for her in his own hand. He would long remember Jack's blonde wig that covered half her face, the extra large mouth drawn in lipstick, and the black beauty spot that dominated her visible cheek.

Kristina was delighted. At the age of eight, cunning enough to pause in the door of the Rolls so that everybody, but everybody should see her stylish departure, she was more used to envying others for their visitors and outings than to enjoying such grand moments of privilege. Once they had left the school grounds, she did not mind that they swapped cars, and accepted readily Jack's explanation (that small cars were better for forests and country lanes) because that would be yet another tale to tell on her return.

Some thirty minutes later, an unmarked dark Cortina sped along the path to the main entrance of the school. 'Police,' said ex-detective sergeant Loveday jumping out of the car. Maxon followed him running into the building. They demanded to see the head. They both wore the sort of gaudy clothes that would be remembered more readily than their faces in which the starkest features were artifical: Maxon's thick moustache vied with Loveday's bushy eyebrows for attention. In the headmaster's office, while Loveday fumbled for his poor fake of a police card, Maxon blurted out why they were in such a tearing hurry: they had received information that Squadron Leader Tucker's daughter might be in danger of being kidnapped. In his consternation, the head ignored Loveday's identity card. They were late, he told them. He had to sit down as his legs began to fail him. 'Why ... why didn't you telephone?'

'We've just heard it on the car radio,' said Loveday and asked for a description of the woman. The headmaster remembered only the Rolls, the long blonde hair, and a few details that would have identified any of a dozen women in the area. 'It'll have to do for the time being,' sighed Loveday and started towards the door.

'Yes, raise the alert for the Rolls, sergeant, perhaps it's not too late.' Maxon then turned to the headmaster: 'How did the woman identify herself to you?'

The man just buried his face in his hands.

'You mean you let the child go with a stranger? ... I see. Well, did the child know her?'

'I ... I don't know. ... No, she didn't ...'

'Was she reluctant to go with her?'

'No. Not at all.'

'Ah! Perhaps she expected a visit. Perhaps her father wrote to her about it. Has she had any letters?'

'We can ask her house-mistress.'

'No. That's one thing we can't do,' Maxon ruled. 'This isn't an ordinary kidnap for ransom.' He lowered his voice: 'It's political. Without my personal permission you're not to mention it to anyone at all. You understand? Perhaps I don't need to remind you that you already bear a grave enough responsibility, and you'll probably be questioned by Special Branch. Now let's see, have you got her father's address?'

'Only a Post Box number, if I remember correctly.'

'But you must have a phone number for emergencies.'

Yes, there was such a number. The 218 prefix indicated that it would probably be a direct line in the Ministry of Defence. That was no help to Maxon, but it was not unexpected. What he hoped was that Biggles (like other loving, absent and guilt-ridden fathers) might have given Kristina a special and personal emergency number. It would be a breach of security, but in Maxon's experience, it would help to reassure him that the child boarder was not entirely neglected and cut off from parental care.

Loveday returned with the news that road blocks had been set up and the hunt for the Rolls was on. The three men then went to search Kristina's belongings. Among her little treasures, on the back of a snapshot, Maxon spotted a long telephone number. It began with 010-1 – the United States. The area code 402 identified Omaha. Maxon felt jubilant. He would contact Tucker, and use the offence of 'divulging a service number without authorisation' as a lever and frightener. Unfortunately, his flight to the States would lengthen the child's retention. Maxon had contingency plans for that, but Jack might refuse to see them through. For in order to avoid causing any mental anguish to the little girl, the idea was to sedate her heavily for twenty-four hours. Maxon knew for certain that the special knock-out drops he had given to Jack would be perfectly safe with no side-effects. Although he could reassure Jack wholeheartedly about the drug, he had to admit to himself that he, too, would be most reluctant to go that far. Better not to think about it, he urged himself. It was time, yet again, to be an optimist.

Rummaging through a shoebox full of papers, the headmaster picked out a picture of San Remo casino. 'That's a recent postmark,' he said and held up the card. Maxon read the brief note telling 'little Kay' that 'Papa Biggles' was 'on business' in Italy and he would arrange for her to come and stay with him for a long weekend. 'Oh yes,' said the headmaster, 'her house mistress mentioned something . . . shall I . . . oh no, you said we mustn't reveal the situation to anybody . . .'

Before leaving the distraught man to his long, agonising wait, Maxon emphasised that absolute secrecy was essential; not even the emergency number must be called because, he confided with a meaningful nod, 'there might be, in fact, a leak at the top'. The headmaster appeared to be totally shaken and convinced. Loveday would telephone him from time to time to reactivate the warnings and make him feel that things were in hand, that the prospect of finding the child safely was brightening.

With the passport Loveday had bought (not a very good one for three hundred pounds) the previous night, Maxon then took the first flight to Nice. Loveday telephoned Jack at the restaurant where she had planned to lunch with the child. 'Stay put and wait for me,' he said and rang off before she could ask questions or argue. They would have to arrange a breakdown of her car and delay the child's return to the school possibly well into the night. The child would not suffer, might even enjoy it all, he was sure, but he was quite willing to take risks: Maxon had told him that the stakes were big enough to justify almost anything, and he trusted him.

In Nice, Maxon hired a car and drove himself to San Remo. Although it was only early afternoon, his man would already be in the Casino, he was sure. Tucker was what Maxon had once described in a confidential security assessment as 'a compulsive, semi-pro., play-safe gambler' who would play blackjack or roulette at every given opportunity, who might spend an entire fortnight's holiday in a casino with only reluctant breaks for short stretches of sleep, who would play the odds without ever taking undue risks, and who would stop and even return home without any regrets when he lost a strictly predetermined sum – which was how almost every one of his gambling binges ended. He wanted to win but did not mind losing because it was the mood of the big casino he loved. He seemed to get high on the hush, the clicks of the ivory ball, the hiss of the card leaving the shoe, the chant of the croupiers, the mingled fragrance of baize, perfumes and fear. No, his gambling hobby was no security risk, and Maxon knew him to be 'not particularly bright but utterly reliable'. That was how he had got him the job at Omaha, just after Tucker's squadron had been disbanded; when he was out on a limb with a bleak employment prospect and when the first hefty bill from the Berkshire school had just landed on his doorstep.

Maxon knew that Tucker was most grateful to him and would do anything he asked him to, but would divulge nothing operational even to the man from GLEW security – his superior, in a way. So Maxon had no choice but to shock him by playing dirty – and loathed himself for it.

From the brilliance of the sea, the sunshine, the vibrating heat on the wide white stairs, a single step transported Maxon into the palatial naves of eternal midnight. Lording over a fair pile of chips, Biggles sat at a roulette table. He looked up, his eyes swept over Maxon, stopped, returned, paused, then lit up, at last, recognising the familiar face that had been distorted by that unfamiliar moustache. He smiled and his mouth opened to shout the name, but Maxon shook his head almost imperceptibly, and Tucker read the message.

They met at the bar. Tucker enthused over bumping into a friend. 'What are you doing here? When have you arrived? Is it work or play?'

'Bits of this and that.' Maxon did not smile.

'Okay, play mum if you must. I won't let it spoil such a happy coincidence. We'll drink this town dry. What's your tipple, old boy?'

'Later, Biggles, later. Let's go for a stroll first.'

'Ah-ah! Am I getting bad vibes or am I getting bad vibes?'

Their eyes struggled to readjust to daylight, and they walked in silence until they had left the main thoroughfare with its colurful crowds and reached a quiet street off the fishing harbour.

'You got me worried,' said Tucker.

'Good.'

'What's up?'

'You tell me.'

'I've been cleared for this holiday, they know I'm here to play a little in the casino, everything is according to the letter of the law *you* wrote, even though it's a silly law, but who cares, ops. personnel love you, my boy ...' he was slowing down, the glitter of his voice faded away.

'It's serious, Biggles. Is there anything you feel you ought to tell me?'

'Lots and lots. We haven't seen each other for ages ...' His last attempt at keeping it light faltered. 'Did I do something wrong?'

'As I said: you tell me.'

Tucker looked puzzled. He thought, then shrugged his shoulders to begin his confession: 'Okay, you win. Occasionally I do sleep with the station chief's wife, but so does everybody else. She's the only screw-worthy female we come across over there.'

'It's a question of security, not morals.'

'She's no security risk. She has the same clearance as any of us. Besides . . .'

Maxon's eyes silenced him. 'That's enough, Biggles. I'm here semi-officially, and only because everybody knows that we're old pals, and that I got you your job. So I'm badly embarrassed, if not compromised. If you're not frank with me, you'll have to answer the posse that's after you and may arrive within a few hours if not minutes.'

'I don't understand. Ask any questions and I promise to give you honest answers. What else can I do?'

'All right. What did you say to anybody about your work?'

'Nothing. I swear.'

'Not even to your daughter?'

'Of course not. She wouldn't understand.'

'Then why did you give her your Omaha number?'

For the first time, Tucker was shaken. He did not know what other blows were on their way. He tried to smile it off: 'Oh that. It's just a telephone number . . . probably listed . . . you know, something to keep her happy . . . she'd never use it . . .'

'Maybe not.' Maxon paused. 'But I think you must have told her other things, too. About Omaha. Or your work. Perhaps to amuse her.'

'I haven't.'

'Then in your opinion, why would anybody want to kidnap her?' Maxon looked away. He did not want to see the man's pain.

'Kidnap?'

'Probably. A strange woman picked her up this morning.'

'But . . .'

'No, Biggles, I don't know how the school let her take the child. But they did. There hasn't been any ransom demand. I expect they'd want to get on to you.' Maxon looked at his watch. 'It may be time for us to check if there's any news.'

From a cafe they called the school. The headmaster

apologised to Tucker profusely and said that according to the sergeant in charge, the police had already found the Rolls and were hopeful. Tucker had virtually disintegrated by the time he finished the call.

'Look,' said Maxon, offering him a drink, 'we must try to go through this logically. I'll have to ask questions I'm not supposed to ask and you're not supposed to answer. If you dislike the idea, we'll leave it until the others get here. But we have no time to waste.'

'I understand. Go ahead.'

'Again, I'm not supposed to know, but I do know that there's been a rather serious leak from Omaha.'

'You mean GLEW Center?'

'Of course.'

'That's bloody ridiculous. What's there to leak? I mean if anybody, it's you who knows jolly well that the job there is a doddle. Plain sinecure, thank you very much.'

'You'll have to be more specific if you want to help both of us.'

'Okay, chocks away.' He downed his coarse Italian brandy, and ordered another.

'Tell me the routine. From the moment you come on duty.'

'What routine? You must be joking. You know better than anyone that it's home away from home, without a nagging wife or *any* routine.'

'Oh yes,' Maxon was getting irritated with him, 'just croquet on the lawn – or is it bowls?'

'Both, as a matter of fact, and squash and tennis, too. The facilities are fantastic. Even so, there's only the two of us on each shift and we get bored with each other because you, you've kindly forbidden any fraternisation even with the SAC personnel. Some of our guys just crack up, as you must know.'

This was news to Maxon whose patch had always excluded Omaha, but Tucker was not to find out. 'Sure,' he said, 'sure I know all the bullshit you're giving me. It's your work I know least about even though that's where the leak must have come from. So tell me about the work.'

'What work? The trouble is that the whole thing flies itself by the seat of its computer, and loops the loop while we sit and watch.'

'That's what you're paid for. GLEW is a complex

operation, it's got to be automated, because you wouldn't know how to handle it.'

'Bloody right, too. That's why if there was a leak, it couldn't have come from me.' His drinking began to accelerate and made him talk louder. Maxon led him to a table on the small terrace where they would be alone: the sun kept all sane locals indoors, and there was nothing around here for the tourist. Indignantly, Tucker carried on with his self-defence: 'Look, I could have given away everything I know, you understand? Everything, and it still wouldn't amount to what you call a leak. Because all I know is just the basic facts, nothing about the purpose of the whole charade, nothing about the effect. All I know is that we get this constant flow of high-speed garbage from the satellite trackers, and we only make sure that it goes back and forth between Omaha and Tasmania, Fylingdale, Guam, Diego Garcia, the Cape, and all the other stations. The job is to receive and re-route the stuff non-stop.'

'After decoding, of course.'

'Decoding? What decoding?'

'Well who the hell would do it if not Omaha?'

'Ha, ha, and even more ha.'

'It can't go any higher than Omaha, so the decoding must be done there,' Maxon insisted.

Tucker's face went Ferrari red. His lips opened to let rise a burst of air that sounded like a misfiring sportscar. 'But what the fuck is to be decoded when the code itself is the message!?'

Maxon looked bewildered. He drank hastily to conceal the fact that he had not the faintest idea what Tucker could be talking about.

'Look, old boy,' Tucker's voice weakened. 'I'm really worried about the little lass. So stop pulling my leg, will you? ... Well, for Pete's sake, you know the score! I'm innocent ... No, you won't intimidate me with that famous Maxon stare ... Look, we're pals. I swear I didn't tell anyone that we do nothing, that we can't do anything, because we don't exist.' He tried to laugh. 'See what I mean? Who'd believe me anyway? I mean I have a feeling that the whole thing was set up so ingeniously that suddenly, even you and Locke begin to believe that GLEW does exist. ... Hey ... Maxon ... are you all right?'

'Yeah ... sure ...' Maxon's brain refused to accept that

Tucker could be right. Yet instinctively, he knew at once that he must be right. Because the mystery fragments of the giant mosaic would then find a meaning and fall into place. The naive elements of secrecy that advertised rather than concealed GLEW. The stupid charade of code words. Skylark in Red Square. The minuscule staff. The drunk at Diego Garcia. The Russians' failure in breaking the code or finding a traitor. Kowalski's puzzled eyes trying to see how such high-speed computers could work . . .

'You look sick.' Tucker was genuinely concerned.

'It . . . it must be the drinks and the sun.'

Tucker rushed inside and returned with some coffee. He placed a wet serviette on his friend's neck.

Maxon felt more and more ashamed of his cruel scheme and the deception of an anxious father, but he was regaining his composure and getting ready to reap more benefits. If Locke knew the truth, and intended to use GLEW and the entire magnificent bluff to further his own secret aims, he must be stopped. And Tucker could provide the proof Maxon was looking for. 'Listen, Biggles, you're still not answering my questions. Of course I know how the system works. But I want to clarify your role. If GLEW is only a successful scarecrow, it couldn't have warned us about that missile attack.' Of course not, he thought: Sarian had supplied the advance information to Locke. 'So you received no satellite signals, yet I know for sure that it was you, personally, who alerted the button-men in Washington to broadcast the alert.'

'You think I wasn't authorised? Locke himself gave the orders. He identified himself with the code known only to him and Omaha. Then he called back to check. . . . What a cackle!'

# VIII

Still dazed and bewildered on his return from San Remo, Maxon knew he had reached a crossroads with 'no entry' signs in all directions. He had to unload his burden of knowing the truth about GLEW, alert all good people, DO something and shout stop! stop! all of you! – but he had nowhere to turn. Somebody (was it Locke, Sandy or the Russian smear campaigners?) had succeeded in isolating and discrediting him completely. And now Chuck Parkin, his reluctant yet last remaining ally, had disappeared without trace. In his White House office, the phone was manned by strangers, probably CIA operatives, who took messages, asked questions aplenty, but offered no information about Parkin's whereabouts. At his home, the number had been changed to another unlisted one which remained unavailable even to Saul Robinson, Maxon's friend at the FBI. The rumour in Washington was that Parkin had been sent on some confidential mission for the President, but Maxon suspected it had been a deliberate removal from his reach. If so, it would have been done by someone who had the President's ear, someone who knew about their contacts if not the contents of their conversations in London Zoo.

Tucker might have reported the San Remo meeting to Locke himself, but that was unlikely: he was a friend, he had been fooled completely by the kidnap story, he trusted Maxon, had nothing to gain from breaking his promise 'to keep mum', and had his job to lose if somebody called attention to 'certain irregularities' in his own conduct.

Loveday, the ex-police sergeant, made some discreet inquiries and told Maxon about the manhunt. 'They want you badly, guv. There's been some shooting at the Wembley industrial estate. A PC and an unidentified civilian are dead – both have been shot by the same gun – and another police officer is on the critical list. No, guv, don't tell me nothing, I don't want to know if you were involved or not, but some people think you might have been, and if you were, you're no friend but a bigger shit than I thought you were, sir.'

Jack alone remained loyal to Maxon. She would help in every way he asked her to, but her enthusiasm for his cause had cooled a great deal since the 'kidnapping' of Tucker's daughter. 'Is the world worth saving,' she kept asking herself, 'if in the process we must act like the Lockes and Sandys of this world?'

On top of it all, it became more and more obvious that the world was preparing faster and faster for yet another war nobody wanted. The headlines were dominated by fear, gloom and dejection. The Kremlin denounced US aggression. The White House hit back with warnings and threats: nobody, but nobody would ever be permitted to take advantage of the preparations for the presidential elections; a single Soviet breach of any space or test ban treaty would be regarded as a 'warlike stance if not outright hostility towards the free world'.

In utter despair, Maxon telephoned Sandy who, for the first time since Toronto, accepted his call. 'Ah, Maxon, I'm glad you've called. I assume you're beginning to see sense. That's wise in the circumstances. So what do you propose to do?'

He spoke so fast that Maxon could not interrupt him without a rude shout: 'Sandy! Will you listen?'

'Just tell me where and when you want to give yourself up.'

'It's not that simple.'

'I know it isn't. But whatever your game is, you're going to get yourself killed if you don't run for home fast.'

'You'd have to hear me out.'

'No conditions, Maxon, not this time.'

'You'd have to hear me out.'

'I always do. So where do we pick you up?'

Maxon felt tired. And badly tempted to accept Sandy's advice: give himself up, take the chance that Sandy or somebody would believe him right away, before the world went up in a mushroom cloud. But had anybody in his position the right to take the soft option, throw away his freedom of decision, and gamble? Besides, what was there to guarantee that somebody would not prevent him from reaching Sandy alive?

'You haven't answered me, Maxon. I presume you have a problem. Well, go ahead, let's discuss it.'

'That was cheap, Sandy – and you know I won't stay on this line long enough for your boys to trace the call.'

There was a few seconds' embarrassed silence. Sandy disliked cheap tricks, his own included, and even less did he like being caught out. 'It's your fault,' he counter-attacked. 'You call me, but you don't say what you want. If you don't want my advice, what *do* you want?'

It was Maxon's turn to pause. He decided he had nothing to lose by trying at least to alert Sandy. 'Would you believe me if I told you' – in a grave tone he emphasised every word – 'that the organisation I'm supposed to be looking after does not exist?'

'Come again . . .'

'You heard me. And I wasn't joking.'

'Then you must be out of your mind.'

'Okay, Sandy, you make up your own mind, but first listen. Our system never detected the launch. The information came as advance warning from Sarian.'

'Rubbish.'

'You check it. Go to . . .'

'This is an open line!' Sandy yelled desperately.

'I know. I wasn't going to name the place. But you go and see him. He told Locke.'

'Then he would have told me.'

'That's what *you* think.'

'And what is that supposed to mean?' Sandy was furious: he had never tolerated innuendos against friends and allies. Even if they were mere upstarts.

'Ask Chuck Parkin of the White House. If you can trace him. And try to contact Squadron Leader Tucker. Biggles, you remember? He's at Omaha. Twist his arm. Do what you can. He's told me everything.' Maxon stopped. What if Biggles had been instructed to set him up? What if Biggles had lied? 'Will you do it, Sandy? Will you try to believe me for old times' sake?'

'I'd find it easier to believe you face to face. You need help, Maxon. I'm offering it to you.' It was easy to tell that his compassion was genuine. 'You can get killed if this goes on, and that's the last thing I want. Now Locke's over here, staying at the Needle for a few days. We could meet there. Or anywhere. You name the place.'

227

'Don't involve Locke. There's something seriously wrong with him.'

'I know, old boy, I know. He tends to wear brown brogues with blue suits. So let's leave him out of it. Where do we meet?'

'We don't, Sandy. I must take my chances and you must take yours. If you don't believe me that GLEW is a monumental bluff, none of us may live long enough to prove me right.' He rang off. This time Sandy did not need to say it: Maxon knew he was on his own. And even complete hopelessness could not revive his flagging optimism. He was most annoyed with his own irrational behaviour. It had always been his forte to work out the odds, his own position and other people's likely reaction, yet he approached Sandy on the spur of the moment, only to blurt out an astounding statement in the worst possible light. 'How on earth could I expect him to take me seriously, let alone believe me?' he fumed. 'And why would he listen to me at all when obviously, the only thing on his mind was how he could get me? For why else would he offer me Locke's hotel so readily? It's got to be a trap. Got to be. Thank you, Sandy, for telling me never to go near the Needle.'

Standing in the open door of the red telephone booth, Jack was glancing anxiously up and down the street. 'Let's go,' she urged him, knowing full well that Sandy's men might be on their way to capture Maxon if they had traced the call. But Maxon did not seem to hear her. He stared at the cradled receiver and the ready-to-oblige dial – and he had nobody to call. There was no one left to inform, nobody to share his secret. 'Except the Russians,' he mumbled incomprehensibly, but the sudden, painful realisation was all too clear to him.

'What about the Russians?'

'I ought to tell them the truth about GLEW.'

'You're crazy.'

'That's no news, my love, but would you think I've got what it takes to be a traitor?'

'Watch out! . . . Over there! Get him, son, shoot!' Locke let go a vicious, inarticulate cry. 'Let's go boys . . . Chaaarge!

Kill the bastards! Chaaaaarge!' With flailing arms he was fighting some battle, dozing in the rocking chair of his hotel suite.

'Sir . . .' Captain Beck hesitated. 'Wake up, sir . . .'

The general's chair reared up, then dived perilously, like a small boat in heavy seas.

'You're having a nightmare, sir.' Beck touched his shoulder.

'Nightmare?' Locke opened his eyes in fierce bewilderment. 'I saw them coming over the top . . .'

'Who?'

'The Chinks . . .' he groaned, closed his eyes to complete his waking up, then rose to cross the large living room to the window. He pressed his head against the pane. From the twenty-fourth floor, the whole of sleeping London was at his mercy. That was what he liked so much about the Needle.

'I've got the papers you asked for, sir.'

'Thanks. Pity you didn't give me a chance to win that battle.'

Staring at the general's back, the captain shrugged his shoulders. 'I sometimes think you miss your wars, sir.'

'Wars? I don't know. I miss my comrades. The exhilaration of victory. Even the sweat of fear.'

'I understand.'

'No, you don't, Alvin. But Maxon would. Because he's a fighter. And I love him for it.'

'Yet you're ready to see him destroyed.'

'He left me no choice. And I respect him for it. For he'd destroy me if he thought it was necessary.'

'But what is he after? What could there be he doesn't know about GLEW?'

Locke smiled as if it hurt him: 'Perhaps something you don't know either. But then, perhaps, he already knows that – and now he wants to face the truth.'

'Truth? What truth? What is the truth?'

'War to the death is the only truth, Alvin.' He walked over to the stunned younger man, and touched his face with fatherly affection as if mourning him. 'And Mutual Assured Destruction is not MAD but the ultimate truth. The difference is slight yet vast, the borderline is only the credibility of menace, and if Maxon knows where that line is drawn, he must also know that he's wanted dead or alive by both sides.'

Having changed taxis several times, Jack met Maxon at the foot of Tower Bridge, from where they walked through the marina, along rows of yachts and other well-planted photogenic sights to entice the tourist. At last they came upon a cunningly converted warehouse (not converted enough, that is, to deprive it of 'character') that was named 'suckerland' by the indigenous population of the docks. The building, packed with luxury pads at extortionate prices to offset the marketing razzmatazz, smelled of illicit affairs, both the sexual and commercial varieties, and served the rich and corruptible the same way as the Wembley hide-out serviced the criminal and the corrupt. With its strict privacy and numerous concealed entrances, it was ideal for Maxon's lying low and thinking in peace for a few days. Jack was duly impressed when he found his way in this maze.

Samantha's pad, frequent setting of its tenant's blue films, left little to the imagination. Books, paintings and exquisite tapestry on the back of dining chairs carried the message – the salt cellar was just one of numerous phallic symbols. From the monstrous waterbed, engulfed in a suede-clad array of electronic gadgets, a conglomeration of vulgar gimmickry and valuable museum pieces could be seen with the aid of subtly positioned mirrors. The proud owner of this sex-maniac's lair would have been greatly disappointed if she knew that her visitors would spend all day and most of the following night in the kitchen, sipping coffee and brandy alternately from phallic mugs with testicles to grab.

Much of the time they sat in silence, holding hands, lost in their thoughts. Occasionally, Maxon burst into long, disjointed monologues to escape his new discovery that loneliness could corrupt even more than the possession or desire of that proverbial absolute power. 'When you're alone, you make compromises with yourself, the silence, the walls, you get corrupted by your own thoughts as you're looking for explanations and stumble only on excuses,' he said and refilled the mugs with Samantha's best cognac. 'Excuses? What excuses? Excuses for your own gullibility? For not seeing through it all earlier? How could I? Even the KGB couldn't because the unbreakable code itself was the message. They couldn't find a single traitor because nobody had any secrets to sell. They couldn't guess that Sarian gave us advance warning, that Locke arranged the public alert, and that it was no good to smear Kowalski or me because Locke, and perhaps someone even higher up, very high up, knew we had nothing to commit our alleged treason with.'

'How about your famous great pals? You think they also were ready to sacrifice you?'

'I don't know. May be.'

'Charming.' She drank. 'Makes me puke.'

'It would be a waste of good brandy.'

Maxon sank into yet another of his protracted silences from which he emerged with a solemn 'yes' and a few slow nods: 'At least Ellsberg has died for his conviction. He knew about the plans for an EMP test, he knew it would be war unless he warned me and I warned our people not to overreact. It's not his fault that they can't be told or they refuse to listen. So what else is there but to warn Moscow that it's a bluff?'

'That's the one thing you can't do.'

'Why not?'

'You know why not.'

'So how do you stop someone who doesn't care about us or even the Russians because he has a third party's interest at heart?'

'You're obsessed with this traitor theory.'

'I wouldn't be if Locke didn't fit the bill.'

'Then how come that nobody else has thought of it?'

'Chuck has. So what happened to him? He disappeared. How convenient. And why? Because he recognised Locke's probable motive. Many of Locke's best contacts and closest friends are said to be Arab and other Moslem leaders. His loyalty may well be questionable on that score alone.'

'You can't be an objective judge of his character. Because you hate him.'

'You don't know how wrong you are. I respect the man. Even love him.'

'Don't be ridiculous.'

'I can't help it. Because I often see myself in him. I know how he operates because I know what *I* would do in his place if *I* wanted to engineer a war that could wipe out the superpowers and leave the Moslem world relatively unscathed. Which leaves me but one course.'

'Treason.'

'No. To do what's right. It's a matter of guts.'

'Not conviction?'

'Ellsberg had both. He had the guts to live up to his convictions.'

'Yes, after you'd given him the final push, the convincing argument.' She tried to take the bottle from him but he would not let go of it.

'Yes, the final push. And now he's dead.'

'While you're drunk.'

'Rise from the grave, Volodya, rise and talk to me!'

He started towards the bedroom. His legs were unsteady but his memory was clear: the red leather case he had left with Samantha was in her huge, concealed safe. She had given him the code to the main lock, but the inside of the safe was all compartmentalised, and he alone knew the combination that would open his box.

To Jack's great surprise, the leather case was brimming over with bugging devices and toy-like tapes. She knew how much Maxon disliked electronic gadgetry, and how reluctant he must have been to bug all his conversations with Ellsberg, but she said nothing. He slipped an extra-long-play cassette, a CIA monopoly product, into a miniature tape-recorder, ran the tape, stopped it seemingly at ramdom, and pressed the REPLAY button.

In the distance, wind whistled and waves gurgled in Toronto harbour. It was an eerie sensation when Ellsberg spoke to them – and Maxon argued with the dead.

*'I'll be perfectly honest with you.'*

*'Yes, I did expect you to be devious.'*

Maxon laughed. 'You see, Volodya? You *are* devious: you're dead when I need you most.' He ran the tape fast. Jack noticed it had been marked at several points. Maxon must have listened to it many times.

*'Telling the truth to the enemy is treason, young Maxon. It's against orders.'*

*'Disobeying unlawful orders is a duty. At Nuremberg we found the accused guilty of failing to disobey criminal superiors beyond a certain point.'*

Maxon's face twitched and distorted with the argument the tape had revived. His pain explained to Jack that he had to listen to himself even more than to his friend whom he was attacking now, in his death, ferociously. You can't have it both ways, Volodya, Maxon thundered from the machine, you can't have one morality for the victors and another for the vanquished. But now his words were hitting

232

back. Maxon could not have it both ways either. If Ellsberg had been disallowed to claim dual standards for the East and West, Maxon, too, was deprived of the same luxury. Ellsberg had tried the *my country, right or wrong* tack. Maxon would not have it: that principle had been ruled dead at Nuremberg – if the principles behind the judgment failed to apply to everybody equally, *'the sentences we passed at Nuremberg would be plain murders.'*

Maxon's attack was now in full swing. He was out to break Ellsberg. In this nuclear age, he argued, *'we're not talking about petty, mischievous misdemeanours like genocide and mass extermination – this time round it's the real McCoy. There's no excuse for not stopping your madmen.'*

Ellsberg resorted to the *'who am I to judge everybody and everything'* ploy. *'Who am I to know what's right and wrong?'*

*'That was Eichmann's defence in Jerusalem ... Humans can tell right from wrong, honour from dishonour.'*

*'And how do you want me to measure my honour against my loyalties – the loyalties I owe to myself, my nation, my kind? Mankind.'*

*'Yes, you got the ascending order right ... The greater good of the larger group must have priority. And your country is NOT the top on your list.'*

The tape was still running, but it delivered only the grave message of silence. It was the voice of a broken man when Ellsberg asked: *'So what the hell do you propose? Treason?'*

And up came Maxon's merciless demand: *'It's got to be your answer.'*

In that underground garage, blurting out the information on EMP, and dying to save Maxon, Ellsberg had found and given his answer. Maxon was still searching for his. He sought guidance in his military oath of allegiance. But there was nothing in it to encourage just and dutiful disobedience – nothing to elevate it to moral superiority over the code of an SS henchman's conduct.

'I love you,' Jack whispered. Nobody could do more for him.

They huddled together on the bed, made love, fell asleep, woke up, made love again, and lay still in the darkness, but the joy of touching and belonging was frozen by the presence of the muted tapes. 'You convinced him,' she said.

It was true. But she never heard the final outcry of

233

Ellsberg's crumbling resistance, the words – almost his last –
that had opened the floodgates. Maxon had lived with them
ever since the shoot-out. He could still see the old Buick
reversing into a parking slot, and hear Ellsberg's questions:
*Have you ever tried to put a price on silence? Would silence
be the greatest betrayal in some circumstances?*

Maxon stared at Jack without seeing the tears in her eyes,
and without realising that he gave voice to his thoughts: 'It's
moral suicide to betray your nation even if it delays the
doom of mankind.'

He reached for the telephone and dialled 103. Interna-
tional Directory Inquiries gave him the number of the
Soviet Baltic Fishing Commission. He called Stockholm. If
Nadia Buzinova was still running some KGB operation
under that cover, there would be a night duty officer on call.
There was one. The man wanted to know who was calling.
Maxon said 'John Smith,' and asked what time Comrade
Nadia Buzinova would be in. 'At nine in the morning like
everybody else,' came the terse answer. Maxon rang off and
dialled flight reservations to book a seat on the first morning
flight to Stockholm. Jack held up two fingers while he spoke
and whispered: 'Make it two.' He shook his head: his was a
mission for one.

'Will she believe you?' Jack asked.

'She's bound to. They know I'm bad news over here.
Which must be good news to her. She knows the stuff
traitors are made of.'

'Not you,' she protested. 'You're no traitor, it's the
others. All those who fail to speak up or listen and think.'

He laughed. 'Oh yes, I know ... It's always the others.'
He began humming a little tune, rose from the bed, hopped
away and back with clumsy dancing steps, clapping the
rhythm all the time.

She watched him in disgust. 'You're drunk.'

'Me?' His humming grew louder, the steps bolder.
'Haven't you ever seen a morris dancer?'

'Am I seeing one? I'd have never guessed.'

'There was this school group, see?' He reverted to the
long-suppressed Mancunian he had last used when talking
about his mum's lover and the lighter that was supposed to
lend class to the lad.

'What group?'

'We was the best!' He danced away, only to dance all the

234

way back with a drink in hand. 'That's why we was taken to the Easter fair at Heywood, see?' He clapped out the rhythm on his naked thighs. 'The teachers in charge promised us oranges for the journey. We never got 'em. They promised us a ride in carts and buggies from the station. We had to walk. They promised we'd dance on a real stage in a big, big marquee. But no, we was to dance in the rain! The lads went mad. I wasn't all that angry, I didn't understand nothing, but I was the youngest, and I tried to copy them big'uns. They decided to sabotage the show. Sabo what? What's that? "We mess it up, that's what. Fool about. Do it wrong. Let them teachers blush! Yeah, yeah!" they all shouted.' Maxon stopped dancing and stared at the floor.

'You're not saying . . .'

'But I am, that's just what I'm doing, love. Because like a little fool I was wandering out of step all over the place in the rain while everybody else made the right moves as we was taught, see? People laughed,' it sounded *luffed* in a choking voice, 'and laughed, but I soldiered on until one of the big lads shoved me aside and a teacher pulled me away from the group by the ear . . .' He began to hum again, but stopped after a couple of bars. 'But who was the traitor? Them or me?'

It had to be done then – it's got to be done now. He went to have a shower to be alone. It's got to be done, he told himself, then closed his eyes hoping that the water might wash away the dirt of the thought. He stayed on and on, delaying the moment when once again he would have to face Jack and tell her that it had to be done knowing full well that it was no answer to her original question: was the world worth saving if in the process we had to act like the Lockes and Sandys of this world?

'I must go to Stockholm,' he said aloud, face up as if challenging the shower to drown him.

Wrapped in a towel, he returned to the bedroom. 'It's got to be done,' he said quietly.

'I understand,' she answered without even a hint of dramatics.

'Except that it can't be done.' He paused, but she said nothing. 'Not without turning my whole life into a lie.' His voice was cool and deliberate. He combed his hair to emphasise finality. 'It would reduce to mockery everything I lived, cheated and killed for, everything for which I was ready to die and send others to their deaths. That's why I mustn't do it. And because ultimately, it would be wrong. And humans can tell right from wrong.' He put down the comb and kissed her lightly.

'I understand,' she said.

He telephoned to cancel his seat reservation on the Stockholm flight. 'There's got to be some other way. Better or worse, crazier or more dangerous, but different. I have some ideas. We'll sleep on it.'

She brought in a silver tray with two glasses of champagne. 'I knew it was going to be an occasion,' she explained. 'I thought we might drink to say good-bye. Now it's welcome back – okay?'


Sunshine perforated the edges of the curtains and Maxon's eyelids. He did not want to wake up. His head felt heavy and his hands refused to move, no matter how much he wanted to reach out and touch Jack before pulling up the blanket for protection against the light. He forced his eyes open slightly. Everything in the room looked fuzzy. A massive fuzzy hang-over, he thought. Unusual for him. His head turned at last. Jack was not there. Must be in the kitchen. Or the bathroom. He fell asleep once again.

It was past noon when Maxon was sufficiently awake at last to look at his watch. Startled, he tried to sit up, but that peculiar hangover had still not gone. Only once had he ever felt anything like that – after recovering from a knock-out inflicted by an over-eager PT master. Nobody knew whether the man was a sadist or a genuine talent scout with a highly individual approach, but his technique worked: at the age of twelve or thirteen, his boys would get a brief lecture, a feel of the boxing gloves, and a 'taste of the leather', served up in a most unceremonious KO punch. The boys who came back for more next day would be taught the art of self-defence. Maxon was one of them. But he never forgot the taste of the leather, the fuzziness of the first sights from a horizontal position in the ring, and the feel of existence devoid of will to move. 'Who the hell was I fighting with?' his thoughts wandered drunkenly. His gaze fell upon two champagne glasses. One was empty, the other half-full. Oh yes, Jack had prepared them for saying good-bye or welcome back. Although his mind would still not be harnessed by the straps of logic, deep down he suddenly knew that this time, the knock out had been chemical rather than physical. He remembered raising the glass to his lips, but he had no recollection of actually drinking the champagne. 'Jack?'

He climbed out of bed, almost fainted, tried to walk, staggered and, finally, crawled to the bathroom. He stopped shouting for Jack. He felt sure she had gone. A long, cold shower hastened the waking-up process and left him feeling rejuvenated: if the champagne had contained the drops he had given to Jack to drug if necessary, as a last resort, Tucker's daughter, the recovery would be complete with no adverse side-effects. Returning to the bedroom, he noticed Samantha's tape recorder: it had not been on the bedside table during the night. He started the tape.

'Josh, my love ...' Jack's clear voice rose from the speaker. 'Isn't it odd? I can call you Josh once again. I hope you don't mind. I couldn't do it before. I mean not since visiting you in that hospital in Washington. Because I tricked and cheated you there. I've tried to live it down ever since. Perhaps you haven't even noticed it. But it's true. I knew all the time that our love would be doomed because nothing could last if it's rebuilt on a lie. And I lied to you in Washington ... Forgive me if I sound a little sentimental, but that's how I feel just now, thinking about my chance to balance the books and wipe out my debt to you ... keep this tape as a momento of my love ... Okay, okay, stop frowning, I promise not to go on like this. Are we friends? ... I love you, Josh ... and I find it hard to speak to this damned machine and say farewell. By the time you'll listen to this, I'll be in Stockholm. I'll give your love to Nadia ...'

Maxon hit the STOP button. He thought for a few seconds, his right fist punched his left palm – and with the clapping sound he activated, inadvertently, some of Samantha's electronic gadgets: the lights changed to a flaming orange glow and Aznavour crooned from somewhere inside the mattress. Maxon wanted to telephone a friend in Stockholm but more clapping only changed the lights and he could not find the right switches to stop the show in the bedroom, so he hurried to the living room and closed the door. He dialled the direct number of a small, obscure but potent unit of Swedish counter-intelligence that kept all 'hostile aliens' under constant surveillance. He hoped that Colonel Wennstrom, the head of the unit, would not yet be at his customarily endless lunch in the Operakellaren, the nearness of which was said to be the only real perk going with his job.

'Yah.'

Maxon recognised the colonel's gasping for air. 'Hi. Maxon here.'

'Ah! How are you, my friend? Are you in Stockholm, and if not why not?'

'Because I'm going to catch the next flight. Meanwhile, you've got to do something for me. I mean right away.'

'You name it.'

'Thanks. You know, I suppose, that the *secret sex weapon* of the opposition is stationed in Stockholm.'

'Very much so,' Wennstrom chuckled. 'You can't help knowing it when she's around.'

Nadia Buzinova's sexual appetite had been a standard joke among the international intelligence fraternity. Allegedly, the KGB hoped that her nymphomania would weaken the entire western alliance singlehandedly. 'Are you still jealous of her?'

'Of course. I can't let her out of sight for a moment.'

'Good.' That meant that the Soviet Baltic Fishing Commission would be under round-the-clock surveillance. All visitors would be logged and photographed for urgent identification. 'Now listen,' Maxon said gravely. 'A major criminal is on the run. She's a confidence trickster. You've got to protect diplomatic missions from her.'

'Yah. I understand.'

'Her name is Mrs Jacqueline Kowalski, but she might have used a false passport. I believe she was on the morning flight from Heathrow.'

'I can check it.'

'Please. But if I'm right and she's already in Stockholm, she'll try to approach the *sex weapon*. She must be prevented from entering the building – whatever it takes.'

After a brief pause the Swede asked: 'Did you say *whatever* it takes?'

'Correct.'

'And do I ask her to stay with me until you arrive?'

'Right again. But the snag is that she may already be inside the building.'

'I can check that, but I must go there. We have . . . er . . .'

'I understand.' Maxon knew they would not have any telephone or radio contact with the surveillance unit. 'Please go and check it right away. But if she's already in there, you must not let her leave.' He anticipated that Nadia would probably try to smuggle Jack out of Sweden at the first possible opportunity. 'Break all rules, cause a diplomatic scandal, but no car, nothing leaves that building without a thorough check.'

'It's difficult, you know.'

'I know. I'll explain everything but you must trust me until then and do it for me, for old times' sake . . . Will you?'

'Oh sure. She's a common criminal as far as I'm concerned. Yah. But I'll need a description.'

'Right. She's five-foot-eight-and-a-half, slim, willowy, with soft dark hair that tends to fly in her face . . .'

'Maxon!' the colonel interrupted him with mocking indignation, 'this is a declaration of love, not the description of a fugitive.'

'I'm sorry. I hope you got the picture.'

'Sure. But is this official business?'

'Strictly official. And for the time being, strictly between the two of us, okay?'

'Whatever you say. Where do I call you?'

'I'll call you.'

'Make it fifteen minutes.'

Maxon rang off and returned to the bedroom. Aznavour was still singing from the heart of the bed, and Maxon could still not find the switch. He clapped and clapped his hands until the music stopped and the lights returned to normal. He then began to dress while listening to the rest of Jack's message.

'. . . in Stockholm. I'll give your love to Nadia . . . I'll imply that it was you who sent me. Only to make them believe me. Wish I could ask you what'll happen to me. I'm terrified. But I know it's got to be done. Ellsberg and you convinced me. It's just that betrayal is alien to your character. Perhaps it isn't to mine. That's why I can go through with it . . . I think.' There was a clink of glasses '. . . Cheers! . . . Isn't this spooky? I mean that my farewell will share your ears with Ellsberg's last words? And isn't it

239

weird that betrayal is the one right thing I can do for the man I love? I hope you'll forgive me one day. Wish I could have done more for you while we were together. The trouble is you're too independent and self-sufficient. Except that now, just this once, you need someone because you've been too loyal too long to change . . . You need someone to whom right and wrong are meaningless . . . or mean something else . . . Cheers . . .

'Mm . . . You see what I'm doing? I'm trying to delay my moment of departure. Maybe I'm hoping that the drug doesn't work, you wake up and don't let me go. Or perhaps that your breathing may become erratic because the drug is too strong, and I must stay to save your life. It would be right, wouldn't it? Kowalski once quoted some maxim, from the Talmud, I think, that someone who saves a life, saves the world. Am I not even luckier? By saving the world, I can save a life. Your life . . .' There was a long pause. Maxon tried to imagine if she was crying with or without tears. 'I'd better go now bec . . .' A hissing sound from the machine signalled that Jack must have run out of time and tape. He dialled Wennstrom's number again.

'Yah.'

'Maxon.'

'Yah, you were right. She was on the morning flight, and went straight to see the *sex weapon*. She's still inside the building.'

'Is it extraterritorial?'

'Not quite. I mean it hasn't got full diplomatic immunity, but we can't just go barging in to get her.'

'You mean *you* can't,' Maxon paused, 'but that's all right, you only have to make sure she doesn't leave until I get there. Meet me at the airport. Can you get some architectural drawings of the building?'

'Er . . . the fire brigade may have some . . . I'll try.'

'Thanks. I'll need some help from you, but officially I won't involve you, don't worry.'

'Is she that important?'

'Yes.'

'To you? Personally?'

'She's a traitor. She has to be stopped. That's all.'

# IX

At five in the morning, the darkness of Lenin Hill belonged to hungry cats and nervous sparrows that made up Moscow's fauna. Like all Moscow inhabitants, both the cats and the sparrows knew their places and fled fast when a black and graceless Pobeda approached. It was followed by a bulldozer and a Wartburg of East German extraction that sounded like cutlery shaken in a dustbin as it trundled along the road, skirting precariously the edge of the hill with a sheer drop to the ski jump and the river. The convoy stopped opposite the Lomonosov university tower, where a paved terrace jutted out offering panoramic views of the town below. The two passengers of the Pobeda showed no interest in Moscow at night. They glanced up and down the road to ensure that both ends were blocked by guards, examined the railing at the edge of the terrace, and cut the metal bars with the aid of a portable power-saw.

As soon as the two men had returned to the Pobeda, the Wartburg was driven right up to the broken rails. The driver alighted, pulled a slumped body from the passenger to the driving seat, and closed the door. He then joined the men in the Pobeda, while the bulldozer shoved the Wartburg through the railings.

Throughout the operation, not a single word was exchanged. They all heard the sound of crashing metal, the thuds of the bouncing, somersaulting vehicle, the minor explosion and the crackle of fire, but none of this was their concern. As they drove away, a police car took their place on the terrace, and uniformed men alerted the fire and rescue services.

Before sunrise, the dead driver of the Wartburg had been identified as Lt Colonel Vorodin, 'a most loyal and hard-working officer on Marshal Beryov's personal staff,' and an investigation began with several arrests to 'uncover the corrupt and negligent practices at Autoservice No. 1' where Vorodin's Wartburg had last been serviced.

Over breakfast, KGB collator Kobelyev heard about the 'tragic accident'. It made him feel most uncomfortable: he knew that Vorodin was an enemy of the state, but it worried him why these days, nobody high up could ever be convicted of treason, corruption, nepotism, misappropriation of funds or any other ordinary crimes. But when he heard about the 'cleaning up' at Autoservice No. 1, he realised that Vorodin's accident had vacated a few highly desirable positions for applicants who would know how to be grateful with the annual allocation of the limited new car quota. Kobelyev felt sick and unable to perform any useful work all day.

At five in the afternoon, he was preparing to go home, when he received an urgent assignment of highest priority, straight from the Director's office, to trace, identify and cross-check every possible reference to 'Jacqueline Kowalski, Mrs, *née* Davis'. Why don't they all just go and drown in a sea of paperwork, Kobelyev thought as he removed the dust-cover of the computer terminal. Not even the sight of his beloved BC 202 could cheer him up. But then he began to think. This Mrs Kowalski was connected with Maxon, Maxon with Ellsberg, Ellsberg with Vorodin. The 'accident' would conceal from the imperialists that their friend, the puppet Vorodin, had been unmasked. This reasoning filled Kobelyev with renewed admiration for his superiors: it was good to work for an organisation that was clever enough to out-think the opposition. It would have annoyed him if he knew that his orders for a trace had been delayed for some three hours because nobody dared to do anything until it had been okayed at the top.

Nadia Buzinova spoke in Russian on the phone. Jack pretended to concentrate on the remnants of her lunch, but listened carefully: although she did not understand the language, the tone left her in no doubt that Nadia was furious. The stunning news about GLEW had been transmitted to Moscow at eleven in the morning; at the same time, Nadia had requested, most urgently, all available information on Jacqueline Kowalski; now it was two in the afternoon, five p.m. Moscow time, and Nadia had not yet received anything apart from instructions to continue the interrogation in a friendly manner, and await the arrival of a high-ranking specialist from the Centre.

Nadia hung up at last and apologised for the interruption. She tried to reassure Jack that she would soon be seen by somebody at the very highest level, and asked if in the meantime they could go through everything just once again.

'You know, I'm disappointed in you,' said Jack without looking up from her plate. 'Maxon said you were a bright woman who'd grasp the essence of his message, and recognise how urgent it was to pass it on.'

'But that's exactly what I've done.'

'Then what is it? Don't you believe me? Or perhaps your people in Moscow refuse to believe you? What's the point in repeating and repeating it all? I've told you everything there was. I've given you as much proof as I can. I've told you that GLEW is merely a bluff, it can't detect any space-launched missiles, the alert that triggered off the whole affair had come from a defector not a satellite, and I've told you that my statements can be checked quite easily. All you have to do is to launch another missile programmed to test this so-called early warning system and then have it destroy itself.' She stopped and stared back at Nadia. 'No, we're not getting anywhere.'

'Coffee?'

'No thanks.' Jack walked round the room. She noted the thickly padded double-door, the unlived-in emptiness of Nadia's third-floor office – not her real one, presumably – and looked down on the darkening Stockholm street: was it really getting dark outside or was the tinted windowpane misleading her? She returned to Nadia, facing her across the desk: 'I'm disappointed in you.'

'I know, it's most frustrating, but I'm sure that deep down you're capable of appreciating our problems. And it's difficult to be more helpful and forthright when you still refuse to explain why Mister Maxon sent *you* with such tremendously important secrets.'

'He trusts me. Obviously.'

'Why didn't he come?'

'You'll have to ask him one day. All I know is what he told me. "Go to Stockholm, find Nadia Buzinova, she'll know what to do with the information because she's a clever woman and a pro." That's all he said. No, to tell you the truth, he also warned me never to lie to you because you'll separate fact from fiction in no time.'

'Oh, he's such a charmer. But you see, he must have overestimated me. Yes, I do know a little about Baltic fishing and things like that, but when it comes to early warning systems and the secret world of spies, I'm ignorant and innocent like any other working housewife. So I had to find out where to forward Maxon's message, and now we must rely on my clever friends in Moscow.'

'And they don't believe me?'

'They do. Of course they do. Why else would they study all your information so carefully? And why else would they bother to send a very, very high-ranking specialist? He's already on his way solely to talk to you.'

'It's a waste of time. I did offer to go to Moscow if necessary, didn't I?' She poured some coffee into her cup.

'We couldn't risk that. If your information is correct, you're invaluable. What if you were caught on the way? Or shot! It's our duty, for your sake and our sake, to protect you. But just to reassure you, I think I can give away a secret even if I'm not yet authorised to tell you: you've already been granted full political asylum.'

'Which I haven't asked for!' Jack put down her cup with such violent force that coffee splashed all over the desk.

Nadia answered with a sad, most conciliatory half-smile: 'There was no need to *ask* for anything. Asylum was granted because we knew you wouldn't have any other choice.'

'But I do have a choice.'

'What? To go to jail?'

'It's my neck. I can risk it, can't I?'

'It would be very unkind and impractical if we allowed it. You must be praised and rewarded for your brave decision to come to us and perform a potentially enormous service to mankind.'

'But that's just it.' Frustration blunted her tone. 'I'm no Communist. I didn't tell you about GLEW to show my love for Russia. It was Maxon who discovered that GLEW was a much too dangerous bluff. He tried to force our people to call it off. When he failed, he had no choice but to expose the bluff to avert nuclear war. It called for living up to higher loyalties than one has for a single nation. I agreed with him, and when it became clear that he had to stay on to fight for peace, I accepted the mission.'

'And we appreciate it.'

Jack noted that Nadia was fiddling with something under the desk: a tape recorder, presumably. 'It was a moral duty. I performed it, so now I must be free to leave if I want to.'

'You must be protected from hasty decisions.'

'You mean you'd keep me here against my wish?'

'No-no. We're on the same side, we're fighting for peace ... together ... that's why we're anxious to find out some important details that would support your own position.'

'What details?'

'Anything you might have forgotten to mention. That's why I'm asking you to go through it all once more.'

It took Jack another two hours to tell her story again. She was pleased when the phone rang. 'Excuse me ...' Nadia gestured towards the pot indicating that Jack could help herself to some coffee while she answered the call. '*Da ... Kak? ... Da ...*' She kept nodding as she listened. '*Ponimayu*' She rang off, looked at Jack and pouted to express her displeasure: 'You haven't told me when Mister Maxon will come over.'

'Of course not. Because he won't.'

'I've just received a coded telex. My friend in Moscow finds it most odd that Maxon doesn't come. People in his line of business have only one way to run when they're in trouble.'

That's what Maxon said, thought Jack. She tried to sound casual and disinterested: 'Who says he's in trouble?'

'My knowledgeable friend in Moscow.'

'He must be very, very knowledgeable.'

The irony did not escape Nadia, but she chose to ignore it. 'He is. And he finds it odd that Maxon uses a messenger in such an important case. But then, there may be another explanation.'

'Such as?'

'Perhaps Maxon only wants to be sure that he'll get a friendly reception when he comes. Perhaps you're his insurance that his message will get through to us even if he himself can't.'

'Your friend must have a lot of spare time to dream up such fancy theories.'

'It's his job.'

'Must be most interesting.' Jack pretended to yawn.

'Perhaps you could help him one day.'

'Oh, I'm no good with theories.'

'It's not just theories. He needs people who know the situation in the West. His helpers have a very, very good life, Mrs Kowalski . . . I mean, my name is Nadia, may I call you Jack?'

Jack hoped her face would not show that she began to feel scared: the last phone call might have begun to provide Nadia with background information; if so, Moscow might have begun to accept her credibility. 'Of course, Nadia,' she said with a formal nod, 'except that my name is Jacqueline.'

'Oh yes, it's just that my friend tells me that your real friends, I mean closest friends, call you Jack. Or was it just a special friend? I can't remember . . . how awful . . . But I'm sure that my friend mentioned something . . .'

'And he's very, very knowledgeable.'

'That's right. But he's never quite sure about anything. He knows he may be wrong about Mr Maxon, too. Because Mr Maxon may only be playing some trick on us. Perhaps he's trying to get himself out of trouble by sending us false messages, hoping that his messenger could then simply walk away . . . Mm . . . Knowing him, such deviousness wouldn't surprise me.'

'You mean you know him well, Nadia.'

'Quite well, Jack.'

Suddenly, invisible claws protruded from every finger in the room. 'How well is *quite well*, Nadia?'

'Oh, a beautiful woman like yourself has nothing to fear from a plain and plump one like me.'

'Fear? No, not even if he finds you most attractive. *His* words.'

'Isn't that nice? I must thank him for it. Even if he only meant to make you jealous – which makes me jealous. But then, I'm sure Maxon would tell us that jealousy is a bad adviser.'

Jack laughed with a ring of sincerity. 'No, you don't know him at all. He'd never dish out such banalities.'

'We'll ask him one day, shall we? We'll say "listen Joshua" . . . I mean Josh . . . Do you *also* call him Josh? . . . No, you don't have to answer . . . But we'll ask him, okay?'

'You're crazy, Nadia.'

'That's what Josh said sometimes. Isn't that interesting?

246

Did he tell you that I was crazy?' The phone rang and she picked it up impatiently. 'Yes ...?' She then listened, switched to Russian and sounded astonished. '*Kak? ... Akh, kogda? ... Chto on imenno skazal? ... Ponimayu ...*' Her eyes began to laugh. Her mouth wanted to share their fun. She struggled to control it and keep up an official tone: '*Gde on seyches nakhoditsya? ... Oprosite yevo pogrobno,*' her voice grew sharper, '*a zatyem shazu privedite komne.*' She hung up with determination. Her eyes were not laughing any more. 'Well, perhaps I'm not that crazy after all. Maxon is here.'

'I don't believe you.'

'He'll soon be on his way up. First a few formalities must be attended to. I hope, for his sake, that he's not armed. More coffee, Mrs Kowalski?'


In London it was four o'clock when Gloucester received Maxon's call from 'somewhere abroad'. It then took him an infuriating hour to track down Sandy.

'Are you sure he was speaking from abroad?' Sandy asked.

'No, but that's what he said.'

'What else did he say?'

'He was rather cautious and mysterious. He said he was on a mission, and if he couldn't return within twenty-four hours, I would receive a package by special delivery. He said it was his insurance. My job would be to get the package to you, personally, and tell you that he had *not* lied to you about Locke and all that. Does it make any sense to you?'

'Sure ...' It's another of his tricks – Sandy swallowed the words. He could not tell Gloucester that he had fought for permission to raise a general alert and place Maxon right at the top of the international 'most wanted' list. Locke had opposed him, enlisting the support of the Prime Minister's security adviser, overseer of all British intelligence operations. Eventually they had agreed that Maxon's photograph should be circulated by Interpol, though his name would have to be withheld, temporarily, for security reasons. What these reasons were, Sandy was not told. But half a victory was better than none. He now thanked Gloucester for his call, and promised him that his helpfulness would not be forgotten.

Maxon submitted to a search willingly enough, but then refused to go anywhere further inside the building. He insisted that Nadia Buzinova must come down to see him, and he would wait near the wrought-iron grille of the plateglass front door, where he could be seen from the street. As he paced up and down impatiently, two burly figures with standard-issue cauliflower ears stationed themselves sandwiching the door. They tried to look aloof, but the effect was as subtly inconspicuous as the presence of a bunch of Highland gillies at a Brazilian Cup Final. Maxon hoped he would never need to tangle with them.

Nadia came down the stairs. She smiled politely. They shook hands. She had already been told that Maxon was not carrying weapons or hidden transmitters, but she took the precaution of bringing a radio with her and playing it loudly as they talked in the glass cage the porter had vacated for them.

With the furled issue of *Time* magazine, Maxon pointed at the radio-cab outside the entrance. Yes, she had already noted it. 'Swedish intelligence,' he explained needlessly. 'So they know that I'm in here and that Mrs Kowalski is also in here, but they only *think* they know *why* we're in here.' Nadia tried to ask something but Maxon silenced her. 'Please listen carefully, we haven't got much time. For reasons I'll explain to you, I couldn't set up a better prepared ... well, defection. If you accept my conditions, I'll place myself at your command and will co-operate with whatever plans you make for getting us to Moscow.'

Nadia thought fast: had they been at the Soviet embassy, any Soviet embassy anywhere in the world, she would have access to contingency plans and secret routes for the transport of any willing or unwilling 'passenger' out of the extraterritorial building; at the Baltic mission she had no such facility, and if Maxon's presence was known to the Swedes nothing could be achieved without his co-operation or the risk of a very major diplomatic scandal. 'If I agree to what you want, will you get rid of the watcher?' was her only question.

'Naturally,' Maxon smiled. 'I haven't come here to be watched by them.'

'Okay. What are you offering and what are your conditions?'

'I presume that you've already got my message.'

'Yes, she told me, though she claimed all along that you'd never come.'

'She didn't know. I couldn't tell her.'

'Just as I guessed: she was only the advance party and your insurance, right?'

'Of course you were right and she was wrong. But then she hasn't got your experience and field sense.' Maxon did not believe that anybody could be buttered up *too* much, and Nadia's face, beaming with tickled vanity, told him that the principle was still valid. 'Now take me to her, Nadia.'

'Why? Because you love her?'

'Because she's my insurance, as you said. I want to get her signal that you've treated her and my message correctly.'

Nadia was on her guard: what if Maxon was here to kill Jack? She tried to stall. 'Suppose she gives you the signal – what then?'

'Then you could order a really good dinner for three and make arrangements for me to see someone at the very top in Moscow.'

'Someone just like that is already on his way here. A happy coincidence.'

'Not happy enough. What I have to say is too big for you or me or anyone who could be dragged at a moment's notice from Moscow. No, you'll have to get me there – and I'll have to see the Director himself.'

'You're playing for high stakes, Maxon.'

'I know. I haven't changed.'

'Haven't you?' She looked coquettish, but her voice was strictly businesslike. 'I'll have to consult Moscow. It'll take time.'

It was obvious what it would really take: some quick thinking. Could they afford to accept his offer? Could they afford not to accept it? If meeting Jack was a precondition, it might be because he loved her – or wanted to kill her. But apparently, she had already told Nadia everything she knew. Her death would be an embarrassment but no great loss. An important gain, in fact. It would prove that she had

249

been telling the truth, that her information about GLEW was vital enough to justify Maxon's desperate bid to get in here and kill her.

'We have no time to lose, Nadia, I'm sorry.'

'I know,' she said. With something of this magnitude, she could not trust even her direct scrambler phones to the Centre. Coded telexes would take too long. There was nobody in Stockholm she could turn to for authorisation and backing. She decided to take the plunge. 'Okay, I'll take you to her.'

'And then to your leader,' Maxon said lightly and gestured towards the lift. 'After you, Nadia.'

She did not move. Her eyes were on the magazine in his hand. 'Is that the current issue?'

'Yes. Would you like to see it?'

'Please.' She held it by the corner of the front cover and shook it. Nothing fell out. She flicked through the pages, then handed it back to him.

'Congratulations.' Maxon gave her the thumbs-up to acknowledge her vigilance. 'Your goons forgot to check it.'

She passed the lift door and led him up the stairs. He understood: the goons could follow them and others could keep an eye on them all the way. Maxon welcomed the opportunity to catch a few glimpses of the lay-out of the building and compare it with his mental pictures of the architect's drawings Colonel Wennstrom had shown him at the airport.

As the padded doors closed behind them in the face of the two heavies outside, Jack and Maxon exchanged rather formal greetings under Nadia's watchful eyes.

'May I use your telephone?' Maxon asked and dialled a number at random. To reassure Nadia about his intention of sticking to their deal, he told the astonished Swedish stranger on the line that everything was okay, she could remove the radio-cab from outside the building. Only then did he turn to Jack to announce that they would go together to Moscow. 'Sorry I couldn't tell you in advance, but this was the safest way.'

Jack said nothing.

Maxon looked at his watch: another ten minutes before Wennstrom and his team would be ready. To justify his checking the time, he asked Nadia if it would be too early for having a vodka. She said she would arrange some to be sent in while she went to see what urgent arrangements could be made. She thought it might take some time. When they were alone, Jack was about to say something, but Maxon's frown warned her not to. 'I suppose you had some doubts but I think I've proved again that you could trust me. Do you?'

'Yes.' Her voice was weak. She did not know what to think any more. She had tried to do the right thing for him, now she did not know what was right and wrong any more. It was easier to sit back and trust him. She took out a cigarette.

He gave her a light, and glanced at his watch: another seven minutes to go. The desk looked heavy: it could block the door.

One of the goons brought in a bottle of vodka, some beer, glasses and chopped up cucumbers. He put the tray on the desk. Maxon dismissed him with an impatient wave: as expected, the man knew how to recognise genuine authority and left hurriedly.

With three minutes to go, Nadia returned. That was unexpected, but could not be helped. They drank to success, peace and comradeship. 'Everything is in hand ... we should hear soon ...,' Nadia said reassuringly to break the apparently uncomfortable silence. She was pouring everybody a second round of drinks when Maxon caught her by the throat. Her mouth opened but no sound came out. Her face went white, then red in quick succession, and she gasped for air. She tried to wriggle free but the pressure on her throat increased. 'You're more beautiful than ever,' he said in a loud voice for the benefit of hidden microphones if there were any, then whispered into her ear: 'it would be such a pity to hurt you.' Suddenly her weight increased: she had passed out. He lowered her gently to the floor and gestured towards Jack, mouthing the words without a sound: 'Lock the door.' She turned the key slowly to kill the click.

Maxon took another look at Nadia, then picked up his *Time* and put a light to it. The magazine, impregnated with a magnesium-base chemical by courtesy of Wennstrom, flared up and emitted an astonishingly disproportionate amount of thick smoke. Maxon held it up to the smoke-detector nozzle on the ceiling. Jack watched him, mesmerised. Within three seconds, both the internal and external fire bells began to ring. At the same time, the alarm signal would be received at the nearest fire station, Maxon knew, but the time gap between that and the arrival of the brigade could be fatal to him. His only hope was that Wennstrom had already surrounded the building with fire tenders and turntable ladder units. He pushed the desk against the door. In a daze, Jack helped him.

Through the padded doors, faint knocking could be heard. At the same time, the quiet street below came to life. Fire vehicles roared in with wailing sirens. The knocking grew louder. Maxon scribbled on a piece of paper: WE'RE OK IN HERE, NOBODY IS TO COME IN, KEEP OUT THE FIREMEN. He splashed the vodka on Nadia's face. She opened her eyes, and recoiled with a fright as Maxon grabbed her throat again. He forced her to pick up the telephone, read his note and give orders in Russian to be left alone. Panic and pain distorted her voice. That was a risk: her men might become suspicious. But even then, the call could gain them a few vital seconds. As soon as Nadia put the phone down, he hit her on the chin, hoping to cause the minimum pain, and caught her in his arm when her eyes glazed over.

Behind the window, two rising ladders with firemen atop could be seen. Both seemed to waver. The turntable operators were looking for would-be escapees. Maxon let Nadia collapse. He tried in vain to open the window. It had to be broken. He used a chair. Falling glass might hurt people in the street below, but that was another risk he had to accept. 'Shout for help.' He turned to press the desk harder against the door. Jack hesitated. 'Shout!' She moved like a robot. She had given up thinking for herself. Her shout was not much more than a loud whisper, but the first ladder was already close enough for her to be heard.

On the outside of the door, furious hammering had begun. Leaning against the desk, Maxon could feel the increasing pressure. The fireman was calling out to Jack. She stood there, watching Maxon.

Nadia opened her eyes. 'Don't go, Jack,' she croaked with great effort. 'Moscow knows everything by now ...'

'Go!' Maxon yelled. He felt furious: he ought to have hit Nadia harder.

'He's cheated you, Jack, he's cheating again.'

'Are you, Josh? Tell me ...'

The door began to give, only the desk and Maxon seemed to hold it, but he rushed to the window and thrust Jack into the arms of the fireman.

The second ladder appeared as soon as the other had swung away. The door broke with a crash at the top and the desk began to yield. The ladder was still too far for Maxon to reach. The two heavies came stumbling through. Maxon pointed at Nadia on the floor: 'Help her!'

The men turned to look as ordered. Nadia struggled to squeeze a painful sound out of her throat – and the delay was long enough for Maxon to step on the window sill, lean outwards until his balance was lost, hear the collective gasp from the street, and hope that he could join hands with the fireman reaching towards him.

Colonel Wennstrom was about to pick up the telephone when a call came through.

'Locke here. You promised to call me.'

'Yah, I was about to. Everything is fine. They'll soon be boarding. Skylark asked me to call Sandy. Shall I?'

'What did he want?'

'He wants Sandy to meet him at Heathrow. It's got to be Sandy and nobody else.'

Sandy was the last man Locke wanted to involve. 'Okay, I'll pass on the message. Don't bother to call him. Just keep an eye on those two and make sure that they are on that flight.'

Locke rang off. He hated to sit back and wait. He hated to be anywhere but in the firing line, and he hated decision-making. He also felt hatred radiating towards him from every direction. How much would they hate him if he chose the direct method for an easy solution to the problem? He could arrange some accident with a fighter aircraft. The Stockholm flight would simply disappear from the radar screens. It would take years for anyone to suspect anything. Why couldn't somebody else decide? Because you're a general, he said to himself and stood up. His vanity demanded that he should make his decision and act fully upright, exposed to imaginary bullets that were about to fly.

He reached for the telephone. He hated Sandy whom he now needed if he wanted to avoid complications with

Maxon at Heathrow, and he hated the thought that Sandy might be loved by everyone, including subordinates.

Sandy opened a soft leather case and eased out his gleaming piccolo. The sight of the instrument had the immediate effect of driving his wife's precious poodle out of the room The first high-pitched scales would keep his wife out, too – might even chase her all the way to her bridge club. The piccolo was Sandy's only infallible safeguard against marital conversations; the sound of his practising was the only silence he knew in his home. Yes, it was going to be a fine and peaceful evening.

Before he could lift the instrument to his lips, his wife appeared. 'Te-lee-phone,' she sang gleefully.

Locke spoke with apologetic impertinence. He wanted Sandy to go to Heathrow, pick up Maxon and companion, and bring them, under armed guard, to the American Air Force base at Rickmansworth.

'I'm no policeman,' Sandy said angrily. If only Maxon had been right about Locke, if only it was not sheer nonsense that GLEW did not exist ... Sandy had tried to find something damaging about the general, but all his discreet inquiries led straight to the top: if Locke was a traitor and there was a conspiracy, at least one of the western leaders would have to be implicated. Sandy loathed the man who had ruined the high degree of independence of his 'special projects' group, who had the backing of Sir Gerald, the PM's pet who had forced Maxon's transfer to that obscure upstart of a security outfit. 'I should have resigned when Sir Gerald made that special request,' thought Sandy. 'I should have foreseen that *helping* Locke would mean plain servicing with no questions asked.' Months of anger and humiliation collected now like nicotine on Sandy's lips: 'I'm sorry, I've got to say no to this one. I'm too senior to play bumbailiff or errand boy. We have professionals for effecting an arrest, and I'll arrange it for you if you wish.'

'Too bad, Sandy, it's got to be you and nobody else. I'm conveying Sir Gerald's personal message.'

'Then Sir Gerald will have my resignation.'

Sandy hung up, and began to compose his request for immediate retirement. A few minutes later, it was Sir Gerald himself on the phone, giving him the sort of bollocking Sandy had not heard since his earliest parade ground days: 'I don't give a shit what you think of Locke. And you may think what you like about me, but I want *you* at Heathrow. Why? Because that's what I want. And because Maxon expects you to be there, and I want no trouble from him in public. He must not contact anyone, he must not get away, and you alone are responsible for both.'

Sandy reacted to the crudity of the voice like a well-trained battle-horse to the sound of the trumpet. He had not been drilled to pick and choose his duties; he thought when thinking was his job, and he knew how to keep his mouth shut when unquestioning loyalty was demanded. Pompous principles of his oft-delivered lectures rushed to his aid. 'There was no price tag one could attach to the silence of obedience' ... 'One could not resign in the middle of the battle ...'

He packed away the piccolo, slipped his old Browning into his pocket, and had the consolation of not telling his wife where he was going and when he might be back.


Jack and Maxon walked hand in hand down the aisle: nobody could notice the handcuff he had borrowed from Wennstrom to bind them together. They refused food but ordered champagne – to hold the glass, each needed only one hand.

'Relax,' he said.

'Will you tell me how?'

'Try more champagne. May be our last for a long time.'

'Damn you,' she said.

'To absent friends,' he raised his glass.

She drank up with him and held out her glass for more. 'Will your Swedish friend be in trouble?'

'Why should he? He wasn't involved. There was an alarm, the fire brigade responded with *admirable* speed and rescued some frantic damsel in distress.'

'Who'll accept that when Nadia stirs it up?'

'She can't. She has nothing to go on. Officially, we've never been in that building. And even if we have, she'd have no right to detain us.'

'And since when do they respect such rights? No, you're bluffing Maxon, you were plain lucky to pull it off.'

'Wrong. I played the odds.'

'What odds? I could have refused to help and lock the door.'

'Why didn't you?'

'I don't know ... I was kind of dazed ... It was quite sudden and it was good to see you ... Was that one of the odds you played?'

'I hoped you'd trust me.'

'What if I hadn't? What if I had refused to leave? I could have helped Nadia. I could have fought you.'

Maxon tried to smile but failed. Grooves of bitterness ran from the corners of his mouth. 'I'd have killed you.'

She closed her eyes. She needed no visual confirmation that he had meant it. She let the sentence circulate up and down her veins, cool her body and numb her mind. Then she stared through the window, chasing the last of daylight as it dived from the poolside of the horizon.

The three-car convoy, its headlights on full beam, sliced through the Moscow night with total disregard for traffic lights and speed limit. Fortunately, the traffic was sparse at this late hour, and all policemen on point duty helped to keep the route clear when they recognised the elongated limousine in the middle as part of the Politburo membership regalia.

The Director of the KGB and Marshal Beryov of the missile forces sat side by side in heavy silence. Only the *Nachalnik* himself could have detected the fact that both men, two of the most powerful dozen in the world, were sulking like schoolboys. He had invited them to a private meeting that would precede the joint emergency session of the Politburo and the war cabinet. The invitation was about the greatest accolade to the two men's status – the sulking was their own doing. Each would have preferred to have the *Nachalnik*'s ear to himself, at least briefly, before the meeting, because war or no war, their private clash in public could ruin them both and sink them without trace; and because each man regarded the current crisis as chiefly the other's doing.

The upheaval had begun at the Centre with the news from Stockholm about a defector and her astounding allegation concerning GLEW. First the credibility of the source, that Kowalski woman, had to be scrutinised. The evaluation was positive, but then the news of her abduction turned it all upside down. Foreseeing the grave implications, the Director could not keep it all to himself or restrict the investigation to the intelligence circuit. Leading scientists and GLEW-watchers had to be consulted, and the result convinced the Director that many of the key men sided with Beryov and the hawks. They claimed that no amount of theorising would solve the puzzle fast enough, therefore an empirical approach should be used which, in plain terms, meant another test, another firing of a missile from a space station, another gamble on GLEW detecting or not detecting the launch before the missile would destruct itself, with the renewed risk of being caught redhanded and ridiculed once again. Over my dead body, the Director was inclined to argue, but he chose not to because it would have been a sheer challenge to fate. Catching a glimpse of the building that housed the Borodino battle panorama, he reflected on his current unalterable position: perhaps it had been a mistake to change the KGB's traditional position from the hawkish to the diplomatic, but at the time it had seemed the best short cut for him to inheriting the *Nachalnik*'s chair.

The silhouette of the Kremlin began to loom up at the top end of the Kalinin Prospekt. The confrontation was only minutes away, and both men knew that it could deteriorate into a mutually fatal showdown unless some sort of deal could be struck; but their positions were too rigid, they knew each other's argument by heart, and there was little they could add now.

At the meeting Beryov would allege that the KGB had failed to glean sufficient intelligence about GLEW, and if a missile was an unacceptable risk to *test* GLEW, then an immediate EMP test could silence everybody who dared to ridicule the weapons of the Soviet Union. The Director would argue that nuclear strategy was not a matter of weapon capability because everybody had the weapons these days: it was a matter of credibility, the credibility of the will to use those weapons.

The *Nachalnik* would sit on the fence and mock them both as usual. How come that the Mad Monk of the KGB could not tell fact from fiction, and bluff from likely double-bluff? How come that all the money Beryov had spent on scientists and their expensive toys could produce nothing but the urge to have a really big bang? Yet ultimately, he and the Politburo might back the EMP, bury their collective head in the sand and pretend that they were not turning the world into a desert but a Socialist paradise, unless . . . unless the Director could give them full assurance that the 'Stockholm episode' was not just a trap. And that assurance he could not give. The principal wares of his trade were not facts but menaces and make-believe, and these thrived on time – a commodity that had joined the current shortages of Soviet life. So he would have to fight for time to unravel the 'Stockholm episode'.

The fate of Maxon and the Kowalski woman would be the key to it all. IF she was caught and shot or killed in some 'accident', the conclusions would be obvious: she was a traitor and had told the truth. GLEW did not exist, and Maxon had done a good job. IF he died with her, she could still be a traitor and his death might be a cover-up punishment for unauthorised activities. IF both were praised: the 'defection' and 'rescue' must have been a trick. IF they were imprisoned, the KGB would get to them one way or another, no matter where they were kept. But IF they managed to escape, the race would be on to capture them first and question them under duress. The Director had no doubt that they would confess everything. He would conduct the interrogation personally. It would be a privilege. Almost as great a privilege as to interrogate Beryov himself, one day.

The convoy flashed through the gates of the Kremlin and the headlights burrowed into the onion shadows.

Jack appeared to be asleep. A stewardess cruised down the aisle and awarded Maxon the smile that was reserved for passengers who refused free food and drank champagne. Jack, oblivious to their favoured status, mumbled incredulously: 'You really would have killed me . . . How could you?'

'I'm sorry.'

'That's a great answer.'

Maxon made a furious turn towards her. The sudden

258

move yanked the handcuff and hurt them both. 'You think I'm enjoying this? You think it's fun to hunt you down and march you to jail?'

'We could run away.'

'We can't, Jack, it's too late.'

'It wouldn't take you any time at all to organise an escape route, a set of papers, new names, new identities . . .'

'And new memories? How do you propose to forget what happened?'

'We'll start afresh.'

'Yes, we will – once the dirt is washed off.' He sounded uncertain. His thoughts were drifting in search of answers.

Her tired eyes scrutinised this stranger who would have killed her. 'You reckon that throwing me to the dogs will cleanse our souls?'

'Our suffering may. And the fact that we may have saved millions of lives. But whatever excuses we have, we've committed a crime. The punishment is due and just.'

'I didn't know you were a catholic at heart.'

'I'd be a fake, a cheat and a hypocrite if I failed to bring my loved ones to justice.'

The aircraft landed with a soft bump, Heathrow shimmered past the windows, but Jack ignored it all. 'What justice? Whose justice?' she shouted over the roar of the engines as they went into reverse thrust.

'Keep your voice down.'

'What if I don't? Will you kill me?'

The Tannoy clink-clunked to life. The stewardess sounded immensely pleased with having enjoyed her passengers' company, and urged them to remain seated until eternity or a complete halt of the aircraft – whichever might occur sooner.

Jack spoke right through the announcement, and Maxon knew no way to stop her.

'All right, Mr Prosecutor, tell me what's the charge. Was it really wrong to do what logic, *your* logic told us to do? Can you be wrong if you do the right thing?'

'I don't know what's right and wrong any more.'

'You wouldn't have accepted that from Eichmann or from your great friend Ellsberg.'

'I know. It's just that I don't know anything any more.'

'But I do know something. I know that for once I've done

the right thing for the man I love ... Don't take that away from me.'

'I won't. I promise.'

As always, the passengers were restless. They stood up, sweating, waiting, luggage in hand, squashed against each other, as if it would speed up the opening of the doors and shorten the arrival procedure.

Jack stared out of the window, then turned back to Maxon. 'Good,' she whispered, 'then I'll go through with it. It was me who gave away the secrets. I'll face the music. But you stay out of it. That's my only condition.'

'Thank you, but no thank you.'

'You caught me, you bring me to justice, you'll be a hero – why should we both go to jail?'

'Mm. Good question. I'll think about it.'

'Don't mock me, Maxon. If you stayed free, you could visit me sometimes. Bring me things ... cigarettes ... give me a light ... seriously ...'

'And seriously you think I could live with myself? If you're the traitor, I'm the instigator. I'm the one who knows all the details, and if we, both of us, tell Sandy what we know, he may be able to minimise the damage.'

'It's too late!' She said loudly. When people turned towards them, she kissed his ear, and whispered: 'It's too late. Moscow knows it all by now.'

Maxon knew that unfortunately she was right: GLEW was a dead duck – and once again, Moscow had the window of opportunity wide open for a sneak attack.

The passengers surged forward impatiently. Maxon remained seated. Jack looked down on the tarmac. 'That's odd,' she said. 'Don't they usually go right up to one of those jetties for disembarkation?'

Maxon shrugged his shoulders. It would be pointless to worry her with the explanation that Wennstrom must have alerted Sandy who, in turn, having made special arrangements with the airport authorities, would keep his reception committee out of sight until the last possible moment.

The passengers filed round the wing of the aircraft. A couple of stragglers had to be warned to duck under the low-hanging engines. Sandy watched the stairs. He knew that Maxon would probably appear last in the door at the top. At Sandy's signal, two unmarked saloons and four men moved in swiftly. Maxon led Jack down the stairs.

Adjusting his eyes to the dim lights, he recognised Sandy's stooping figure and noted the strategically positioned motorcycle police further away. He frowned when Sandy failed to return his greeting except with a disdainful wave of three fingers that directed Maxon towards the larger of the cars.

They rode in silence. Sandy found it hard to play the deaf, dumb and mindless executive arm of authority. He was not supposed to ask or answer any questions, so he rudely ignored Maxon's hesitant attempt at some conversation. A spasm of anger sent ripples down Maxon's arms. Jack put her free hand on his clenched fist to cool him. He then removed the handcuff and dropped the key on the floor. It was a petty gesture, but he had run out of grand ones.

At the Air Force base, they were saluted through the gate without stopping. The cars followed the road along the perimeter, and came to a halt at a dark building that stood apart behind a clump of sycamores. A civilian with a submachine-gun opened the door for Jack and Maxon. Sandy stayed in the car and called to Maxon in a low and bitter voice: 'You of all people ... why?' Before Maxon could answer or Jack could protest that there was nothing against Maxon, the cars and motorcycles pulled away, and a second armed civilian led the two of them into the house. They were ushered to a small, rather dark room, lit only by a single bulb under a green glass shade on a brass stand. Locke joined them a moment later, and they heard the key being turned behind him.

Locke sat behind the tatty, sergeant's-issue desk, and gestured a little formally towards the two chairs opposite: 'Take a pew, as Sandy would say.'

'Why isn't he here?' Maxon demanded.

'Because this is something strictly between ourselves.' He took a sheet of blank paper out of the combination lock briefcase he had brought with him. 'Would you like to start with a summary of what happened in Stockholm?'

'No. We have nothing to say to you, but we'll make a full statement to the proper authorities.'

'Very well, then let me say it all for you.' Locke placed his fingertips with great precision on the edge of the table. 'You've conducted a series of unauthorised investigations, and discovered that GLEW doesn't exist. You've then tried

261

to dictate to me and all of us what course of action to take, how to treat Ellsberg's information about an EMP plan and how to avoid that plan being put into operation by the Russians. When you failed, you grew desperate enough to contemplate high treason. Am I right or am I right?'

'You're wrong in many ways, but your summary is fair,' said Maxon. 'I'll take full responsibility.' He raised his hand to silence Jack. 'Full responsibility.'

'I thought you would, Maxon.'

'But in all fairness, General, I must warn you that in a closed court, I'll make a statement about your conduct throughout this affair. More as an explanation than an excuse, I intend to prove that you've refused to pass on the vital information I supplied, that you've isolated me quite deliberately, that I was cut off from all possible support, and that I had to reach my own horrible conclusions without a chance to test my views in the light of my colleagues' experience. In all, if my acts amounted to treason, yours might be seen as high treason.'

Locke nodded thoughtfully. 'But what would you do if there was *no* trial? What if you could choose not to go on trial?'

'Are you suggesting some sort of plea bargaining?'

Rocking his creaky chair, Locke leaned backwards. 'Let me just clarify something. Am I right that it wasn't you who actually approached the Russians in Stockholm?'

'It was me,' Jack blurted out.

'That's immaterial,' Maxon objected.

'It isn't.' Jack addressed Locke without looking at Maxon. 'I acted on my own.'

'On my behalf!' Maxon raised his voice.

'Is that a fact?' Locke asked her. He rocked forwards, let his upper torso land on top of the desk, and stuck out his jaw this time towards Maxon as he repeated the question: 'Is that a fact, that she acted on your behalf?'

'It is not,' said Jack with quiet conviction. 'I had slipped some sleeping tablets in his drink at Samantha's, our hiding place.'

'Why?'

'That was the only way to prevent him from stopping me. Once I alone had decided that telling the Russians was the only right thing to do, I had to be free to act without any interference.'

262

'Rubbish. She's only trying to keep me out of it.'

She smiled at Maxon. 'I can prove it. I can show where I've hidden the leftover tablets. How can *you* prove that you weren't drugged? You chased after me to stop me. But why the long delay?'

'Because you were the advance party. To test the water for me – according to plan.' It was Maxon's turn to smile. If he wanted to prove Locke's guilt, he had to be the accused at the trial.

Locke rose and rounded the table. He stood between the two chairs. 'Well, I must say, I envy you, Maxon. I envy you from the bottom of my heart.' His face reflected solemnity – a new experience he seemed to find painful. 'You see,' he rested his hand on Maxon's arm, 'all my life I was hoping to meet a woman who'd be my equal in putting duty and logic before emotion when it comes to making unpleasant decisions.' He turned to face Jack, and honoured her with a stiff little bow that would have done credit to a Prussian officer paying homage to his prince. 'I think you're just the woman, Mrs Kowalski. Please allow me to toast you in style.' He crossed the room to the metal locker that should have held an athlete's soiled kit but housed, this time, a magnum of champagne with three crystal goblets. He poured out drinks and delivered them on a tray. Maxon watched him with a mixture of disgust and suspicion.

'You sure saved my plan ... and my neck, Jacqueline,' Locke raised his glass. 'I thank you both.' He looked hurt momentarily when they failed to reach for their glasses, but accepted the rebuff with equanimity. He returned to his chair, drank his glass dry, and poured himself some more. 'Would you prefer to drink to success? Our success?'

'Let's stick to business, General.' Maxon was past emotional outbursts. 'Unless you kill us here and now, I'll prove your guilt. Yes, we may go to jail first ... but when we have nothing to lose any more, you become equally vulnerable.'

'True. I admit. You could ruin me, and I, in turn, would bring down two or three governments with me. Between us, we'd hand world domination to the Russians on a plate. But I don't like the idea. It's too big a price for a mere gesture. So sadly, I must make a deal with you.'

'You want to buy our silence?'

'I'm asking for the ultimate sacrifice.'

'The answer is *no*, General, I've risked my life many times without a word. But this time, I'll not die without speaking out. And I've taken out insurance. If we're not charged properly by tomorrow, my voice and evidence will reach everyone concerned. So if you're asking for our lives ...'

'It's worse, Maxon. I said it's the ultimate sacrifice. I want you to live. For as long as possible. In fear.' He sipped some champagne. 'And shame.'

'What the hell are you talking about?'

Locke opened his briefcase and took out some documents. 'I want you two to go away. With new identities. I'll give you three hours before we leak it that you're traitors on the run. Then I'll start a proper manhunt, of course, with the hunters authorised to shoot you if necessary. And needless to say, the Russians will try to catch you first. Your job is to be elusive and survive as long as you can ... or until we can bring you home.'

'Go on.'

Locke seemed to be completely preoccupied with his fingernails. He examined them from every possible angle as he spoke to avoid the eyes of his audience. 'I ... I guess I owe you something. No, not an apology,' he hastened to add. 'I'm a soldier, not a favourite in a high-school popularity contest. And you don't have to accept my explanation. It's not a pretty story and you may judge me as you wish, you won't break my heart.'

Locke refilled his glass and pushed the bottle towards Maxon, then stared at the ceiling as if looking for celestial inspiration and approval. He recalled the day when intelligence first confirmed that the Russians had perfected the Fractional Orbit Bombardment technique. Their FOB vehicles in orbit could launch missiles from anywhere in outer space, and so had reopened the window of vulnerability by rendering all early warning systems obsolete at a stroke. It was a tremendous blow to the West at a time when crisis was succeeding upon crisis, inflation, recession, oil blackmail and the menace of worldwide banking collapse, when the arms race was demanding incessant spending sprees on ritzy nuclear hardware of short strategic life, while both decent intentions and prudent electioneering were begging for vast social and peace programmes.

Against FOB, defence seemed impossible, and deterrence grew ruinously expensive.

'Time was what we needed most,' said Locke, mostly to himself. 'Time and funds to produce a major breakthrough in our nuclear capability instead of more junk to patch up defences and make the menace credible.' Under these combined pressures, with no aces held by the West in this treacherous game of nuclear poker, bluff was the last resort – and GLEW was invented.

The bluff grew into an industry (even dummy satellites needed astronomical fund allocations and a stormy passage through budget debates), but GLEW became immensely successful in baffling and worrying Moscow.

Locke accepted that the Mad Monk would laugh at him and his conspicuously amateurish network, and that 'Skylark' and other spooks on his own side would despise him for the childish security regulations. All this would help to needle the KGB until massive Soviet intelligence resources would have to be tied up to break the secret. Yet they would be wasting their time. They could not guess that GLEW security was impenetrable because GLEW did not exist: those incrediably fast and jumbled computer signals meant no more to the sender and receiver than to the eavesdropper.

Until a solution could be found, the Kremlin had chosen to counter GLEW with a bluff – a counterbluff, in effect. They had begun to pretend that GLEW would be neutralised because its secrets had been cracked. In order to shake Western confidence in GLEW, faked leaks of a Russian scientific and intelligence breakthrough were planted. The measure of their success was that even top White House aides like Chuck Parkin were taken in and driven to issuing anxious warnings to Western leaders. When these warnings were suitably magnified and leaked back by Locke to Moscow, the KGB operation became a boomerang: if the West worried, it was a proof that GLEW did exist and there *was* something of enormous importance to be penetrated and uncovered.

The Russian disinformation campaign continued with the smear against Kowalski, to imply that through him even the computer secrets of GLEW had been compromised. Locke had to be seen being rattled enough to confirm that there were, indeed, some great secrets Kowalski could have given away.

'And for that you refused to clear him?' Jack asked, looking sick. 'He was hounded and dubbed a traitor. Had you no pity?'

'Couldn't afford it.'

'And you let him die for this charade.'

'His suicide was unforeseeable. His death was a miscalculation, I admit, but a sacrifice rather than a waste.'

Kowalski's fate had not been the only miscalculation. When Ellsberg had made his move and Jack had involved Maxon, there was no way of telling whether the Russian was acting as an enemy or a friend. Only his death had been some proof of his integrity but by then the KGB smear campaign was in full swing against Maxon: once again, the West had had to pretend that they had been taken in and that he had become a suspect. 'We had to allow them to feel successful,' said Locke.

'Naturally,' Maxon agreed. 'What's a Kowalski or two?'

'You know I had no choice.'

'And *you* know that I would have had one – if you told me what was going on.'

'How could I be sure that you'd rise to the challenge?'

'I had a track record, hadn't I?'

'This was a new track.'

Locke's plan had evolved step by stumbling step rather than by grand design. The Russians were watching Maxon. His despair was the gauge of their success. It was essential that he should be seen to be worried and on the run. And Locke refused to rely on his play-acting ability. It had to be for real. When the Russians grew determined to carry out an EMP test, it would have been counter-productive to admit the bluff: they would not have believed the confession. The only answer was to push and squeeze Maxon until he really became a traitor. 'I wanted you to convince yourself that you alone could block the road to holocaust, that you had to reveal all to Moscow to avert their EMP test and war. Unfortunately, I misjudged you.' Locke was now bent on outstaring Maxon. 'Because I thought you'd be more pragmatic. And if it hadn't been for Jacqueline, we'd have failed.'

'I hope you're proud of yourself,' said Jack.

'No. I don't measure action in terms of pride. When decisions must be made, somebody must make them.'

'I'm glad it's not me.' She turned away. She felt he was

too repulsive to look at. But she could not help listening with a degree of shame.

'Of course you're glad. Most of you are glad to make the simple decisions: if it's edible, eat it; if it's desirable, take it; if it moves, kill it before it kills you. Easy. But what do you do with the hard ones? What if it's you and you alone who has to get your hands mucky? Then you delegate. Leave it to the politicians and scum like me. Don't sneer, Maxon, I'm the man with muck on my hands. I'm the one who captured those kids who'd planted the bombs in a Saigon department store. There were hundreds of women, children and good American soldiers in there, and I knew we'd never find the bombs in time. What was I to do? Try to reason and argue? Yes, you know damn well what I had to do. I ordered the green berets to beat the kids and torture them. With water. Until one died. And the other confessed. I didn't want to know any of the technicalities. Only the answers. And that's what I got. I retrieved the bombs. It was victory. And it wasn't my fault that the bombs turned out to be dummies. Harmless dummies . . .'

Locke looked and sounded broken and exhausted, but Maxon was not prepared to soothe him with violins. 'Yes,' he said, 'we all know that you were a great hero.'

'And you think I was wrong? What do you think, Jacqueline? Was I wrong to let Maxon suffer? Was I wrong to push him to the brink of justifiable treason? Didn't I gain what we wanted most?'

'Did you?' she asked as casually as she could, lighting a cigarette. 'Did you gain time?'

'Yes, but we need more. What you told them and what Maxon did must puzzle them. They must evaluate, check and double-check every bit. Could Sarian have really given us the vital clue about that missile? Why would Maxon send you? Why would he then snatch you back? Difficult questions – and anybody who answers them takes a chance. And in the Kremlin, it's a bigger chance than anywhere else. That's why when it comes to decisions, they also love to delegate. They're even more reluctant to grasp the nettle than our people. Their bureaucracy is even slower than ours. If we feed them enough alternatives, they'll chew and chew until they choke on them.'

'You're taking one hell of a risk,' a subdued Maxon mumbled.

'We can't save peace without taking risks. Not any more. And the biggest risk is that we must rely on people like you. People with doubts and confused loyalties, people who must think for the whole of mankind.'

'And people you can sacrifice without too much belly-aching.'

'I won't beg for your sympathy, Maxon.'

'And you won't get it.' Maxon walked away and stood gazing at the locker in the corner. Slow down, he told himself, slow down, play for time. He began counting the scratches on the metal door.

'You see, General,' Jack began with growing pity for the emotionally blind and uninitiated, 'you've just explained why you've never found the woman you talk about. Because she doesn't exist. Perhaps some men can turn traitor through logic. Yes, I also needed a lot of convincing, but to *do* it, that I could only do out of love. That's why you're wrong about me and the whole infernal scheme.'

'Am I?'

'Damn you!' Maxon exclaimed and punched the locker. His knuckles cracked and blood began to seep.

Locke's face lit up. 'You mean you agree I was right?'

'Yes, damn you, yes, I hate you for it, and I hate myself even more because I'm unable to disagree. But unlike you, I can't live with it. Not with the memories of treason and deaths.'

'You can't afford the luxury of suicide, Maxon.'

'My staying alive hasn't been a part of my oath of loyalty.'

The phone rang and Locke picked it up angrily. He listened, grew pale, and rang off saying, 'We'll have to wait and see. What else can we do?' After a pause he told Maxon in a flat voice that intelligence had signalled incessant Politburo and war cabinet meetings in the Kremlin. There was also news of increased activity with FOB vehicles in Space Sector Saturn Blue. 'One day, there'll be a bluff too many,' he said quietly. 'One day, somebody will call that bluff. The game is to put that day off. We've been putting it off for forty years.'

Maxon returned to his chair and picked up the two sets of documents. He glanced towards Jack. 'We'll have to go along with it. Okay with you?'

'You know it is.'

Maxon studied his new identity, held pages of a Brazilian passport to the light, frowned, then threw the lot on the desk. 'The British entry stamp in the pass is a poor forgery. I don't want to be caught on the way out.' While Locke checked the passport, Maxon began to scrutinise the papers Jack would use. He paled with anger when he came to her airline ticket. 'Another bloody mistake! What sort of amateurs have prepared this? Her destination is shown as different from mine.'

Locke nodded. 'I know.' For the first time, his face suggested a faint but undeniable acquaintance with shame. 'Sorry about it, but it can't be helped. You mustn't stay together. I don't even want you to know where the other is going to, so your final orders will be given privately.' He paused to clear his throat repeatedly, then tried, in vain, not to sound apologetic. 'If the KGB captures one of you, they'll want the other, too. They'll ask questions, and if you know the answers ... well, they'll get them out of you.' He flicked the pages of the passport to avoid their eyes. 'Yes, this must be put right. ... It should give you time to say good-bye and cancel your insurance.'

He knocked hard at the door until it was opened from outside, stormed out and swore with venom at everybody in sight as the door closed behind him.

The late night antics of the news-room reached a crescendo. All the phones rang simultaneously. Reports of international sabre-rattling were pouring in. The superpowers' attitudes were hardening. There were threats and counter-threats. Gloucester put down one phone and picked up another. It was Sandy on the line: 'Come out and wait at the entrance. I'll pick you up.'

The heavy Fleet Street traffic did not react kindly even to momentary hold-ups. The black Rover was hooted at hard even though it took Gloucester only a few seconds to get in. He had never seen Sandy looking so haggardly and dishevelled.

'I can't stay long,' said Gloucester as the car pulled away with a racing start.

'You don't have to, dear boy. I'll drive you round the block.' He forced his way through moving traffic to make a right turn as if bent on causing a crash. 'It seems I've misjudged Maxon all along.'

'I don't want to know, Sandy.'

'Oh yes, you do. I'm returning your favours, as promised. He's on the wanted list. Interpol is circulating his photographs but without naming him, as yet. If you're quick, you could be the first to identify the face.' He sounded drunk or bilious or both. 'So run along, Glossie, old sport, and try to look suitably surprised. You'll have a real scoop.'

'It's ... it's not my doing, is it?'

'Don't try to guess and don't worry. Just spit in his beer if you ever see him again.'

THE END

**NO COMEBACKS** BY FREDERICK FORSYTH

A rich philanderer plans to kill the husband of the woman he loves in NO COMEBACKS, a skilfully contrived piece with a savage twist in the tale. It is the title story in a marvellously exciting and varied collection by a master story-teller.

To this, his first book of short stories, Forsyth brings the narrative power and the wealth of meticulous detail that have made his novels bestsellers around the world.

'The ten stories vibrate with drama and the shock of the unexpected ... chillingly effective.' *Publishers Weekly*

'A diverting collection of short suspense fiction that should both surprise and delight Forsyth fans.' *New York Times Book Review*

0 552 12140 1      £1.95

**THE CANARIS FRAGMENTS** BY WALTER WINWARD

During the interrogation of an ex-Abwehr officer, Heinrich Arndt, the name of Langenhain, friend and right-hand man of Admiral Canaris, is mentioned, and a mysterious reference is made to a fragment of colour photograph, one of four that Canaris handed to selected officers before he was executed by the SS. It appears that Arndt's mistress, Hannah Wolz, has the first fragment, but who has the others and what do they all mean? Who are these men prepared to rape and murder in pursuit of the fragments?

In Nuremberg, Munich and Berlin, Major Quinlan, a pre-war journalist, and Major Hadleigh of the US Intelligence, together with Hannah Wolz, try to find the answers in a race against the clock. They know that something is due to happen before January 10, 1946. The climax of this brilliant new thriller is explosive in true Winward style. It is a worthy successor to his bestseller, THE BALL BEARING RUN.

0 552 12119 3          £1.75

## RUMPELSTILTSKIN BY ED MCBAIN

Beautiful Victoria Miller is making her comeback as a singer. That night, she makes passionate love with successful attorney Matthew Hope. The following morning, Vicky is found brutally murdered and her daughter has been kidnapped ...

Matthew Hope becomes embroiled in a welter of hatred, greed and jealousy that filled the dead woman's life. And at the end of the trail is a little girl – worth twelve million dollars ...

0 552 12021 9      £1.50

# THE MAN FROM ST PETERSBURG

BY KEN FOLLETT

AS LONDON SOCIETY WALTZED TO THE BRINK OF
THE GREAT WAR, AN IRON-WILLED FANATIC
RELENTLESSLY PURSUED HIS PRINCELY QUARRY ...

In the summer of 1914, at the British government initiated
Anglo-Russian talks to counter the threat of German aggression, a
fanatical Russian assassin arrived in London ...

His name was Feliks. He was an anarchist, pledged to prevent the
deaths of thousands of young Russians in a futile war – prepared to
kill in order to stop the treaty from being signed ...

But as Feliks closed in on his victim, he met the woman he had
loved – and lost – years ago in St Petersburg ...

0 552 12180 0          £1.95

**RED DRAGON** BY THOMAS HARRIS

RED DRAGON

'... is an engine designed for one purpose – to make the pulses pound, the heart palpitate, the fear glands secrete.'
*New York Times Book Review*

RED DRAGON

'... is an extraordinary book. A thriller in its own right, with pace, tension, and a capacity to prickle the skin with excitement, but more than this, a superb study of character, seen and understood and created in depth ...
Enthralling, frightening, totally professional. It is quite simply the best of its kind that I have read in twenty years.'
Lord Ted Willis.


RED DRAGON

'... simply comes at you and comes at you, finally leaving you shaken and sober and afraid ... the best popular novel published since THE GODFATHER.'
Stephen King

Over two months on the American bestseller list.

0 552 12160 6      £1.95

# A SELECTION OF FINE
# NOVELS AVAILABLE FROM
# CORGI BOOKS